DIRECT FIRE

The Jake Mahegan Thrillers
by A.J. Tata

Direct Fire

Besieged

Three Minutes to Midnight

Foreign and Domestic

DIRECT FIRE

ANTHONY J. TATA

Zebra Books
Kensington Publishing Corp.
kensingtonbooks.com

ZEBRA BOOKS are published by

Kensington Publishing Corp.
900 Third Avenue, 26th Floor
New York, NY 10022

ISBN-13: 978-1-4967-0664-5 (ebook)
ISBN: 978-1-4967-6069-2

First Zebra Trade Paperback Edition: August 2026

The authorized representative in the EU for product safety and compliance
Is eucomply OU, Parnu mnt 139b-14, Apt 123
Tallinn, Berlin 11317, hello@eucompliancepartner.com

156593254

For Chuck Schoninger, a friend for all seasons

CHAPTER 1

JACKKNIFE CRACKED THE SHADOW BOX AND REMOVED THE COLT .45 PISTOL, thinking, In case of emergency, break glass.

To Jackknife, the need for this specific pistol wasn't so much an emergency as it was part of an elaborate plan.

Keeping a towel wrapped around the punching hand, Jackknife was able to avoid any incriminating lacerations from the razor-sharp shards of glass. Knowing what kind of pistol was in the mounted display on the wall of Major General Bob Savage's oak-paneled study deep in the bowels of the man's secretive Vass Estate, Jackknife had already secured the magazine and ammunition from the desk drawer. Savage was the enigmatic commander of JSOC, or the Joint Special Operations Command, at Fort Bragg, North Carolina. Jackknife knew that Savage was not home this evening, that someone had sent the general a secure text message asking him to meet at a discrete location.

The pistol slid easily from its red velvet background into which two mounting pegs had been secured. Jackknife's latex-gloved hands caressed the pistol as if holding a large, precious gem. The weapon was heavy and perfect in every way for tonight's mission.

Jackknife retraced the route used to breach the secure compound, hiked a mile through the forest, cut through a golf course, and located the cash-purchased, gray 2002 Ford Taurus. Cranking the engine, Jackknife laid the Colt .45 on the towel on the passenger seat, folded the towel over the pistol, then placed it beneath the driver's seat with the magazine and ammunition.

The drive to Charlotte took over two hours because Jackknife drove the speed limit the entire way. Passing a few police officers around nine p.m., the vehicle gave off no suspicion of DUI, speeding, or reckless endangerment.

Though Jackknife's mission was completely reckless and dangerous.

Arriving at the preplanned spot on the far side of the Country Club of Charlotte, Jackknife parked in a dirt lot used to gain access to the golf course maintenance shed. It was out of the way, hidden from the members who didn't care to see the maintenance personnel who kept their course in pristine condition.

Jackknife walked across several golf holes and followed a rehearsed route along number five, went around a pond, hit some muddy spots, and walked into the backyard of the target. Having scouted the security system and overall security posture of the home, Jackknife knew that, despite all of the warnings to the person who was about to die, this part of the plan might actually go smoothly.

Now, at ten-thirty p.m., Jackknife came up the back deck of the Georgian brick mansion. After retrieving a lock pick set from the inner coat pocket, Jackknife first checked the doorknob that led to the kitchen.

Unlocked. This was that kind of neighborhood. Friendly neighbors. Tall pines and magnolias dotted the mature gated community like sentries keeping watch. Signs said NEIGHBORHOOD WATCH. Gate guards were at the road entrances, though no guards protected against cutting across the twice-mowed golf greens and fairways.

After returning the pick set to the coat pocket, Jackknife carefully opened the door, listening for any alarm beep or indicator. After a minute of remaining perfectly still, adapting to the environment, Jackknife quietly closed the door and navigated through the house to the stairs. The muddy, rubber-soled boots were too big but necessary for the job, in part because they ensured quiet movement. Jackknife ascended the stairs thinking, The master bedroom is on the left at the end of the hallway.

Approaching the open door, Jackknife noticed the woman and her husband sleeping soundly amidst rumpled sheets. Both of them were snoring, the husband louder than the woman.

Jackknife wanted to kill only the husband but thought that killing the woman first would be a nice touch. A misdirection that in the grand scheme of things might prove useful, buying some time. With that in mind, Jackknife moved to the far side of the bed, where Vicki Sledge was sleeping soundly.

Vicki Sledge had at one time been Vicki Savage, wife of Major General Bob Savage. A recent divorce landed her in Charlotte, where she married Charles Sledge, the CEO of United Bank of America, the fifth largest bank in the nation.

Having walked the length of the expansive bedroom, Jackknife stood above Vicki. She was sleeping with her mouth slightly open, dyed blond hair scattered across her face. Jackknife imagined that she would have a serious case of bed head in the morning.

Especially with a bullet in her forehead.

Jackknife wasted little time, placing the weapon near the forehead of the sleeping woman, who suddenly awoke. Her eyes popped open, big and round. She was roused either from a bad dream or the realization that she was about to step into one. Her gaze shifted up, and she stared into Jackknife's own eyes and recognizable face.

"Oh my God. What are you doing here?" the wife said. Jackknife recognized that even with a pistol to her head, Vicki couldn't get past herself. Well, that was about to end.

"This," Jackknife replied, and pulled the trigger. The Colt .45 sounded like a cannon in the bedroom. The husband was jolted awake, as if someone had placed defibrillator paddles on him. Vicki's head kicked back into the pillow. Blood splattered in both directions, toward Jackknife's outstretched arm and along the path of the exit wound toward the pillow and the mahogany headboard of the poster bed.

"Vicki, what the hell?"

Suddenly the husband was looking up at Jackknife, eyes wide with fear. "What are you doing? What have you done?"

Jackknife held the pistol steady at the man and thought, Aw shit, he's seen me. *Then an unexpected voice came from the hallway.*

"Mom? Dad? Everything okay?"

"Run, Danny!" the father shouted.

Jackknife pressed against the far wall, pistol held high. Yes indeed, run, Danny. *Jackknife was solid with killing the husband and wife, but the kid had never been an option, or even a thought for that matter. Still,*

Jackknife, stood square with feet spread into a balanced shooter's stance, prepared for this unexpected turn of events.

But Danny didn't run, at least not away. He ran into the bedroom and spun around. That was when Jackknife shot him in the face. With that task done, Jackknife walked up to the trembling man and shot him in the heart point-blank. Jackknife was careful to use a small Maglite to find and secure the three shell casings ejected by the Colt .45.

Retracing the path out of the house, Jackknife retreated quickly, mission accomplished. Tossing the gun and shell casings into the golf course lake, as good a place as any, Jackknife felt unburdened and moved quickly toward the car. Unconcerned about the footprints that would clearly reveal the path that Jackknife had taken from the murder scene, the killer turned the ignition, pulled gently onto a state road, and turned on the radio, hoping for some news.

After some time driving the speed limit to the northeast, Jackknife arrived at the next destination, parked the burner car, wiped it down, and thought for a second. The feeling of perfection was close but not at hand. Jackknife wondered if there had been a mistake somewhere along the way. It didn't seem likely, but mistakes were possible. Not having time to contemplate what might have occurred, Jackknife focused on the next mission.

Jake Mahegan was next on the list.

CHAPTER 2

FORMER ARMY PARATROOPER AND EX-DELTA FORCE OPERATIVE JAKE Mahegan turned his head slowly and looked in each direction. To his left was a man holding a pistol and to his right was another man holding an AR-15 assault rifle. The assault rifle had a rail with a Maglite attached beneath it and an infrared aiming light secured on the opposite side. Neither man wore night vision goggles, but the presence of the high-tech device gave Mahegan some insight to his adversaries' capabilities. This was not their first rodeo.

Both weapons were aimed directly at him.

"It's going down right now," the man to his right said in a thick Middle Eastern accent. "Everything, all at once."

Mahegan was standing in a rustic cabin on an exclusive golf resort in the middle of North Carolina's golf mecca, Moore County. He had received a text over his secure Zebra communications application developed by his former Delta Force teammates, Patch Owens and Sean O'Malley. The text had instructed him to meet Owens and O'Malley at cabin number two, Longleaf Pine Golf Resort, at midnight. The text had included the code words *en fuego*, which meant "on fire" in Spanish and "hurry, be armed" to Mahegan. And even though he had intended to head from Wrightsville Beach up to the Outer Banks today, General Savage's text trumped all, as it always did.

Mahegan said nothing. He stood there and waited. He understood that someone had probably breached the secure Zebra application. He didn't know if Owens and O'Malley were dead or alive, and now he wondered if Savage had sent the secure text for him to meet here. They rarely communicated on the Zebra app, but when they did, their texts and phone calls were immediately eliminated from any server or digital storage system. Gone forever. One of his teammates could have sent the text message in extremis, at gunpoint, but he didn't think so. They, and he, would take a bullet for one another before sending a secure coded message luring one of them into a trap.

Mahegan sized up the two men in the dimly lit cabin. The pistol man was almost his height, placing him just under six foot six. The man was broad shouldered and muscular, holding a balanced shooter's stance. Sweat glistened on his shaved head. He wore a black T-shirt and dark cargo pants. Muscles strained the fabric of his shirt as he held the pistol, locked forward in large hands. Behind the pistol man was a small river-rock fireplace and a doorway, from which he had emerged as Mahegan had stepped into the cabin.

"Do as we say and no one gets hurt," the man with the AR-15 said.

The assault rifle came closer as the man stepped slowly through an open door that led to a screened porch, holding the rifle at eye level like a soldier conducting a room clearing. He was dressed in similar dark clothing. Because of the moonlight pressing through the screened porch, Mahegan could discern the dark features of this attacker. Olive skin, dark eyes, hard planes on his face. His cocked elbow flexed at a right angle to the weapon, the forearm muscles looking like steel cables beneath his skin.

The two men had moved simultaneously from opposite sides of the cabin. They had checked him, like chess pieces cornering the king.

Fortunately for Mahegan, *en fuego* also meant for him to come armed and ready. It was a code that the hackers must have seen before the texts vanished on previous communications. They would only surmise it meant to move quickly, perhaps, but not that Mahegan would also come armed with his Tribal Sig Sauer pistol and his Blackhawk knife, both readily accessible.

The open family room, dining room, and kitchen design gave advantage to his two attackers, who had been lying in wait. Mahegan's was not too far from the home of his mentor and chief aggravator, Major General Bob Savage. Mahegan had assumed the code was for a quick meeting to act upon a new threat to the homeland. So far, since his dismissal from the Army for killing a handcuffed enemy prisoner of war, Mahegan's chief role had been to thwart nefarious schemes operationalized by those intending to harm the country.

Truthfully, all he was really looking for was a good-hearted woman and some peace to counterbalance all of the violence he had endured so far in his young life. Thirty years old with multiple deployments to Iraq, Afghanistan, and other countries not to be named, Mahegan was a Native American from a small town called Frisco in the Outer Banks of North Carolina, a series of sand spits formed by the violent clashing of the Atlantic Ocean's Labrador Current and the Gulf Stream.

His birthplace foreshadowed his life so far. Love of the ocean and its beauty were offset by the danger of the currents and tides colliding. Love and violence, his twin curses, seemed to be his fate. When the call to duty rang clear, he surrendered the possibilities of a stable home life like so many of his peers. Even as a former soldier, Mahegan never saw a different path than that of defending his nation. Like the black-and-gold, half-moon-shaped Ranger tab tattoo inked on his left shoulder, the lazy *Z* scar just beneath it, and the TEAMMATES tat on his right bicep, Mahegan's call to duty was part of his DNA.

Not sure what the two gunmen were waiting for, Mahegan was never one to be stymied by indecision. He analyzed his situation. First, the two men were opposite one another, Mahegan being the center point in a straight line. If both fired and missed, there was a fifty-fifty chance they would shoot each other. Second, Mahegan's right hand hovered inches away from his Tribal 9 mm pistol, which had a round chamber and was hidden beneath his loose Windbreaker. He didn't know how good his two attackers were, but he was pretty damn good. He gave himself a fifty-fifty chance at beating the pull of the trigger of at least one of the men. Third, if they wanted him dead, they could have shot him as soon as he walked into the unlocked cabin. So there was a probability they needed him for something. What did they want from him?

Mahegan's body was coiled tight, as if flexing would make the bullets bounce off his sturdy frame. In the end, there was only one decision to make. The fifty-fifty chances of the world usually worked in his favor when he acted first. The geometric problem that Mahegan faced was that he needed to first kill the man aiming the AR-15, the more lethal and accurate weapon, but that man was to his right. The movement would require Mahegan reaching into the hip holster on his left side, angled slightly forward for a quick draw, and then crossing his arm 180 degrees to his right. He could do that fast, but not fast enough to beat two gunmen.

Mahegan had wrestled in high school and had retained the flexibility required for that timeless combative sport. His right hand slid perfectly onto the textured pistol grip as he dropped low to the ground, spinning as if performing a single leg takedown. He raised the pistol and fired three times, walking the sight up the AR-15 guy's torso, stitching him with 9 mm hollow point bullets. The AR-15 fired wild and high, like a baseball closer losing control of his fastball. Mahegan rolled toward the rapidly dying man, who was no longer holding the AR-15, and came up to one knee, using the arm of the leather sofa as a prop for his shots at the man with the pistol.

He scanned the room, but didn't see the man. In his attackers place were the pockmarks from the AR-15 bullets riding up the pine paneling. Blood was splattered around the lower bullet holes, looking like those fake gunshot stickers that rednecks put on their trucks.

From his protected position, he quickly checked the AR-15 guy, who was slumped dead against the screened porch door, blood still blossoming onto his dark shirt. Rising slowly, Mahegan kept his pistol aimed in the direction of the pistol-wielding man until he noticed that the attacker had taken two shots in the torso—one lower left and the other upper right.

He was still alive as Mahegan approached him. His breathing was a labored wheeze.

"Who?" Mahegan asked.

He stared at the man whose neck and head were slumped against the wall. The body was splayed at a forty-five-degree angle to the river-rock fireplace, as if he was just resting in the nook between the wall and the chimney. Blood was running out of one corner of his mouth, and his eyes looked milky. After just a few shots from three weapons the cabin smelled like a gun range, cordite wafting into the open chimney flu.

Mahegan held his Tribal to the man's forehead and asked again, "Who?"

The man shook his closely shaved head twice before it lolled to one side, lifeless. Mahegan confirmed the man's death with a finger to the carotid artery. He searched the men and found nothing on either. They had removed any revealing information prior to entering the cabin. Mahegan didn't know who they worked for or who else might be headed his way. These two men had obviously compromised Zebra, and so he couldn't use it to communicate with Owens or O'Malley. The last thing he wanted to do was reveal their locations, assuming they were secure.

He replayed in his mind what the men had said.

It's going down right now. Everything, all at once.

Mahegan carried a government-issued smartphone that was encrypted with the latest technology to include the Zebra app, which was a combination secure locator service, distress signal, text eraser, and classified telephone. Once Mahegan read a text on his phone, it was automatically erased in five seconds. Texts that were not read in twelve hours were automatically deleted. It was better than Wickr and other secure e-mail and text apps, but not impenetrable, apparently.

Walking into the bedroom, he found a set of car keys, which he presumed belonged to the crew he had just disabled. He cleared the rest of the cabin and found nothing of interest, but he did collect the AR-15 and a Glock 19 from the two dead men. He took one last look around to make sure he wasn't missing anything. It was a basic golfer's time-share. Green and burgundy cloth mixed with leather upholstery. Mahegan stepped into the warm September night, glad to get the gunpowder out of his lungs. He walked along the asphalt parking lot looking at the random cars. He looked at the key fob, which had an Audi logo on it. Fancy car for two hit men.

A white Audi A5 was about twenty yards to his right. It was parked away from all of the other vehicles. Mahegan's Cherokee was on the far side of the parking lot, nearly a hundred yards to his left. Standard security protocols.

He knelt behind a pickup truck and aimed the fob at the Audi. The lights flashed twice, and he heard a beep. He clicked it again and heard the other door locks pop open. He wondered if a timer would lock the car doors or detonate a bomb. While he discounted the possibility of this car being rigged, someone had left the keys in the open.

Sure enough, after about a minute, the locks reengaged.

Then the car blew up, creating a massive fireball that billowed orange and yellow into the sky like a small nuclear explosion.

He wondered if the bomb was meant for him or the two would-be assassins.

CHAPTER 3

MAHEGAN TUCKED HIS TRIBAL INTO HIS HIP HOLSTER AND ZIPPED his Windbreaker up a third of the way as he walked quickly to his gray Cherokee. Once inside, he turned the ignition and drove the long way out of the resort, following the golf holes with no homes lined along the fairways. In his rearview mirror flashed the blue and red lights of emergency responders.

He exited the resort and wound his way through the small village of Pinehurst, then followed U.S. Route 1 to the town of Vass and pulled into another golf community called Wood Lake. There, he looped around a big lake and two golf courses until he came upon an old, white farmhouse with black shutters. Behind the farmhouse was a garage, in which he parked the Cherokee. Making sure to close the garage door, he walked into the thick pine forest just off the garage and circled to the backyard, where tall pine trees stood like sentries.

Standing amidst the thick forest on General Savage's twenty-acre compound in the calm September night, he breathed deeply, glad that he had survived the ambush. He'd survived others.

The worst ambush—perhaps the one that defined his life path so far—was when he was fourteen and already freakishly over six feet tall. He had walked in on a road crew in the process of raping and murdering his mother. He had killed two of the drunken men at the time. Two had survived, and one of those survivors had murdered his father within the past year. Recently, he had sought and delivered justice on behalf of his parents. He had no brothers or sisters, except his comrades in the military. Now his family was the tight-knit group of soldiers with whom he had served.

Mahegan walked from the garage along a two-acre field framed by a low, electric cattle fence. In the middle of the field was a copse of pine trees, which Mahegan entered. From the protection of a thick pine trunk, he stared at the two dark green doors that sat at an angle to the flat ground. Beyond them was Savage's country house and the garage where he had parked his car. The field was essentially Savage's backyard. The storm shelter was like a Kansas tornado shelter, but here he was just outside the gate of Fort Bragg and the Joint Special Operations Command. There were occasional tornadoes, but the true safety that lay beneath the storm doors was that of communications and situational awareness.

Reasonably sure that no one was watching, he walked to the storm doors, where he used his phone to shine a light on the combination lock. He spun the dial from memory and got the numbers right on the first attempt. This was a heavy-gauge lock built into the door so that every time someone wanted to enter, they had to use the combination. It was purposefully low tech so that no maintenance was required. As far as Mahegan was aware, exactly four people had memorized the combination. With the last number aligned, he snapped the handle open with a flick of his wrist and then pried open the right-side storm door. Using the flashlight app again, he descended the steps and closed the door behind him, listening as the lock snapped shut.

It had been five years since he had last been in the continuation of operations protocol command center, known as the COOP. When he was active duty, General Savage had Mahegan, Owens, and O'Malley come out here and establish the hard-wired capabilities to command and control deployed and domestic forces should Fort Bragg be neutralized in any way. They were the four combination holders.

Mahegan had no reason to suspect that Fort Bragg had been

compromised, but he had every reason to believe that something had happened tonight that could have serious ramifications.

It's going down right now. Everything, all at once.

He found the master circuit breaker and pulled down the main switch, bringing the lights on with a flicker. In the middle of the room was a bank of forty-eight-inch fluorescent lightbulbs. Mahegan remembered helping to install those but doubted they were the same ones. They all came on and cast a bright hexagon of light in every direction.

Secretly he had hoped to find Patch or Sean already here. That was the plan. If any of them detected an unusual threat or breach of their communications protocols, they were to immediately rally at the COOP. Savage owned the property and had purchased most of the equipment used in the communications center. Some of the gear ran continuously, because the servers that powered and filtered the Zebra app were in this shelter also.

To his left was a bank of computers, all MacBook Pros that looked relatively new. Their lids were closed, as if they were resting. On the far wall were weapons racks that held a variety of rifles and pistols. To his right were a series of server racks that blinked and winked with every transmission. The power switch he had thrown was for everything but the servers, which ran on underground cables connected to the main house, which was vacant. Rampert used the house as an alternate command post and retreat for his men. Behind the pine forest from which Mahegan had emerged was Wood Lake, a 200-acre boating and fishing respite for the property owners in the resort.

Beneath the fluorescent lights were two conference tables pushed together to make a workspace for Rampert, Mahegan, O'Malley, and Owens.

While the law of Posse Comitatus forbade employment of military force on U.S. soil, Savage had an agreement with the chairman of the Joint Chiefs, director of the CIA, and the president that he could have a few men on retainer to respond quickly while the Homeland Security bureaucratic machinery decided how to counter a domestic attack.

Mahegan, O'Malley, and Owens were the three men Savage had tried to convince to stay in the army, but all had left of their own accord for one reason or another. Once Mahegan was forced out by an aggressive and corrupt inspector general, the rest of his men saw little reason to stay.

Again, he wondered if the others were alive. He didn't want to activate Zebra, because he knew it was compromised. He could fall back on unsecure communications, but he had to assume those were compromised as well. Owens lived in Charlotte and O'Malley lived in Raleigh. It would take them some time to get here.

If they were okay and if they knew anything was amiss.

Mahegan turned on the flat-screen television that hung on the support post to his right. It flickered to life, set to Fox News. He turned and walked to one of the MacBook laptops, fired it up, and let it spin through its protocols. He used his password and he was in. He pulled up Google and typed in "attacks in North Carolina."

It's going down right now. Everything, all at once.

About thirty minutes later, the crawl on the news program caught his attention.

Charlotte, NC: A family was murdered around eleven p.m. in the Myers Park neighborhood of Charlotte. Charles Sledge, CEO of United Bank of America, and his wife, Vicki, were gunned down along with their 14-year-old son, Danny.

Mahegan read the news stub. It was obviously a first report.

Vicki Sledge was formerly Vicki Savage, now General Savage's ex-wife. And Charles Sledge was the CEO of the fifth largest bank in the country, with just under five hundred billion in assets. Danny was Sledge's son from a previous marriage. Vicki and Charles Sledge were married a year ago after she and General Savage divorced.

Footsteps above Mahegan made him quietly close the MacBook and mute the television. He retrieved his Tribal and moved to the near corner, where he would have the best protection and shot in relation to the entrance.

The lock spun, tumblers ratcheting loudly. A pause. Someone was calculating perhaps that the lock was warm and not cold to the touch, as it had first been when Mahegan had spun it. Mahegan had his pistol aimed at the entrance as he rested his arms on shelving that held electronics equipment. The fluorescent lights flickered overhead as if they were flinching in anticipation of a gunfight.

The door swung open, Mahegan listening to the creaks of rusted hinges. His hearing was in the top range of every Army auditory exam he had ever taken, and he listened to the footsteps beneath the octaves of the hinges. They were lighter than he anticipated. Could be a small man treading lightly, or it could be a large man with soft-soled shoes, but he didn't think so.

Or it could be a nimble woman.

The first thing visible was a black suede ankle boot covering the intruder's left foot. The matching boot appeared on the next concrete pad as long, slender legs covered by tight-fitting jeans moved carefully into the storm shelter. Mahegan could shoot to wound right now, because he was certain those legs did not belong to Savage, Owens, or O'Malley.

Next, two slender hands were cupping an Army officer's 9 mm Berretta pistol, its distinctive black finish reflecting the nervous lights. The hands had fingernails manicured with clear polish as the intruder carried the pistol in a right-handed shooters grip.

The pistol swept right and then left, toward him. A black, long-sleeve polypro athletic shirt covered toned arms and an athletic torso as the feet continued to reach for the next concrete steps.

Again, he could have a full torso shot, but he was intrigued as he noticed shoulder-length brunette hair come into his view. The locks framed a smooth, alabaster face that had a nose with a slight upturn at the end. The woman's pistol swept to her right and then left again.

Mahegan waited until she cleared to her right again, her back one third exposed to him when he leveled the pistol, his finger firm on the trigger.

"Stop," Mahegan said in a calm voice. "You've got a Sig Sauer

Tribal aimed at you that will blow a hole the size of a bowling ball in your torso."

She froze, lifting her hands instinctively into the air, her right hand still firmly gripping the pistol. After a pause, Mahegan said, "One knee, put down the Berretta." He wasn't sure, but he believed that he was speaking to a military officer. By saying "Berretta" he was communicating to a friend or foe that he knew the weapon she was carrying.

The woman began to slowly kneel as she lowered the pistol to the floor of the ersatz command bunker. She placed it next to her right foot and said, "Don't make me kick it away. I hate scratching up my guns."

"Then step away," Mahegan said. "And face me."

"Okay, Jake, I'll do that," she said. Her voice was professional, a neutral tone intended to disguise its origin. Southern women often tried to hide their accents the same way someone from Boston may work on his *r* consonants.

Mahegan had never met this woman before in his life, he knew that much. He wasn't certain how she knew his name. As she turned, her nose profile was prominent again. Not too big, but distinctive. Something anyone would notice and generally appreciate. She had smooth skin under high cheekbones and full lips. Her eyes appeared light brown, the color of new pennies in the weak light.

As she turned and faced him, Mahegan still had no recognition of her whatsoever. She stood just below six feet tall in the low-heeled boots, which he found to be an unlikely choice for an assassin or terrorist. And by mentioning his name, she was communicating something to him. Perhaps that she was friend, not foe. Or maybe not. Mahegan had been on the U.S. government's gray list—possibly detain—for two years now, and maybe she was a bounty hunter.

"Name?" Mahegan asked.

"Alexandra," she said.

Mahegan processed the first name she provided and still registered nothing. He had never seen her before, and she had no business in this top-secret, off-the-books, compartmented storm cellar turned continuity of operations command center.

"Last name?"

"Russell," she said.

Still nothing to Mahegan. Owens, O'Malley, and Savage were the ones who should have come pouring through the door.

"But they call me, 'Alex,' " she added.

A gear caught in Mahegan's mind. He had heard General Savage refer to an 'Alex' before but had always visualized a male, not a beautiful, young thirty-something woman.

"Alex?" he said. "What are you doing here?"

"I think we've both got the same problem," she said cryptically.

"I wasn't aware I had one," Mahegan replied.

He watched her toss her hair behind her shoulders but was still tracking both hands closely.

"You're trying to figure out whether to shoot me. I 'm trying to figure out why you're on the North Carolina State Bureau of Investigation's recently updated most wanted list."

"Most wanted list?"

"It's got a far more technical name, but you get the idea," she said.

"Humor me," Mahegan said.

"Murder? In the first degree? Apparently they found your pistol in a golf course lake in Myers Park, Charlotte. Along with some size twelve muddy Doc Martens bootprints." She looked at Mahegan's Doc Martens as she spoke.

Her voice was cool and crisp, like a spring breeze whispering past his face. Mahegan's mind raced through the weapons he had owned throughout his life. While he had owned several pistols, he had only ever purchased one that he had registered under his name.

"What kind of pistol?" Mahegan asked.

A phone began playing its musical tone from her pants pocket. She pulled it out and stared at it, then turned the large screen toward Mahegan.

The screen read "State Bureau of Investigation." She showed it to him.

"Shall I get this?" she asked.

"What kind of pistol?" Mahegan reiterated. She appeared to shut off the phone.

And he already knew that the pistol was going to be a Colt .45 Ranger Spirit Tribute that he had purchased on behalf of his unit to present to Savage on his promotion from colonel to one-star general. With the gift, Mahegan had included a document that Savage signed declaring he would have the weapon registered in his own name. He had done so partly because he didn't fully trust Savage—theirs had been a turbulent relationship—and because Patch Owens was a stickler for detail, having drafted up the military "hand receipt" with the transfer verbiage already typed on it. Apparently Savage had never followed through.

"A Colt .45 Ranger special," Alex Russell said.

Mahegan nodded. "You seem pretty calm staring at the pistol of a murder suspect," he said.

"We're pretty sure you didn't do it," she said. She braved a step closer to Mahegan, putting her about fifteen feet away from him.

"Who is 'we'?"

"General Savage and me."

"What's your connection to Savage?"

"I'm not sure I can trust you with that information, Mahegan, but you should know me."

"Okay, how do you know who I am, then?"

"I've seen pictures. And you're one of five people authorized in this alternate command post."

"Four."

"Five, including you, Patch Owens, Sean O'Malley, Bob Savage, . . . and me."

"You?"

"Yes, me. I'm Savage's JAG. His attorney. The one who stands next to him every time we shoot a Hellfire missile up someone's ass and says, 'Valid target' so I can cover his."

Mahegan wanted to believe what she was saying, but he needed more authentication.

"What is Savage's call sign?" he asked her.

"Jackknife Six, of course," she said without skipping a beat.

Mahegan lowered his pistol and stood from his kneeling position.

"I didn't get any communication that you had been added to the list," he said.

"Zebra is compromised, as I'm sure you know by now. There's a decapitation action occurring as we speak. CENTCOM Commander has been arrested on charges of child pornography on his computer. Commander in Iraq was killed by a sniper about two hours ago. The family of the commander in Afghanistan has been killed in their home. The president is locked down in the situation room with his national security team."

"What about Savage? What's this murder got to do with anything?"

"Someone killed his ex-wife, who lived in Myers Park in Charlotte. Killed her husband and son, also. The husband is CEO of one of the biggest banks in the country, United Bank of America. CEOs and generals are the targets. It's almost certainly a precursor to some follow-on attack. In particular, the cyber capabilities of this enemy appear formidable. I missed a call from Yves Dupree, the number two at United Bank of America. He's supposed to be calling me back soon."

Mahegan processed this information. He already knew about the news report on Savage's ex-wife but wanted to see what Alex Russell knew and didn't know. If she was correct, four of the Army's eleven four-star generals had been neutralized in some way, plus Major General Savage, who led the Joint Special Operations Command. Alex Russell had used the word *decapitation,* and he thought it fit the situation well. The Central Command general was prosecuting the war efforts across the Horn of Africa to Iraq and Syria and into Afghanistan and Pakistan. The JSOC commander—General Savage—supported that effort by employing

Special Operations Forces throughout the region to accomplish strategic and tactical objectives in support of national security.

He did not know the general who led the effort in Afghanistan or his family but couldn't imagine the dilemma in which that put the general and the president. Does he leave the combat zone permanently to bury his family and grieve, or does he return and drive on with the fight? And while it was unfortunate that the four-star general in Iraq was killed, they would just pump a new general in there to keep the machine rolling. The cumulative effect, though, of a felled four-star commander, coupled with the other actions, was significant.

And he recalled Al Qaeda putting out a fatwa, or assassination order, on American chief executive officers nationwide a year ago through their trade magazine, *Inspire.* Perhaps the murder of Vicki Sledge was a by-product of her husband's assassination, consistent with Al Qaeda's edict. But why would the JSOC JAG be talking to a murder victim's friend?

"Why are you trying to talk to this Yves guy?"

"Because he reached out to me. Said he had some information that could help."

"Help who? I'm assuming Sledge was his friend. Wouldn't he want to get after me or whoever did this?"

"Apparently it's more complicated than that," Alex said. "He has information."

Mahegan nodded, thought for a minute, then asked, "Where's Savage now?"

"Thought he'd be here," she said. "We were supposed to meet at the compound. When he didn't show, I came here. Protocol."

"Patch? O'Malley?"

"That's different. I've got distress signals from both of them. Those came in before I realized Zebra was compromised."

She walked over to one of the idle MacBook laptops and opened it, then typed in a password and logged into a map function.

"I've disabled Zebra but kept the tracking function enabled. These two red dots in the mountains just west of Asheville represent the last known locations of Owens and O'Malley. At least the last two locations of their phones."

Mahegan looked at the map, leaning over her shoulder a bit. She smelled of freshly washed hair with a whiff of laundry detergent. Alex Russell's cleanliness permeated her space. He looked at where a well-trimmed and manicured nail pointed at the two dots somewhere south and west of Asheville, North Carolina.

"What the hell are they doing *there*?"

"I'm not sure," she said. "They both must have recognized that someone had compromised Zebra, because they went into stealth mode about the same time. Only we can track them in stealth mode."

Owens and O'Malley could have called each other on burner cell phones to coordinate going into stealth mode, but it made no sense that they didn't come to the rally point. After all, it had been his first instinct and they were both good soldiers as well.

"Not right," Mahegan said. "They'd come here if they knew Zebra was compromised."

She looked over her shoulder and stared at him a minute. She nodded. "You may have something there, Mahegan.

"Look at that," she said, pointing at the screen.

Mahegan looked at the monitor and saw a third red dot appear next to the ones representing Owens and O'Malley.

"General Savage is with them?" Mahegan asked.

CHAPTER 4

ABOUT 193 MILES AT NEARLY A PERFECT 270-DEGREE AZIMUTH FROM Wood Lake, North Carolina, was a man who hated Jake Mahegan and General Bob Savage with great passion. His name was Zakir Lecha, and he walked the perimeter one final time to ensure there were no campfires or other indicators that might reveal their hideout near Asheville, North Carolina.

He had a Mack truck to hijack tomorrow morning, which was no small task.

But now he sat at his command center and looked at the large Ultra-High-Definition screen that served as a monitor. He pulled on a Bose headset that he used to cancel any external noises, allowing him to focus on the mission at hand.

Through the lens of a butterfly drone, the monitor showed his five-man team dressed in Army blue uniforms. The feed used Ku band satellite; it wasn't high definition, but it wasn't grainy. His men walked through the white headstones of Arlington National Cemetery looking as if they had just concluded a burial detail.

The five men quickly stepped over a low stone wall that separated the cemetery from adjacent Fort Myer. They walked to the parking lot of the commissary and then began walking toward Generals row nearly a mile away. They didn't walk in formation and appeared to be a group of officers returning from an evening at a formal event, perhaps. It was Thursday night, and officers' social calendars would be full. One man walked with a severe limp, as if he might have an artificial leg.

Zakir and his adopted uncle Gavril had hacked the calendar of the chairman of the Joint Chiefs of Staff, General Bartholomew "Bart" Bagwell. He and his wife would be returning from Andrews Air Force Base just outside of Washington, DC, in fifteen minutes, about the time his five man team would be arriving.

Previously, Zakir had one of the men launch the butterfly drone that flew nearly invisibly above the men, like a member of the team, which in a way it was. The butterfly piped back images of the five men, the streets of tranquil Fort Myer, and the homes of the high-ranking officers.

They cut through a set of tennis courts across the street from the chairman's three-story brick mansion that overlooked Washington from the bluffs of Arlington. The butterfly drone showed that the driveway was a narrow alley, something they had already reconnoitered.

The moon was high, and streetlights shined like stage lights. The man with the limp actually carried a disassembled Sig Sauer Commando assault rifle with a noise suppressor screwed to the muzzle. He knelt behind a low wall that separated the tennis courts from the General's home, quickly assembled his weapon, and then lay down so that no one could see him except his four "friends," who were talking casually, as if discussing the merits of tactics and strategy.

In Arabic.

None of the men turned as they saw the armored Mercedes and its chase car pull into the driveway, but one of them rubbed his hand across his sleeve, like a signal to a base runner to steal second base, which the sniper noticed.

As the security team stepped out of its car, the sniper rose quickly and fired two rounds from fifty meters using a Leupold scope. The butterfly drone was actually over the chase car now, and Zakir could see two security guards, one male and one female, drop to the ground from headshots.

The group of ersatz Army officers chuckled and continued walking across the street, remaining calm. The butterfly drone was flying in front of the windshield of the armored Suburban, and Zakir could see the driver pointing at it and laughing to the guard in the passenger seat. The drone was slightly larger than the average butterfly, with a wingspan of six inches.

As the driver was smiling and laughing with the chairman and his wife in the backseat, one of the men dressed in blue knocked on the window, so the driver began to roll it down. The pistol was quickly inside the car and pressed against the man's head. It fired, and brain matter splattered on the security guard in the passenger seat. The second shot killed the guard as he was reaching for his weapon.

Zakir secure chatted Gavril, who was in a safe location in Charlotte, and said, "Good job, but get the locks."

Gavril secure chatted back, "Didn't forget. Doing it now."

Gavril was able to hack the fully electronic vehicle and unlock the doors. With two men on each side, they used Vipertek VTS-989 heavy-duty stun guns to subdue the chairman and his wife.

The limping man moved from the tennis courts to the chase vehicle and secured the keys from the driver, who was dead. He opened the trunk to the up-armored Mercedes and stepped aside as the four men carried the chairman and his wife to the back of the car—the most vulnerable point in the mission—and dumped them into the trunk side by side. The team had quickly zip-tied their hands and feet and placed duct tape over their eyes and mouths. The man who could possibly have an artificial leg passed the keys to another man and then walked to the end of the driveway, where he stood with his hands clasped in front of him, as if he belonged, like an aide-de-camp.

The butterfly drone showed the trunk close. Then the four men entered the car, backed out, and picked up the man at the end of the driveway. Then the drone itself dove inside an open window.

It hovered inside the car as the team drove toward the exit at the bottom of the hill. They passed a security guard who was checking identification credentials of vehicles entering the base but not those departing.

They steered onto a series of roads that led them to Interstate 66, and began driving west. The team would ditch the stolen chase car in Haymarket and transfer to a cash-purchased Buick SUV, and then in Asheville they would transfer to a new car waiting for them in a Walmart parking lot.

Zakir looked at his watch and thought, *Perfect timing.*

He knew that simultaneity was the key to his operation and that Jackknife wanted everything to happen very quickly. His snatch team should have the chairman and his wife in their mountain redoubt before sunrise.

With the kidnapping under way, Zakir walked into the small cabin and saw the final two jihadists that he had smuggled in with his Syrian refugee immigration scheme. The two men had arrived yesterday from Birmingham, Alabama, and brought his total to thirty-eight fighters, five of whom were in Washington, DC, right now, plus another two on Fort Bragg as Zakir began this phase of the operation.

As his boots crunched the gravel road, Zakir remembered his path to this point. He was a Chechen war orphan, raised in a refugee camp along the Syrian border with Iraq. He quickly learned to speak the languages of his tentmates from Iraq, Syria, Serbia, Bulgaria, Turkey, Russia, and his homeland of Chechnya. Now thirty years old, Zakir had befriended a Bulgarian boy and a Syrian girl in the refugee camp when he was ten. Four years later, when America was attacked in 2001, Zakir was fourteen and his friends, Malavdi and Fatima were sixteen. The boys were both ripe for the picking by the jihad recruiters who patrolled the camps looking for mujahideen to fight the West. The girl, Fatima, was striking and tough, fighting off predators daily.

Zakir, Malavdi, and Fatima had no interest in fighting anyone. In their dusty tent, they slept on straw mats and talked about a world beyond the concertina wire. A world beyond the pallets of water bottles and combat rations that the United Nations High Commissioner for Refugees fed them. When Fatima recommended they escape, Zakir and Malavdi were on board with the plan.

Because their refugee camp had minimal security, fleeing was relatively easy. They slid under the wire in the middle of the night. Zakir stole the sleeping guard's keys that unlocked a Renault 19. But with no money and little fuel, their trip to Bulgaria was fraught with peril. Ultimately, they had avoided sex predators, criminals, police, and the jihad recruiters to find Malavdi's uncle Gavril in a small apartment in the Bulgarian town of Burgas on the Black Sea.

While not thrilled to have three additional mouths to feed, Malavdi's balding, stout uncle was happy to see his long-lost nephew and the nephew's apparent love interest. Zakir viewed Fatima as an older sister, and he understood why Malavdi viewed her as a potential mate. They were in love.

Gavril saw that, also. Shining to the idea of having three young people in his life, Gavril told them he could use some help with a new thing called the Internet. In his dining area, Gavril had several keyboards and computer monitors. Zakir, Malavdi, and Fatima knew what these computers were because the Red Cross and UNHCR had used them to process the refugees. And every day at the refugee camp when they had to line up to be accounted for, they walked past the gray-haired Italian woman who counted them as present, filing some report somewhere.

Today, Zakir was sure of two things.

First, "Uncle" Gavril and his computers had taught him and Malavdi to be two of the best computer hackers in the world. Fatima had balked and said her passion was to help the orphans back in Syria. As their love grew, Malavdi and Fatima vowed to be married and to visit the refugee camp where their love had blossomed.

Second, four years ago, the American military's Operation Groomsman had changed their lives forever. And that operation led Zakir to this very moment in time.

He walked up the steps of a small camp cabin a few hundred yards from his command post, entered, and nodded at two men.

"Take off your clothes," Zakir directed. He spoke in Arabic, though his native tongue was Russian.

One thing Zakir had in common with the fighters who stood before him today was that he no longer had any reason to live and so it didn't matter what chances he took. Death and danger had always been twin reapers waiting in every refugee camp tent, every Raqqa street corner, every Turkish souk, and even every grungy Burgas basement where Internet thieves were beginning their boot camps that would fifteen years later make Bulgaria the number one producer of the most proficient hackers. If hacking were an Olympic sport, Bulgaria would receive the gold medal every four years. The difference now, though, was that the twin reapers didn't scare him. Death was inevitable, and he would prefer to die seeking justice for his friends than to grow old and weak.

The two men stared at Zakir with wide eyes, as if expecting some kind of torture. These were strong, military-age men, but despite their shaved heads and prominent muscles, he needed to ensure the U.S. government had not sent him any spies. Zakir himself was a strong, military-age man who had, since the U.S. military Operation Groomsman, fought alongside ISIS forces solely to inflict as much damage on the Americans as possible. Then, when the American president had called him and his fellow Islamic State warriors "The Junior Varsity," he had begun cycling between Bulgaria and northern Syria as he wrote code, planned logistics, and determined to demonstrate to the Americans that they were the real junior varsity.

Working with his commander, codenamed Jackknife, Zakir had marshaled a sizeable force over the past two years. The sanctuary cities in America and their religious charities had welcomed the Syrians with open arms and lax documentation inspection procedures. Even without the bribes to American security personnel and the resultant cut corners, Zakir was confident that the passport and document creators he used produced authentic-looking paperwork that would have passed muster regardless.

In the end, though, Zakir had the best of connections.

His thirty-eight men had been dispersed all over the country for the past year. His objective was to infiltrate one fighter with every five hundred refugees. Sometimes he got three per five hundred, and sometimes he got none. His goal had been thirty within the year. When Interpol found a Syrian passport on one of the November 2015 Paris bombers, he decided to stop his flow for a few months. He had resumed terrorist migration in the spring of 2016, when the Americans had not led NATO to enact Article 5 of the North Atlantic Treaty, despite President Hollande's call to do so. Then came the attacks in Belgium, Turkey, Bangladesh, Orlando, and so many others. Again, Zakir had to delay each time. He found the American attention span for terror to be about two months.

Zakir had resumed migration the following summer and now had two teams. One team was focused on home invasions and kidnapping senior military personnel and corporate chief executive officers. The second group was with him in his mountain redoubt awaiting the arrival of a Mack truck.

His fighters had received their American Instagram accounts in Raqqa prior to deployment in the United States. They were told whom to "follow" on the application and to look for the code words "fall colors" accompanied by a picture of the Blue Ridge Mountains outside the city of Asheville, North Carolina. Zakir had selected "fall colors" because everyone raved about the changing of the tree leaves in the mountains in the months of September and October. Two months ago, he had posted a picture of the mountains covered in colorful splendor as the green leaves were turning red, orange, and yellow. Zakir had taken the picture from a scenic overlook with the mile marker evident in the photograph. He had met the first few men at the overlook, the rendezvous point, then trained those men on the route into the base camp where he stood now. Those men became the guides using the scenic overlook as the link-up point. Each man was on his own to find his way to the scenic overlook using resources at their disposal and field craft.

He looked at the two men, knowing that he had other missions to execute tonight.

"Now," he said. "You received your briefing in Raqqa, correct?"

The men nodded in unison, appearing almost like twins. The Nexus Command in Syria—an ISIS splinter cell—had briefed all of the sleeper agents prior to their infiltration with mass exodus refugees. The instructions were basic: get to America, stay alive, and watch their Instagram accounts. So far, the plan had worked. The two men stripped naked, revealing honed bodies that were devoid of fat but showed the scars of combat.

"Turn around," Zakir said. The men did so and then turned around again, facing him. "Now put your clothes in this bag."

They placed their clothing in the brown paper sack and handed it back to Zakir, who walked to the fireplace, placed the clothes in the mouth, and lit the bag with a long-nosed butane lighter. He placed the lighter on the mantel and turned to the men.

"Now, put on the clothes on your bunks. I have personally ensured that there are no U.S. government tracking devices in these clothes." He pointed at the bunks.

The men nodded and began dressing in the black dungarees, black athletic stretch tops, black pullover shirts, and black tactical vests that held ammunition magazines, hand grenades, medical equipment, and knives. While the U.S. government had no tracking devices in these clothes, Zakir had made sure that each tactical vest was outfitted with wearable technology that he could track twenty-four hours a day, seven days a week, from his warren here in the North Carolina mountains. Gavril also tracked the personnel from his basement apartment in Charlotte, North Carolina.

"Now rest and prepare. We have an important mission tomorrow morning. We move out at first light and will establish an ambush location."

Zakir paused for that information to sink in. The men nodded. They understood. They were eager, so he whetted their appetite with grandeur.

"Then, in the next two days, you will attack a city. We have selected a city that controls much of the economy of the United States but is less well protected than New York City. I will give you the name of this city tomorrow after the ambush."

The two men nodded, eager.

Zakir did the hand-to-forearm warrior clasp with each man and bumped shoulders, a sign of acceptance from him, their commander. He left their cabin and walked fifty yards along a dirt road to the more substantial log cabin that served as his command post. He ascended the three wooden pine planks that led to the covered porch, passed the two rocking chairs, and opened the heavy oak door. Two years ago, when he first inspected this building, there were a few desks, a fireplace, and some cots along the far wall. Today, the cots remained, but he had fashioned the interior into the complex server farm and satellite transmission station he stared at presently.

Red and green diode lights winked at him as he checked the connections to make sure everything was secure. Zakir was a thorough man, leaving nothing to chance. While this was his nature, the ramifications for him would be severe if he were to have, as Jackknife described it, an "unforced error." Zakir figured it to be an American term, but he understood the concept.

And he also understood the concept that even he, Zakir, had a boss to whom he must report. Jackknife was unrelenting and harsh. Regardless, Zakir's path to vengeance was through Jackknife.

If they were able to decapitate the military and execute the remaining missions, he had a chance of lighting the fuse that would blow up America.

The team that was to snatch the family of the U.S. commander in Afghanistan had performed a similar mission on Fort Bragg, North Carolina, with less success. The butterfly drone there showed that they had seized a wife and two teenage children, but one of the children had a rifle and fought back. Zakir had issued instructions to execute the family if any complications arose. Kidnapped or slaughtered were the same in his mind. The deployed commander would be unable to continue his mission with his family murdered. The two men, dressed as military policemen, fled in their fake military police car and prepared for their follow-on mission.

Capturing the White House, destroying the Capitol, and similar grand gestures were all the stuff of Hollywood movies. However, crippling the United States economically and taking advantage of arrogantly weak security for their military and civilian leaders was entirely possible, as he was demonstrating.

He chatted securely with Gavril, who was tracking many things all at once. The most important part of his mission was to keep tabs on a Mack truck that was scheduled to turn off I-26 onto I-40 in Asheville at approximately nine a.m. tomorrow.

The truck looked like 99 percent of the other Mack trucks pulling nondescript trailers. But it was not a normal truck. It was on its way to the Y-12 National Security Complex in Tennessee.

Zakir was determined that the truck would not make it that far.

CHAPTER 5

JACKKNIFE FELT THE PHONE VIBRATE. LOOKING AT THE TEXT, JACKKNIFE knew that everything was going according to plan. The one stray electron, as Zakir called it, was Jake Mahegan.

How much could one man really do to stop what was becoming a massive ball of momentum rolling downhill crushing everything in its path? Jackknife was confident in the plan.

There had been so much preparation, sometimes it drove Jackknife crazy. The stress, the secrecy, the purpose, the higher meaning of what was happening were all important. This mission and its outcome, though, were intensely personal to Jackknife. So very personal.

Jackknife had practically lost everything during Operation Groomsman. And even though Groomsman was not the proximate cause, those events had started a series of incidents that spiraled out of control.

Status, reputation, finances, everything was lost.

It was time to rebuild.

It was time for revenge.

CHAPTER 6

ALEX TURNED HER BACK TO MAHEGAN AND LOOKED AT HER PHONE. Her shoulders slumped as she lifted her head up in an apparent sigh.

"What's the deal?" Mahegan asked.

She turned back and stared at Mahegan.

"The chairman of the Joint Chiefs and his wife have been kidnapped."

"Kidnapped? From from Fort Myer?"

"Apparently so. Cameras show five military officers dressed in Army Blues conducting the takedown."

Mahegan decided to let the moment pass and focus on Savage, O'Malley, and Owens.

"It's all part of the same thing. Savage, Sean, and Patch were most likely kidnapped as well," Mahegan said.

"No way anyone kidnaps Savage," Alex said, regaining focus.

"Nobody's perfect, especially Savage."

"I know you guys have a love–hate relationship, but he really respects you. You should respect him."

"I do," Mahegan said. "I'm just saying nobody's perfect. Savage and I have had our moments, but that doesn't mean I wouldn't take a bullet for him."

Mahegan took in Alex's dark features—smoky brunette hair, almond eyes, high cheekbones, nose a bit larger than she probably wanted it to be. An altogether attractive package, he thought. Despite her allure, Mahegan kept wondering if he had missed a cue. Was he in the right place? Were Savage, O'Malley, and Owens waiting for him somewhere else? Never one to need a lot of guidance, Mahegan suddenly found himself reviewing the last few hours. He had received the text to arrive at the golf lodge, *en fuego*. Stat. Armed. Prepared for a mission. The text was from Savage's phone. Had he sent it? And would Mahegan take a bullet for him? He thought he might.

"And he'd do the same for you, Jake," Alex said.

"I'm not so sure about that one, but I figure we'll see one day, won't we?"

"Perhaps."

Mahegan nodded not in agreement, but in knowing he understood something that perhaps she did not. Unless Alex had a similar experience on her way to the COOP, Mahegan had insight on a simultaneity of action happening locally, nationally, or globally. He wasn't sure which of a long list of enemies was the culprit, but that was precisely the issue; there were a variety of ne'er-do-wells who wanted to cripple the U.S. economy, destroy its freedoms, or so threaten the people that the blessing of liberty evaporated like a shallow summer puddle in a hot North Carolina sun.

In Mahegan's view, no amount of vigilance could stop every attack and no amount of wishful thinking or foreign dictator ass-kissing on behalf of American leadership could deny that Islamic extremism was a major threat to U.S. vital interests at home and abroad.

"Could the Sledge family murder be connected to something bigger?" Mahegan said.

"Like what?" Alex responded with a scoff.

"Something larger. Cyberattacks. Zebra has been compromised, which shuts us down. Army leadership has been decapitated, as they call it. And now that I think of it, Vicki Savage, or Sledge, might not have been the target as much as her husband, Charles Sledge. We're getting three pings on Savage, O'Malley, and Owens ten miles west of Asheville in some of the most forbidding terrain, someplace that has no relevance to us."

"Okay, let's pretend some of these events have something to do with General Savage's ex-wife, her husband, and son being murdered . . . by your pistol."

"Simultaneous operations are never simultaneous," Mahegan said. "At best they're near simultaneous. If you get it done in twenty-four to forty-eight hours, you're doing well. The Carbanak bank heist took two years and netted the cybercriminals nearly a billion in siphoned funds.

"Carbanak?"

"Yes. Ukrainians and Russians that employed something called the Anunak virus to steal the money."

"You know about all this?" Alex asked, smiling.

Mahegan shrugged. He made it his business to understand the vulnerabilities of the nation, physical and cyber.

"I don't have it figured out. All I'm saying is, we should operate under the assumption that everything is connected tonight . . . and for the next twenty-four hours."

Alex looked at him and nodded when her phone rang. She turned away from Mahegan and answered, pacing into the middle of the rustic operations center. Mahegan could hear her speaking a few words, but the conversation was mostly directed at her, it seemed. She rang off and turned to Mahegan.

"You're a wanted man. That was the Fort Bragg provost marshall asking me if General Savage had seen you. I replied that, to my knowledge, he had not. Then he asked me to please let him know if Savage does run into you, because Charlotte police have placed an all-points bulletin across North Carolina, South Carolina, and Virginia. I told him I would certainly notify him if General Savage saw you."

Mahegan said nothing. He understood that she had played coy with the provost marshall.

"We should get going," Alex said.

"Where did you have in mind?" Mahegan asked.

"You're the operator, Mahegan. Where do you think?"

"Let me put this a different way," Mahegan said. "I know where

I'm going, which is a wholly different location than where you're going."

"If we're talking about the fact that you're going to hell, then I'm with you. Right here, right now, I'm you're only option."

"Hell would be an upgrade from having you as my only option," Mahegan said.

Alex laughed. "Good one, Mahegan. Savage always said you could be funny."

"Wasn't joking," he affirmed.

Mahegan assessed the situation. The North Carolina State Bureau of Investigation and State Highway Patrol had his picture, his name, and his last known location near Fort Bragg. He was in the clandestine storm shelter cum continuous operations center with a woman whom he had heard about from Savage but didn't personally know. Could he trust her? Did he have a choice? With a phone call she could have him arrested. That damn pistol. He knew he should have made Savage sign the transfer documentation right there on the spot. But there had been too much whiskey as he, Patch, Sean, and the others had been celebrating their boss's promotion.

Alexandra Russell. Savage's confidant. Perhaps lover? Mahegan didn't spend much time with Savage, as he had just been a low-level captain. The headquarters was unfamiliar turf to him. Alex was an enigma to the team members—rarely seen, elusive. What was her stake here, Mahegan wondered? Personal? Professional? If she had any interest in figuring out what had happened to Savage, then their interests overlapped. And with that, he could move forward, using her as he needed to, fully realizing that she would be using him for something as well. Mahegan's stake was his compulsive desire to protect the thin fabric of what he could call family, his former teammates.

"Got it figured out, Jake?"

"Not even close. You ever hear of a kill sheet?" Mahegan asked, changing tack.

"Of course. Snipers use them. Special operators use them all over the world. It's a hit list. Savage used one."

"Exactly. That's what we're dealing with here, a kill sheet. Someone planned a near simultaneous takedown of military leadership coupled with an attack on the CEO of United Bank of America."

"And on top of that, someone's trying to frame you," Alex said.

"Or Savage. How would they know I had bought the gun?"

Alex stared at him a moment too long.

"Did you know?"

"Yes. He told me, as his lawyer. He kept meaning to register it in his name, but he's been rather busy."

"Did you tell anyone?"

"Of course not," Alex said, offended.

Mahegan eyed Alex for a moment, gauging the veracity of her statement. Deciding to focus on the task at hand, he said, "So, the pings we're getting on Savage, O'Malley, and Owens. What makes you think we can trust them? They could be misdirection if someone has hacked into the system."

"They could, but what else do we have to go on?" Alex replied. "Besides this."

Mahegan watched as Alex produced an iPhone from her black purse, which was strapped tightly across her chest.

"A phone," Mahegan said, knowing it was more than a simple smartphone.

"Yes. A phone." Alex paused. "This phone can override Zebra and shows us exactly what information the intruders have accessed. It also contains a list of every protected member of the Department of Defense and their location. It's our proprietary technology that O'Malley developed."

O'Malley was constantly working on new technology to assist Mahegan's vigilante efforts to maintain the appearance that Mahegan was operating alone, off the books. Not always in the loop on O'Malley's latest development, Mahegan wasn't surprised that someone close to General Savage might have the most recent evolution of Zebra or related software.

"Did someone hack that to get to the military leadership?" Mahegan asked.

"It's possible, but doubtful. Other than Savage, our military leadership doesn't take their personal security that seriously when back here in the United States."

"And yet Savage was captured, it appears."

"That remains to be seen."

Just then the phone buzzed with a 704 number with the name "Yves Dupree" displayed in large letters across the screen. She already had the number two from the United Bank of America in her phone. Interesting.

"Better take that," Mahegan said.

Alex punched the SPEAKER button and said, "This is Major Russell with a colleague standing by, and you're on speakerphone."

Code speak? What was the preexisting relationship between Dupree and Russell, Mahegan wondered?.

"Major, this is Yves Dupree. I'm the general counsel and chief of staff for Charles Sledge and United Bank of America. I have his will and am the executor of his estate. In his will, which I prepared, you are listed as a point of contact should General Savage not answer his phone. I am required to personally notify you that Vicki Sledge was murdered a few hours ago."

The man spoke with a slight French accent.

"I've seen the news, Mr. Dupree."

"I understand, but my obligation is to personally notify you. And so I have."

"You have. And I will notify General Savage whenever I can find him."

"Find him? I thought you always had a tether on your general?" Dupree asked.

"It seems he has slipped the tether," she replied.

"Of all nights to do so. I've been watching the news as well. Seems as though someone has it out for our leaders," Dupree said.

"You indicated in your message that you also had information regarding the shooting?"

"I'm at the house now with the police. They've found the pistol and three shell casings in the lake. They have size twelve boot prints but no fingerprints. That's what we know right now."

"Thank you. I'll let you know once I've made contact with General Savage."

"Thank you, Major."

They hung up, and Alex looked at Mahegan's face, then at his large feet.

"Those look like size twelve to me," she said.

Mahegan said nothing. He turned his head up at a noise outside the storm shelter doors. There was a hint of familiarity in Alex's voice when she spoke to Dupree. Tires crunched in the gravel above.

"Expecting someone?" he asked Alex.

"No. Where's your car?"

"Garage."

She nodded. They both moved quickly to either side of the doors, Mahegan assuming the same position he had when Alex had entered. Alex moved toward the stairs when they heard knocking. How would anyone know the coop existed, yet not have the combination, Mahegan wondered?

"Go up," he said. "But don't let them in."

Alex walked up the same steps by which she had entered the underground facility. She unlocked the doors and pushed one of them to the side, leading with her pistol. When the door was open far enough, the flashing blue and red lights of police or emergency vehicles bounced inside the dugout.

Military police, he thought. Either Alex had given him up or the MPs had a way of tracking her. He had been off the military police radar for over two years. He readied his pistol, less sure about Alex by the moment now.

"Hey, guys," he heard her say. "How can I help you?"

"We're looking for Jake Mahegan, ma'am."

"Why would he be here?" she replied.

Ever the lawyer. Instead of denying his presence with a lie, she answered their question with a question.

"We got an anonymous tip that he might be somewhere on this property."

"An anonymous tip?"

Another question.

"Yes, ma'am. Have you seen him? Do you know him?"

"I'm here monitoring the situation we have going on right now. Kidnapped military leaders and United Bank of America CEO and family murdered. Something is happening right now. Do you really think I have time to look for a has-been renegade murder suspect?"

"So that's a no?"

"That's a no, Sergeant," Alex said. Again, she hadn't directly answered the military police officer.

"Mind if we look down there?"

A flashlight swept the steps beyond Alex's feet.

"This is a top secret facility, Sergeant. What's your clearance?"

After a long pause, the sergeant replied, "Not top secret. But we'll be back with a warrant." Then after a noticeable hesitation, he added, "Ma'am."

There was something off about the sergeant's voice. Too old? Maybe trying too hard to hide an ethnic undertone?

"Anything else, guys?"

Guys.

More than one MP. There was tension in Alex's voice as her hand tightened on the pistol grip. She stood on the step with a perfect balanced shooter's stance, feet spread evenly and knees flexed.

"Just this," the older voice said.

Alex's pistol was up and firing as she dove opposite of Mahegan's protected position. He heard a grunt from the top of the stairwell and saw a shadow move across the opening to the COOP. The body belonging to the shadow took two tentative steps into the stairwell, and Alex used her Berretta to blow the kneecap off the intruder. The man bellowed and fell down into the cavern with a thud. He was dressed in standard issue Army combat uniform with the digitized olive and tan pattern. There was an MP armband around his left deltoid, and he had a high and tight haircut like many of the paratroopers at Fort Bragg. It crossed Mahegan's mind that this could be a legitimate soldier conducting official business.

Regardless, Mahegan was on top of him with one knee in his back and his pistol to his skull.

"Check up top," he said to Alex. She moved swiftly up the steps. Initially he had been concerned she might have been wounded, but if so, she was doing a good job of hiding it.

Mahegan bounced the man's head against the hard floor of the COOP, knocking him unconscious. Soldier or not, Mahegan could not have him see his face. Lifting him, Mahegan climbed the stairs and dumped the attacker on the ground next to the dead man dressed as an MP sergeant.

Mahegan looked up at Alex, who was pacing back and forth, muttering something unintelligible. He checked the unconscious man first. He found a Berretta 9 mm pistol, standard Army issue, in a hip holster. Upon further inspection, he found a Makarov PM, a Russian pistol, strapped to his ankle. This was unusual but not out of the ordinary. Many soldiers, including Mahegan, had carried personal weapons into combat or while on duty. A military policeman was "in combat" when he was on patrol whether near Fort Bragg or in Kandahar. MPs were targets everywhere because they were law enforcement.

Studying the man's facial features, Mahegan did not discount that he could be of Middle Eastern or Russian origin. He lifted the man and carried him to Alex's Land Rover. By now, she had gathered herself and moved back to the second body.

He turned as Alex was lifting a pistol to the man's head.

"He's already dead, Alex. No need for that," he said. The air outside was warm and muggy. Alex was sweating. He placed his hand on hers and shifted the pistol to the side. "Plus, you don't want another bullet they can trace from your pistol. I see the first was a through and through on the neck. Nicked his carotid artery."

"More like blew it wide open," she said, regaining some composure.

"Are you sure these are not real military police officers who were doing their duty?"

Alex looked at Mahegan with a cold stare.

"The only thing that matters now is that we do ours," she said. "Lift him and throw him in my car. I've got a painter's tarp back there."

"I saw it," he said. "I need a first aid kit."

Alex looked at him. A cloud moved across her eyes. Something registered in the back of Mahegan's brain. Again he asked himself, *Is she friend or foe?*

"We need to get moving. They're after you. Legit or not, we can't afford to have you off the chessboard. That's what they want. All of you incapacitated so they can do whatever it is that they're doing."

Mahegan lifted the dead man and placed him next to the unconscious, wounded MP in the back of Alex's Land Rover. He grabbed the first aid kit from the side well of the car's hatch. The bullet had ripped off the man's kneecap. If he lived, he would probably need to have the lower half of his leg amputated. There was no way he was putting any pressure on that knee unless a doctor could reconstruct it or do replacement surgery. He used Betadine, Neosporin, and gauze as best he could. Flashbacks of patching teammate combat wounds popped in his mind like firecrackers.

He spoke in Arabic to the wounded MP.

"What's your name?"

The MP coughed and started to say, "Haf—" but then looked at his name tape on his uniform and said, "Smith." It was no kind of confirmation, but also a good clue that these two military policemen were not legitimate. The throaty Arabic voice shifted to something more trained and smooth when he said, "Smith."

He searched their uniforms and came away with weapons and ammunition. Another clue that they could be part of the decapitation team, here to clean out the COOP, which would mean him, O'Malley, Owens, and Savage. Which meant that whoever was running the operation did not actually have his COOP teammates in captivity, or this team had not received the word. Or perhaps they were after Mahegan alone.

Alex went into the COOP, and Mahegan closed the Land Rover back door. He walked over to the military police car and switched the idling vehicle off. He removed the keys and pocketed them. On the dashboard he noticed a GPS indicating the vehicle's location. He was certain that it was transmitting back to Fort Bragg or somewhere else if these men were not authentic MPs. Regardless, as Alex had said, someone would be coming their way shortly.

He climbed into the COOP and saw Alex hovering over one of the computers. She looked over her shoulder and quickly closed the MacBook lid. After unplugging it, she tucked it under her arm and said, "Let's go. They're coming."

Alex climbed back up the steps and Mahegan followed, closed the doors, secured the locks, and spun the dial.

"We should drive their car wherever we're going to drop them off," Mahegan said.

"Too obvious. Just move it a mile up the road and I'll pick you up."

Mahegan sat in the MP sedan and used a dark green cloth in the backseat to wipe his fingerprints and hold the steering wheel. He cranked the engine and the vehicle came to life. He debated the next move. He had enough information—the Russian pistol, the lack of identification, and the Arabic accent—to reconcile in his mind that the men were part of the operation that was happening tonight.

He followed Alex's taillights as they bumped along the dirt road that led past the main house, a white farm-style home with a covered porch. It was unassuming and blended with the homes of the region. Savage had done well. They hit the blacktop and pulled a right turn, driving about a mile before Alex slowed to a stop on the country road. She pulled into the oncoming lane and waved him forward. Through the open window, she said, "Drive it into the ditch, like they were drunk or something."

Mahegan snapped his seat belt across his chest as he pulled forward, eyeing the drainage ditch just off the narrow shoulder. It was steep and would require a tow truck to recover the vehicle once it was found. He nosed over the lip and gravity took over as the hood of the sedan slammed into the watery bottom. Black muck splashed onto the windshield as the car slapped the water and then settled up to about the top of the grill. He wiped away his fingerprints again and opened the door, barely able to escape through the narrow crack. Clawing his way up the ravine, Mahegan saw Alex waving her arms, motioning for him to hurry.

He climbed into the backseat of her Land Rover SUV. The back windows were tinted, but he chose to lie down on the bench seat as she cranked the engine. Holding his Tribal pistol in one hand, he steadied his large frame with the other as Alex rocketed along the asphalt road.

"Stay down. They're right around the corner, waiting. Another cruiser was called to the scene when someone reported gunshots."

"These could be real MPs in the back of your vehicle, Alex," Mahegan said from the backseat. Although he didn't believe them to be, Mahegan was pushing on Alex. There was something that seemed out of alignment. He couldn't put his finger on it, but it was there. Everything was too convenient. She happened to arrive after him. She happened to have a backup to Zebra. She happened to shoot the MPs.

Mahegan didn't doubt his ability to fend off the two faux military policemen. He was unsure if he wanted an aggressive, shoot-first-ask-questions-later partner. He had no problem with rapid action, but they needed intelligence and information, not dead and dying MPs or assailants.

"Whatever. They don't realize I'm a lawyer, and these guys were and are off base with no jurisdiction," Alex said.

She continued for a minute without talking, then said, "Okay, I'm past them. They've started following me but haven't turned on any lights. They could call state troopers or Southern Pines police, but we're going to have to risk it. I'm just going to stay on Route 27 through Troy and into the Uwharrie National Forest. If you need to bail out, you can bail. But that's where I was thinking we could dump the bodies."

They had a good forty-five minutes before they were in the national forest. But it was reassuring that they would be passing through the Uwharrie, because Mahegan had walked every trail from the land navigation training he had performed as a paratrooper, Special Forces soldier, and Delta Force operator.

After about fifteen minutes, Alex said, "They turned back toward Fort Bragg."

She drove another thirty minutes until Mahegan could tell that the ambient light had diminished and they were in the countryside, perhaps passing through the Uwharrie. He sat up and got his bearings.

"Just entered the national forest," she said. "I'm guessing you know your way around here. Route 109."

"Some," Mahegan said.

"Where's the best place to dump these guys?"

"There's no good place to dump wounded and dead soldiers, Alex," Mahegan said.

"These guys aren't soldiers. I can promise you that."

"So enlighten me before I use this Tribal on the back of your head."

He watched her eyes in the mirror. Saw the wrinkle of crow's-feet, indicating a smirk.

"I'll flip this car so fast, that pistol will fly through the window, Mahegan. You have no idea who I am or what I can do. I killed that imposter without even thinking about it. Shot him through the neck, which is where I was aiming because I *wanted* a through and through. Think about *that*."

Mahegan did think about it. She was a good shot and a quick thinker. She was also an enigma. Alex claimed to have connections to General Savage, and he had heard Savage talk about an "Alex," but there was no way he could be certain that Savage's Alex and the one driving this Land Rover with two military policemen stuffed in the rear compartment were one and the same.

"Got it figured out?" she asked.

"Not even close," Mahegan said. Usually the one driving the action and in control, Mahegan had to admit that he had relinquished his positional advantage to Alex once she shot the military policemen. Knowing that he was wanted for murder added a layer of complexity to the equation, also. Mahegan needed to find his team: O'Malley, Owens, and Savage.

That's where he needed to be, needed to go. Whether Alex was who she said she was or, worst case, an imposter allied with the elements wreaking havoc on the country right now, he didn't know. But he did know she had a vehicle with a full tank of gas that could get him to Asheville.

"Make a right up here at this milepost. It's a well-known spot for everyone doing the land nav course. Gravel road. We can drop these guys there and get to Asheville."

"Now we're talking," Alex said.

Alex slowed the vehicle to a stop on a gravel road about one hundred yards off the main highway. Mahegan opened the hatchback and lifted the dead man first, carrying him about fifty yards off the road into some of the thickest forest in North Carolina. It would be less than twenty-four hours before animals, most likely bear, had devoured this corpse. Mahegan was still conflicted, but he convinced himself that this was the right course of action. The military policeman had drawn first on Alex, or so it seemed. And there was a personal Russian weapon strapped to the ankle of the man who fell to the basement floor. If these men had anything to do with the disappearance of the senior military officers and their families, then they were fair game. Mahegan was going to treat them as such until he had further evidence that they weren't.

After dropping the dead man on a rock outcropping, he doubled back, found the road, and saw the dim outline of the SUV in the low moonlight. He retrieved the wounded man and set him next to his dead partner. He walked back to find Alex standing outside of her vehicle, closing the door.

"You made a mess back here," she said.

"Let's go," Mahegan replied.

Alex turned toward him, holding her pistol in his direction.

"Things are about to get messier," Alex said. "I'm thinking it would be good for my career to turn you in."

In the moonlight, Alex' face was set, the left jawline visible in the weak light, the right side of her face shaded. She had shut off her vehicle, and the engine ticked as it cooled. What was her play? Why draw down on him now? Perhaps she just needed to rid herself of the two dead military policemen and now she could pin it on him. The weight of his Tribal on his hip, a one-second draw away, beckoned him.

"Hand me your pistol, Jake, and tell me everything you know about Operation Groomsman."

"What are you doing?" he asked, buying time. "You know Groomsman was a classified operation and a disaster."

"It was worse than a disaster. Trust me."

Mahegan remembered the mission clearly. He had been the team leader and was tasked with taking seven other men to a long stretch of road leading to a compound in Syria near Mosul, Iraq, to kill or capture a high value target. Savage had ordered the mission, and he presumed Alex Russell had been standing next to him saying, "Valid target," as the Predator drones and B-2 bombers annihilated what they thought was an SUV convoy of bona fide bad guys.

Instead, what they found was a wedding party. Of course, all along, the convoy had been referencing a wedding, but the intelligence analysts thought that was a ruse. They had confirmation of the high-value target's voice on the target's cell phone, and they had the cell phone active in a specific vehicle of the convoy. The bombing run had destroyed all of the vehicles and killed more than twenty people. As Mahegan's team descended on the carnage along the cratered road at twilight, they saw no survivors, no runners, and no high-value targets. Just a bloody and dead bride in her white dress and SUVs full of dead groomsmen, family members, and the groom.

Why Alex was asking for more information on this mission, he didn't know and frankly didn't care. That was a different lifetime for Mahegan, and he was trying to move beyond the violence and find something stable, something to call his own.

"What could I possibly tell you about Groomsman you don't already know?"

Alex looked away and then back at Mahegan. "Jake, you were on the ground there. Tell me what you saw."

"I reported everything to Savage. My understanding was that you guys were in Mosul, not that far. It was a murderous mission. The intel was bad."

"Tell me!" she shouted. Mahegan heard her voice echo into the deep forests on either side of the road. Birch, oak, and maple trees rose all around them as if standing in judgment. Hardwoods. Hard decisions. Mahegan looked at her pistol, its dull black finish a shadow in the dim moonlight. Saw her balanced shooter's stance. She was prepared to pull the trigger.

"What do you want to know?"

Alex had tears streaming down her face. Her countenance slackened, as if her mind was spinning backward in time.

"The bride," she whispered. "Tell me about the bride."

Mahegan paused, took a breath, considered his options. While the road was sparsely traveled, it *was* traveled. He looked left and saw the light gray gravel spilling away to the east where it met Highway 105, swallowed by the darkness. He looked right and saw the gravel rise slightly in a long, straight line until it merged with the horizon. No lights were coming from either direction. Not even a hint. He could hear a million crickets chirping and the clarion call of owls on the hunt. Animals were moving in the bush, probably smelling fresh blood fifty yards away.

Operation Groomsman. Savage had been hell-bent on attacking that convoy. They'd had no clues on future ISIS commander al-Baghdadi until twenty-four hours prior to the mission. The intel team picked up al-Baghdadi's phone pinging from a specific location. Savage directed the Air Force to move Predator over the location, and the live streaming showed a group of SUVs at a compound. From his headquarters in Mosul, Savage monitored the compound for nearly a full day and night with little activity other than children playing in the courtyard near the SUVs, making a Predator shot impractical. Mahegan and his team had watched from a separate compound twenty miles away from Savage's location. The farther, the better, in Mahegan's mind.

Savage had laid out two quick options. One, Mahegan and his men air assault into the compound and capture Baghdadi alive, which would lead to better intelligence, or, two, wait for the SUVs to move, kill the nascent leader, and call it a day. For any operation involving ground troops, Savage liked to have two confirming sources of intelligence. A human spot report coupled with signals intercept, for example. Streaming video and voice recognition. Any combination of confirmed intelligence from reliable sources was the trigger. For dropping a bomb, the same standard held but the commander felt more discretion. The U.S. Air Force pilots were flying out of range of enemy surface-to-air missiles and weren't necessarily at risk other than the normal hazards of flying combat missions.

Savage had a known phone number for Baghdadi with his voice in the phone. The voice match was weak, but it was there. Savage told Mahegan that he considered the phone and the voice match two distinct sources, though Mahegan believed neither was reliable. Mahegan never went into the operations center. He and his team were always remote from the headquarters. He rarely saw Savage during deployments, if at all. But he was watching the Predator streaming video from his remote viewer, called a ROVER. He watched as the Hellfire missile struck the middle SUV and then JDAM bombs lawn darted into the remaining vehicles. It looked as spectacular as anything shown on television or YouTube. His little bird helicopters had spinning blades, awaiting Savage's word to launch his raid to gather intelligence from the detritus. Savage gave Mahegan the word to execute sensitive site exploitation. He remembered the carnage at the scene.

"Wasn't much to see. A Hellfire missile struck her vehicle, and everyone in there was charred. Weren't you in the Mosul JOC?" Mahegan used the acronym for Joint Operations Center.

"Tell me!" she shouted again.

Suddenly Mahegan felt that she had a personal connection to someone in the wedding party. The pistol remained aimed at his chest. He figured she was about done asking him questions.

"Why draw down on me, Alex? I was there, but I didn't kill anyone that day. And I didn't kill anyone today or yesterday."

She laughed a high-pitched squeal. "You? You killed so many people over there and now you're wanted for murder here. I have no idea if those MPs are real or fake. My gut tells me they're fake and bad guys, but at the end of the day my career is too important to me to risk it. I should put a bullet in your head. You've killed one person already tonight. Let's make it a killing spree. Murder–suicide. You get the gist."

"Really? This is all about your career?"

"What else is there in life? Relationships? Family? You know better than anyone that those things hurt you more than they help you. This right here, this is what counts." Alex patted her identification card clipped to her belt on a retractable lanyard, her credential for getting behind the fence. Now Mahegan was convinced that Operation Groomsman had wound up killing someone she knew or had been close to.

"So tell me, Jake Mahegan, what is it that you care most about?" Alex asked him.

She shifted her weight. Mahegan guessed she was positioning her feet to absorb the kick of the pistol when she pulled the trigger. He studied the geometry. She was five feet from him. The vehicle was to her left. The wooded forest was maybe ten feet behind him. If he dashed toward the SUV, he figured he could use the vehicle as protection as he angled toward the wood line. Once in the forest, he didn't believe she would come after him.

"I care about my teammates, Alex. And at one time I guess General Savage considered you worthy of the JSOC team."

Alex nodded her head. She appeared on the verge of losing control.

"That's right. Teammates. JSOC. Friends. All of that happy horseshit. Now give me your pistol," Alex emphasized. "Not asking again."

She tightened her grip on the gun, and about the same time that she pulled the trigger he leapt to his right, toward the SUV. The shot was loud, an echoing report that rumbled for miles. Mahegan landed on his right side and rolled toward the SUV. Two more shots plinked off the side of the SUV, chasing him. He removed his pistol and opened the passenger door as he slid across the hood. He hoped the white light from the dome would blind her as he escaped into the woods. Alex pressed her body against the back of the SUV as he jogged into the woods on the opposite side of the road. He quickly positioned himself behind a large oak. Watching as Alex carefully made her way to the driver's door, Mahegan aimed the pistol from less than fifteen yards away.

It was an easy shot.

CHAPTER 7

IT WAS WELL PAST MIDNIGHT ON FRIDAY MORNING, AND YVES DUPREE stood in the familiar master bedroom of his boss, Charles Sledge, the CEO of United Bank of America. That he had previously taken certain liberties with Vicki Sledge gave him pause.

The police and crime scene techs were milling around, and he was, frankly, surprised that he had been allowed inside. His status as a lawyer and the executor of the Sledge family estate most likely played a large role in the Charlotte police chief and Mecklenburg County sheriff granting him access. After all, somebody had to identify the bodies, and it would be hours before they moved any of the three.

He wore light blue booties over his Ferragamo high-top calfskin sneakers, freshly pressed designer jeans, and a Ted Baker pinpoint cotton shirt with silk collar and sleeves. He ran a hand through his wavy, light brown hair as he stared at the body of Danny Sledge. There was a hole the size of a fist through his body. The blood splatter against the wall above Vicki Sledge's head was grotesque, an artist's gruesome rendering of death. Vicki looked as if she were sleeping, and it appeared that someone had closed her eyes. Her head was cocked toward him, and he expected her to awaken and say, "Hello, Yves, what brings you here tonight?"

But he knew that wasn't going to happen. Looking at his boss, Yves could see and smell the urine that had been voided from his body either directly before he was shot or during the shooting.

Yves could only imagine the fear the man must have felt for his wife and son.

Yves was single. He never planned on getting married if he could help it. He was raised in the small town of Lille, France, on the Belgian border, attended both the Sorbonne for his undergraduate and masters in finance and accounting, then Oxford for his JD in Law and PhD in Political Economy. His primary focus was on international trade, foreign exchange, and markets.

A rising star in the French government, Yves had worked for Barclays as an investment banker before being recruited by the General Directorate of Security, or DGSE in French acronym parlance. The DGSE was the French equivalent of the CIA. He had become a field agent, which included interacting with groups such as cutouts for ISIS and Hezbollah as they secretly made ransom demands or threatened French officials. Yves had even deployed to Syria and Iraq to work with the UN High Commissioner for Refugees, a legend for his spy work. The Arab Spring had created chaos . . . and opportunity. There he had met Lieutenant General Bart Bagwell, the commander to whom he had proven a reliable source of intelligence.

While he had enjoyed the cloak-and-dagger work, he found that for it to be lucrative he had to skirt the law, which he had little problem doing from a moral standpoint. With his connections he was able to establish a profitable side business in the world of information sharing and manipulation in the wake of the mass exodus during the Syrian civil war. People needed to safely exit Syria and get to Europe. Dupree figured there was a market there. His business plan catered to the Syrian elite, who were arguably also the most targeted. The equivalent of one hundred thousand dollars or euros cash got a potential migrant processed in a single day. Within twenty-four hours that individual and up to two family members were cleared to leave Syria and enter the European country of Dupree's choosing. Similarly, the equivalent of fifty thousand dollars or euros resulted in a five-day processing time, which was a deal given that visas were taking months to clear. Those were his only two offers. Anything else and he felt he would be exposing himself to the hapless, but sometimes effective, UN auditors. Ultimately he could not have done this business venture alone, and he and his business partner had cashed in nearly $15 million over the course of a year.

But then it had all disappeared. Stolen. Cyber hacked.

The loss had been devastating, forcing him to sell his Biarritz beach house and his Paris apartment and to find a higher salaried job. His business partner had a connection that landed him with United Bank of America.

Because Charles Sledge and the board of directors had hired him for his financial expertise, Yves had an idea what Sledge's murder would mean for him. He would immediately become Interim CEO, according to the Board of Directors succession plan that had been in place for years. His salary would more than triple from $600,000 annually to $2 million.

Having fulfilled his first duty of executing the will of Charles and Vicki Sledge, his mind wandered back to Alex Russell. They had met on a few occasions. She was certainly a beautiful, exotic woman, if not a tad rough-hewn. He figured the military did that to a woman, diminished her feminism.

Nonetheless he had been somewhat smitten with her, causing him to use his DGSE sources to dig deeper into the backgrounds of the men with whom she worked. He studied General Savage, her boss, and the team that worked for him, such as Jake Mahegan, Patch Owens, and Sean O'Malley. He knew that Mahegan had been on the gray list, meaning to possibly detain if found. He had heard about Mahegan's dustups in other parts of North Carolina, though he had discovered that information through unofficial sources.

Looking at the bodies lying on the bed and floor, like the remnants of a combat zone, Yves Dupree knew that these killings were motivated by money, not radical Islam, which was certainly a threat.

He looked again at Vicki Sledge's face and shook his head. Someone was one step closer to what they wanted.

"Seen enough?" the police chief asked.

"Seen too much, Chief. That's Vicki. That's Charles. That's Danny. Positive ID. Can I go now?"

The chief nodded with his thick neck and heavy jowls, a sympathetic look on his face.

"Sure thing, Counselor. But first can I see those fancy sneakers?"

Dupree chuckled, "Of course." He lifted his foot and removed the blue bootie so that the police chief could see his two thousand dollar tennis shoes.

"Emily?"

A young woman wearing surgical scrubs, blue booties, a blue surgeon's cap, and latex gloves came over, placed a sticky piece of paper against the sole, got an imprint, and then walked away.

"Thanks. Since you've been in here before, we need to make sure we're not chasing the wrong shoe prints."

"No problem," Dupree said with confidence.

"We'll be in touch." The sheriff nodded and held out his hand. "You okay?"

Yves shook the man's hand and nodded. "It's quite a shock." Of course, only Dupree knew that he had seen worse, much worse.

Yves Dupree had the stomach for death. He was simply bored and had work to do.

State Bureau of Investigation agent Tommy Oxendine leaned against the jamb of the kitchen door and watched with a wary eye as Yves Dupree departed the crime scene.

Not ruling him out, Oxendine thought.

Oxendine was a Lumbee American Indian from Lumberton who had been with the State Bureau of Investigation for seventeen years. A Lumberton High School football star, Oxendine had graduated from the University of North Carolina at Pembroke prior to joining the SBI. Now a seasoned investigator, Oxendine had been given the lead on the murder of Charles Sledge, one of the most prominent citizens in Charlotte. Aside from being rich and the CEO of a large national bank, Sledge was a frequent donor to political candidates and to charities that promoted literacy and education for children.

A quick search of the golf course pond behind Sledge's house revealed a Colt .45 Ranger Spirit Tribute pistol that looked brand new once his weapons man had cleaned it. A quick check of records showed the weapon was purchased in Fayetteville, North Carolina, and was registered to Chayton Mahegan.

Oxendine knew of Mahegan. They were both Native Americans, and Mahegan had once lived in Maxton, not far from where Oxendine had gone to school. Although older than Mahegan, Oxendine had been on the scene of his mother's murder in Maxton, one of his first cases as a young agent. Oxendine also checked the Homeland Security black/white/gray list and saw that Mahegan was listed as "gray," meaning possibly detain. Mahegan's name had come up a few times in the last couple of years regarding possible connections to terrorists.

A young woman named Emily Jones walked up to Oxendine. Emily smelled of antiseptic hand wash and was average height, white, her blond hair tied up in a bun beneath the surgeon's cap. She wore blue surgical scrubs and booties and latex gloves. She had been making casts of the boot prints inside and outside the home. She had just printed Dupree's shoes.

"Yes?" Oxendine asked. He was a good foot taller than the petite technician. She looked up at him with narrow eyes and a furrowed brow.

"I've got size twelve Doc Martens patterned soles," Emily said. "In case you were wondering, Dupree wears size nine."

"Okay, log it in," Oxendine said.

Emily nodded but didn't move.

"What else?" Oxendine prompted. He had worked with Emily before and knew she was always just the facts. Now she looked confused or uncertain.

"Just something freaky about the prints. As I study them, each one looks like the boot slid a fraction of an inch with most every step," Emily said.

Oxendine thought about it a moment. Studying shoe and boot prints was a standard part of any crime scene analysis. He had seen hundreds of prints, and all varied to some degree. He thought about Emily's relative inexperience and weighed that against her renowned thoroughness.

"What do you think that means?"

"I'm not sure. I just wanted to let you know. I'm going to put them in the computer and then compare all of them and see what I come up with. I know what you're thinking, that I'm young and inexperienced, but I've seen a lot of these prints, sir."

"Don't pretend to know what I'm thinking, Miss Jones. Run it through the computer and then speak to me with more certainty. Thank you for your thoroughness."

Sufficiently chastised, Emily nodded, said, "Thank you, sir," and walked into the family room where the rest of the technicians had set up a makeshift command post.

Oxendine got back to thinking about Mahegan. He was accused of murder in Afghanistan, but Oxendine heard that Mahegan had his dishonorable discharge overturned on a technicality. Mahegan was on the possibly detain list, which was as good as saying, "Detain." In Oxendine's mind there wasn't much difference between the black and the gray lists. And the white list, for that matter, if you pissed him off enough.

Mahegan was rumored to have been involved in a fracking scheme that nearly melted down a nuclear plant in the Raleigh area, and Oxendine had read a report that Mahegan had gotten into trouble with the Coast Guard in the Outer Banks. And now, his team found Mahegan's pistol in the pond.

Oxendine held the pistol with a latex-gloved hand. It was a beautiful weapon, with the words "Ranger Tribute" inscribed on the trigger housing. He popped the magazine out of the well and counted five bullets. He would have those fingerprinted immediately by the team in the family room. It was a newer eight-round magazine. The math certainly added up for Oxendine. Three dead victims, each with one bullet in them apiece. Eight-round magazine missing three bullets. Three casings in the pond. No-brainer.

Mahegan went from gray list to black list in Oxendine's mind. Moreover, Oxendine had worked with the Lumbee community in

North Carolina and was proud of his Native American heritage. Protective. He wasn't going to let a bad seed like Mahegan feed into the negative stereotypes of American Indians everywhere. He was going to be harder on Mahegan than anyone else could ever be.

Tommy Oxendine was a role model for his people. He volunteered in Lumberton sometimes on his weekends, when he had weekends. Work pretty much consumed him. Still unmarried, he was career driven and equally motivated to show everyone that a Lumbee could compete in the white man's world.

And Chayton Mahegan, the Hawk Wolf, was an embarrassment.

He pulled out his secure phone and punched speed dial back to Raleigh; got Officer Lucy Cartwright, the night watch officer; and gave her his report.

"Put out a BOLO on one Chayton Mahegan. I need the state helicopter here within the next two hours. I'm setting up a command post at the Concord Airport conference room. Need a SWAT team on hand by six a.m. Any questions?"

"Getting bossy, Oxendine?" Cartwright said.

"I'm on the ground. You're in a comfy air-conditioned office, Lucy."

"I hear you're chilling in a three-million-dollar mansion," she replied.

"With three dead bodies."

"Watch yourself, Tommy," Cartwright said, a subtle reminder she outranked him. "One SWAT team heading your way. Roger, out," she said.

Oxendine hung up. Most people didn't question Tommy Oxendine, the linebacker with the fierce black eyes and thick black hair mowed nearly into a Mohawk. No, most people nodded and said, "Yes, sir," to Oxendine, because whether he liked the analogy or not, people said he had more scalps than any other special agent in the SBI.

"Adding one to the list," he muttered.

CHAPTER 8

MAHEGAN DIDN'T TAKE THE SHOT ON ALEX RUSSELL.

He watched as Alex got back into her Land Rover and sped west on Route 109 through the Uwharrie National Forest. They had stopped about the five-mile mark after passing through the town of Troy. Mahegan broke brush due west through the hilly terrain. At times the undergrowth was thick, and in other places it appeared and smelled like the Forest Service had performed a controlled burn. If he kept going west he would hit the Yadkin River, which flowed southeast out of Badin Lake Dam. On the opposite side of the Yadkin would be the town of Badin. Perhaps he could find a rental car there and head toward Asheville and the last known locations of the blinking lights of Savage, O'Malley, and Owens. When he was safely away from the road, he checked the time on his smartphone. Three in the morning. Peak circadian rhythm time for human sleep. It was also peak hunting time for nocturnal animals, such as owls, wolves, and bobcats, all of which he knew inhabited the Uwharrie Forest.

His goal was to reach the town of Badin by sunrise, which would be around six-thirty. His walk was surprisingly uneventful other than knowing he was going to have to check himself for ticks when he reached a hospitable location. He spent the balance of his time wondering about Alex Russell and why she had flipped on him so awkwardly. She'd acted like a different person when he returned from dropping the bodies of the men she had shot. He remembered her affect when he was attempting to inspect the two men in Savage's backyard. She was worried about potential backlash on her, but then why had she taken the shot? Mahegan had observed that the military policeman's pistol was in his hand. It was conceivable, however, that while Mahegan was confronting the man who had fallen inside the COOP, Alex was up top placing the man's pistol back in his hand. Perhaps she had drawn down on him because she had recognized him, or he had recognized her.

A few twigs snapped him in the face as he felt the ground begin to slope downward. Thus far, he had been on a fairly steady climb with some level spots in the middle. His pace count put him about four and a half miles from where he had started. The river, by his estimation, would be another quarter to half mile down the slope. He navigated the terrain, still wondering about Alex. She was an enigma. Initially, she was all about saving him, protecting him so that they could find Savage, O'Malley, and Owens. Then, suddenly, she had a pistol in his face, asking about Operation Groomsman, a cluster if he had ever seen one.

Baghdadi had most likely placed his phone and a voice recording inside the back of one of the SUVs, deceiving American technology into believing he was in the convoy. Mahegan had found the splintered remnants of Baghdadi's phone and a chip that indicated it was his. The document exploitation team had found a single picture of Baghdadi on the cut-out cell phone. It was a photo of him smiling and flipping the bird to the camera, and of course to anyone looking at the image. That pretty much confirmed the idea that Baghdadi had duped the American intelligence system.

Perhaps Alex felt remorse for giving Savage the "valid target" confirmation. But then again, she was simply basing her professional judgment on the intelligence and information provided at the time. But guilt weighed on people differently, particularly if there was a personal connection.

As Mahegan navigated the slope and approached the expanse

of the river, he was certain that he had not seen the last of Alex Russell.

Wading thigh deep in the river, he made sure his Sig Sauer Tribal was secure and began a simple Australian crawl directly toward the far bank.

The water was cool but consistent with the air temperature, some fog lifting off the surface in cloudy puffs of mist. Ghosts of Mahegan's past escaping, perhaps. As he pulled through the water he felt the scar on his left deltoid bite back at him. The scar was left by a chunk of metal blown from his best friend's vehicle during a roadside bomb attack. Mahegan figured that if his wound never healed, then he would never forget Sergeant Wesley Colgate. Even if it did heal, Colgate remained a fixture in his life, a pivot point for so many things. That day, Mahegan had killed an enemy prisoner of war still handcuffed, albeit attempting to escape by charging Mahegan. Nonetheless, the Army Inspector General was bent on dishing out a dishonorable discharge to Mahegan. And while his present life path rotated around that one night, there were many other nights when anything similar might have happened.

Such as Operation Groomsman, Mahegan figured. He remembered pawing through the remnants of the attack. With each charred body, each female passenger, each child, Mahegan's worst fears were confirmed. Savage had ordered the strike on the wrong target. Al-Baghdadi had tricked them. It was a twofer for the terrorist leader. Not only did he dodge a missile, he also set a trap for the Americans to kill innocent bystanders. It was great theater. In all societies there was nothing more joyous or sacred than a wedding. The beginning of joined lives and potentially new lives to be created. And here the Americans had squelched it all with a few precision guided bombs to his cell phone. Like candles snuffed, the lives were no more. Al-Baghdadi couldn't care less other than the theatrical effect his misdirection had created.

The Americans issued a statement saying that it was a "valid target." Then they retracted the statement. Then the Army Inspector General conducted an investigation. Given the wide latitude of the IG, he went after midlevel officers who had the responsibility of vetting the intelligence. Mahegan remembered that two majors and a colonel had been demoted. Perhaps it was warranted, who knew? But a female military intelligence captain had been spared, he remembered. Something caught in the back of his mind.

And there was Alex Russell. Why would she instantly flip on Mahegan? The man needed medical attention, and as soon as he was able he would make an anonymous call to the closest police department, tipping them as to the location of the two men.

Mahegan waded in the water, assessing the best place to step onto the steep bank. He spotted an area about thirty yards upstream and swam to that. He was able to stand in knee-deep water and pull himself out of the river using tree roots and vines. The undergrowth was thick, but he powered through the renowned thorny vines that infantrymen had dubiously labled, "wait a minute vines." They ripped through his skin and clothing. Soon he was clear of the bank and walking through knee-high grass. A dull oval of light bounced against the early morning clouds. It had to be Badin's small downtown reflecting its wakening moments upward.

As he walked the town glow diminished and the edge of morning began creeping toward him, erasing the darkness and shedding dim light on what had been a treacherous path. He could feel the ticks crawling on his skin and wanting to burrow. Figuring it would be a waste of time until he got completely out of the field, he chose not to slow down and remove the bloodsuckers just yet.

As he approached the road, two vehicles sped past him without slowing. One was a Ford pickup truck and the other was a sheriff's white and tan cruiser with a rack on the top. They turned to the left, so Mahegan angled to the right. He figured that, like any small town, there were probably two decent restaurants people frequented. The sheriff was heading to breakfast, he was certain, and Mahegan didn't need to be seen by the sheriff looking like he did. If there truly was an all-points bulletin out, Mahegan probably should just forage and not risk being seen in public. But he needed to eat. It had been a long night, and he liked his chances at the north end of town, the opposite direction of the sheriff.

He walked through a field and saw a family restaurant at the end of the block. Its light was on and a red OPEN sign flickered twice and then held steady. Mahegan figured it was six a.m., and the town of Badin was waking up. He walked to the restaurant door, nodded at the man taking chairs off the tables, and opened the door. The white-haired man took a second to assess Mahegan and then nodded, most likely figuring he was a hunter. It was deer season and Mahegan could very well have been hunting. The man was dressed in cook whites and carrying a dingy dish rag he was using to wipe down the tables.

"Been spotlighting?" the man asked him. "Because if you have, I won't serve ya."

Mahegan shook his head. "Truck issues. Had to walk here."

"Looks like you swam," the man said. He turned his head when the lights in the kitchen came on. There were two women tying aprons and preparing to cook.

"Did a little of that, too," Mahegan said.

"All right. Have a seat. Sheriff usually flips a coin. He either comes here or goes to Sammy's at the end of the street. If he ain't here by now, he's probably at Sammy's. Just letting you know I know where the sheriff is."

"Saw him go there. I just want to order some food and make a phone call."

"Assuming you've got a cell phone. No freebies here. What can I get you?"

Mahegan ordered a full breakfast of pancakes, two eggs over easy, bacon, hash browns, and orange juice. He was never much of a coffee person, but he'd just swum through the cool waters of the Yadkin River and so he ordered a cup of coffee, also. The food arrived quickly as did the coffee. Mahegan ate in less than ten minutes, pulled some wet ten-dollar bills from his pocket, and laid two on the table. He figured his tab was less than fifteen dollars and he would overtip in hopes that the proprietor would keep quiet. Doubtful, but even if it bought him a few minutes, that might be all he needed.

He stepped outside and turned to the north, away from Sammy's and the sheriff, and walked diagonally across the street to what he could now see was a park that overlooked the river. Ensuring he was out of view of the diner in which he just ate, Mahegan removed from his cargo pocket his government-issued cell phone, which he kept in a protective pouch along with his pistol. He continued walking north, following the river, thinking that worst case he could seek refuge in the dense brush and perhaps even the river if the police came after him now. He knew that he could make himself invisible in the Uwharrie National Forest, where he had trained so many times before.

Looking at his phone, he unlocked the screen and stared at the red and white candy-stripe image of the Zebra app that had been his lifeline to his teammates, past and present. Savage, O'Malley, and Owens had been there to support him just as he had been there to support them. Now, the app and the phone seemed to be a liability. The enemy, whoever that might be, most likely knew where he was exactly at this moment. If they were smart, and they certainly seemed to be, they would make anonymous calls to the local police departments to chase him down wherever he went.

He called the Stanly County Police Department and reported the two military policemen as dead or wounded and gave them as precise a location as possible. It was a brief call, and the young deputy who answered the phone continued talking as Mahegan hung up. Then he did the unthinkable.

He opened the Zebra app and hit the ZERO OUT function, which removed what little data were stored on the SIM card. He removed the SIM card, snapped it in half, slipped one half into his cargo pocket and the other half back into the slot, closed the SIM card door, and palmed the phone. He felt its weight, then placed his index finger along the side of it, his thumb on top, and he flung the phone into the Yadkin River as if he were an outfielder making a play at home plate after catching a fly ball on the warning track. He heard the phone land with an ominous plunk into the current.

Standing there briefly, Mahegan felt the nakedness that comes with being without communications. While never reliant on communications devices, he was reliant on situational awareness. Technology aided that greatly. Real-time situational awareness, knowing exactly what was happening at the moment it was happening, was a critical necessity in combat. Devoid of technology, especially the Zebra app, he would continue to rely upon his instincts and his last known orders, which were to move to the sound of the guns, so to speak. Mahegan was a civilian and had no true orders, but his calling derived from his unit bond ordered him to find Savage, O'Malley, and Owens.

That was his mission.

He stood behind a large oak tree at the very north end of the town, having moved another quarter mile away from where he had tossed his phone into the river. As he predicted, the sheriff's car came to a screeching halt in front of the Main Street diner where he had just finished breakfast.

Knowing the owner would rather stay tight with the sheriff than protect a deranged looking drifter, Mahegan followed a trail behind a stand of pine trees and found a hollow. He took ten minutes to inspect his body for ticks, removing a total of seven. Then, emerging onto the road, he spotted a gas station a quarter mile away and walked toward the busy venue. Drivers were gassing up, customers were buying coffee and donuts, and hunters were prepping for the kill. He approached the business from the rear, using a low ditch that fed into the river. He heard sirens in the distance, most likely converging on his last known whereabouts. A helicopter chopped in from the south, its blades a reminder of the observation threat from above.

An air pump was behind the gas station along with a nonoperational car wash. A white Subaru Crosstrek was at the pump. Subaru was a subdivision of Fuji Heavy Industries in Japan. He had flown in aircraft made by Fuji but licensed to Boeing or Lockheed Martin. Subaru had started out as a tax write-off for the company but emerged into a viable enterprise. The car was packed with camping gear, tents, sleeping bags, propane stoves, and backpacks. It was that time of year to be in the North Carolina Blue Ridge Mountains. The gold and orange hues of autumn blanketed the rolling terrain.

He walked around the vehicle where he found a young woman squatting next to the left front tire, cursing.

"Help you?" Mahegan said.

"Damn flat," the woman said. Her voice was sharp. She had short hair that naturally ranged somewhere between blond and brunette. Mahegan guessed she was in her midtwenties. She was dressed in cargo shorts, Teva hiking shoes with vents along the side, and a light green tank top with a sports bra showing over each shoulder.

"Got the spare?" he asked. "That's like using a coffee cup to bail water from a sinking boat."

She continued to hold the air pump against the valve in a vain attempt to fill the flat tire.

"Yeah, but no jack."

"I think we can work around that," Mahegan said. "Mind if I grab the tire?"

She paused, looked up at him. Green eyes, perfectly pursed lips, clean face with a smattering of freckles.

"Nobody does this shit for free. What do you want, sex?"

"Just a ride," Mahegan said. "If you're headed my way."

She looked around, perhaps wishing that she had someone with her.

"You get my good tire on here and you've got a deal. I carry a pistol, and if you have thoughts of anything beyond a ride, just be aware that I'm a damn good shot."

"No thoughts of anything but a ride. My name is Jake," he said.

She stood and reached out her hand, which Mahegan shook.

"Cassie. Leave it at that for now. I'm headed to Sparta. Meeting some friends to hike the App Trail. Where are you going?"

"Asheville for now."

"Okay, let's see what you can do."

Cassie walked behind the Subaru and opened the rear hatch, then unloaded half her camping gear. She lifted the floorboard to reveal a full-size wheel in the well.

"The actual tire," Mahegan said. But he was looking at a muddy pair of Doc Martens, maybe his size, stacked beyond the bay for the spare tire. She had camping gear as well, but he lodged the information in his mind that there was a guy somewhere in the picture.

"Smartest thing I've done is get the full tire instead of that stupid fake one."

Mahegan unscrewed the wing nut and lifted the tire out. "A full-size tire doesn't do any good without a jack, you know?"

"Long story. Bottom line is, the jack is in my garage in Fayetteville. Was taking the shortcut to I-40 and took some time in Uwharrie yesterday. Must have run over a nail or something."

"Fayetteville? You military?"

"I am. On leave for a few days." She assessed him for a few seconds. "You might have been former military, but right now you look like something out of a horror flick. Can't believe I'm standing here talking to you."

"I had a rough night. Now let's get this tire on."

Mahegan rolled the tire to the left front, grabbed the lug wrench, and removed the nuts from the existing wheel, placing them carefully to the side.

"Okay, I'm going to lift your front end up, and I want you to pull that tire off. Then I'll put the front end down while you get ready to slide the new tire on."

"You're going to lift my front end?"

"Well, you know, the car's front end," Mahegan said.

She blushed. "I know what you're talking about. That's a heavy engine you're going to be lifting."

"Engine looks fine to me," Mahegan said. "Let's get to work."

She positioned the wheel, and Mahegan pretended he was doing a dead lift with his hands under the front bumper. He pushed up from a squatting position, and his arms and shoulders strained, but he could feel the tire come off the ground.

"Now," he said through gritted teeth. She worked the tire back and forth across the threaded wheel bolts until it came free.

"Got it," she said.

Mahegan lowered the car and took a few deep breaths.

"Ready?"

"Roger," Cassie said.

He did another squat and then lifted the car again, straining and holding it as still as possible as she fumbled with the heavy tire against the wheel bolts. A couple of "damnits" later, she said, "Okay."

Mahegan lowered the front end again and came around the driver's side. He placed the lug nuts on the bolts and threaded them as far as he could. Then he used the lug wrench and tightened them as much as possible, then handed Cassie the wrench.

"One more time. Crank down on each nut as hard as you can so the tire's straight. Won't do us much good if this thing is wobbling and falls off."

He lifted again, and she was quick this time. With each tightening, though, he could feel the downward tug of the wrench. The scar in his left deltoid was about to tell him enough was enough when she said, "Done."

He lowered the car. He put the old tire in the compartment and then they repacked the back, where he took further inventory of her supplies. There was a box of Meals Ready to Eat, or MREs. These were high-calorie combat rations. He also saw a shotgun stuffed in a camouflaged carrying case along with two boxes of buckshot ammunition. Buckshot was for home defense, mostly. Cassie wasn't going bird hunting. Perhaps she'd had a bad experience when camping in the past. Conversely, there were also two tennis rackets and a can of unopened tennis balls.

"I see you taking inventory, Jake. Mind your own business."

"Just making sure you're a safe ride, is all," he said.

That got the first smile out of Cassie. It was a full grin showing good teeth and a perfect dimple on her right side.

"You're all about the ride, aren't you? Well, let's ride."

CHAPTER 9

ZAKIR STOOD FROM HIS CHAIR AS HE RECEIVED AN AUTOMATED ALERT from the security camera that indicated the vehicle carrying the chairman and his wife was arriving from northern Virginia.

His kidnap team had made a brief stop on the outskirts of Asheville, where they had switched cars in the designated scenic overlook. There, they had stripped their Army blue uniforms, donned their black pants and shirts, and had done a final strip search of General Bagwell and his wife.

They had found an interesting anomaly, which he had immediately messaged to his superior. Behind General Bagwell's left ear had been a device that looked like a bandage. Perhaps it was. Their metal-detecting security wand had discovered the device, giving off the slightest beep. Then, upon searching Mrs. Bagwell, they had found the exact same microdevice behind her ear. In the soft padded portion of the "bandage" was a nano-transmitter. It was a tracking device that he assumed their security teams made them wear. He was proud of how his kidnap team had neutralized their weak security very quickly but was concerned that their footprint could be followed to Asheville.

If someone was monitoring these small transmitters behind their ears, they would be able to identify the last known location at a rest stop on I-40. He had instructed his men to tape the devices to another vehicle. They had done so and reported that the vehicle was heading west through the mountains. This was good.

The car could be on its way to California and would provide sufficient misdirection for the next twenty-four hours.

On the camera in his command center at the camp, he watched the nondescript sedan park across the river near the security cameras he had installed several months ago. The headlights flashed twice; a "friendly" vehicle. The sun was nosing over the horizon, but the deep valley in which they had burrowed was still dark, awaiting the morning glow.

He also knew it was one of his teams because he had installed a satellite GPS tracker on the link-up car prior to the mission. Looking at his screen, he confirmed that the blinking blue dot was the car he was viewing on the grainy black-and-white camera feed. The trail upon which the car had traveled was an unimproved dirt road that paralleled a fifty-yard-wide creek. He had positioned a small, flat-bottomed duck hunting boat on the far side, where the vehicle was parked. Per his instructions, one of his team members opened the door and lifted a woman and then a man out of the trunk of the car. He could see that they were bound and gagged. The woman stumbled as her husband attempted to help her. His team member led them to the boat. Once they were in the boat, the car departed and would exit out the far side of the trail onto an asphalt road.

On the near side of the creek, two other team members helped the chairman of the Joint Chiefs of Staff and his wife out of the boat. Zakir switched security cameras and saw them enter the cabin, which had two cages inside. The man was locked in one cage, while his wife was locked in a cage across from him.

Zakir had taken the time to install prison-grade bars inside the cabin, along with extra soundproofing. He was glad that the first delivery had been made. Others might still arrive, but the biggest prize had been snared. Bagwell had killed many of his Syrian brothers and sisters. He also was close friends and West Point classmates with General Bob Savage, the American general who had killed the most Arabs over the past fifteen years. Both generals were intimately involved in Operation Groomsman, as well.

Zakir had already made his move against General Savage and his off-the-books team of commandos. The only one not in his control was Jake Mahegan, but he knew where Mahegan was and when he would be near Asheville. With Savage and Bagwell in his control, this devastating deep strike against the Americans had a chance of taking hold.

He walked the one hundred yards from his command post to the cabin to greet his fresh prisoners. The small bungalow was set back in a copse of pine trees toward the eastern end of the valley. The morning air was cool, alerting him to the excitement of the day. He was about to meet a general and then hijack a Mack truck. It was going to be a great day. He walked up the steps of the cabin and entered.

"General," he said. The general was tall and lanky. He was wearing khakis and a denim dress shirt. His face was haggard and unshaven, with white whiskers around his jawline. Zakir noticed he wore a large ring atop his wedding band—his West Point ring, no doubt. General Bart Bagwell had risen rapidly through the ranks after repeated tours in Iraq and Afghanistan. Ambitious to a fault, Bagwell had stayed overseas rotating between theaters, leaving his family behind in the United States while he lobbied for the top job in the military. He had been the three-star general in charge of all operations in Iraq and Syria in 2011 when the Arab Spring had unleashed evil like a cyclone throughout the Middle East.

Zakir's kidnap team had flex-cuffed Bagwell and his wife, who was lying on her side with a distant look on her face, as if perhaps she was not surprised by their predicament. She was an attractive blond woman with disheveled hair and was wearing gray slacks and a white blouse. They had been traveling from Fort Hood, Texas, for a speech and returning to their Fort Myer mansion.

Looking at Bagwell made Zakir think of his boss, Jackknife, who was none too happy with the general. Bagwell had secrets and Jackknife wanted answers. Thinking of Jackknife led to thoughts of Operation Groomsman.

Zakir was supposed to be in the convoy that had been bombed—what the Americans had called Operation Groomsman—but his

Ford Explorer SUV transmission seized up from the desert grime prior to making the final turn into the compound. Zakir recalled watching with horror as the bombs rained down upon his friends and family, slaughtering them all. And he had refrained from calling Jackknife, even though he should have.

Zakir had run toward the charred wreckage when suddenly two American helicopters flew into the area. The men disembarked and began clawing through the debris. Zakir remembered seeing a large man clearly in charge of the team on the ground. They were wearing helmets and body armor as they held their rifles at eye level. Later, Zakir learned that the air assault mission commander had been a man named Jake Mahegan.

Today, almost four years later, Jackknife's revenge was coming to fruition. As Zakir stared at the chairman of the Joint Chiefs and his wife, he felt satisfaction that he was able to help Jackknife pull this plan together. Here was tangible evidence that things were working. He would know precisely at nine a.m. if the auto repair worm had worked across many of the different car manufacturer service shops and DMVs nationwide.

To his knowledge, General Savage, Sean O'Malley, Patch Owens, and Jake Mahegan would all be dead or also captured by the end of the day, if they weren't already.

"Lock them in their cages," Zakir said to his kidnap team.

CHAPTER 10

SPECIAL AGENT TOMMY OXENDINE LISTENED TO THE TROY POLICE chief's report over the radio. He was standing in the glassed-in conference room of the Concord Airport, looking at the jets of many of the NASCAR racing drivers, such as Dale Earnhardt, Jr. and Jeff Gordon. They were painted with the drivers' car number on the fuselage. Oxendine was a NASCAR fan and thought it was pretty cool to be staring at those airplanes.

"We've got one dead body and one severely wounded. Got an anonymous tip from an untraceable phone that pinged the tower near the town of Badin. Gave us the exact location of these two individuals. They are dressed as military police officers, but the one who is alive is unconscious right now. Might be a few hours. They don't have any credentials on them, and their weapons are missing. I got a call from Sheriff Williams over in Moore County, and his guys found the car they were probably in. They're fingerprinting it right now, but they've already got one hit on a guy named Chayton Mahegan."

"Stop right there, Sheriff. That's all I need to know. Keep building evidence on Mahegan. His pistol was used in the murder of that family here in Charlotte. His boss's ex-wife was murdered right next to her new husband. In fact, she was the first one murdered of the three. We're looking at a love triangle thing with Mahegan. I'm sending a team to Badin right now."

"I'm not far if you need me to head that way," the police chief said.

"He'll be gone by then if he's not already. Focus on the evidence there. I want this case rock solid."

"Roger that."

Oxendine clicked off and looked at the jets, then saw the helicopter land. Six men in black suits poured out of the doors. They were carrying their helmets and AR-15 rifles.

"Better turn around, boys," Oxendine whispered. But truthfully he wanted to look the men in the eyes and make them understand the importance of this mission. He was going to push his finger into the chest of the team leader and emphasize that he could not under any circumstances screw this up.

He turned to his aide, a young sergeant with a blond crew cut and chiseled face of an Icelandic boxer.

"Get me Sheriff Bubba Wilson of Stanly County, now."

In less than a minute, the aide handed him the phone and backed away. Oxendine continued to look at the SWAT team striding into the small VIP terminal, where he would brief them.

"Sheriff, this is Special Agent Tommy Oxendine. I know it's early, but I'm chasing this gruesome murder down in Charlotte and we've got evidence that a person of interest named Chayton Mahegan, goes by Jake, made a call within the last hour that used a cell phone tower near your town. He's about six and a half feet tall, big, strong, armed and dangerous with possible ties to terrorists."

"Roger that. Finishing up breakfast now," Sheriff Wilson said.

"Breakfast?" Oxendine barked. "We've got a cold-blooded murderer on the loose in your county!"

"You may be some big, badass special agent, Oxendine, but you damn sure ain't my boss," Sheriff Wilson said.

After a pause, Oxendine said, "You're right. My apologies. I've been up all night on this case, and I saw three dead bodies, one of them a fourteen-year-old boy."

"Now that's all I need to hear. I'll call you when and if I find out something," the sheriff said.

Oxendine hung up and looked across the room as the SWAT team poured in.

"What we got, boss man?" Lieutenant Chuck McQueary asked. Known as "Q," McQueary was the leader of the Charlotte–Mecklenburg Police Department SWAT team, called CharMeck. After a lengthy argument that Oxendine wanted nothing to do with, the director of the SBI, secretary of public safety, sheriff of Mecklenburg County, Police Chief of Charlotte, and the governor of North Carolina had all agreed that regardless of where they would find Mahegan, they needed a mobile response force that could move quickly to the location. And while the governor had put every county's SWAT teams on standby, the CharMeck SWAT team would be the main effort with Special Agent Tommy Oxendine in charge of all decision making on the ground.

Oxendine was fine with that. The CharMeck guys had a great reputation, and he liked having the men briefed and ready to go. Mahegan was making mistakes, and Oxendine would find him and kill him. Oxendine preferred that. No questions asked. The evidence already indicated that Mahegan was guilty. Why waste the time and effort to capture, detain, try, and imprison a man for murdering the Sledge family in cold blood.

"Hey, Q," Oxendine said as the men laid their helmets on the table. There was considerable noise as they removed their ballistic vests, leaned their rifles against the wall, and pulled out chairs to sit in.

"Understand we've got a lead?" McQueary prompted again.

"Yes, don't get too comfortable. We think Mahegan pinged off a cell tower near Badin about an hour ago. I've got a definite on the murder weapon. Ballistics match the bullets to the weapon. That just came in. We've got a fingerprint on a military police vehicle, one dead MP, and one wounded MP who can't talk yet. All roads lead to Mahegan."

"This guy must be pretty stupid to use his own pistol and then toss it in a lake," McQueary said.

"Well, I thought of that. Not saying Mahegan's stupid. He was Delta or whatever they're calling those special mission units nowadays. But I'll say he may not be thinking right and not give a damn if he's caught. As I'm time lining this thing, he kills the Sledges about eleven p.m., makes it back to Moore County, maybe gets pulled over by the military police, runs them off the road, shoots both, dumps them in Uwharrie, and now he's near Badin. So we need to load up and be ready to pounce."

"He on foot or in a car?"

"Don't know. We checked with DMV and there's no vehicle registered to Mahegan. Military records don't show anything, either. Word is he does off-the-books stuff for JSOC, or at least that's what he brags about in the bars."

"Which bars? Do we know where he hangs?" McQueary asked

"We don't know much about him, Q. I've given you what I've got. Want this guy more than I've wanted anyone in a long time," Oxendine said.

"You know the saying, right, boss? You want it bad, you get it bad," McQueary warned.

"I want it *good.*" Oxendine smiled. "Here's his picture." He passed around a photo he had pulled from the Department of Homeland Security files from the gray list. "It's about four years old. He may have changed his hair color, don't know. But for right now, we're hunting a big guy, skin the color of mine, light brown or blond hair, and dangerous as hell. Now let's saddle up, get in the air, establish comms with Stanly County, and find us a murderer."

Oxendine looked at McQueary, who squinted as he stared back. Oxendine just nodded, as if to say, *Get your ass moving.*

CHAPTER 11

MAHEGAN CLIMBED INTO THE SUBARU'S PASSENGER SIDE, RACKING back the bucket seat as far as it could go with all of the gear haphazardly thrown in the back. Cassie simultaneously slid into the driver's seat. He would have stopped her to reorganize everything, but she shot out of the gas station parking lot as the sirens grew louder.

"Damnit," she said again.

"Running from the law?"

She looked at him and shook her head. Her thin hands tightly gripped the steering wheel as she raced the Subaru to seventy miles an hour.

"Just going camping," she said.

Mahegan doubted that. The shotgun, the mention of a pistol and her expert marksmanship, her Army background, and the fact that she was speeding away from sirens gave Mahegan the impression that perhaps she was more concerned about law enforcement than he was.

After an hour of sharp turns and rapid accelerations to over one hundred miles per hour, Cassie turned to him and said, "So what's your deal, Jake? Not that I really give a shit."

"Ex-soldier. Just going camping," he replied. "Not that you give a shit."

They merged onto I-40 headed west after cutting through the town of Salisbury. It was approaching nine a.m. They had another ninety minutes or so until they reached Asheville. From there, Mahegan wasn't sure what his plan might be. Without Alex Russell and her magic override phone, which he continued to find suspect, he had no idea where Savage, Owens, and O'Malley might be.

Cassie ran her hand through her clipped blond hair. Just above the collar, military regulation.

"Where are you camping?" she asked.

"Mountains."

"Just trying to narrow down where I'm supposed to drop you off. You helped me. I'm returning the favor."

"I think if you get me to Asheville, I can figure it out from there."

She nodded, as if that would do the trick and she would be free of her obligation.

"I'm sure you get this quite a bit, but you look familiar to me. Were you in Iraq? Afghanistan? Both?" Mahegan asked.

"Both. Multiple times. Intel."

He said nothing, nodded, and looked over his shoulder.

"Tennis? Really?" Mahegan asked, recalling the rackets in the back of the car.

"Played at West Point. Force of habit to bring them."

Mahegan had been processing her face since he first saw her at the gas station. He didn't believe he knew her from combat. It was something more remote, like he might recognize a movie star or public figure. Mahegan recalled when Prince Harry from Great Britain had served as an Apache copilot and gunner. He wasn't sure, but Henry, Prince of Wales, might have saved his ass a few times with some covering rockets and missiles.

Mahegan latched on to what he was seeking when he thought of the long version of Cassie: Cassandra. He knew of one notorious Cassandra, and that was Cassandra Bagwell, the renowned daughter of the chairman of the Joints Chiefs of Staff, General Bart Bagwell. As one of the first women to graduate Ranger school without recycling, "Cassie" Bagwell was a rising star in the military. Mahegan had not seen many pictures of her but knew the name and had followed with interest her graduation from

West Point, trek through Ranger school, assignment to military intelligence at Fort Bragg, and then some of the news of her redeployments. Like Prince Harry, Cassie Bagwell's deployments were off the radar, but the media usually caught wind when she and her unit returned from a combat zone. With a reputation for selfless but aggressive service, Cassie Bagwell was known mostly for trying to shake the notion that she was sailing along on her father's following winds. That and the fact that her father had publicly and solidly opposed her attending Ranger school.

"You?" she asked.

"Both theaters. Other places. Pretty much combat or prepping for combat twenty-four/seven," Mahegan said.

"Unit?"

"Yes," he replied.

"I meant, which . . ."

She caught herself. Often Delta Force was referred to simply as "The Unit."

"I know what you meant."

Her countenance shifted, perhaps a new measure of respect or envy.

"Why'd you get out?"

"Didn't really have a choice. Killed somebody I shouldn't have."

That gave her pause. She eyed the pistol she kept in a holster sewn into the front of her seat. He had seen it earlier, a Beretta 9 mm with a magazine in the well. It was perfectly positioned between her legs, where she could rapidly draw down on a passenger or someone approaching her vehicle.

"Wait a minute," she said. "You're *that* guy?"

"Depends."

"Mahegan. You killed Hoxha on the border in Nuristan."

"I'm that guy."

Cassie continued to speed past vehicles on I-40, the speedometer routinely above ninety miles an hour.

"WTF," she said. "What are you doing out here looking like a lost zombie?"

"Among other things, I'm looking for your dad."

"Looking for my father?" Cassie asked. "What do you want with that son of a bitch?"

Mahegan determined that she had to be a better soldier than she was an actress.

"Cassie Bagwell. I'm not the only one who has some notoriety," Mahegan said.

Her shoulders slumped, and suddenly the weight of her parents' kidnapping seemed to pull at her every feature. Her face tensed, her arms flexed, her hands tightened, knuckles whitened.

"I did a pretty good job of staying incognito until I met you, I guess."

"I wouldn't be too sure of that, Cassie. There's some bad stuff going down."

It's going down right now. Everything all at once.

"More than my parents?"

"As central as that is to you and all of us, yes, more than your parents."

"How do you know any of this? You're not with your unit anymore," she said.

Mahegan treaded carefully.

"I've got sources, still. My question is, why aren't you with *your* unit, assessing this enemy? And what's up with your dad? I mean, I've read some of the media, but he's kidnapped. Can't you cut him some slack?"

"My unit looks at combat ops overseas. This is a domestic terror event, and the FBI and Homeland aren't going to be rolling out the red carpet for me anytime soon," Cassie said. "And my relationship with my father is my business," she added flatly.

"I get that," Mahegan said. And he did. The last thing any of those bureaucracies would want is a competent family member to be on hand to get any credit for saving her parents. "So, what intel do you have that's bringing you west?"

Cassie looked at Mahegan with an untrusting gaze. He got the vibe that she didn't trust much, if at all. Her wariness was probably warranted in most cases. In her cohort, hangers-on and suck-ups probably surrounded her, and her superiors probably remained suspicious and distrustful that she wasn't running home to Daddy every time something went wrong. General Bagwell was known as a ruthless leader. He did not suffer fools and, most suspected, would not suffer anyone who mistreated his daughter. Even if that "mistreatment" was her version of the story.

"After reading that article about Al Qaeda putting out a fatwa on American CEOs and senior government officials, I had both of my parents use wearable technology. I'll just leave it at that. I've tracked them as far as Asheville, heading west. They made a stop and now I'm no longer able to track them."

"Okay, let's just head to their last known," Mahegan said.

"That's the plan."

The outline of the Asheville skyline was a smattering of low, pastel-painted buildings etched against the undulating green hues of the Smoky Mountains rising toward the intermittent clouds in the background. The I-40 and I-26 intersection loomed to the south.

As he was assessing the traffic, which was building and steady, Cassie shouted, "Hold on!"

Directly to their front, a Chevrolet Suburban rapidly decelerated to a stop in the middle of the road. To their left a Ford F-150 did the same. All around them, vehicles were grinding to a halt without provocation. A Mack truck slammed into a group of cars in the middle of I-40 and created a fireball that exploded upward in yellow flames.

Cassie slowed and swerved hard right onto the shoulder, narrowly avoiding the developing pileup. Mahegan began looking for an exit like a running back trying to find daylight. He spotted a sign for four gas stations about a quarter mile ahead as Cassie nearly flipped the Subaru, taking it up on two wheels, swerving to avoid a flaming hood that was spinning like a top in the road.

"There," Mahegan said. He pointed at the exit and the wide shoulder that could get them there. Neither of them had been able to process what had happened. They were strictly in survival mode. So far Cassie had handled the first five seconds well. She maneuvered the car through an array of stopped and crashed vehicles that looked like air strike remnants. Briefly he flashed on Operation Groomsman and why Alex Russell had been asking him about that mission, but then refocused on the task at hand: helping Cassie get them to the exit.

She passed several cars that had simply stopped, as if they had run out of gas. A few cars continued, such as hers, but the majority were stalled. As Cassie navigated the melee, Mahegan looked at the make of each of the stalled cars: Chevrolet, Ford, Chrysler, Mercedes, BMW, Honda, Lexus, and Toyota. He looked at the interstate road in the distance as it rose into the mountains and saw nothing but taillights and accidents.

"What the hell is happening?" Cassie said through clenched teeth.

"Some kind of accident, but more," Mahegan said. He made a mental note of the brand of her vehicle, Subaru, and those of others that were still crawling through the wreckage. A Hyundai swerved past the flaming Mack truck. Further up a low-slung Porsche was turning around in the middle of the interstate. The fire had spread across the entire road, blocking movement. The side-view mirror showed an old Chevy Nova with fat wheels and lift suspension. It was following them out of the morass.

"Okay, I've got a clear shot at the exit if the fire doesn't spread," Cassie said.

"Gun it."

She did. The Nova followed, and the Porsche driver saw them and fell in line. There were stopped cars on the ramp and on the adjoining road. People were turning their ignitions and getting nothing, not even the clicking sound of a dead battery. At the bottom of the ramp a Chevy Cruze that had been turning left was stopped in the oncoming lane, which was okay because the Dodge Charger that looked like it might T-bone the Cruze was frozen in place also. By now, drivers were standing outside their stopped vehicles. Some had the hoods up and were blankly staring at dormant engines, while others were talking on cell phones.

Cassie wound her way around the Cruze and the Charger and found a less traveled road that went south.

"We've got to keeping moving toward Asheville," she said. Cassie's jaw was set with determination. Regardless of whatever was happening to the cars, or the nation for that matter, her car was fine and therefore her mission remained unchanged: save her parents.

Mahegan had his knife and his Sig Sauer Tribal pistol, the clothes he was wearing, his Doc Martens boots, and a thin leather wallet that held his driver's license, an ATM card, and a stack of twenties totaling close to four hundred dollars. He would be okay for a while, depending on what exactly was taking place. What he didn't have was his phone or its all-important Zebra app that prior to yesterday allowed him to securely communicate with Savage, Owens, and O'Malley.

As they turned west onto a two-lane road with few stopped cars and fewer moving cars, Cassie said, "Okay. So what was that?"

"I've been thinking," Mahegan said. "Not sure if this is happening anywhere else, but it could be some type of cyberattack. I don't know."

"EMP, you think?"

Mahegan considered an electromagnetic pulse attack and thought it was a possibility but unlikely.

"EMP would be more inclusive. For example, why are we still moving? And the Porsche and Chevy Nova behind us?"

The two cars had followed them as if they knew precisely what they were doing and what was happening. Perhaps they knew more than the others, but they were all flying blind to a degree.

"So some kind of attack through the GPS of newer cars?"

"Something like that," Mahegan considered. "Maybe only specific cars that someone could hack. We're in a Subaru, sort of a one-off brand. A new Porsche is two cars behind us. And the Chevy Nova directly behind us is at least thirty years old, no GPS. I saw new Chevys, Fords, BMWs all stopped."

"The Internet of Things," Cassie said.

"Heard of it. Can't say I know much beyond the basics."

"Instead of just connectivity for your computer or smartphone, the Internet of Things is the connectivity of machines, devices, cars, buildings, all networked together and sharing data. When your smart-refrigerator senses your milk carton weighs less than 'x' ounces, it orders you more milk, or at least sends you a text to buy milk."

"An automated honey-do list. Great," Mahegan said.

"It's more than that, as you know. If a car has an alternator go out, the onboard computer communicates with the parts shop and orders you one at the same time it is making your service appointment after it checks your calendar in Outlook, for example."

"So, like every other use of the Internet, good stuff can be used for bad stuff."

"That's a bit technical for me, but yes," Cassie quipped.

"Okay, so let's use some of that technology. What was the last known grid coordinate of your parents?"

"Well, the ear patch dropped a pin in my app. So that's what we'll have to go by."

Cassie drove up the winding road as she simultaneously thumbed through her phone and found the monitoring app named Find-Aid.

"Usually used for seniors with Alzheimer's. It's a bandage you put behind the ear, under the hairline, and it has a tracking device in it not unlike Find My iPhone."

Mahegan took the iPhone from her and looked at the picture on the screen. There was a red pin on a rest stop overlooking Asheville from the west.

"The beauty of this technology is that it is powered by body heat. Once it is disconnected from human skin, it stops operating. During the trials, some of the seniors were wise enough to try putting it on a car or a building, forcing the developers to find a way to make it 'senior proof.'"

"Okay, so your parents' kidnappers stopped at this rest stop and found the sensors, I'm guessing."

"That's my guess," Cassie said. "They went dark there."

"Probably a triage point. A final inspection before taking them the last leg into the kidnap holding site."

"Get me there," Cassie said, dropping all pretense of going to Sparta to go camping.

Mahegan eyed her and then looked at the phone, glad to have some situational awareness back, albeit unsecure and limited.

"Okay, you're going to loop south of Asheville and then come up through some mountain roads, then double back to the rest stop. Take this next right."

She did, then continued to follow Mahegan's directions for an hour, until they were at the rest stop.

The rest stop was a scenic overlook, parking lot, and single building. Mahegan imagined where he might try to hide someone in this rather compact lot. There were several cars stopped now, owners pacing frantically and headed toward them. The Porsche and Nova had followed them to the rest stop and pulled up alongside them.

"Grab your pistol," Mahegan said. "This is like one of those end of the world things where people might try to steal your car."

"No worries," Cassie said.

Tommy Oxendine couldn't believe what he was seeing below him. From his vantage point in the helicopter it appeared that there were accidents occurring on every road. He had tactical response teams on standby in each county, and now it looked as if they may be tied up with unscrewing all of these wrecks.

They tracked country roads, major highways, and the interstates and confirmed that every road had multiple major accidents.

He called back into headquarters in Raleigh and reported what he was seeing to his director, Winston Black III, who had little experience in law enforcement but a lot of experience in donating to politicians. He got a plum patronage job as the SBI director, and Oxendine knew the man enjoyed wearing the badge and carrying the pistol. The joke was that he would shoot his own dick off one day. Oxendine wouldn't mind seeing that.

"Sir, we've got dozens, maybe hundreds, of accidents occurring on every roadway in the state that I've seen so far," Oxendine reported.

"I thought you were hunting this Indian?" Black said.

Oxendine paused, biting back a million comebacks he had for the bureaucrat.

"I am, sir. In the SWAT helo trying to find him, and I'm seeing chaos everywhere. It's like the apocalypse. Cars are just stopping in the middle of the road."

"Well, I don't see much out of my window here," Black said.

Black was famous, or infamous, for not leaving his office. He was a paper pusher and political suck-up. He made appearances with the governor and spoke to the rotary circuit, but that was about the extent of his law enforcement capabilities.

"Oh, wait a minute. I just saw a car stop," Black said. "Oh, shoot. It stopped for a pedestrian. It's going now."

"Sir, I'm making a spot report to you. If you would prefer I call someone else, I'm happy to."

"Don't get insubordinate with me, Tommy. You should always know with whom you're speaking. I'm the director."

"Yes, sir. I know. And I'm a sixteen-year field agent veteran making a report to you so that you can call the governor and be the hero, letting him know what the heck is going on."

Black paused on the other end of the call. Oxendine's stomach dropped as they hit an air pocket. Beverly Setz, the pilot in command, came over the intercom into his headset. Her voice was crisp and authoritative. Having earned three air medals in Afghanistan, Setz was known as one of the best pilots of the North Carolina National Guard. "Sorry, agent. Getting windy up here near the mountains. We're over Hickory heading west over I-40."

"Roger," Oxendine said. He had the headphones covering one ear and cocked up on his head, making room for his iPhone so that he could talk to Black.

"My name is Winston, not Roger," Black said.

"Yes, sir. I was talking to the pilot."

"Well, let's just have one conversation at a time, shall we, Tommy?"

"Yes, sir."

"This report I'm going to make to the governor, what are the five 'W's'?"

Black was always asking for the five W's: who, what, where, when, and why.

"Sir, the who is just about one in ten cars, the what is stopping in the middle of the road and causing accidents, the where is every road, the when is that it started about five minutes ago, and the why is I have no freaking idea."

"Well, call me back when you have a fix on that last W, Tommy, and then I'll make my report to the—oh my God!"

"Finally," Oxendine muttered.

"Right outside my window, a van on Peace Avenue just stopped and five cars piled into it."

"Better call the governor," Oxendine said. "And then call a meeting or whatever you guys do to figure this out. I'm going after Mahegan."

Oxendine hung up, shaking his head.

"That bad," McQueary said through the headphones.

Oxendine looked at McQueary. He liked Q. Smart. Dedicated. Good shot. Good leader. Just under six feet tall, McQueary had been a college gymnast. Excelled at the rings, apparently. Oxendine liked leaders who were athletes. He knew that athletes had to make split-second decisions, as did leaders. Leadership was a competition.

And Oxendine played to win.

"Hey, boss," Setz said over the headset.

"Roger," Oxendine replied.

"We've got state-of-the-art tactical messaging up here. Because we work with Homeland and Department of Defense on crisis response, hurricanes, and so on, we get messages from DHS. Just got one about the chairman of the Joint Chiefs of Staff and his wife being kidnapped." DHS was the acronym for the Department of Homeland Security.

"When?"

"About midnight last night."

"Couldn't be Mahegan. Not my concern. Let's stay in the lane, Bev," Oxendine said.

"Well, there's more," Setz said.

"Go on."

"Apparently, the chairman and his wife have a daughter named Cassie. She's a soldier at Fort Bragg. And DHS believes her life might be in danger, too. They've given us a ping to her vehicle GPS, and it shows a route coming out of Badin and heading west not too far from us now."

Oxendine thought a moment. While he was dedicated to North Carolina and the SBI, rescuing the daughter of the chairman of the Joint Chiefs could get him some major props and maybe even a federal position somewhere. FBI, maybe. But he didn't want to detract from the hunt for Mahegan. After a few more seconds of thought, Oxendine reasoned that if Cassie Bagwell had been in Badin, he could legitimately argue that he was chasing a solid lead and trying to help protect the young woman.

"That's something. When did the car leave Badin?" Oxendine asked.

"About a minute before Sheriff Wilson put out the all-points bulletin on Mahegan. I'm assuming you talked with him?"

"Roger that," Oxendine said. "Can you track that vehicle real time?"

"Almost. We get pings on it every ten minutes. You'd think it would be better, but our system isn't futuristic, it's just government state of the art," Setz said.

"Okay, let's go find it."

At the far end of the rest stop was a thicket of trees with picnic tables. There were three parking spots where someone could, without suspicion, back in and raise a trunk, as if they were grabbing picnic supplies.

"Over there," he said. "That's where they did it."

"Don't disagree," Cassie said. She drove over, and the Nova followed, while the owner of the Porsche waved and pulled onto I-40, headed west. They parked, and Mahegan quickly jumped out of Cassie's Subaru and walked up to the Chevy Nova driver's side.

He watched a long-haired man roll down the window and say, "No worries, bro. I'm just freaked about this whole thing, and you guys seem to know what you're doing."

Mahegan briefly studied the man. Dark, stringy hair hung to his shoulders. Thin facial hair covered his jawline and chin. He had a soul patch beneath his bottom lip. Then Mahegan assessed the contents of the car. Old vinyl seats, cracked and dull. Two plastic Harris Teeter shopping bags in the backseat. He could see a carton of milk, some eggs, and other groceries through the tan bags. More important, no weapons were visible, but that didn't mean there wasn't anything beneath the seat.

"You carrying?" Mahegan asked.

"I've got a right to," the man said.

"That you do. What have you got?"

"None of your business, actually. I'm just trying to get out of Dodge and find a partner in case it's like that movie *World War Z*," the man said.

"Something's happening. Not trying to make an enemy here. Just making sure you're not after us."

"Should I be?"

The man was becoming obstinate, and Mahegan was done with him. He had to investigate the last clue that could lead them to the locations of Savage and the chairman, assuming all of this was connected.

"Just FYI, I'm carrying also." Mahegan produced his Sig Sauer Tribal and flashed it briefly. "Probably in your best interest to head home and deliver those groceries."

"You might be right," the man said.

"I know I am."

Mahegan turned and walked back to the Subaru, two spaces over. Cassie was already out of the vehicle and rummaging through a trash barrel.

"Nothing," she said.

"Footprints here," Mahegan replied. "But they could be anything. Two different sets of large boot prints."

"I double-checked the pin and our location. This is right."

Mahegan had a thought. "If they put the patches on a car or something, they don't register?"

"No. Activated and powered by human body heat. DARPA invented it, and it is in the advanced pilot stage."

Mahegan recognized the acronym for the Defense Advanced Research Project Agency. Her father being the chairman would provide him—and her, by extension—access to such technology. Mahegan took a step back. The Nova was still there, the driver doing something on a cell phone. He huffed and stormed out of his car toward the rest stop building. Mahegan noticed the bulge at the back of his dungarees. He was carrying.

"There's a wild card there," Mahegan said. "Been following since the cars shut down. Maybe even before then. Know him?"

"Never seen him before in my life," Cassie said. "But he's got a purple heart license plate from Buncombe County. Probably served in one of the wars and was wounded."

"Prob." Mahegan absently stared to the north and west, where he could see the Blue Ridge Parkway snaking along the mountain rims. He gently took Cassie's phone and looked at the Google Maps function, zooming in and out, following roads, studying terrain features.

"I've got Google Earth on that, too," Cassie said.

She punched it up for him and he repeated the process, pinching the screen and then using his thumb and forefinger to widen it. There were three possibilities: a Bible camp, a summer camp, and an old mining village. Asheville had been a micro-version of San Francisco during the gold rush days. Speculators had dug their fair share of gold from the Blue Ridge, and the federal government had given Charlotte its own mint, its beginning as the second largest financial capital in the world.

"Which one is the closest to some sort of communications network?" Cassie asked.

'There are power and cell phone towers near all three. How much gas do you have?"

"A little over half. Filled up at that station where I had the flat."

"So we prioritize and go inspect," Mahegan said.

Cassie was pensive, standing next to him as they gazed out over the valley falling away to the north. "Seems so random. If we think for fifteen minutes it might save us fifteen hours."

Mahegan, who was accustomed to acting on operational intelligence immediately, was growing impatient.

"If we wait fifteen minutes, we might miss something. We can talk and drive at the same time. All three points are on the Blue Ridge Parkway. We go there and decide north or south."

"You're everything they said. GI Joe action figure."

"No, just know we don't have much time to waste."

The owner of the Chevy Nova came running from rest area and dashed up toward them as Mahegan drew his Tribal and held it low.

"Shit's happening everywhere, man. All across the country. It's like that zombie movie!"

Mahegan replied calmly, "Except there are no actual zombies. This is a cyberattack. My guess is that your car doesn't have a GPS and isn't serviced through the automated system most car dealers use nowadays."

"Nah, man. I do my own stuff. I'm a mechanic. Live just up the road in Avery Creek. Got a garage and everything."

Mahegan felt the seconds ticking away. Could Nova guy be any help? Doubtful. He looked at the map and saw that Avery Creek was about ten miles adjacent to one of his three best guesses. Then he thought, *mechanic.*

"What's your name?" Mahegan asked.

"Ronnie. Why you asking?"

"You followed us, remember? Just trying to get to know you. Let me ask you, Ronnie. Over the past year has your business picked up, been steady, dropped off? Anything change?"

"Not much change that I can say. One of my main competitors was bragging about some pick up, but not me. I'm thinking things are looking good for me right about now, though. Good time to be a mechanic." Ronnie looked across the parking lot at the stalled vehicles and their frustrated owners.

"Who's your competitor?"

"Look, man. If you need some work, I can do it. Don't pick that douchebag."

"This is important, Ronnie. It's got nothing to do with future work. Did the competitor talk about the uptick and what kinds of vehicles?"

Mahegan was thinking it was a long shot but worth a phone call or a visit given Avery Corner's proximity to one of his suspected hideout locations.

"I'll call him," Ronnie said. He wasn't happy but retrieved a Droid phone from his jeans pocket and pressed a few buttons. He repeated the process several times before saying, "This mass shutdown of cars has everyone on their phones. Can't get through. Might as well follow me."

They got in their cars and picked their way along several narrow, winding country roads. Ronnie, it seemed, knew the back way around all of the stopped traffic.

"Where the hell's he taking us?" Cassie muttered. "We don't have a lot of time."

Mahegan watched her, eyes focused on the road, but he also sensed that her mind was working through something else. How to get her parents back, most likely. But he wondered about her relationship with her father. The chairman had been an outspoken opponent of women training as Rangers, and Cassie had been the first to graduate without being recycled. Sucked it up for sixty straight days. Probably a fair amount of hazing and abuse prior to and after that. How would that lack of support from her role model impact her?

"This is our best lead to find a starting place. Other than this, we've got nothing."

"I'm just worried. Mother doesn't do well in small places. She's claustrophobic."

"What about your father?" Mahegan asked.

Cassie swerved the Subaru and pulled back into the lane, avoiding an obstacle unseen by Mahegan. She didn't answer the question, and soon they were pulling into Jasper's Garage and Repair.

Ronnie was already out of his Chevy Nova. Cassie pulled up next to him, then they exited quickly. A man about Ronnie's age—maybe late thirties—came barreling out of the shop office door with a shotgun, aimed it at Ronnie, and said, "What in the hell do you want, you slimy weasel?"

"Hey, man. I'm just bringing you some business."

The man whom Mahegan assumed was Jasper kept the shotgun trained on Ronnie but averted his gaze to Mahegan and Cassie.

"You ain't never brought me nothing but trouble, and I'm sensing you're doing it again. They look like cops."

"They're soldiers. They're trying to stop whatever is happening," Ronnie said.

The shotgun came down a fraction.

"What unit?" Jasper asked.

"I was with Delta Force. She's with military intelligence at Fort Bragg."

"Bullshit. Ain't nobody with Delta says they're with Delta."

"Fair enough," Mahegan said. "I said I *was* with them. I'm out now."

The shotgun came down another fraction.

"What do you need?" Jasper asked.

"Need to know if you've had any unusual pick up in business. Anything out of the ordinary."

"Other than Ronnie the Weasel here trying to steal my customers, not really. One new steady customer. That's it," Jasper said.

"Who was that?" Mahegan asked.

"What's this got to do with?"

"We're looking for someone who might have wanted a car fixed without computers involved."

The shotgun came all the way down.

"I've had one new steady client for the past ten, eleven months.

You don't see too many people nowadays that insist you don't use a computer, but I've had some trucks and the owner insisted. Hit them for a grand or two a pop for my trouble, and that's some good income right there," Jasper said.

"Same person, different people bringing the cars in?"

He paused, looked at Ronnie, then Mahegan, and then Cassie. "Y'all ain't mechanics, so I ain't so much worried about you stealing my business as I am that asshole, but I'm still curious as to how this might help."

"We think that whoever did this to the country," Mahegan said, waving his hand at some of the stalled cars, "may be holed up somewhere in the mountains."

"Like that Atlanta bomber guy?"

"Like that, but different. More lethal and still planning stuff," Mahegan said.

Cassie joined the conversation. She pointed at Jasper's pickup truck parked next to the garage. "We see your purple heart license plate. Which war?"

"Both. Two of them damn things. Now I'm all jacked up in the head and the VA wouldn't piss on me if I was on fire. But I'm better off than that weasel," Jasper said, pointing at Ronnie.

"So you're a veteran and someone who cares about his country," she continued.

"Care about my buddies. Country can kiss my ass for all they've done for me."

"Okay, well, some of your buddies are probably being impacted right now by whatever is happening. So tell us, who's bringing you the cars?"

Jasper paused, scratched the scraggly hair on his chin, and sighed.

"Two people. They have a fleet of Mitsubishi trucks and some other cars. A lot of them camps do that. I'm glad to have the business, so don't go messing it up. Plus, one of them is a hot babe. She gets a rise out of me every time."

"What's this babe's name?" Mahegan asked.

"Prettiest name ever. Ameri. Asked me to inspect her Land

Rover to include her chassis. I told her I'd be happy to inspect her chassis."

Mahegan looked at Cassie, who rolled her eyes.

"Smoking hot," Jasper said.

Mahegan paused. "You got a picture?"

"Nah, man. We don't take no pictures of our customers. She's got brown hair, gorgeous body, carries a pretty, black Berretta pistol with her everywhere."

Mahegan turned to Cassie and said, "Do you know Alex Russell?"

"Of course. She's part of the Fort Bragg female officers' informal hangout group."

"Got a picture?"

Cassie pulled up her Facebook page and showed a picture of her and Alex at the beach.

Jasper looked over her shoulder and said, "Yep. That's her. Smoking hot. Told ya."

CHAPTER 12

THE MACK TRUCK SKIDDED TO A HALT, BRAKES LOCKED, TIRES SMOKing, the smell of burning rubber filling the air as it was making a turn down a steep incline. Zakir understood that he would never be able to get the timing perfect and so had established an ambush zone of a five-mile radius. His team was within a mile. Not bad.

He led fifteen of his men through the rugged terrain with steep crags in the mountainside, where the North Carolina Department of Transportation had blown a gap in the granite to make the road grade navigable.

Zakir had the sniper teams set up on a ridge overlooking I-40 from about eight hundred yards, essentially a half mile.

"Shoot anyone that gets out of any vehicle," Zakir said. "Kill everyone."

His two sniper teams had SR-25 sniper rifles with Leupold Mark 6 scopes and suppressors. They had been training in the base camp for a one-mile shot. Zakir figured that a half mile would be far enough to protect them and allow for their eventual egress to the base camp several miles away.

The chaos of the network attack reigning around the country, of course, was his and Gavril's doing, and it served multiple purposes, the theft of the Mack truck being the primary one.

With his four-man support team in place, Zakir led the remaining men toward the truck, which had jackknifed.

How appropriate, Zakir thought.

"Two vehicles in the front and two in the back," he said into his handheld personal mobile radio, alerting the assault and support teams as to the defenses they would face. Four Suburban SUVs that had also stopped near the truck disgorged three men apiece, each with helmets and rifles.

Twelve men, plus the drivers.

Time for the snipers to get to work.

Zakir had his assault force brace in a ditch next to I-40. He could hear people shouting, asking what was happening. There were innocent bystanders whose cars had stopped, and there were armed men protecting the truck cargo.

"Execute," Zakir said, losing patience.

The metallic ratcheting of the SR-25 hissed with each shot, coupled by the coughs of the sound suppressors. The idea was to kill as many guards and witnesses as possible and then attack to secure the truck and its contents.

After six shots from his snipers, the security personnel began to return fire, but it was not accurate fire. His snipers were doing well.

"Medic! I need a medic here! Five down. We've got five men down!" someone shouted several times. Then his voice was cut off in midsentence.

Six down.

After another minute of sniper fire, Zakir said, "Follow me."

He wound his way out of the ditch, over the guard rail, and took up position behind the last black SUV. Three men lay in the road, dead from head shots. The SUV driver was slumped over his steering wheel. Beyond the Mack truck were several dead civilians with a few scrambling away from the onslaught. His instructions were clear. No one lives in the ambush zone. He couldn't afford to have video or pictures make it to the media. Zakir raised his rifle and snapped off several rounds, killing each civilian whose car had the misfortune of stopping near the Mack truck. He couldn't rule out that someone had not already uploaded the video or had been streaming live on Facebook, but he hoped that

Gavril was monitoring all of that and erasing anything that appeared on the Internet.

His guidance to his assault force was to secure one vehicle for cover and potentially as a getaway vehicle. Zakir carried a flash drive with the antidote to the virus that Gavril had attached to all the major auto manufacturers' service center software updates.

The flash drive would work on the Mack truck as well. The eleventh man in his team was a techie named Ratta, and when the time was right, Zakir would give Ratta the flash drive.

His assault force moved to the second SUV as the snipers provided deadly accurate suppressive fire. Having killed all eight men in the last two SUVs and every civilian they could find, his team swarmed around the jackknifed truck, its cab at a ninety-degree angle to the trailer with its precious cargo.

They were taking sporadic small arms fire from the lead two SUVs. Zakir could hear the supersonic zips of 7.62 sniper rounds buzzing past him. One of his men was shot in the leg, but they kept moving.

He approached the passenger door and had his penetrator team use a crowbar to pry open the door while two of his men fired repeatedly against the bulletproof windows. Once the door was open, the close-quarters combat resulted in two of his men wounded and two dead men in the cab interior. Using an Uzi submachine gun, Zakir sprayed the sleeping compartment of the cab, where two more security personnel were lying in wait.

Blood sprayed in his face as both men caught multiple bullets to the neck, severing their carotid arteries. He backed away and had another member of his team help him pull the driver and passenger from the two truck seats. They dropped them from the cab on the rumble strip of the interstate shoulder.

"Ratta, now," Zakir barked.

Ratta scrambled up to the open passenger door and climbed into the well of the driver's side. He opened the access panel with a screwdriver set he carried specifically for this mission.

"Turn the ignition off and then on," Ratta said, lying on the floor of the cab.

Zakir placed one foot on the brake, just above Ratta's back, another foot on the clutch, and shifted the truck into neutral. Then he removed the key and immediately replaced it. The dashboard lights flickered, and a warning light for the parking brakes shone red.

He watched Ratta insert the flash drive beyond an access panel. They waited thirty seconds, then Ratta looked up and said, "Try to start the motor."

Zakir placed his foot on the brake and punched the start button. The diesel engine coughed to life. Zakir then engaged the parking brake and slid out of Ratta's way.

Ratta climbed into the driver's seat, racked it forward, and then began a series of Y-turns to remove the truck from its jackknifed position.

Meanwhile, Zakir's men had subdued the remaining security personnel. Zakir leapt from the cab and shouted, "Rally on me!"

His men moved from one SUV to the next, firing suppressive shots simply to provide cover from any survivors. Soon he had four men in the sleeping cab sitting on the dead bodies and another four men holding on to the sides of the cab.

Ratta began driving the heavy rig west on I-40 and took the first turnoff at the Blue Ridge Parkway. He then drove a few miles before taking a gravel turnoff that led to a road that would wind them toward the base camp.

Zakir's hopes grew as they descended into the valley and passed the fire tower where he kept a sniper on sentry duty.

"Did you disable the GPS?" Zakir asked Ratta.

"Yes, of course. That and four RFID tags," Ratta replied. "Does not mean there are no other tracking devices, but the primary ones are not functioning right now, and I've got the portable JackRabbit to block the signals."

Zakir had purchased a JackRabbit Jammer expressly to block any hidden sending unit on the Mack truck.

"Good. We will want it to work Saturday, but not now."

Ratta drove the large tractor trailer into the valley where the Bible camp had once been. Zakir's men flocked around the truck and began performing their duties.

"Over there, as we discussed," Zakir said. He pointed at camouflage netting stitched tightly beneath a thick canopy of trees. Ratta pulled the truck beneath the netting and shut the engine.

Immediately men began to work on opening the door to the trailer. Zakir expected to find more security personnel in the trailer, so he had his fighters assume covered positions behind rocks and the Mitsubishi trucks he kept on hand. Right after the two men opened the doors with bolt cutters and crowbars, they spilled to either side of the opening, avoiding the fusillade of gunfire that rained at them.

His support team fired precision shots at the two security guards, avoiding striking the precious cargo inside. Eventually, his commandos overwhelmed the two men inside the trailer.

Zakir had no time to relish the victory. Gavril texted him, and Zakir immediately dispatched a two-man team to address a developing situation.

He watched them bounce east along the dirt road as he thought about the enormity of what he had just done.

He turned to Ratta and said, "Follow them with the Skunk Copter."

Ratta looked up at Zakir and said, "Yes, sir."

Zakir turned and studied the trailer, its doors angled open wide, like a hungry beast.

In the beast's gullet was the bounty he had anticipated: an SB-61 tactical nuclear missile.

Special Agent Oxendine pressed his PUSH TO TALK button and said, "Why are we putting down?"

Prominent to the north was the Biltmore Estate; to the south the French Broad River.

"Running out of gas. Just be a few minutes," Setz said.

"Where is the car?" Oxendine asked. They were still talking through the headsets over the internal communications system.

"Last ping on it was at a rest stop just west of Asheville. I didn't want to get over her, spook her, and then have to turn around. Better to let them think she is unobserved."

Oxendine agreed but couldn't let Setz's independent decision making stand.

"Not your decision to make, Bev," Oxendine said. "I'm the tactical commander."

"Au contraire, sir. I'm the pilot in charge, sir."

"Don't be a smart-ass with me, Setz. You know what I'm saying," Oxendine said.

McQueary looked at him and shook his head, as if to say, *Lay off.*

"I do, but when it comes to the safety of this aircraft and my crew and passengers, I'm in charge. End of discussion," Setz countered.

Oxendine seethed for a moment, knowing the pilot was right and had checkmated him. Anything he said would be said simply to get the last word in and appear to be in charge.

"All I'm saying is, let me know next time. Time is of the essence," Oxendine said.

"Roger that, sir," Setz replied.

Oxendine felt the aircraft bump down on the ground and watched the pilot talk to who he assumed was the fixed base operator, who would be providing the fuel. Several other commercial and private aircraft were on the ground moving to the terminal or runway. It was a busy time of year around the mountains with the leaves changing color.

Oxendine continued to see stopped vehicles everywhere, wrecks, a few ambulances and emergency personnel tending to injured citizens. People were standing in the roads looking dazed and confused. Not wanting to talk to Director Black again, he called the operations center and found a longtime special agent named Bud Hathaway from Down East in Morehead City.

"Bud, man, what's going on with these cars?"

"Word we're getting is that the military's Strategic Command is saying that someone planted a bug in the service centers and it was dormant for some like a year or something and set to activate at exactly nine o'clock this morning."

"Just in North Carolina?" Oxendine asked.

"Hell no. It's everywhere, man. All over the damn country."

Oxendine looked out the window. There was still no gas truck heading their way. Holy shit, he thought. Maybe the gas truck was hit with the cyberbomb, or whatever it was.

"It's obviously not all vehicles. Was it certain makes and models?" Oxendine asked.

"Roger that. They're narrowing that down, but it is mostly General Motors, Ford, Chrysler, BMW, Mercedes, Honda, Toyota, and Nissan right now. Still getting info," Hathaway said.

"Roger, thanks." Oxendine shut off the phone.

"Hey, Bev, you up on the net? Who makes the engines for most of the refueling trucks for aircraft?"

"General Motors, mostly, but there's lots of independent companies like Westmor and Garsite. Just depends, but most of them contract out the big stuff like engines," Setz said.

"All these stopped vehicles? STRATCOM thinks it was a bug put in the service center network. The Internet of Things. Laid dormant for like a year and then boom, they all activate this morning at nine a.m.," Oxendine said.

"Meaning my refuel truck might not be here anytime soon?" Setz asked.

"I think that's why we're seeing all these aircraft trying to figure out what to do. I've been to this airport a lot and never seen it this busy."

"Come to think of it, me neither. I need aviation gas. Can't be from a pump at the gas station. Especially if we're headed up into the mountains. So maybe take your SWAT guys there and see what you can find."

Oxendine was thinking the same thing. Without replying to Setz, he said to his SWAT commander, "Q, you know the deal. Let's see if we can find a fuel truck and get it here."

The SWAT team dismounted with Oxendine and moved in formation toward the small terminal building. On the south side were two fuel trucks in a garage with their hoods up. Small airplanes were parked in front of the garage, and there was no way to have the helicopter land closer to the fuel trucks. Oxendine looked around inside the garage and saw two small airplane tow tugs.

"Grab those and drag them over to the first fuel truck. Tow it like an airplane," Oxendine said. He walked along the concrete apron, noticing the chaos inside the terminal. Men and women were shouting at one another, and the overwhelmed airport manager was getting it from all sides. Once the SWAT team had the tow tug jacked beneath the fuel truck, Oxendine chipped in and helped pull the rig filled with 2,500 gallons of gas weighing about 15,000 pounds. It was heavy and took considerable effort to move, but after ten minutes they had traversed the parking ramp and moved to the helicopter.

One of the SWAT members had been a truck driver in the Army and had experience with operating Army refuel trucks. This was similar, and he was able to refuel the UH-60 Blackhawk helicopter that was their transport.

After climbing back in, Oxendine sat down in his command seat, put his headset on, pushed the button, and said to Setz, not in his most politically correct way, "Now fly this bitch and don't stop until I say so."

Setz turned her head and locked eyes with him. Oxendine gave her his linebacker stare as if Setz were a quarterback who was going down hard on the next play.

"Roger that," Setz said.

Oxendine felt the aircraft power up and lift into the sky toward the rest stop just north of their position by ten miles.

CHAPTER 13

MAHEGAN STUDIED JASPER'S MECHANIC'S LOGS, NOTICING THE monthly inspections of vehicles. Cassie stood to his side, then began walking the length of the garage and back. She was pacing, arms folded. Impatient.

"Keep that weasel out of here," Jasper said. He pointed at Ronnie. Mahegan figured they'd had a falling out of some sort, but that wasn't his concern now. He nodded at Ronnie, indicating for him to stay outside.

"Shit ain't right," Ronnie said.

Jasper began talking as Mahegan thumbed the logs.

"Started out with me just doing a state inspection. I'm kind of a shade tree operation here and was a little surprised that someone just dropped in like that. I mean, don't get me wrong, I do better than Ronnie and his little one-bay operation, but mostly it's repeat clients that I've developed and known for years. They're steady and loyal, and they help me keep food on the table."

"You notice anything different about these cars and people?" Mahegan asked. They were standing in a single bay of a two-bay garage. Outside, the parking lot was gravel and in need of a new load. Two giant oaks cast a dark shadow across much of the garage, dissipating the heat. To Mahegan the garage looked exactly like that, a home garage that Jasper had added on to with decent construction of another bay. He had a hydraulic lift and an assortment of tools and tool bins scattered around the rim of the cement garage floor.

"First thing I noticed is the man looked different than most of us up here in the mountains, but Asheville gets all sorts of different folks with all the art and bullshit they've got going on there. So I didn't think much of it. Second thing I noticed was the trucks they were bringing in. These were pretty new L200 Mitsubishi Barbarian pickup trucks. They specifically asked me to unplug the computer and to not use any kind of computer device, not that I have one. Saving up for that, but ain't got the diagnostic machine just yet. They wanted an old-school mechanic, and they got one. Last thing I noticed was that Ameri is going to be the next Mrs. Jasper Jernigan if I have anything to do with it."

"I wouldn't put too much stock in that last observation," Mahegan said. "Your future wife may have something to do with all these cars stopping."

"My two ex-wives might also. Maybe they're teaming up," Jasper quipped.

"You get an address on any of these vehicles?"

"Well, to do a state inspection there has to be a home of record. So I've got those. They always paid cash, which I appreciated."

"Can we take a look at the address they listed?" Mahegan asked. He wasn't hopeful, but it was a rock they had to turn over.

Jasper snatched one pink carbon copy and read aloud. "John Smith. PO Box 1720, Asheville, North Carolina." He looked up. "That ain't much help is it?"

Mahegan shook his head. "No. And they're all bogus, I'm sure."

"Hey, man. Don't get me in any trouble here."

"You're not in any trouble. Just need to find these people."

He watched Jasper scratch his chin, thinking. Then he turned toward Cassie, who was staring at something in the corner.

"You ever tear down any of these cars? Put them back together?" she asked.

"A couple. All the suspensions were bad. Two needed new shocks."

Cassie looked at Mahegan. "That might be all we get," she said.

Mahegan paused, looked at Jasper.

"What did you do with the computer components you removed from these vehicles?"

A slow smile spread across Jasper's face.

"Damn. That's why you was Delta and I was a mechanic."

"It all counts," Mahegan said. "Can't fight with broken stuff."

Jasper disappeared for a few minutes and came back with two items that looked like thumb drives.

"They had a 2014 BMW X5, and I tore the computer system out of that. Here's that," Jasper said as he handed him one of the flash drives. "And here are the modules for all those Mitsubishi trucks."

"You got something I can use to look at the data?"

"Hell no. Those machines cost about a million dollars. Told you, I do basic shit here."

"Let me ask you. Did a red flag go up when these people started asking you to pull out their computers?"

"At first, yes. But it went down really quick when they started paying two thousand dollars cash every time they came in. That's a lot of coin."

Mahegan nodded. There was no way Jasper could know the future. For all he knew, it was a cheating spouse trying to get rid of GPS data. But the GPS data were what Mahegan wanted.

"Closest place I can look at this stuff?"

Jasper scratched his face about the time Ronnie stuck his head in and said, "I don't want to get involved in nothing, but I saw that shit going down today. You ain't getting nowhere with anybody unless you got a real mechanic with you. I got a friend who has a machine. He's probably up to his ass in alligators right now, if he's at his place at all, but it's worth a shot."

Jasper looked at Ronnie and said, "Sometimes my brother is a real asshole, but sometimes he can be useful. I'd listen to him on this one."

"Ronnie's your brother?"

"Yeah, not getting into it, but we both joined the Army, became mechanics, and then got all fucked up by the wars. What he's saying? It's worth a shot."

"You miss every shot you don't take," Cassie said.

"Damn, I like that, woman. Gonna use it in the future, if that's all right," Ronnie said, stepping into the garage.

"I'll drive," Cassie said, walking to her car.

"And I'll stay here, if it's just the same. All that crazy shit going on out there. Don't want nothing to do with it," Jasper said.

"We'll bring Ronnie back here," Mahegan said.

"Please don't," Jasper said.

They piled into Cassie's car and followed a series of turn commands from Ronnie until they were dodging cars and people along a main strip.

"Here. Turn along this alley and come in the back way. Sam's office is in the back."

They found Sam sitting in his office staring at his phone. Without looking up, he said. "I can't help you."

"Sam, it's me. Ronnie."

Mahegan watched Sam slowly turn his head. He had gray hair that was tossed, possibly from running his hands through it. His black T-shirt was stained with salt lines around the armpits and stomach area, where his ample gut protruded. The office smelled of greasy fast food and cigarettes.

"Ronnie, the owner of every car I've worked on in the past year is calling me, telling me I fucked up. They're stopped on the road between here and California. My insurance is going to drop me, I'm sure."

"Sorry to hear that, Sam. I've got a couple of people here who might be able to help."

"Help? I'm a damn General Motors franchise service shop and I've done close to a thousand cars in the last year. State inspections make it close to two thousand. Every one of them, far as I can tell, has stopped on the road like I purposely did something to them. How the fuck can someone help me?"

"There's a lot more going on, Sam. This here's a terrorist attack. I've got two people that need to read some car chips and see the GPS data."

Sam eyed them warily, then pushed up from his gray metal desk and squeaky chair. They followed Sam into his garage, a six-bay operation with everything in place. Lifts, toolboxes, and tires were all neatly aligned and where they should be, in stark contrast to Jasper's garage. Sam walked them to a laptop computer sitting atop a red toolbox.

"Let me see it," Sam said.

"Where's all your people?" Ronnie asked.

"What the hell you talking about? They're like everyone else. Their shit shut down at nine a.m. sharp. They're standing on the road somewhere. Not everyone has a mullet and drives a Chevy Nova as if they never grew up from the eighties," Sam said.

"Let's focus, guys. This is important." Sam looked up at Mahegan, who towered over the man. He nodded and grasped the flash drive. He powered up the laptop, slid the drive into the USB port, and let the computer work for a minute or two.

"Okay, here's the GPS," Sam said. "Looks like they drove along the Blue Ridge Parkway a lot. Spent some time in Greenville, South Carolina. And made a trip to the beach." He kept scrolling through the data but came back to the Blue Ridge Parkway. "There's a spot here where they pick up and drive into Asheville. I know this area like the back of my hand. That right there is Walmart and the strip mall."

Sam pointed at the screen. Mahegan nodded and said, "Okay, what about the other chip?" He was thinking, though, that this was something. The origin in the Blue Ridge Parkway was near one of his three guesses for the terrorist camp.

Sam unplugged the one drive and inserted the other. He went through the same machinations and said, "Same thing. Almost identical. Instead of Greenville, it's Spartanburg, South Carolina. Practically the same thing. Lots of movement along the Blue Ridge Parkway. They get on it here, the satellite picks them up and starts tracking them to Walmart. Both have suspiciously been to Ronnie's brother's auto shop. I'd arrest his ass right now."

Sam's moment of levity led to Cassie's deadpan: "Yeah, I think that's a good move."

Ronnie, completely missing the sarcasm, said, "No way, bro. I brought you here!"

"Chill, Ronnie. She was only joking," Mahegan said. "You've been very helpful. We've got some good intel here." Then to Sam, "Can you give me a grid coordinate or a lat-long on the location they enter the Blue Ridge Parkway?"

"Am I going to get a medal from the president or something?"

"Look at it this way. You'll avoid getting your ass kicked all over this garage. That's better than any medal you'd ever receive," Mahegan said.

Cassie punched him lightly on the arm. "Come on, Jake. Don't threaten Sam. He's helping us. Plus, we'd already agreed to waterboard him if he didn't."

Mahegan played along. "Roger. So what's the location?"

Sam had already printed out the two pages of information on where the vehicles had entered the Blue Ridge Parkway. They were identical.

"We've got a location," Mahegan said.

"If it's them," Cassie said. "Maybe it's just preachers at Bible camp getting their cars fixed."

"It's them," Mahegan said.

"They was just joking about the waterboarding," Ronnie said to Sam. He elbowed him.

"Like hell. Look at that dude. He don't joke about much," Sam said.

Mahegan looked at him. "You've got every employee stuck somewhere. You've got every car and truck you've worked on stuck somewhere on the highway. Tell me, exactly, what is there to joke about?"

Sam sighed and looked up at him.

"Nothing, man. Nothing. I've been thinking about sucking the long end of my pistol."

"Well, no need to do that. We'll figure this out. You'll be okay," Mahegan reassured him.

Ronnie had disappeared into the waiting area and came back in a rush, waving his debit card. "Hey man, how come your ATM ain't working?"

"Was fine yesterday," Sam said.

Mahegan looked at Cassie. They both said, "That's next."

CHAPTER 14

ZAKIR WATCHED THE ACTION UNFOLD FROM THE ARMED SKUNK Copter drone he kept in the base camp. It was an eight-propeller riot control drone that Zakir had purchased on Amazon.

The drone was originally rigged to shoot paintballs, but Zakir had Ratta upfit it to fire missiles and .50-caliber bullets. At the moment, though, he was using it to provide intelligence on the local auto repair shop they used to have their vehicles inspected. As he purchased the trucks before Ratta arrived in the base camp, Zakir needed to have the computer systems neutralized so that they were not subject to the very Trojan he and Gavril had planted in the network.

After returning from the ambush, stowing the Mack truck in its hide position, and defeating the remnant security in the back of the container, Zakir had received a secure message from Gavril that the FBI were tracking Cassie Bagwell's car, perhaps to warn her that her parents were missing. And he didn't consider it a coincidence that her car was at the remote garage he had chosen to have their vehicles inspected. To stay off local police radar, Zakir had to have current license plates. So he had picked Jasper's garage, a one-man operation that he fully intended to shut down today. The presence of Bagwell's daughter's car bugged him. She was hunting for her father. The ear patch had led her this far. How good was she, he wondered?

Zakir's two-man team approached Jasper's garage. This impromptu mission was useful because he needed to kill Jasper anyway. Of all the major tasks he had on his to-do list, killing Jasper was at the bottom, but it was still there. The new information about Captain Cassie Bagwell gave him the possibility of a twofer.

He could eliminate Jasper as a source of connectivity to his operations, and he could deal with Bagwell's daughter.

The Skunk Copter hovered just above the tree line and tilted forward, panning its camera at the back of Jasper's garage and home. Within the camera's picture, Zakir viewed his two commandos stalking the buildings through a pine thicket. He could see the backs of their heads as they took slow steps down the hill. He noticed the backpack on one of his men, whose mission it was to use the pack contents in the best tactical manner possible.

The sniper took up a position about one hundred yards behind the garage. The backpack man continued walking to the south and found an old Buick Electra about a quarter mile below the garage. The Skunk Copter showed him unloading the contents of the backpack into the Buick. The commando then hot-wired the car and prepared to drive it toward Jasper's garage.

It would be quite the stroke of good fortune to have Captain Bagwell on hand so soon in the operation.

Mahegan and Cassie drove back to Jasper's shop to return Ronnie to his Chevy Nova. She parked next to the Nova, and they all got out of her Subaru Crosstrek and walked into the garage. They spent a few minutes there looking at Cassie's phone, studying Google Maps, devising a plan for going to the location and determining how they would approach the church camp, which was their suspected location of the terrorist base camp. Jasper was nowhere to be found. Ronnie walked next door to a small trailer that must have doubled as his brother's home.

"We need to get moving," Mahegan said to Cassie. He looked at her car in the gravel parking lot. The sunshine was a dull blade. Beyond the gravel lot was a hundred yard drop-off that Mahegan had noticed on the drive into Jasper's garage. The garage was situated on a knoll that jutted northeast above the entrance road, which required a switchback, and below the mountain that angled away to the north, dominant.

As often happened in his military career, Mahegan felt that if they didn't move quickly, the situation could slip away from their control. Call it gut instinct or combat awareness, Mahegan sensed that he and Cassie needed to get moving quickly.

"What?" Cassie asked.

"We need to roll," Mahegan said.

Ronnie came running back from the trailer. "Can't find Jasper. We may hate each other, but we love each other, too. If you know what I mean."

Mahegan nodded. He understood.

"And, hey, I ain't no strategic genius, but I think I just heard a car down below. First of all, not many people are moving now. Second of all, he don't get many customers up this way that I don't know about ahead of time," Ronnie said.

"You have any weapons?" Mahegan asked. Then he looked at Cassie. "Shotgun?"

"Damn straight. Jasper's got an AR-15, a Remington shotgun, and a few others."

"Get the fifteen for me and the shotgun for you," Mahegan said.

"All I've got is buckshot. But I've got an AR-15 . . ." Cassie said.

It was too late, though. Mahegan was already moving to Jasper's home thirty feet away. Cassie's car was at the other end of the garage.

The first shot came through from the elevated terrain behind the garage. It was full of trees and thick underbrush, rarely traversed. The rifle shot echoed down the hill as a bullet crashed through the grimy window. The first bullet hit Ronnie in the side. He clutched his ribcage and muttered, "Not again."

Wounded twice in combat, the mechanic knelt down and said, "Better get the hell out of here."

Mahegan grabbed Ronnie and pulled him out of the line of sight of the window. Cassie had her pistol up and her back to the far wall, waiting.

"AR-15?" Mahegan asked as he applied a dirty, oil-soaked rag to Ronnie's side.

"House. Under the sofa. Got a full mag," Ronnie said. The bullet had run its course through the mechanic. Blood spread rapidly from his sides. His eyes faded. Having done all he could do, Mahegan sprinted through the side door of the garage that connected to the house. A couple of shots snapped past Mahegan as he entered a single-wide trailer, found the sofa, and pulled an assortment of detritus from beneath the sofa before feeling the reassuring stock of an assault weapon. There was a full fifteen-round magazine taped to the stock. Mahegan was in business.

Mahegan heard a few pistol shots, assumed they were from Cassie's weapon, and checked the bedroom quickly. Then the bathroom. Jasper was wide-eyed in the tub with his throat slit from ear to ear. Blood ran down his neck, looking like a bad Halloween costume.

Two brothers go to war and come back a little messed up but alive and okay. And now they both eat it on the same day. Not right.

He ran back to the garage where Cassie was in a shooter's stance, feet spread, arms locked, eyes focused on the car rushing their position.

Pop. Pop. Pop.

Her shots were well aimed and splintered the glass windshield of the car fishtailing in the parking lot. Mahegan raised the AR-15, flipped the selector switch to single shot, and fired through the shattered windshield at about where he thought a driver and passenger might be. Then he knelt down next to Ronnie and felt for a pulse. Nothing. Ronnie's blood pooled with the oil and grime of the garage, its blackness stark on the floor.

"Let's move," Mahegan said, standing. He led Cassie out of the garage, past the trailer, and up the spine of the hill. There was a minor trail that led behind Jasper's garage, up the incline and toward the crest of the hill. Two shots snapped past them, and Cassie said, "Never been shot at until now."

"Get used to it," Mahegan replied. She was to his left, holding her pistol. Mahegan held the AR-15, glad that he had a long weapon to combat whoever had come for them, or more likely, for Ronnie and Jasper. The enemy was erasing loose ends, perhaps those that they didn't have time to eliminate previously. They found a small bump in the terrain, a rock that had been there for centuries, and Mahegan clasped Cassie's hand.

"Hang tight," he said. Pausing, assessing, Mahegan listened for any anomalies. A car idled in the gravel lot. The wind whistled through the tall pines.

Then he heard the slightest metallic click. It could have been the turning of a sniper scope dial or the flipping of a selector switch, as he had just done. Regardless, it was from his two o'clock direction. He lifted the AR-15 and sighted along its iron sights, scanning, catching a wink. Maybe the glimmer of a wristwatch, or possibly of a sniper scope, or even binoculars. It was the faintest reflection. But it was something.

"I see it, too," Cassie whispered.

Mahegan put the iron sight where he last saw the reflection and snapped off three rounds. With their position compromised, Mahegan said, "Hunker down behind the rock."

But he was talking to himself.

Cassie was up and running toward where Mahegan had fired his shots. She was sprinting, like a hurdler whipping along a track. She had her pistol up and was firing.

Mahegan covered her advance, leading her with the AR-15. Waiting. Watching. Wondering what the hell she was doing. Cassie stopped, sucking in deep breaths, about one hundred yards from their rock hide position. He watched her kneel, reach out her hand, and possibly feel for a pulse.

She looked back at Mahegan and waved him forward.

Joining her, he looked down at a midtwenties man dressed in olive and black cargo pants and shirt.

"Wounded," Cassie said, gasping for air. Next to the man lay a state-of-the-art ORSIS T-5000 sniper rifle with scope. The rifle that had killed Ronnie. He looked at the man's belt and saw a sheathed knife, its handle still wet with sticky, red residue. The knife that had killed Jasper. Two decent men who had fought for their country and come back to scratch out a living were now dead because of what? The terrorists were covering their tracks? It was D-day and they were eliminating loose ends?

Everything is happening now. All at once.

Mahegan was reminded that even planned simultaneous operations were often near simultaneous or even sequential, but rarely did everything happen all at once.

"Look outward. Pull security while I frisk him," Mahegan directed. Cassie took a knee, cupping her pistol and scanning in each direction.

There were two bullet holes—one in the leg, which was probably Mahegan's shot given the smaller diameter of the wound, and one in the upper left torso, Cassie's shot. It was a big hole. A sucking chest wound. Mahegan searched the man's pockets, found a Pop-Tart wrapper, and placed it on the aspirating wound. He slapped the man in the face a couple of times and said, "Talk to me."

"Help me," the man said.

"You need to help me first. Where is your base camp?"

"Ask him who his commander is," Cassie said.

"Nothing," the man said. His voice was a hoarse whisper, meshing with the wind.

Mahegan put his thumb on the leg wound and the man screamed.

"Tell me something," Mahegan said. "Where?"

"Hurry. The car," the man said. Those were his last words. His head lolled to one side and he stared blankly down the hill where the car sat idle, like an inert bomb.

Mahegan quickly checked the rest of the shooter's pockets, and they were unsurprisingly empty. Trained operatives usually sanitized their clothing and equipment prior to executing an operation. Plucking the dead man's weapon from the grass, Mahegan peered through the scope, assessing the sniper's perch. Through the shattered window, he could see Ronnie lying dead on the floor of the garage.

"Let's go," he said to Cassie, who followed him back down the path. As they rounded the corner by Jasper's trailer, the car—which Mahegan could now see was an old Buick Electra—exploded with a fury that he hadn't seen since Sergeant Colgate's vehicle burned and spit shrapnel that horrible night four years ago in Afghanistan. The heat licked their faces, and hot metal whipped past them like flung ninja stars. They dove beneath the trailer, avoiding the bulk of the debris. A few seconds later, they were up and running, avoiding bullets coming from somewhere.

Muzzle flashes sparked like bad fireworks near where they had left the dead foreign fighter. While Mahegan laid down suppressive fire, the commando used cover and concealment to evade and escape into the mountains.

Special Agent Oxendine was frustrated. They had flown over the rest stop but had not seen Cassie Bagwell's car.

Oxendine had Setz land the helicopter in the scenic overlook, and he began interviewing people. On his third attempt an elderly couple admitted to seeing a white Subaru with a big man and a woman with short blond hair.

"They appeared to be together, though," the elderly woman said.

"You're sure you saw both of them and the woman was not under duress?"

"Well, I can't be certain, but it didn't appear so," she said. Turning to her husband she asked, "What did you think, Eldon?"

Oxendine looked at Eldon, who had been gazing over the scenic overlook at the colorful array of trees sweeping down into the valley.

"Looked pretty normal to me, but what do I know. Ain't nothing normal about a brand-new Honda Civic not working either," Eldon said. "Should have had one of those Chevy Novas like the fellow with them."

"What fellow?" Oxendine asked.

"Redneck-looking guy they was talking with," Eldon said. His wife nodded in agreement.

"Did they leave together?"

"Appeared that way. They jumped back on the interstate heading the only way you can go," Eldon said.

"Thanks."

Oxendine jogged back to the helicopter and sat in his command seat. When Oxendine had his headset on, Setz said, "Got another hit on the car. It's south of here. Parked. Maybe ten miles."

"Let's go, now."

Oxendine turned to McQueary and said, "SWAT ready, Q?"

"Roger that," McQueary said.

Then in the distance, a fireball erupted, looking like a mini nuclear explosion boiling into the sky.

"My car," Cassie said.

Her white Subaru was charred black on one side and across the roof. She tried the key fob but got no response. She inserted the key in the metallic door lock, then immediately withdrew her hand, singed from the heat.

"Let me try my side," Mahegan said. She tossed him the key, and the passenger side worked. He manually unlocked the doors and opened the driver's door from the inside. Cassie slid in, avoiding the exterior, and pulled the door shut. The car started on the first try, but Mahegan noticed the onboard computer was not displaying in the dashboard. Out of habit, he had been watching the GPS map to remain oriented.

"Your GPS looks shot," Mahegan said.

"I've got Google Maps on my phone," Cassie replied. She used her thumb to access her phone via fingerprint identification, tapped Google Maps, and handed it to Mahegan.

"You're my navigator," she said as she shot out of the parking lot.

"Roger. This thing's just spinning, though. Cell towers maxed out," Mahegan said.

"You've got the printouts?" she asked.

Mahegan flashed her the two pages of rudimentary maps that pinpointed the cars operating somewhere just south of the Blue Ridge Parkway and almost due west of Avery Creek, their current location.

"If we take Route 191 north, we can get on the parkway and find the exit they must have been using. We'll park up top and walk down with the AR-15 and shotgun," Mahegan said.

"Why not the sniper rifle?" Cassie countered.

"Single shot. Bad condition. Not enough ammo."

"Was good enough to kill Ronnie back there," Cassie said.

"A blind kid could have made that hundred-yard shot. We'll keep the rifle as backup, but I've got a fifteen-round magazine plus about ten rounds left in the AR-15. How much buckshot do you have?"

"Two boxes. Twenty-four rounds."

"Okay. We stay together and we find your parents," Mahegan said.

Cassie dodged stalled cars everywhere on the road. A police officer was trying to wave them down, but Mahegan said, "Keep going. He needs us, we don't need him."

The officer drew his pistol at the same time a helicopter buzzed them from maybe thirty yards away. Mahegan slid the sniper rifle out the car window so that the cop could see it. He lowered his pistol, and Mahegan kept the optic trained on the policeman until they were past him. In the rearview mirror, the cop was shouting into a personal mobile radio that Mahegan doubted would get much response.

Meanwhile the helicopter made a wide, arcing turn and came back at them. There were six men in black uniforms—three on each side—with their legs dangling from the open door of the aircraft into the breeze. They were carrying long rifles and wearing body armor and helmets.

"We've got a SWAT team above us. Not sure why, but I'm certain they're not here to help me," Mahegan said.

"They may be here to help me, but I don't want anything to do with them," Cassie said.

"Then haul ass onto the parkway and get somewhere in the trees quick. They won't shoot if they're tracking you and your car. They will shoot if they think it's just me."

They looped up onto the Blue Ridge Parkway, and Cassie asked, "Why would they be tracking you?"

"No time to explain," Mahegan said. Alex Russell had told him about Savage's pistol. Then there were the military policemen and their car. Someone may have some hard evidence against him right now and believe that a murderer was on the loose.

"Well, what the hell is in this for you? Why take the risk? What are *you* running from?"

The helicopter raced ahead of them, presumably looking for a landing spot, but too many cars littered the roads. Power lines hung like spiderwebs. The trees were tall, thick and tightly bunched. All factors combined to prevent a direct landing in the road. They could go offset, but the SWAT team would never catch up with them. The helicopter circled around and settled into a fixed altitude as it followed them.

Cassie dodged dozens of stalled cars and passed stranded motorists reaching out to her as she followed the winding parkway. They snaked between steep mountain peaks and tunnels of trees that gave way to brief, wide panoramic views of valleys that ebbed away endlessly. The noise from the helicopter was a constant reminder, urging them forward. Cassie drove through another tunnel of trees for about a mile, and Mahegan looked at her and offered his explanation to her question.

"I've got two teammates missing and my former boss. And we've got an attack right here, right now on the homeland. The country has literally seized up from gridlock. The cell towers are jammed, and people can't communicate. If Ronnie's bank account is any indication, and granted he might have just had insufficient funds, then yours and mine are probably locked up, also. How does all this get undone? And who did it? We've had so many spineless politicians weakening our defenses that we lack even the basic tenets of national security. Everyone is focused on the Capitol, or the White House, or big landmarks. All of that is symbolic. What's happening now? This is real. Hits Joe Six-Pack right in the wallet. Hits Joe Millionaire in the wallet, too. Equal opportunity terror. Hell with that. Equal opportunity attack."

Cassie nodded. Her tired eyes showed the worry, the stress. It was all there, etched across her furrowed brow.

"This looks like it might be it," Mahegan said. They were approaching a small gravel turnout that appeared to have a dirt two-track running off to one side and then curving beneath the parkway. There was a thick forest on either side of the gravel road. Cassie pulled off the parkway, slowed through the gravel, centered the Subaru on the two-track, and followed it about fifty yards. The helicopter hovered, unable to land. Mahegan wondered if their pursuers had fast-rope or rappelling capabilities.

"Pull over here," Mahegan said. "They could have cameras or even remote sensors and IEDs." It was unlikely that the trail had improvised explosive devices, but he couldn't be too careful. To attack the sensors in automobiles and trucks by infecting the code took months of planning and execution. Likewise, the precision execution of the decapitation attack that occurred last night required rehearsals and communication capabilities.

The power lines rose and fell with the undulating mountains. Their skeletal towers and heavy-gauge cables were foreign to this otherwise mostly unspoiled environment. Up on the tower nearest the parkway he noticed cellular phone and satellite dishes and drums that fed the communications needs of those who lived in the mountains and traveled on the scenic parkway.

And perhaps those who were attacking his country.

As the helicopter lifted away and flew south, no doubt to land on the road and dismount its SWAT team, the distinctive whoosh of a surface-to air-missile or rocket-propelled grenade thundered above. He looked through the trees and saw the helicopter immediately take evasive action and spit flares to decoy the heat-seeking missile.

Mahegan watched as the helicopter disappeared over the mountain ridge. This was their opportunity, and certainly the presence of a SAM from the valley below was an indication of a fortified enemy encampment.

* * *

Tommy Oxendine slammed into the side of the Blackhawk helicopter as the vapor trail of a missile smoked past them.

Alarms and buzzers wailed in the cockpit. Setz's face tightened into a grimace as she worked both hands on the controls to tilt ninety degrees, fire chaff to fool the missile's heat-seeking guidance, and prevent a crash.

McQueary and his men hung on as the helicopter nearly did a barrel roll. Somehow Setz kept the aircraft in the air as Oxendine was at one moment looking at Cassie Bagwell's white Subaru and the next staring at blue sky . . . below him.

After thirty seconds of evasive maneuvers, Oxendine's adrenaline leveled off, as he imagined Setz's might have as well.

"What the hell was that, Bev?" Oxendine barked into the headset.

"You know damn well what that was, Agent Oxendine," Setz said. "A surface-to-air missile from our nine o'clock. It's not safe up here in the mountains, and I'm taking us back to lower ground."

"Like hell," Oxendine said. "We've got eyes on Bagwell's Subaru and two eyewitnesses who described someone the size and looks of Mahegan with her."

"You can file a report on my ass, I don't care. I'm not putting Q and his team in jeopardy, and as much as I don't give a shit about you, I'm not putting you in jeopardy, either."

"You can let us fast-rope out about a mile down the hill and we'll walk up, if that is any kind of compromise," McQueary said.

"Maybe two miles down the hill," Setz said. "That had to be a Stinger missile, and it has a range of five miles. I'm staying out of that range."

Oxendine felt helpless. Pilots. Always worried about their damn machine and their careers. Right here, right now was the biggest thing happening in the state of North Carolina, and Setz was blocking him from executing. He let his temper boil and then took a few deep breaths.

"Okay, here's what we're doing," Oxendine said. "Bev's right. Can't risk the team or the chopper. If they've got one SAM, then they probably have another. Not sure who it is, but it's clear they were gunning for us. It's probably Mahegan. We'll head back to the rest area where they were last seen and set down. We can save fuel and track the car once it starts moving. Then we'll pounce. And Q, be ready to fast-rope your men in. We need to rescue Cassie Bagwell and kill or capture Jake Mahegan."

"Kill or capture?" McQueary questioned. "Who put the kill order out on Mahegan?"

"I did, Q. He's armed and dangerous. Shoot first, ask questions later."

"I really can't believe you're saying that, Tommy. He's not even been charged with anything," McQueary said.

"I want your men ready to shoot. Mahegan is ex-Delta. He's good. He'll kill quickly and efficiently. If we don't take the first shot, he will and your men will die."

The entire team was hooked into the internal communications system via their headsets and could hear the conversation. Oxendine had just put McQueary in a bad position and he knew it. Either McQueary cared about his men and would give them the green light to shoot first, or he didn't care and would let Mahegan have the advantage.

McQueary stared at him and said, "We'll discuss once we're on the ground at the rest stop."

Oxendine nodded.

Setz said, "Roger. Headed to last touchdown location."

Mahegan listened as the helicopter rotor noise diminished and finally faded away beyond the front range of the Blue Ridge.

Convinced they were in the right location based on the surface-to-air missile, he decided to strap the sniper rifle across his back as he pocketed the box magazine with five 7.62 mm bullets. He checked his Tribal pistol and then his knife secured to his ankle. He lifted the AR-15 from the foot well of the Subaru as Cassie grabbed her shotgun and Berretta 9 mm pistol.

"Here. Couple of Clif Bars and some water," Cassie said. Mahegan motioned to her to sit behind the Subaru, facing up the hill they had just driven down. He accepted the chow, powered it down quickly, and then chugged the entire bottle of water.

"Remind me never to go to dinner with you," she said.

"Deal," Mahegan replied. He stared at her as she took a couple of bites of her bar and then pocketed it in the wrapper.

"No, eat it or leave it," Mahegan said. "Wrapper's too noisy."

She nodded, removed the bar, and finished it. Then she drank the water and left the other bar in her kit bag in the back of the Subaru.

"Satisfied?"

Mahegan ignored her question and outlined the basic plan.

"We walk on either side of the road, staying to the low ground. Look out for anything that might be emitting infrared beams at ankle level and for anything that might be recording us up in the trees. You saw they fired a Stinger or an SA-18 Russian missile. Stinger can go about four to five miles, and the eighteen can go about two to three miles. Maybe we've got a small window here."

"Well, being in the intelligence field, I would say that if they have surface-to-air missiles, they are protecting something pretty significant."

"Which we are about to poke. So keep that in mind. Could be a few dudes or could be an army."

Cassie nodded. As they began to stand, the first shot whispered silently between them, kicking up dirt at their feet.

"Probably an army," Mahegan said as they dove away from the follow-on shots.

They entered separate sides of the woods that paralleled the two-track downhill. Mahegan kept Cassie in his peripheral vision, reminded himself that she had graduated from the U.S. Army Ranger school. She knew what to do. By now, she'd even been under fire. Mahegan noticed some tire tracks on the dirt and gravel road that were too wide to be a regular four-wheel car or truck.

Scanning ahead, he stepped over rocks and logs that impeded the awkward downhill walk. Cassie whistled a high-pitched animal noise, like a bird call. He knelt and slowly turned toward her. She was kneeling behind a thick tree and pointing to her one o'clock, across the road. He looked to his front and saw a tower. It was an observation tower used by the North Carolina Forestry Service to watch for forest fires.

A muzzle swiveled from left to right as if searching for them. He rolled his back against the tree and removed the sniper rifle from his shoulder. He retrieved the box magazine and fed it into the well. Slowly working the bolt, he quietly slid a 7.62 M118LR round into the bore. He looked at Cassie, who was watching him with her back to the tree providing her cover. He nodded. She understood. Stay back and stay alive.

Mahegan slid to the ground and splayed his legs out into a Y position, inching his right knee up just a bit. He slid the rifle along the ground directly toward the tower, keeping all movement perpendicular to the line of sight of his target. The human eye was less capable of detecting coincident movements as it was lateral shifts. Turning the rifle upright, he slowly brought the scope to eye level. He walked the crosshairs up the base of the tower, noticing the metal crossbeams and supports that narrowed gradually as they reached the tower at its peak. There was a circular stair that had protective handrails and mesh to keep people from falling off the steps.

The tower had a four-way rectangular opening about chest high on an average human being. It was maybe two hundred feet above ground level, giving the occupant clear views in all directions . . . and clear fields of fire. The tower was maybe two hundred yards away and on a ridge that angled to the right. Mahegan did the calculus. He would need to kill the occupant and then move along the ridgeline under Cassie's covering overwatch, ascend the stairway, gather intel, and then link up with Cassie to revise the plan, be that what it was.

The tower guard kept a low profile, sliding his rifle slowly in a forty-five-degree arc that began about fifty yards to his right and ended about fifty yards to Cassie's left. He would need to lean forward to scan the ground closer to the tower, and eventually he did. This was most likely the same person who fired the surface-to-air missile. He could see in all directions from the tower.

The guard elevated just a bit, used his scope to scan the same arc like a sweeping beacon. As he got to the side of the arc that aimed to Cassie's left, Mahegan planted the crosshairs on the man's head. With this upward angle, the elevation change, and the unfamiliar rifle, Mahegan hoped the first bullet would strike the man somewhere. He anticipated the lead dropping, but not much at this altitude.

He pulled back on the trigger, felt its pressure less than what he preferred, slowed his pull, and felt the firing pin strike the cartridge. The shot echoed loudly down the canyon. To some, it could have been a deer hunter. To anyone in a proximate terrorist base camp, it was the first shot of the war fired at them.

The scope allowed him to draw a second bead on the man, who just stood there. He was looking down at his shoulder. Mahegan could see a red spot blossoming on the guard's shirt as Mahegan ratcheted another round into the bore. It appeared he had struck the man in the left shoulder. The bullet had caused the guard to elevate, and now Mahegan took a full body shot at his right pectoral, expecting the gun to be off again a bit to the right.

The second shot seemed louder than the first. Red mist exploded from the man's chest. As he predicted, the bullet had drifted right, or the weapon's zero was off for him, and the guard was down.

He turned to Cassie, who was already running toward him.

"He's down. Cover me with this rifle. I'm climbing the tower."

"Roger."

Mahegan sprinted along the ridge. The tower was at least two hundred yards away, but he found it and the ladder. He had the AR-15 in one hand and used the handrail to pull himself up as he took the steps two and three at a time.

Upon reaching the top, Mahegan found the guard dead, eyes open, flies already buzzing. Quickly pawing through the man's pockets, he found a wallet. He opened it briefly and saw an Arabic name on a South Carolina driver's license issued three months ago. Then he closed the wallet and put it in his own pocket. He plucked a full magazine from the man's hunting vest. Grabbing the silenced SR-25 sniper rifle, Mahegan scanned with the optics. About a mile south along the two-track were several cabins in a circle with a larger cabin in the middle. There was a small pond and what looked like a mess hall. Residence cabins, a command post, and a chow hall. The sheer cliffs of mountains on three sides created a narrow valley heading east where a river cut its path. Along the south wall was a dark opening, perhaps a cave or maybe a mine shaft.

This was a terrorist base camp with all of the trappings an invading force needed.

Men in black uniforms emerged from the cabins, running and pointing in his direction.

They all had weapons.

CHAPTER 15

ALEX RUSSELL LOOKED THROUGH BINOCULARS AT THE FIGHT RAGing on the ridgeline to her right and in the valley below her position. She was curious about the helicopter that had flown over and narrowly avoided the missile. Most likely state police tracking Mahegan for the Charlotte murder. Then she turned and saw Cassie Bagwell's white Subaru parked about a mile away in a gravel turnout on the north side of the Blue Ridge Parkway.

Interesting, Alex thought.

Alex stood leaning against a tall pine perched on a short ridge about a mile off the Blue Ridge Parkway. For the better part of the morning, she had been observing the minor activity in the abandoned Bible camp only to be surprised by the surface-to-air missile and then a sudden outbreak in rifle fire.

She jumped when the missile zipped over her head and then again as she heard the first shots. She admonished herself for startling. Alex' routine doctor appointments were no longer frequent enough. She needed to see the doctor soon and get a refill on her PKCzeta shots, called Boradine. Not one to get surprised easily, she had been jumpy this morning. Even worse, she had begun to get dizzy on the drive to Asheville after abandoning Mahegan on the side of the road in the Uwharrie National Forest.

As she observed the melee below, her mind spun with anxiety. She thought about her life as Alex Russell. She had a faint recollection of her role as the JAG lawyer to the elusive special operations commander, Major General Bob Savage, known as Jackknife Six to his legions of devoted Delta Force, now special mission unit operatives. Most days she was confused, depressed, and anxious. Today she felt disoriented. She needed to see the doctor, for sure, but she also had a small supply of the treatment at her Asheville condo. She thought that she would head there after figuring out precisely what was happening here.

Prior to the killing of those civilians in Syria, Alex had been an outgoing social butterfly, but her posttraumatic stress had made her mostly a loner. She avoided contact with her real, live social network, but she did keep a Facebook page where she posted pictures and tried to maintain some semblance of the person she had been. Her many Facebook friends "liked" the photos, keeping the idea of the old Alex Russell alive—gorgeous, friendly, patriotic, single, available, dedicated.

But the truth was that Alex's mind played tricks on her. She suffered from severe posttraumatic stress. Her memories of Operation Groomsman had haunted her for four years. Rare was the night that she did not awaken in a cold sweat, screaming. Ghosts of those she killed with her confirmation of "valid target" danced nightly in her visions like smoke-filled apparitions wafting through the darkness. Doctors initially treated her anxiety with low-grade medications such as Valium and BuSpar. When those did not work, they upgraded her to clonazepam, which briefly stabilized her but quickly ebbed as an effective method of holding her demons at bay. Still she chewed the pills like candy, numbing her brain the best she could. All the while her doctors were having her attend cognitive behavioral therapy, where they assessed her responses to specific questions. Alex found this treatment ineffective for her, though she knew others for whom it worked. The military psychiatrists demanded that she use all of her thirty annual vacation days, and so she did.

On one vacation to a Caribbean island, she met a man who was a psychiatrist. Their brief affair led to a discussion about her anxiety when the doctor awoke to Alex standing over him at three a.m. holding a kitchen knife. She had little memory of doing so but did recall him sitting her on the sofa and quietly taking something from her hand. He spent no more nights with her but encouraged her to visit Dr. Charles Boras, who specialized in PKCzeta protein inhibition and blocking. This experimental treatment focused on erasing trauma from the brain and blocking memories. Alex visited Dr. Boras in northern Virginia, and he changed her life. She was now sleeping most nights, though the nightmares still came.

She took four seven-day vacations a year. The first and last days of each vacation always included a visit to the doctor to get the shots and stock up on supplies of the medicine. She explained to her bosses, including Savage, that for the last four years she had medical and family commitments that were set in stone. Even General Savage supported her work–life balance, especially after Operation Groomsman and the trauma created for all. And because of the doctor visits, she never worried about the lie detector tests she had to take when she returned from these absences.

Did you visit any foreign countries?

Did you have any contact with known terrorists?

Have you given away any classified information?

Did you receive any large sums of money you have not disclosed?

Do you have any bank accounts which you have not disclosed?

Alex always passed those tests easily. She never even worried about them. The PKCzeta shots temporarily erased her memory, especially the memories of Operation Groomsman. At the beginning, the PKCzeta shots nibbled away at the fringes of her most traumatic memories. Dr. Boras was able to isolate the portion of Alex's brain that stored the more stressful, long-term memories. Protein kinase C zeta, or PKCzeta, was one of two proteins doctors believed stored long-term memories. Boras had been working on experimental treatment in addressing posttraumatic stress that focused on isolating the proteins that harbored the memory. Boras, seeking a Nobel Prize most likely, believed he had been able to isolate the protein that would play the Operation Groomsman video in her mind, like selecting a movie on Netflix, but instead of Alex selecting the movie, it selected itself and played at its own choosing. All Boras had to do was disable the movie or at least diminish its ability to play. Just like some benzodiazepines controlled anxiety by enhancing a neurotransmitter that muted the anxiety response, Boras's PKCzeta treatment that he modestly called Boradine muted the video held within the protein in Alex's brain.

At this moment, she stood on the ridge looking through binoculars into the old Bible camp about twelve miles to the east of Asheville. Alex felt the Boradine wearing off, the memory climbing over a ledge in her brain, pulling itself up so that it could return to its dominant, haunting form.

She heard more rifle shots and decided to back away and see what Cassie Bagwell was doing up here and how she might have gotten involved in all of this. True, Alex remembered that Cassie's parents had been kidnapped, but surely Cassie did not believe she could rescue them on her own.

Or did she want to rescue them? Alex and Cassie had been friends at one point in time, even doubles tennis partners. Cassie had played at West Point, and Alex was a natural athlete with ability in most sports. Immediately after Operation Groomsman, Alex had returned to Fort Bragg on the same plane as Cassie Bagwell, who had been an intelligence officer in Mosul with the coalition forces. They had discussed the mission that had gone so wrong, and while Alex's primary angst was that she had delivered the go-ahead to drop the bombs, Cassie couldn't stop talking about how much she hated her father because he had taken a public stand against her attending Ranger school.

So perhaps Cassie was happy her father was kidnapped, Alex thought. She smiled. The world was twisted and dark, and why would Cassie Bagwell be any different from Alex or General Savage? Cassie had even provided some of the preliminary intelligence on Operation Groomsman, so as far as Alex was concerned, she was as liable as anyone else. It had been Cassie's report that al-Baghdadi's cell phone was in one of the SUVs in the convoy.

She needs to pay, too, Alex thought.

Alex next thought about Jake Mahegan. She knew that she should have killed Mahegan. It had to be him who had led Cassie in her white Subaru to the periphery of this base camp. Truthfully, Alex was glad he had done so. She needed him here.

A muzzle flashed from a fire tower. Down below men in black clothing were taking well-aimed fire at the tower. She determined that it could only be Mahegan at the top of the mountain. He had most likely memorized the locations she had shown him of the Zebra indicators for Savage, O'Malley, and Owens. Now he was playing hero and had come to rescue them.

How noble.

A dark-skinned man moved quickly to the edge of the base camp and knelt next to two men fumbling with a rocket-propelled grenade and launcher. One man placed the launcher on his shoulder while the other man secured the rocket inside the tube. As the loader knelt down next to the shooter, Alex heard another loud shot echo throughout the valley. The binoculars provided her a front row seat. The loader's head exploded in a fine spray of pink mist. The rocket launched, but it was wide, poorly aimed if aimed at all. The white smoke trail of the rocket wound harmlessly through the sky, landing somewhere unintended. If the pilots were still flying that state helicopter, they would think another missile had been fired at them and put themselves in for air medals, she figured.

She watched a few men with AR-15 rifles on semiautomatic fire three round bursts at the tower. It was too far away, maybe five hundred yards, but perhaps they would get lucky.

The men moved through the woods. Black-clad soldiers were taking the hill, shooting, moving, and communicating. They were getting close to the tower. If this were a lone shooter, even Jake Mahegan, he wouldn't be able to fend off the balance of the advancing force.

She needed to act quickly.

Before she could move, though, the stress immobilized her. She took a step and crumpled to one knee, heaving and sucking in deep breaths. The emotions were like a python, strangling her, choking the life out of her. The scene replayed itself again and again in her mind.

Four words scrolled across her mind's eye as if they were on a Jumbotron.

"Yes, sir. Valid target."

Then she was back in Mosul, in the Joint Operations Center, not on this ridgeline watching terrorists defend a base camp.

The Netflix in her mind had chosen to replay the movie. The PKCzeta shot was wearing off. Now, in her mind, she was on the Iraq–Syria border. The Predator drone launched the Hellfire missile, which was winding its way to an SUV. Exploding in a giant fireball of dust and flames, the missile had been enough to kill everyone in that one vehicle and probably injure the others. But no, Savage took her "valid target" designation to the extreme and had a B-1 bomber drop five JDAM precision guided missiles on the entire convoy. All that was left were five smoking holes in the ground and some shards of metal.

She remembered watching from the forward command post in Mosul. The grainy live streaming video feed delivered by the Predator showed the two helicopters as they swept into the picture, landed, and disgorged eight soldiers.

"That's Jake Mahegan," she remembered saying. Though she had never met him, she recognized his bulk from pictures and other videos she had seen. She had also seen him walking in the compound before, but he was a recluse, always 100 percent professional, cleaning his weapon, shooting on the firing range, or lifting in the gym. Now it was Mahegan's team looking for the confirmation that Savage had killed al-Baghdadi.

Mahegan's team took a long time on the target. Were they killing the survivors? She didn't know. Were there survivors? There were no enemy counterattacks. That was the first clue that gave Alex a sinking feeling in her stomach that they had done something terrible.

But when Mahegan returned and met with General Savage privately, she knew that something was amiss. She was not authorized to attend the meeting between Savage and Mahegan.

Savage had emerged from the unit compound on the other side of the base in Mosul and met her in the vehicle that drove them to the JSOC headquarters.

"It's not good," Savage had said.

In the end, they had killed her sister, Fatima, and Fatima's fiancé, Malavdi, along with their friends. She was experiencing her own form of shell shock from saying that, unbeknownst to her, her own sister was a "valid target."

She screamed, grabbed her hair, and pulled it straight outward, torturing her scalp.

She had unwittingly approved the murder of her friends and family.

The trauma had been so great, Alex had visited the unit psychiatrist several times. She had cried most nights until there were no tears left. Sleep rarely came, if ever. The sun was a knife blade every morning, poking her bloodshot eyes. The Predator footage was a continuous reel playing in her mind.

"Yes, sir. Valid target." Then the Hellfire missile. Then the JDAMs. Then Mahegan. Then the confirmation that her sister was gone.

And then the forced amnesia.

Alex was now on all fours. She looked up through the stringy hair that fell across her face. The commandos had deployed smoke grenades to cover their movement. A thick haze of gray and white smoke was boiling up the hill. The wind was moving the curtain to the north, toward her. The leading edge of the acrid smoke filled her nostrils.

An idea began bouncing around her increasingly deranged mind. She tried to clutch it. Pushing off the ground, she clumsily stood and hung on to a pine tree branch as if it were her only grasp of reality. Perhaps it was.

The idea. There it was. It stopped long enough for her to see it, then sped off again in her mind like a taunting motorist.

Fueled by the idea, Alex stumbled and then ran to her vehicle hidden in the trees, cranked it, and sped out the back way, taking rough trails along the ridge that led to the Blue Ridge Parkway. From there she sped past the disabled cars littering the roads. A few tow trucks were hauling cars in different directions, undoubtedly to dealerships or service centers. She wondered how long it would take for the auto manufacturers to reboot the cars. She knew that some would do it "over the air" to the shark fin satellite antennae for the newer cars, while many of the cars would need to be manually rebooted at the service centers that had originally unwittingly planted the bug in the cars in the first place.

Alex drove her Land Rover onto the Blue Ridge Parkway, found the turnoff, and then sped toward Cassie's Subaru.

Again, she wondered what Cassie was doing. Cassie was an intel officer. Was she piecing bits of intelligence together and deducing enemy locations? Cassie was a "friend," but only in the sense that it helped her maintain her appearances at Fort Bragg. The sisterhood of Army officers and all that happy horseshit.

She stopped her SUV, noticed Cassie crouching at the base of the tower. Cassie was providing supporting rifle fire for someone—probably Mahegan—in the tower. The attacking men were probably a half mile down the mountain, but she realized that the weapons were now aimed in her direction. She backed up the SUV so that it sat behind a small knoll where she could still see the top of the tower.

The cloud of smoke was rising into the sky to her southeast. The tips of trees were visible as if poking through a low-hanging cloud. The sound of gunfire popped at a steady rhythm. She found it interesting that there was an assault on an enemy base camp in the Blue Ridge Mountains on the same day a vehicle service hack had stopped the majority of the cars on the road, if only briefly. She had no illusions about the speed with which some of the major manufacturers would solve the problem. But for now, there were no first responders arriving on the scene.

She pulled out her cell phone and punched up Cassie Bagwell's number. Cassie answered on the third ring.

"Hello? Alex?"

"Hey, Cass, I know you guys are in a shitstorm right now. I'm behind you and can provide covering fire if you want to escape and evade back this way. It looks like a damn army coming up at you."

"Where are you?"

Alex braved a walk up to the top of the knoll and waved at Cassie, who was turned around, looking in her direction. Just then a machine gun from the Syrian commandos opened up and began peppering the tower. No way that Mahegan would live through that if he stayed up there. Cassie spun around and began firing again with what looked like an AR-15.

This was a full-fledged firefight.

Mahegan was spiraling down the staircase, realizing perhaps that the tower's usefulness had run its course. Cassie was intermittently waving him down, shooting at the black-clad commandos, and shouting something at him. Somehow, Mahegan reached the ground, and Cassie lay next to him. He glanced back at her with a furrowed brow, perhaps trying to figure out if she was friend or foe. He knew the answer, she was certain, but in this case he was probably choosing the devil he knew—sort of—as opposed to the devil he didn't—the apparent army rushing up the mountain to the tower like Little Round Top at Gettysburg.

Cassie and Mahegan low-crawled off the backside of the ridge and then began running in her direction.

Alex found a tree to the right side of the road and leaned against it with her left shoulder as she knelt on her right knee. After retrieving her Berretta, Alex rested her left elbow on the thigh of her left leg and took dead aim.

She would need the stable firing platform at the distance she was expecting to shoot.

With Cassie Bagwell running her way, Alex thought of her sister, Fatima.

For you, Fatima, she thought as she pulled the trigger.

CHAPTER 16

OVER THE PAST TWO YEARS ZAKIR HAD COORDINATED THE RESETtlement to America of thousands of Syrians. His standard was to have one of his aspiring terrorists in every batch of one hundred. One percent. That was all Zakir needed, and he was able to easily obtain his goal.

At first he was a clean-shaven UN High Commissioner for Refugees midlevel politico who processed paperwork. He could speak Arabic, Turkish, Bulgarian, English, and Russian. The UNHCR processing teams were glad to have him on board. Because of his fluency in English, he had been assigned the U.S. desk, something that he had wished for when he had applied but did not want to seem too eager about. In fact, when they asked him, he said he would prefer processing the Syrian refugees to Bulgaria because he had lived there for so many years. The project director had insisted he take control of the U.S. processing station even though the bureaucrats in America were moving the refugees at a snail's pace.

Zakir accepted and enjoyed partnering with a French woman named Isabella. She was beautiful with long black hair, a soft voice, and slender hands that he watched as she talked and smiled. Joining Isabella and Zakir on the U.S. processing team was a young political appointee from the previous administration who believed that everyone deserved a chance at the American

Dream. Rodney Leland was a light-skinned African American who eagerly wished to process as many Syrians into America as possible.

"Because that's what my prez wants, you see?" Rodney would say. And every time he stamped "Approved" on an application, Rodney would say, "Cha-ching! Welcome to America!"

Isabella was dutiful and efficient in their Damascus office, and Zakir was able to report to ISIS leadership in Raqqa that if they did not get greedy, they would be able to infiltrate somewhere between fifty and one hundred terrorists into America.

Zakir's cyber teams in Raqqa and Damascus created for the terror immigrants false paperwork that looked faded and crumpled, just abused enough to appear legitimate. Many of the Syrian refugees did not even require paper other than what they filled out at the processing stations. Rodney was very welcoming to all who sought asylum in the United States. To Zakir, it was almost as if Rodney and his president wanted terrorists in the country.

Based on the ease of immigration, Zakir focused on how his terror immigrants would communicate once in America. He established a Facebook page and Instagram account allowing him to communicate with his charges as they scattered to the winds across the lower forty-eight of the United States of America.

Over the past several months, they had rallied here in this abandoned religious camp near an old gold mine. Purchasing AR-15s around the country was not an issue. Once placed in a sanctuary city, the terrorists secured driver's licenses and then soon thereafter purchased assault rifles. He had also pilfered two National Guard ammunition depots of some ammunition, to include two Stinger missiles.

His men had just demonstrated that one of the missiles actually worked. With the automobile Trojan being so effective, Zakir wasted no time in preparing for the next phase of the operation. Working closely with Malavdi's uncle Gavril, who was now in Charlotte commanding and controlling the cyberattack phase of the operation, Zakir and Gavril had been able to easily hack the state Division of Motor Vehicles mainframe, one of the most unsecure computer networks they had ever seen. From there, they planted the remote access Trojan, or RAT, to be downloaded by every service center that conducted state inspections. While they had been able to infect the auto manufacturers as well, because of their encampment in the North Carolina Blue Ridge Mountains, they chose to attack every vehicle being inspected in a single year. Because more than seven million trucks and cars are inspected every year, each time a service station plugged in the inspection cable to the car, the RAT would leap into the car's computer, provided it was built within the last ten years. By Zakir's assessment, that portion of the operation had been a success so far, based upon reports he was listening to on the news.

Now he thought about General Savage.

Yes, General Savage. The one who had killed Malavdi, his best friend, who was engaged to be married to Fatima Assad. Savage was the one who had ordered the strike on the convoy of Operation Groomsman. Zakir had Gavril hack into the private server of a senior cabinet official who had reviewed the documents at her convenience on an unclassified system. From there, he downloaded all of the investigation documents on Operation Groomsman. Zakir had pored over the documents and learned that all of the intelligence had indicated that the convoy was just a simple wedding party, but then the voice of al-Baghdadi had appeared almost as if out of nowhere. They tracked the cell phone in the third vehicle of six SUVs. Center mass.

That was what Zakir had learned about the mission.

He had also learned that Major Alex Russell had been there as well, standing apparently by General Savage's side. As the documents described the situation in the joint operations centers, Russell had watched the general wrestle with the decision. Al-Baghdadi was an Al Qaeda mastermind who would later become the head of ISIS and a man whom Zakir had met and now reported to, albeit infrequently. How had al-Baghdadi simply appeared in the convoy, and why was he so brazenly on his phone? Zakir had read that Russell said that she wanted nothing to do with the decision. But ultimately when General Savage turned to her and asked her,

"Valid target?" she had confirmed, "Valid target." It was right there in her statement.

He and Gavril had data mined Alex Russell and learned that she wasn't Alex Russell at all. That she had even more of a vested interest than he in what had happened in Operation Groomsman.

Much to Zakir's surprise, as he and Gavril studied the myriad classified documents maintained by the Army's Inspector General, they found dozens of investigations of bad intelligence that led to bombing wholly civilian convoys, many of which were wedding parties.

What was it that made a wedding party look like an enemy convoy, Zakir wondered? Sure, there were often guns securing the convoy because many of these weddings by definition were taking place in hostile countries. But the customs and traditions were different. To ensure safe arrival, the entire wedding party traveled together to the bride's parents' home. While Fatima's parents had long ago abandoned her, Malavdi was going to marry her at the home of her surrogate parents, who had raised the orphan Fatima.

All of these thoughts spun through his mind as he was commanding and controlling the fight against the man in the tower.

Was it Jake Mahegan? The third person on his kill list? Savage, Russell, Mahegan.

They had all played a role in killing Malavdi and Fatima on their wedding day.

They all deserved to die.

And the country that had put them there was going to pay a high price for their indifference to two lives snuffed out like a church candle.

"Capture the man in the tower," Zakir barked into his small handheld radio.

CHAPTER 17

TEN TO FIFTEEN MEN WITH RIFLES CHARGED THE HILL TOWARD Mahegan. They were dressed in black and performing the equivalent of "three-second rushes," a combat tactic to avoid getting shot by staying vertical too long.

With the tower guard's sniper rifle he was able to take five shots and confirm five kills before the smoke became too thick. When large bullets from a machine gun began to chew at the metal tower, Mahegan scrambled out the back door and down the spiral staircase. The smoke and the constant movement would make him a tough target for the enemy machine gunner.

At the base of the tower Cassie was shouting something at him. He dove to the ground, dirt spraying his face as he rolled to the back side of the hillock upon which the tower stood. Cassie slid to the base as well and said, "Alex Russell is back near my car."

Her voice was steady but an octave higher than normal. She was breathing fast, adrenaline pumping through her veins. Mahegan looked back toward the north where Cassie had parked the Subaru. Couldn't see much through the thick forest. Machine gun rounds zipped through the air with an audible whoosh. The sound of rifle fire seemed closer. It was time to move.

Mahegan said, "Follow me."

He was up and running through the trees, allowing the incline to pull him farther to the west for more cover and concealment from the attacking forces. Mahegan believed they had just poked the beehive but that the bees would not stray too far from their hive.

As they neared the Subaru location, Mahegan detected the slightest motion in his peripheral vision to his right. Heard brush breaking. He risked a glance over his shoulder. Two of the terrorists were running at full speed along the road, occasionally glancing into the woods, presumably searching for him and Cassie.

He dropped the sniper rifle and retrieved his Sig Sauer Tribal, saying to Cassie, "Keep running."

He sprinted toward a large oak about thirty yards ahead, dropped to the ground as he heard two shots, and reared up to one knee in a shooter's position.

The men were no longer running. He scanned the road and saw two black lumps lying motionless on the ground. Had Cassie turned and shot them first? Mahegan looked over his left shoulder, up the ridge to the knoll where the car was parked, and saw Cassie still sprinting. Mahegan came up with his gun and carefully stepped toward the road. He cleared it right in the direction of the enemy, and then looked left.

Alex Russell was standing at the top of the hill, pistol in hand. She had fired the shots that had protected them. He moved swiftly to the two men. Both had shaved heads and trim black beards. They wore identical black cargo pants, black shirts, and black tactical vests. They carried AR-15 assault rifles, easily purchased in the United States. A quick check of the pockets revealed nothing, not even a scrap of paper or piece of lint.

"More are coming!" Alex shouted.

Mahegan looked up the road but did not see any threats. Leaving the bodies to rot, he moved to the wooded cordon of the road and found his way to Cassie's and Alex's location.

"You shot them?" Mahegan asked. He fixed his eyes on Alex, who didn't flinch.

"Yes. They were two seconds from seeing you. So I shot them."

"That was a hundred-yard shot," Mahegan said.

"Actually, it was two one-hundred-yard shots," Alex replied. "That saved your ass."

"Okay. Good point. Thank you, by the way. But tell me—" Mahegan said. He considered his next comment carefully. The air was thick with smoke now. A gentle breeze carried the scent of military smoke grenades from the valley below.

"I'll tell you whatever you want, but let's head to my place first," Alex said. "There are more coming. You and Cassie should follow me. And watch out for that helicopter. That's state police. I've been monitoring channels. They found your pistol and size twelve Doc Martens boot prints in the house. And they've got still photos of you in Charlotte around that time."

"Doesn't make sense," Mahegan said.

"They've got you pegged as the murderer of three people, and now they're also saying you killed that MP."

"You did that," Mahegan said.

"Just follow me. I think I know a way out of this," Alex said.

A few shots snapped overhead. A sniper had set up somewhere on the ridge.

"Let's go," Mahegan said. As Mahegan and Cassie returned to the Subaru, they watched Alex pull up and idle next to Cassie's car. Mahegan waved for her to lead the way, and she shot out of the gravel turnout.

"Hell of a coincidence running into her," Mahegan said as they quickly jumped in the Subaru.

"I don't know what to make of it. The mechanic identified her as bringing a car into the shop." Cassie cranked the engine and slammed the car into reverse.

"And she pulled a weapon on me last night after she shot two military policemen who might have been fake."

Cassie followed Alex as they drove east. They were quickly on the Blue Ridge Parkway conducting a slalom around the stopped vehicles. Mahegan scoped the skies for the Blackhawk that had been pursuing them.

"What the hell is going on?"

"How well do you know Alex?" Mahegan asked.

"O-Club, female officer gatherings, tennis, that kind of thing. We don't go clubbing, if that's what you're asking."

"Didn't picture you as the clubbing sort. You said you were friends," Mahegan said.

"Maybe 'acquaintances' is more like it. She didn't shoot me, or try to shoot me, so that's a positive . . . and *much* better than you're doing with her."

Mahegan cast a wry smile at Cassie's joke. Up to this point, she had been all business. Very little personality other than perhaps a deep-seated conflict issue with her father. Professional and focused. He appreciated that she showed some wit within ten minutes of a firefight. To Mahegan, the gallows humor that came from combat was a necessary part of the process. Focus and fear dominated initially until those gave way to relief and exhaustion, which often manifested as humor initially. And later, perhaps much later, as posttraumatic stress. Mahegan didn't like to call it a disorder because he didn't believe that it had to be. He had grown from his own posttraumatic stress and had seen others do so as well. Still, it was true that posttraumatic stress had disabled many veterans, and it was often because they didn't process the events. Some events were so horrifying that they couldn't be processed. Like when he reached into Sergeant Colgate's burning ground mobility vehicle to pull him out, only to have Colgate's skin come off in his hands.

That was traumatic. And he lived with the reality and the memory of a chunk of Colgate's vehicle in his left deltoid and the brain matter of Commander Hoxha, their captured bomb-making target, on the buttstock of his M4 carbine.

"Can you call Alex?"

"Sure, why?"

"I want to park your car in a Walmart or something and then ride with her to her place. That helicopter was following your car somehow, probably GPS, which isn't working anymore, it seems. But they've identified it and will be looking for it."

Cassie pulled out her phone, used her thumb on the home button, and pressed her last call, Alex Russell. She handed the phone to Mahegan.

"Yeah, Cassie, what's up?"

"It's Mahegan. Take us to a Walmart or shopping mall, then we'll jump in with you."

After a pause, Alex said, "The helicopter?"

"Roger."

"Okay. Don't want that thing buzzing my house anyway."

Mahegan clicked off, and they followed Alex's Land Rover to a Target parking lot near Asheville. They parked the Subaru, and Mahegan said, "Grab your pistol and rucksack. That's about all we'll be able to carry."

Cassie eyed him warily for a second, then grabbed those items and a couple others, which she stuffed into the standard-size Army rucksack. She nodded to the floor of her backseat, which was lowered into hatchback mode.

"If you're taking that AR-15 you might want to grab the rest of the magazines from the console," she said.

Mahegan took the AR-15 and all of her magazines out of the center console. She had left Fort Bragg expecting a fight. Did Cassie know what was happening, or was she preparing for the worst?

Mahegan got in Alex's backseat and set Cassie's heavy rucksack next to him. He found it odd that he had been in Alex's backseat twice in the last twenty-four hours. He didn't trust her then and he didn't trust her now, but she knew something about what was happening and he wanted to find out what that might be. If it led to rescuing Savage, O'Malley, and Owens, then the risk would be worth it. Cassie sat in the front seat holding a small bag and her Berretta.

As they were exiting the parking lot, Mahegan pointed out a large gathering of police and emergency responders.

"Looks like they've set up a triage site here for people and for cars," he said. There was a series of operational tow trucks pulling cars into the parking lot. A group of mechanics was working on cars, hoods up, in assembly line fashion. It appeared that the mechanics were able to reboot the onboard computers and eradicate the bug fairly quickly. A mechanic plugged a cable from a rolling cart with a computer diagnostic system into a car, took a reading, and then unplugged. Apparently it was that quick. The car pulled away, and the mechanic pushed the cart to the next vehicle in line.

"Alex, you hearing anything about this?" Mahegan asked.

"Just a sec," Alex said. She stopped the Land Rover and looked at her phone. "Yeah. There's this classified e-mail message. A techie from the FBI figured out the Trojan and created a Diagnostic Trouble Code to identify the Trojan and then a fix that simultaneously erases it. They're pushing it out system wide to every DMV and every major auto manufacturer, affected or not. It's kind of like a cure and a vaccine."

"That's fast work," Mahegan said. Then, "Let's get out of here before someone sees us."

Alex slowly turned around and pulled out of the Target parking lot. They drove about ten miles to the town of Bent Creek, then to a townhouse complex overlooking the French Broad River. The townhomes all had a Bavarian mountain look to them, with wide, crisscrossing wood planks painted dark brown against tan stucco. Window ledges with flower boxes held purple and white mums blooming brightly against the dull exterior. Alex pulled into the gaping garage door.

"Stay in the car until the door is down," Mahegan said.

Alex's garage was neatly arranged, almost devoid of other items, save an upright toolbox. Mahegan looked over his shoulder through the back window of the Land Rover watching the garage door lower. The barely audible hum of the garage door opener stopped and the door was down, muting the light inside the garage.

"Okay, let's go inside," Mahegan said.

"You're making this seem like a kidnapping, Mahegan," Alex said.

There was something different about her that he couldn't place just yet. Her hair was wind tossed, almost deliberately so. Her eyes seemed out of focus. Her voice was less confident than it was last night.

"You okay, Alex?" he asked as they walked to the front of the Land Rover.

"I'm fine," she said, more confident this time, but it seemed forced, not natural. "Just don't understand why you've got all this heavy weaponry. Not good for keeping a low profile, especially when the cops are after you for murder."

"Well, you just saw what happened on the mountain. You killed two yourself. I've got no idea what's coming our way or who those people are. So I need firepower. This being what it is," he said, holding up the AR-15. It was not a particularly loved weapon by special operators, but if that was all he had, he would use it.

"Fair enough. This way," Alex said. The inside of the town house was all neutral tones and hotel artwork. It looked like a time-share, but he couldn't be sure.

"This place yours?" Mahegan asked.

Alex led them through the mudroom and kitchen into a neutral-toned family room with a white sofa and love seat fixed in an L shape. They faced a sliding glass door that provided an ample view of the mountains and their colorful foliage.

"Have a seat, Jake. Cassie."

Mahegan stood with his back to the kitchen counter, looking to his right through the sliding glass and then to his left toward the front door at the end of a small hallway. He detected no movement from either direction. Despite Alex's calm voice, Mahegan was suspicious. Alex was visibly shaking, going through some type of transformation in front of them. Cassie stood to his left in the gap between the kitchen and family room. She was staring intently at Alex, whose eyes were fixed on Mahegan. He continued scanning the home, saying, "Don't feel like sitting. What the hell were you doing on that hill?"

Her eyes fluttered for a second and then she said, "Excuse me. I need to use the ladies' room."

Alex disappeared up the stairs near the front door, and Mahegan used the time to put the rucksack by the refrigerator, which was next to the door to the mudroom. Then he walked the entire first floor consisting only of the kitchen, family room, and small dining room. The sliding glass door led to a deck. He studied the sloping terrain outside of the northward facing glass door. It sloped away sharply beneath the deck, and he could see the French Broad River less than a mile away. The Blue Ridge Mountains angled away to the north with their subtle curves.

Nice view.

Alex returned down the steps, rubbing the inside of her elbow before she made the turn toward them off the last step. She walked up to Mahegan, much more coherent, and said, "I'm sure you are pissed at me for drawing down on you earlier this morning, but I'm also sure you can understand me protecting myself from a wanted man. I'm glad to see that you were able to make it to Asheville. You're every bit as good as Savage tells me you are. And we need you to help stop an imminent threat to the country."

"You're talking to Savage?" But he was really thinking that she just took something. The change in her demeanor was marked. From frazzled and jumpy to calm and coherent.

"I've spoken with him, yes."

"Today?" Mahegan asked. Cassie watched the conversation, perhaps wondering if she had made a mistake by giving him a ride.

"When I have spoken to him is not important, Jake. I'm executing his orders to the best of my ability given the fact that Zebra is down."

"What's Zebra?" Cassie asked.

Mahegan and Alex looked at the chairman's daughter simultaneously. Alex spoke first.

"Zebra is an off-the-books JSOC communications protocol, Cassie. I shouldn't be telling you this, but it has been compromised by some very bad people. I'm certain we won't call it Zebra anymore and that we'll change its platform. So, it's a former protocol." She turned toward Mahegan and continued talking. "Those bad people? I shot two of them today to protect you. So if you want to continue to suspect me of something, Jake, go for it. Search my car. Search my mountain condo. I'm single. I love the mountains. I bought this place with my combat pay, and this is where I come when I need to get away."

"Why did you ask me about Operation Groomsman?" Mahegan asked. He didn't move and thought about taking her up on her offer to inspect her house and car. He was still worried that they could have been followed even though Cassie's car was in a Target parking lot ten miles away. A good cop would look at surveillance video and find Alex's license plate number and then find her house. He wasn't hanging out here long enough for all of that to transpire.

"Because it was personal to me, Jake. You were on the ground. I wasn't. I gave the 'valid target' call to Savage. We ended up killing a bride and groom and their families. That has weighed on me. I've seen military therapists to help me cope with the angst that I feel. Is that what you wanted me to say? That I'm not as tough as you? That I can't just randomly kill people and be okay with it? Well, that's the truth."

Mahegan paused. She had no idea what angst he had suffered from the loss of everyone from his mother to unit members with whom he was close. Everyone counted, to Mahegan. But he didn't let that debilitate him.

"What about those military policemen?" he asked.

"Apparently you called in their location," Alex said.

"What military policemen?" Cassie asked. Mahegan looked at Alex and then Cassie. Alex spoke first.

"That's exactly right. There were none," Alex said. "But there were two terrorists dressed up as military policemen who had been following Jake, most likely through the hacked Zebra app. Even with the Zebra tracking function disabled, once they knew your phone number they were able to get the phone's identity and track that, even if you shut it off."

"She shot them," Mahegan said. "If they weren't MPs, I'm good with that."

Alex looked at her phone, moved some data around with her fingers by touching the screen, and then stood as she flashed the phone at Mahegan.

"Here's a report from the Stanly County sheriff. I'll read it to you. 'This morning at five minutes after six, we received a report of one dead male and one wounded male at a specific grid coordinate in the Uwharrie National Forest. I dispatched two officers to the location immediately and then met them there. We provided life-saving measures to the wounded individual, who is critical but stable and in our protection and care. Moore County also found a vehicle that confirmed person of interest Chayton Mahegan was in the police cruiser in which the military police officers were traveling. I called Special Agent Oxendine from the SBI, who is leading the manhunt for Mahegan. After the wounded military police officer awoke, it was clear the surviving member of the two does not speak or understand English very well. He did, however, speak Arabic. We had a local university professor come to his location and begin an interrogation, in which the survivor admitted he was from Syria. That's all we know. We have alerted the Department of Public Safety, and they are en route with a team from the Department of Homeland Security and the FBI."

"Okay," Mahegan said. "What's the sheriff's name?"

Alex grinned. Without looking at her phone, she said, "Sheriff Bubba Wilson. I go hiking in the Uwharrie quite a bit. Have had coffee with him in Troy a few times. Anything else?"

"Jake, I think we can accept that Alex is on our team, can't we?"

"Alex didn't aim a pistol at you this morning," Mahegan said.

"No, but she shot past me and killed two men who were about to catch up with you and me."

"That's true, but I find it an awful big coincidence that Alex just happened to be in the same spot as us."

"I'm still here," Alex said, interrupting the conversation that was occurring as if she weren't. "I showed you the last known locations of Savage, O'Malley, and Owens. That's the same way you found the location. It just took me longer than you. I stopped by here on my way and looked at maps on my phone until I figured the Blue Ridge Parkway was the best way to look at the two or three areas on the map that I thought correlated with their location. I used to watch Savage do this quite a bit when he was with his planning team back in JSOC headquarters."

"I've served in special mission units most of my life. I've heard your name but I've never seen you before in my life," Mahegan said.

"But you have. You just didn't notice me. I've seen you from the headquarters window heading to the range. I can tell you every detail of JSOC HQ, which you don't frequent much, I might add," Alex said.

Mahegan stared at Alex. "Why would I have ever gone there?"

"Case in point," she said.

Cassie jumped back into the conversation.

"Jake, relax. Let's try to figure out what the hell is happening. The three of us can figure this out better than two. My parents are being held captive by these guys, I'm pretty sure. All of the bad stuff happening? It has to be orchestrated by the same people. We lucked out and swatted the beehive."

"I'm not feeling the luck or the love," Mahegan said. "I don't forget things easily, and I've never met Alex before." He then pointed at Cassie. "For that matter, I had never met you before today. Read about you in the papers, and I know you and your dad had a pretty public falling out that made a lot of money for the newspapers and television shows."

"Right. He chastised me in public for attending Ranger school. I was one of the first female graduates. He couldn't deal with it. Well, tough shit. He needs to handle it."

"It was more than that. He didn't like you being in the Army, much less attending Ranger training."

"It's not his call. I'm not some doting Daddy's girl. I'm my own person," Cassie said with emphasis.

"Jake, it looks like you're pissing off both of us. That's an unwise move, wouldn't you say? She's got a pistol, and so do I. You've seen I'm fairly accurate."

Mahegan said nothing to Alex's taunt. But something stuck in the back of his mind. Had she missed him on purpose? He looked through the sliding glass doors and studied the deck with its table and four chairs. Everything looked new and rarely used, if ever. The sun was well overhead and beaming on a beautiful fall day. He heard a noise coming from the front of the house.

"Expecting company?"

"Not unless it's the police looking for you. Did anyone make you in Cassie's car before we got to Target?" Alex asked.

"No, but I'm sure there were security cameras that picked us up," he said.

She walked to the front door. Mahegan looked at Cassie, whose eyes were burning holes in his. She was pissed. Apparently touching that raw nerve of her father opened a Pandora's box of issues for the captain.

"It's a police cruiser, Jake. Buncombe County. You better get into the garage," Alex said.

"I'm not going anywhere," he replied.

"Your funeral," she said, then opened the door. Alex stepped onto the porch and closed the storm door behind her but left the wooden front door open. Mahegan moved slightly to his left, out of the line of sight of anyone standing on the porch. He brushed past Cassie and put his back to the wall.

"She's not right," Mahegan said.

"Chill, Jake. She saved our asses."

"Maybe. Maybe she saved hers, too."

"She's out there saving yours again," Cassie said. They listened as the sheriff spoke with a country drawl that mixed in some Elizabethan English. Mahegan had heard the dialect before in the Virginia Blue Ridge Mountains.

"I was asked to check on you, Major Russell. There's been some shooting up in the mountains, and someone said they saw a vehicle with your license plate on it. We've got an all-points bulletin out on Captain Cassie Bagwell, whom I am told is a friend of yours."

"That's right. Cassie's a good friend from Fort Bragg, Sheriff."

"Well, we've got a BOLO for her. Something's apparently happened to her parents, and the FBI gave us her car's GPS coordinates to make sure she was okay. We found her car in the Target parking lot. Looks like it has been burned on one side."

"I heard her parents were kidnapped, Sheriff. She came to my home up here to be with me as we await further word. It's nice of you to check on us. I know you've got a lot going on today. Please tell the FBI she's okay."

"We do have a lot going on today. Most of my cars have shut down. Only a few work—the older ones, and why I'm driving that piece of junk."

"What happened to your cars?" Alex asked. "I've seen a lot of them just stopped in the middle of the roads like they're frozen in time."

"Well, I'm surprised she made it to Asheville, to be honest with you. FBI says she drove from near Charlotte this morning," the sheriff said. "Television news is saying that about five million cars around the country were stopped. That's a hell of a lot, even if as they say there's two hundred fifty million out there. All my cars are Dodge Chargers, and we get them serviced regularly to make sure our warranty is good. What the pundits are saying is that someone hacked these cars through the service centers and planted some kind of Trojan virus that activated at exactly nine a.m. eastern time today. Kind of like the nine-eleven attacks, only on cars. Well, I'm rambling now. I just wanted to check up on Ms. Bagwell."

"That's Captain Bagwell, Sheriff. She's an Army Ranger."

"Pardon me, ma'am. No disrespect intended. Well, that's just the thing, Major. We've got a big operation going on in that parking lot and lots of video cameras and so forth, and it showed two people getting out of Captain Bagwell's car and getting into yours. And one of those people looked like Captain Bagwell."

Mahegan grabbed the AR-15 and the rucksack and prepared to ease into the garage.

"Well, I hope you can understand me being protective of her, Sheriff. Would you like to come in? Speak with Cassie?"

"Well, to be honest I'd like to be able to tell someone that I laid eyes on her. And what about this other feller? Was that by any chance a man named Mahegan? SBI tells me he kidnapped Captain Bagwell."

Mahegan looked at Cassie and pointed at himself and the garage door, then at her and the front door. She tucked away her pistol, took a second to straighten herself, and moved into the hallway. Mahegan watched her for a moment. Her face adjusted slightly as if she were deciding how she should appear to the sheriff. Concerned, confused, or surprised.

As Mahegan was stepping through the mudroom door that led to the garage, the loud rumble of motorcycles echoed up the road. Whatever cyberattack had occurred to stop the vehicles in their tracks seemed not to impact the police motorcycles. The sheriff mentioned the word "cavalry" as Mahegan stepped into the garage, quietly closing the door.

Mahegan worked his way around the hood of the Land Rover and opened the passenger side door briefly. He leaned into the vehicle and inspected the interior, finding nothing out of the ordinary. He quietly closed the door and walked around the entire automobile, noticing a splash of mud and a broken tree twig and leaves on the right rear side. He removed the thin branch and leaves, registering that these were maple leaves. He pocketed the twig and opened the side door of the garage, which led to a cement footpath behind a wooden eight-foot-high privacy fence. Making sure the door was unlocked from the inside, he closed it and watched through a gap in the fence boards while palming his Tribal out of his waistband.

Two BMW R1200 police motorcycles slowed as they passed the town house, but they continued their patrol, if that's what they were doing. When the engine noise faded, he could hear Alex walking the sheriff back to his car.

"I hope you figure out what has happened with all of these cars," Alex said. "Where did the motorcycles come from?"

Flashes of movement appeared through the fence gap. The sheriff was walking, dressed in his gray uniform. Alex was behind him, wearing her olive and black hiking attire.

"Turn on the television. It's happening everywhere," the sheriff said. "Lucky for us, I ordered those BMW motorcycles and they came in a couple of months ago hot off the factory floor. We've only got six, but they're patrolling designated routes right now.

I'm guessing whoever hacked these cars didn't think to hit the motorcycles also. Our ambulances and fire trucks are working, also. So that's a blessing. Lots of accidents. I'm sending two motorcycles up in the mountains. Several people have called in about a big shootout up in the hollow. Probably some road rage, but you never know. Anyways, I'm getting reports that say some of the cars have been reactivated already through the GPS systems in those shark fins on the top of cars. They call it 'over-the-air rekey.' Damn if they don't think of everything. Plus we've got us an assembly line of mechanics at Target, so we're doing our part."

"Yes, I heard the FBI figured it out. Well, I hope everything gets sorted out. People have been talking about this doomsday scenario where we get hooked on the Internet and then somebody just shuts it down. Banks. Hospitals. Apparently cars. Scary stuff," Alex said.

"Scary indeed. Call if you need anything, ma'am."

"Roger that," Alex said.

The sheriff stepped into in his car and Alex waved as he backed out and went south, the opposite direction of the motorcycles. Mahegan turned and studied the neighborhood. Alex's town house was an end unit, and he was looking at the adjacent end unit that faced hers. To the north was an unobstructed view of the mountains that rose into the sky and then fell away into the distance. To the south was a steep incline and drop-off toward the river. Inside, Cassie flipped on the television. Next, the motorcycles roared back down the mountain and slowed as they approached Alex's town house.

One of the men snapped photos using his phone. They could have been police doing their job, or they could have been imposters triangulating their location. Given the unknowns involved, one was just as likely as the other. Mahegan sensed that he was transitioning from hunter to hunted. He needed to get back on the offense.

He didn't like the fact that a sheriff and two of his police officers visited Alex's home within an hour of their arrival. Nor was he enthused with the sheriff's comment that they had used the cameras and spotted them transferring to Alex's car. As Alex reminded him, Mahegan was a wanted man in North Carolina. Whether the strange network attack on the vehicles would slow down the police or disrupt their ability to search for him remained to be seen. The helicopter was still out there somewhere, waiting to pounce.

He needed to get back on track to finding Savage, O'Malley, and Owens before it was too late, if he even still had time to rescue them. If Alex Russell was sniffing around Operation Groomsman because of a personal connection to one of the casualties, then Savage was the one who would pay the highest price. He had made the call, and regardless of whether Alex confirmed it was a legal target or not, Savage would have made the shot either way. Killing al-Baghdadi was too important.

What he didn't know was whom he could trust. He walked back into the house, carrying his pistol. Alex and Cassie were deep in conversation, leaning over a map on a glass coffee table.

"I linked up with you guys right in this area," Alex said. She was circling a green patch on a North Carolina state road map that the NCDOT handed out at rest stops.

"Where were you before that?" Mahegan asked. He retrieved the twig and leaf from his pocket and held it up. "Off-road driving?"

Alex paused and looked up at Mahegan, who had walked from the kitchen into the family room. He closed the curtain to the sliding glass door and sat down in a tan leather chair across from the white sofa.

"As a matter of fact, I was, Jake. I showed you the coordinates on my phone. I followed those as best I could. Just as you did. Some of that route took me off-road, just as it did for the two of you. So shall we dispense with the suspicion and get on with the business of finding our team and Cassie's parents?"

Mahegan stared at Alex and then at Cassie. The women seemed to have a bond that transcended today. He nodded.

"Fine. In the hour that we've been here, we've been spotted by three police," Mahegan said.

"*We've* been spotted," Alex said, waving her finger between her and Cassie. "Not you."

"That you know about," Mahegan acknowledged. "The two motorcycle guys slowed and took pictures of the house. The sheriff was here in no time. They saw me get in your SUV."

"What are you saying, Jake? That I'm calling the cops on you? If I wanted to do that, you'd be in jail right now. It's your lucky day that somebody jacked with a bunch of car engines, because everyone seems pretty confused right now."

She pointed at the television with CNN playing in the background on mute. The screen was showing aerial photos from around the country of traffic jams in the Boston Big Dig area. In Manhattan yellow cabs were stopped and blocking the roads. In Atlanta traffic looked no worse than usual, stopped. Every major city along the East Coast was gridlocked. The cameras showed the West Coast cities such as Los Angeles, San Francisco, and Seattle, where there were still major traffic jams, but because the cyberattack had occurred at nine a.m. eastern time, six a.m. Pacific, there were marginally fewer cars on the road.

Before stepping into the ambush in the golf lodge where the attacker had told him, *It's going down right now. Everything, all at once,* Mahegan had been looking forward to heading to the Outer Banks of North Carolina. He wanted to return to his birthplace and spend some time sorting out the past couple of years since his departure from the service. Always one to have a clear mission focus, Mahegan found that he was wrestling with the absence of his parents, especially his mother, and the lack of stability, something that he wanted. Perhaps he was seeking a family, something to ground him, but he continued to follow the clarion call to duty, wherever the mission took him. Meeting the right woman was always something he believed would just happen naturally. Now he wasn't so sure. Circumstances always seemed to overpower or outweigh any budding relationship he might have been considering.

And the main obstacle seemed to always be General Savage.

The JSOC commander needed Mahegan off the books and on the trail of some real threat that either JSOC or the nation faced.

He looked at the two women staring at him and shook his head.

"No. I'm not saying you're calling the police on me."

He watched Alex's left eye twitch and then he looked at Cassie, who was staring intently at him. She had been mostly quiet but harbored a resoluteness that reflected in her strong countenance.

"I will tell you that this place is burned and we'll be lucky to survive another fifteen minutes here," Mahegan said. He had no specific threat information. But he reasoned that if the hayseed sheriff could find Cassie here and if someone could hack JSOC's Zebra application, then it was an easy conclusion that the helicopter would be next on the scene.

"Let's go. We'll find someplace to stay," Mahegan said to Cassie.

"We could stay here," Cassie said.

"Don't be naïve. You heard the man. They know I'm here. He's at the bottom of the hill calling in the helicopter. You want to find your parents? Come with me."

"Like hell," Cassie said. "Maybe I want to be found if something happens. My father hasn't done me any favors lately, anyway. So maybe I'm really just out here showing the flag."

Mahegan cocked his head, looking at the two women.

"Okay. This place is not safe, Cassie," Mahegan emphasized. "I spent ten years in combat. I'm telling you we will not be okay here."

Mahegan looked at Cassie, who was genuinely undecided. He could see the confusion on her face. These were Army buddies, she must have been thinking. Why should she have to choose? Isn't everyone on the same side?

"Get used to it, Cassie. Not everyone has the same objectives," Mahegan said. He looked at Alex as he spoke.

"You guys go," Alex said. "This is my home. You're always welcome, but Jake's right. The sheriff knows he's here."

"Leave your phone. They're tracking that, too," Mahegan said.

"I'm not leaving my phone," Cassie replied.

"Then shut it down and take out the SIM card out. Do it now."

Cassie fumbled with her iPhone and a paper clip she had plucked from Alex's coffee table, powered the phone down, got the SIM card out, and placed it in Mahegan's open palm.

He stood and then began to walk toward the garage when he heard the motorcycles at the bottom of the hill, maybe a mile away. Less than a minute. They whined at full throttle, sounding like dueling chainsaws. In the distance Mahegan heard the distinctive *whup-whup* of helicopter rotors. Had Alex had been stalling for time while Cassie perhaps had been her unwitting accomplice?

"Go now," Alex said. She stood and raced to the front door. "Jake, we need you to stay alive. Take Cassie. There are caves near the river."

Cassie followed as Mahegan led. They bolted through the mudroom and out the garage door, made a left into the backyard, and began barreling toward the fence.

"The fence," Mahegan said, taking Cassie's AR-15.

He looped the two-point sling on the AR-15 across his chest. Holstering his Tribal pistol, Mahegan took on the plank fence at full stride as he heard the motorcycles squeal into the driveway. The helicopter flared overhead as it lowered and dropped ropes into the street in front of Alex's house. As Mahegan scaled the fence ahead of Cassie, four men dressed in black SWAT gear and helmets slid down the ropes from the wobbling helicopter. Cassie and Mahegan both landed on a forty-five-degree slope covered with mostly eastern white pine trees that angled upward with the slope of the ground. The trees were mature, some reaching sixty to seventy feet high. Mahegan clasped Cassie by the wrist, and they powered through the forest. She pulled her pistol from her cargo pocket to have it at the ready.

"Follow me," Mahegan said.

When he had studied the terrain from the sliding glass door, he had noticed a sharp drop-off to the north. He remembered from reviewing the map beforehand that a large creek or river ran just east of this location. Around the river would be rock formations, possibly caves that they could use as a hide position. The problem was that they had four men chasing them and a helicopter overhead, most likely vectoring the capture team to their location.

He was pleasantly surprised that no shots had been fired, yet.

They jumped about ten feet from a rock ledge onto a trail just beneath, then took two more similar ledges as they were straight-line navigating a series of switchbacks. The farther down the hill they ran, the denser the forest became, filling in with hardwoods such as maple and birch. On the last ledge before a long straightaway to the north, Mahegan held Cassie back with one arm and listened for the pursuers. The sound of men crashing through the woods could be heard in the distance, but it was not necessarily drawing closer. It seemed more lateral, to the south. The helicopter was angling to the south as well. The canopy on the trees was thicker the closer they got to the river. Birches, oaks, and maples with dense, bright foliage masked their movement.

"Let's go," Mahegan said. They moved noiselessly to the north, found the river's edge, and kept walking. After two miles of walking upriver, Mahegan pointed out rock formations that gave way to deep carve-outs within the face of the granite. They had moved northeast and uphill, whereas for some reason the pursuers had moved southeast and downhill.

"Feel bad about leaving Alex up there," Cassie said.

"Feel bad about the world. For all we know, Alex is the one who orchestrated that rendezvous."

"Why don't you trust her, Jake?"

"I don't even trust you, Cassie. How would you feel if I pulled a pistol on you?"

"Probably not great," she admitted.

Mahegan led them deep into a cave that was twice his height and wide in some places, narrow in others. They rounded a corner, and Mahegan stopped.

"Good place to take a break here. Wait for night and then move," he said.

"Sounds good," Cassie replied.

It was quiet in the cave. Mahegan had exceptional hearing, and he listened, acclimating to the environment, something he was particularly good at.

"Rotors," he said. He heard the distinct sound of Blackhawk rotors chopping in the sky not far from their location. "They'll have thermal and infrared. They shouldn't be able to see us in here without putting boots on the ground. I'm thinking they picked up the SWAT team and have them on board again. Pine trees get up to one hundred feet. They can rappel with the one hundred twenty foot ropes, if they've got them. Otherwise they can drop into the river and come up from that direction."

"You're thinking out loud. Tactics," Cassie said.

"It's what I do. Think tactics. They're after me, not you. But I have to protect you from the assholes who captured your parents, and we have to try to get back into the terrorist base camp."

"We're just two people, Jake."

Mahegan said nothing. He looked at the roof of the cave, listened for the helicopter, certain they were scouting for him, and decided that he was in the best spot he could be for now.

CHAPTER 18

GAVRIL THOUGHT OF HIS DEAD NEPHEW'S BEST FRIEND, ZAKIR, AS HE stared at his bank of computers and monitors inside the small warehouse in Charlotte, North Carolina. He knew that Zakir was somewhere in the mountains with a group of armed men whom Zakir planned to use to attack America.

And this bothered him. *The mouse that roared,* Gavril thought, shaking his head.

He had stringy black hair that he combed over his balding head. Fat and stout, Gavril was short, just over five feet. In his trench coat, though, he became anonymous walking down the street in Charlotte. Somebody's unlucky uncle living on the outskirts. Indeed, Gavril lived just outside Uptown Charlotte near the dilapidated rail station. He could get most places he needed to go using the Blue Line metro. He would hunch over and wear a baseball cap, keeping the cameras off his face, which was important. In the black screen of the computer monitor was the faint outline of his tired, round face. He was hungry but lacked the energy to get out of his chair in his command post. Tired, Gavril was glad that they were near the end of the operation.

One of the most notorious Bulgarian hackers of all time, Gavril was happy to leave his Black Sea rattrap where he had taken in the three orphans, Zakir, Malavdi, and Fatima, and taught them computer intrusion skills. He knew bad things would happen when his nephew, Malavdi, and Fatima were already in love when they arrived in Burgas as young teenagers. In 2011 as the Arab Spring Awakening was occurring throughout the Middle East, Gavril had warned against the stirring winds of revolution in Syria and advised them to never return despite Fatima's unbreakable will to do so. Love was an enigma, he had told Zakir, Malavdi, and Fatima over dinner of kebapche and cold beer that day. And love or sentiment were certainly not worth going to the Middle East where madmen were leading bands of rebels fighting one another like some three-dimensional civil war. Go to the courthouse if you wanted to get married, he had told Malavdi and Fatima, not Syria. During that dinner a television news report had shown the U.S. commander in Iraq speaking about his strategy to stabilize Iraq in the wake of the Arab Spring.

"See that man?" Gavril had said, pointing at the television. "He's an American general in Iraq talking about something he has no idea about. Peace in the Middle East? Who is he kidding? Stay away." They watched CNN scroll the name of Lieutenant General Bartholomew "Bart" Bagwell as the savior of the Middle East with an "All-In" strategy. But the two lovebirds had forged ahead anyway with plans to marry in Syria that led them into oblivion.

Gavril preferred to manipulate the many 1s and 0s of the code world, away from the shock and horror of combat. Safe, secure, and air-conditioned, or at least cooled by a breeze off the Black Sea. On the ground floor of the Internet revolution in the late 1990s, Gavril saw his opportunity flourish with the stock markets at the turn of the century and then as companies with graybeard CEOs ignored the threat of cyberinvasion.

He had amassed a fortune in bank accounts around the world, most of which came from his participation in the great Carbanak bank heist from 2011 to 2012. Like an army of hackers, Gavril, Malavdi, and Zakir had been assigned the domains in southern Europe, which included the Balkans, Italy, Greece, Switzerland, and Spain.

One evening several months later in 2011 he was scanning the remote-access Trojan work and he looked at the names of the accounts from which he had stolen the money. One Swiss account worth $16.5 million was registered under "Bartholomew Bagwell and Yves Dupree."

Gavril had removed his reading glasses, stood up, and turned on the small television on his kitchen counter. He always worked at the little dining room table, usually with piles of computer printouts and books next to his homemade keyboards and monitors.

He found CNN on the television and kept it on all day. Later that evening his curiosity was rewarded with a press conference given by General Bart Bagwell, the commander of U.S. forces in Iraq. He had just been nominated for his fourth star and was under active consideration to be named the chairman of the Joint Chiefs of Staff, the highest military position in America.

Ever the artist of remote thievery, Gavril was struck with a brilliant idea, but first he needed to do some spade work through the Dark Web.

He quickly called in Malavdi and Zakir and discussed his idea. They both agreed it was a good one. After all three explored separately on their computers, hacking through the Deep and Dark Webs, they learned that General Bagwell and Yves Dupree maintained a secret joint bank account that received weekly deposits between $100,000 and $300,000.

Of course the lay person, or even most expert hackers, could not see this information, but there it was. He was stealing from a French intelligence official and the commander of coalition forces in Iraq.

Secret bank accounts usually meant secrets worth keeping . . . and killing for.

"What do you think?" Gavril had asked Zakir.

"This is too good to be true, but all of our checks have confirmed it is General Bagwell and Agent Dupree."

"Malavdi, are you in agreement?"

Malavdi nodded.

With that, Gavril sent an e-mail to Yves Dupree, whom he was certain was just beginning to notice he had no money in his bank account.

And Gavril was equally certain he would find a way to get a message to General Bagwell.

Now here he was in Charlotte, staring at a bank of monitors and live video feeds feeling at times as if he were just a security guard. However, he had been excited this morning. The television news had reported the thousands of vehicle accidents around the country. All from his remote access Trojan bug he had placed in the service software of many of the major car manufacturers and DMVs. And today, as the automobile companies tried to do their over-the-air reboots of the disabled vehicles, he was having some fun swatting away many of their attempts like tennis balls lobbed softly over the net by an amateur.

It was Gavril's idea to not impact the emergency response vehicles such as ambulances and fire trucks, even though Zakir had wanted that. After an argument, Gavril had reluctantly agreed. A year ago when he had planted these latent viruses in the software, it was a big idea. Today they had so many other big ideas, this one seemed minor.

He stared at the video feeds on the monitors in front of him.

Gavril saw the chairman of the Joint Chiefs and his wife huddled in their cages. In a way, he felt sorry for them and didn't condone capturing them, but this was Zakir's plan. Zakir was a monster, Gavril had come to find out, and he was thankful for that. Zakir was brutal, lethal, and brilliant. Perhaps a psychopath, he didn't know. But he did know that Zakir scared him enough to convince him to go along with the grand plan. Like most computer geeks, Gavril found comfort in the distance and separation between himself and his actions, which created a gap in conscience. He could separate himself from the silent crime he was committing when stealing money or planting child pornography on someone's computer.

He watched the chairman and his wife try to speak to each other. They appeared to be weeping, reaching their hands through the bars in a vain attempt to clasp fingers. The cages were fifteen feet apart. No amount of reaching would close that distance. And while blackmailing the chairman had been his idea, Gavril was now suffering the unintended consequences of his actions. His extortion scheme had been a small brush fire that had turned into a raging forest fire. With each step, Gavril found himself and Zakir deeper and deeper in the byzantine forest of cyberwarfare, throwing punches and counterpunches, sometimes with precision and sometimes blindly.

He looked to the right at another monitor. This one showed a different location. Two men were chained to a wall in shackles, arms outstretched. The recruits had nailed the chains to heavy beams that supported the mine shaft in which they were confined. Both of them were white men, shirtless, gaunt. Gavril knew that the men had not eaten in at least two days, since their capture.

He looked at the next monitor. It showed just one man, naked, staked to the wall like an animal. This man had bristly gray hair that looked like wire. His muscles were honed, his ropey skin devoid of fat. This captive was near the other two but deeper in the mine shaft.

A dark place.

"*A tumno myasto,*" Gavril muttered in his native tongue.

Shaking his head, he turned to the computers that mattered most to him. He watched the root drives of several auto manufacturers as their amateurish cyberdefenders attempted to find him while also trying to reboot thousands of stalled automobiles. He played with this a few minutes more before turning his attention to the real prize, the banks.

He had already delivered to the five biggest banks in country the RATs, which he called "Plukhs."

Five monitors on the top row showed the code from five banks' information assurance firewalls. He had navigated each maze in less than thirty minutes, found his way to the root drive, and planted an exploding RAT that would send "baby RATs" in every direction throughout the system. From there, the Trojans' add on code coupled with a web injection to lock down millions of personal and business bank accounts. As individuals attempted to enter their passwords, the code automatically changed one of the figures in the password. People would continue to try their password until they reached the maximum number of tries, and then the bank's own software would detect a hacking attempt and block the account.

Gavril also employed a sweeping RAT that collected small amounts of money from millions of accounts, usually the remainder from a bank account amount. If the total was $7,302.59, the RAT would sweep the .59 and collect it with millions of other amounts from .01 to .99. Less intrusive and harder to detect, this sweeping RAT would then accumulate the funds into an external account in one of five new Grand Cayman accounts Gavril had established. The money would bounce five times until it landed in Switzerland.

In time, he and Zakir would have a fortune waiting for them after concluding the mission here to achieve retribution for the American Operation Groomsman. Gavril estimated their take would be somewhere around $10 million. Not fully restoring them to their previous level, but good enough for him.

Gavril pressed the EXECUTE command and watched the RATs scamper through the bank systems worth $5 trillion.

Counterpunch.

Zakir stood in the middle of his base camp wondering what had happened. In this action alone, he'd had seven men killed: his guard in the fire tower, two on the road, the rocket-propelled grenade gunner, and three others who had been advancing on the tower.

Who had done this? Mahegan, of course.

With the loss of the seven today, the two who were supposed to capture Mahegan, and the two military policemen who had slaughtered the general's family on Fort Bragg, he had lost eleven of his original thirty-eight In addition, Zakir calculated, he had two men wounded. They would survive but were incapacitated. Nineteen remained.

His medics were performing triage. They were more than medics, though. They were doctors from Syria, educated at the University of Damascus. He had the very best Syria could offer. He even had some Iraqis and Chechens in his group. These were hardened fighting men.

While he had full confidence in Gavril's computer hacking plan and Gavril's ability to wreak economic harm on the United States, Zakir believed in his heart that to properly avenge the American government's murder of Malavdi and Fatima, Zakir needed to kill General Savage, Jake Mahegan, and ultimately, if he could bring himself to do so, Alex Russell.

Those three soldiers had either made the decision to bomb the convoy or execute its survivors. Russell would be difficult for him because of the power she held over him, but he could do it nonetheless. He was angry, standing in the middle of the gravel parking lot in front of the headquarters, surrounded by the circle of cabins about fifty yards away in each direction.

He looked to the southeast, toward the mine shaft where he had secured some of his captives. He would begin his mission tonight by killing Savage. Yes, kill Savage.

But first he summoned two of his best men.

Takir and Nadr, both from Syria, both motivated, both six feet tall with ripped muscles, stood before him, dirty and bloody from the advance on the tower.

"Go find Jake Mahegan. There will be a helicopter hovering near his position in the vicinity of this address," he said. He handed Takir a piece of paper with Alex Russell's townhome address on it. "Don't kill the woman, but Mahegan is fair game. Would prefer him alive, but"—Zakir waved his hand at the dead bodies lying on the ground with olive drab wool blankets pulled over their faces—"he did this to us."

The two men nodded in understanding. Zakir watched as they grabbed their rifles and rucksacks and loaded a new Mitsubishi pickup truck.

After watching them bounce out of the valley toward the Blue Ridge Parkway, Zakir looked at the mine shaft again and whispered, "Savage."

CHAPTER 19

SPECIAL AGENT TOMMY OXENDINE SAID, "THEY'VE GOT TO BE DOWN here somewhere."

"Roger. I agree," McQueary said. "Is the sheriff getting anything out of that Army major?"

"Says she's just talking in circles. One minute she's at the door, the next minute Mahegan has a knife to Bagwell's throat and he's out the door. She said she took aim, but she couldn't get a clean shot. I think I saw that, so I half believe her, but I ain't trusting many people right now."

"Get me on top of them again and we've got him and we'll save her," McQueary said. "This is big time."

"Still trying to sort out what was happening in the mountains. Damn Stinger missile isn't small potatoes. The National Guard Armory in Ashe County said they're missing two. Means they've got one more."

"Also means that somebody's getting fired," McQueary said.

Setz was making lazy circles in the sky. Oxendine knew that they were probably getting close on gas, but he wanted to get the SWAT team on the ground smoking out Mahegan.

"I'm thinking those caves at the north part of the French Broad where it bends," Oxendine said, looking at a map.

"Got about fifteen minutes of fuel, Agent Oxendine. Just a heads-up," Setz said.

"Roger." Oxendine looked out of the starboard window. The afternoon sun was heading toward the mountains. Plenty of daylight left. The river and the trees that gathered on either side were the dominant terrain features. The map sat in his lap, seemingly taunting him to find Mahegan.

"You got anything near those caves? Thermal? Infrared?"

"Nothing so far—wait, I've got movement. Two bogeys, one carrying a long rifle walking down the ridge."

"That's them. Where can we drop ropes? Land?" Oxendine asked.

"I'm twenty yards above the trees and I'm one hundred eighty feet AGL," Setz said.

Oxendine calculated the math and asked McQueary, "How long is your fast-rope?"

"Can't go more than eighty feet on that thing. We've got two rappelling ropes that are your standard one-hundred-twenty-foot nylon ropes. Dangerous without a belay down below, but we can do it."

"Danger is your middle name," Oxendine said. "Rig the rappel ropes. We'll drop you in the river."

"Bitch is cold and night will be colder. Be better to get me and my men on hardpan," McQueary said.

"I've got a spot," Setz said. "About a half mile from the caves."

"That's good enough," Oxendine said.

"Roger that." McQueary nodded.

McQueary and his men had premade tactical Swiss seats that they retrieved from their rucksacks and stepped into in the back of the yawing aircraft. The SWAT team members pulled on their leather work gloves to prevent burning their hands against the L4 Nylon Type 4 rope. The two crew chiefs manning the M240B machine guns on both doors waded into the mass of men prepping for combat in the back of the aircraft, opened the sliding doors, and rigged the ropes by securing them into the half-inch steel cable secured to the anchor points in the floor of the aircraft by twelve-inch steel U-bolts and seven parachute static line snap hooks.

The crewmen secured the ropes inside the aircraft by tying proper bowline knots, and when the first two men were prepared to rappel, the crew chiefs snapped them into the line and then dropped the ropes into the small clearing that Setz had found. Oxendine watched as the two crewmen inspected each man and then looked at each other, gave a thumbs-up, and pointed at the two men, simultaneously saying, "Go!"

The first two men, one of whom was McQueary, were out the door and sliding quickly down the ropes dangling from either side of the helicopter. Oxendine had a bird's-eye view and secretly wished he were going with them, but he needed the communications capability in the helicopter.

The ropes went from taut to loose as they bounced against the side of the aircraft. The crewmen hooked up the next two men, who leaned out butt first into the wind and began their rappels on the crewmen's word. The final two men were out a minute later. Six men on the ground, moving toward the caves.

Oxendine had Setz methodically patrol the sloping woods from Alex Russell's backyard to the French Broad River. He had worked the terrain using thermal and infrared imaging, but other than some deer and bear, they saw nothing, convincing him that Mahegan had taken Cassie Bagwell into the caves that were the infamous make-out spots for Asheville High School kids and the occasional satanic cat sacrifice.

"Blackhawk One, this is Mike One," McQueary said over the radio.

"Roger, send it, Q," Oxendine replied into his headset. Setz had opened a UHF channel for Oxendine and McQueary to communicate from air to ground.

"Team assembled, moving to objective," McQueary said.

"Roger that. Happy hunting," Oxendine replied. "You've got about three hours of daylight left."

CHAPTER 20

MAHEGAN LOOKED AT CASSIE'S RUCKSACK AND SAID, "WHAT ARE you hiding in there?"

"I'll show you," she said. "But first I want to know what you saw from the tower."

Mahegan nodded. The cave was dark and moist. He heard the sound of water dripping deep in the recesses, a ping that echoed like sonar. He knew bats were probably directly above him in their inverted slumber, dreaming about nighttime air raids under some streetlight. He looked toward the mouth of the cave, some fifty yards away, then at Cassie's face, which he could barely see.

"Fair enough. Your parents might be in that stronghold. My friends might be in there. You have a flashlight?"

"Roger," Cassie said.

He withdrew his knife and started scratching in the dirt where Cassie shone her light.

"Here's the tower," he said, making an X. "Here's where you were. The trees were mostly blocking your line of sight into the compound." He scratched another X into the dirt. "And here's the compound. It's about a mile down the valley. It's a circular grouping of cabins, maybe an old summer camp, maybe something else. It looked pretty run-down and shuttered. Obviously it was vacant. Now it's got at least twenty foreign fighters in there. Judging by the two killed on the road by Alex, they're Arabic—Iraqi, Syrian, or somewhere else in the Levant."

Cassie nodded.

"I was slightly delayed in shooting because I was studying what looked like an old miner's cave over here," Mahegan said. He poked the knife at a spot indicating the southeast corner of the valley. "Can't be sure, but it looked like one. Small trail, dark opening distinctive from the face of the cliff. There's one road in and two roads out of the valley. All three have barricades and guards. Nothing's getting past that very canalized terrain. There's a swift creek that runs through it, but I lost sight of it and focused on the mine shaft again. Even from above, the canyon is framed by three sharp cliffs—the one we were on to the northwest, another to the east, and another to the southwest. The cliff faces were sheer rock, straight drop longer than one-hundred-twenty-foot climbing ropes. Regardless, we'd be spotted climbing or rappelling down. If we do a brute force attack against a gate, they'll have time to reposition on the interior from this central area." He pointed at the circular row of cabins he had drawn.

"So it's impenetrable?"

"Nothing's impenetrable," Mahegan said. "But this is tough. We drew them out and gathered some intel. It was a good probing attack."

"Roger. I have an idea."

"What's that?" Mahegan asked.

"You wanted to know what was in my rucksack." Kneeling in the cave, she opened the pack and retrieved two nylon containers that looked like they might hold sleeping bags.

"Sleeping bags?"

"No. Not sleeping bags," she said, holding up the black bags a bit larger than a football. "I'm a skydiver, and this is the latest rage."

"I've seen them. It might work. Why two?"

"My boyfriend does it with me," Cassie said.

Mahegan said nothing.

"But he decided to dump me a week ago. Said I was deployed too much," Cassie said. "Never had time to change out the pack.

Kept it stored in my Subaru, which is probably in the police pound by now."

"Looks like we got all the good stuff out of it anyway," Mahegan said. "Except maybe those muddy size twelve hiking boots." Mahegan had noticed in the pile of stuff stacked high in Cassie's Subaru a few things that were not congruent with a lone female driver. The shotgun seemed odd to him, but he could give her that. It was the pair of boots that seemed oddly out of place.

"Yeah, he left those at my place, too," Cassie said. She averted her eyes, looking down and to the right, as if she were embarrassed about something. Mahegan considered that she might have been hiding something. He remembered Alex mentioning that the Mecklenburg County sheriff and Charlotte Police Department had clear tracks of size 12 hiking boots in the Sledge home. Vicki, Charles, and their son, Danny, were slaughtered in cold blood by someone using a pistol he purchased. Mahegan wore size twelve boots. Would Cassie Bagwell have any reason to frame Jake Mahegan for murder? He knew that she had a public dispute with her father about her attendance at Ranger school, but what could that have to with him? The Operation Groomsman debacle had tarnished General Bagwell and everyone else in the chain of command. Was that enough for Cassie to frame him? He didn't think so, particularly given the hate–hate relationship she at least projected that she had with her father.

"So, knowing this, what are your thoughts?" Cassie asked.

Mahegan caught her eyes down low and with his, brought them back up so that they were looking at each other again.

"My thoughts are that we can try your nylon bags out," Mahegan said.

"You sure you're up for that?" Cassie said. "Can we make it?"

Mahegan eyed her. Nodded. "Your call on that. I could use the help. Getting there on these"—he pointed at the nylon bags—"will be the easy part. Getting out is the hard part. Not that getting there will be easy at all. Risky as hell."

"There's a chance that at night we could get in and out without anyone knowing," Cassie said.

"There's a chance, but it's improbable. I deal in probabilities. I like math. Perhaps there's a one percent chance that we hit it and quit it. There's a greater chance one of us crashes and burns on landing and there's one of us left to see what's in the cave, rescue anyone in there, fight his or her way out with two to five immobile captives, and live to tell about it."

Cassie stared at him. "Yeah. That's a greater probability. I'll give you that."

"But the plan can work. Like anything, the key is that both of us make safe entry with all of our equipment."

"What about Alex?" Cassie asked.

"What about her?"

"She'll probably want in," Cassie said.

"There's no role for her," Mahegan said.

"How can you say that? It's just the two of us," Cassie replied.

Mahegan looked up and turned his head when he heard a noise from deep inside the cave. Figuring it wasn't a threat, he continued.

"Two is one more than I normally operate with, Cassie. But with the possibility of carrying or escorting anywhere from two to five hostages, I need you. I'm hoping they'll be ambulatory, but hope is not a method. So we have to plan on their not being able to walk, which means we need a vehicle. Yours is burned. As much as I'd like to have the things you've got stashed in your car, we can't get to it."

"But maybe we can. I've got 'Find My Car' on my iPhone. Locate it and disable the shark fin and we can go."

Mahegan had considered this. Wanting it to be her idea if they chose to use her car, he soft-pedaled the concept.

"Your car is known to the police," he said. "They're all over that parking lot. And that's if it's not impounded. No way."

"Anything moving will be subject to being stopped. You saw the carnage out there. We could get Alex to get it."

"Alex could be a problem," Mahegan reiterated.

"How so?"

"Too much detail to get into right now. Let's just assume we are going without her help and maybe she could be a hindrance to us," he said, understating the complications.

"So we wait until nightfall and grab my car and then move to one of the three rims?"

"Something like that," Mahegan said. "Or more likely, we walk."

Just then he heard the distinctive pull of a pin from a grenade, the high-pitched ping the spoon makes when it releases from the grenade body. The sound was from the mouth of the cave. He heard the whooshing of the grenade through the air and its impact on the dirt near them.

Most grenades had a five-second cook-off time. From the release of the spoon to hearing the grenade land had been two seconds, perhaps three. In that time, Mahegan had grabbed Cassie by the upper arm with one hand and her rucksack with the other hand as they scrambled deeper into the cave. He found a slight bulge in the wall of the cave, enough to protect from the blast. He pressed his back against the jagged rock while holding Cassie behind him with his left arm. He tossed the rucksack on the ground behind Cassie, figuring the contents were precious to the future missions.

The explosion came milliseconds after they had found semi-protected cover. The deafening roar and bright fireball pushed heat and smoke past them. Mahegan smelled the cordite instantly as the shrapnel peppered the wall, sounding like heavy hail on a sidewalk. Automatic three-round bursts raked the ground in a sweeping motion.

The attackers were advancing.

Mahegan lifted the rucksack and nudged Cassie in front of him, whispering, "Go deeper into the cave."

Given Mahegan's status on the black list for the North Carolina SBI, he didn't know if his attackers were the legitimate SWAT team that had rappelled out of the helicopter or if they were the commandos hidden in the Bible camp in the mountains. Mahegan did not like the thought of shooting a North Carolina SWAT team.

The farther they retreated, the more Mahegan gained hope for some kind of escape without having to use force against possible U.S. law enforcement. In the sweeping arc of lights from the attackers' rifles, Mahegan noticed the smoke moving swiftly to the rear.

"There's an exit somewhere back here," he said to Cassie.

"I'm a rock climber," she said. Mahegan wondered if she had any other gear in the heavy rucksack.

As they rounded a corner, a shaft of gray light cut down from the top-left corner. There was a slight incline, but not much. It would be a tough climb, and Mahegan was no rock climber. He was strong and powerful but not nimble and lithe like Cassie. She assessed the shaft and grabbed her ruck, slinging it over her shoulders. Cassie began climbing the rock face as if it were a beginner's climbing wall. She was forty feet up and had her hands on the lip of the four-foot opening. She sat down, legs dangling in the hole, opened her ruck, and fed rope down to Mahegan.

Mahegan grabbed the rope as the searchlights became more powerful. The attackers were less than fifty yards away. He would be spotlighted by the searchlights as well as the light coming from the cave opening.

He grabbed the rope and looked up, unable to find Cassie. She had probably backed away and found something against which to anchor the rope. He had hoped for some covering fire but understood she was trying to get him out of there.

Looking over his shoulder, he noticed a ledge about twenty feet to his left, back in the direction of the attackers. Forgetting the rope for the moment, he jumped up to the fifteen-foot-high ledge, grasped with both hands, and did a pull-up, swinging his leg up at the same time. Hooking his right heel on the slippery rock outcropping, he levered his body onto the ledge and laid silent, breathing hard through his nostrils, filtering the dank air.

Immediately, two men ran around the corner toward the rope and the opening. They began speaking as they pointed at the rope, the diversion Mahegan was hoping for.

They spoke in Arabic.

These were not friendlies.

Mahegan leapt from the ledge and spread his considerable wingspan to collar both men simultaneously. He landed with his heavy mass on their backs and had each of them in a choke hold as he released one man, keeping one knee in the back of each, and snapping the neck of the man on his right. In a swift move, he retrieved his knife from his ankle sheath and drove it into the neck of the man on his left.

Both men were dead. He looked up at the opening. Cassie was staring down at him in disbelief.

Resorting to his training, Mahegan put his knife back in its sheath and conducted a quick inspection of both bodies. He retrieved two grenades, two AR-15s, a small backpack he didn't have time to inspect, and five magazines of ammunition. Rolling the men over, he checked their pockets for identification, finding none.

They were wearing the exact same clothes as the two men whom Alex Russell killed on the ridge. Black cargo pants, form-fitting black stretch shirts, and hiking boots. Same brands. All relatively new looking. The men looked Turkish or Syrian, perhaps Iraqi.

He looked up at Cassie fifty feet away.

"I'm coming up," he said. He stuffed the grenades and ammunition into the backpack, shouldered it, and crisscrossed the AR-15s across his chest using their two-point slings. Clasping the rope, he began to climb the rock wall.

Reaching the top, he was impressed that Cassie had expertly tied the rope using a round turn and two half hitches around a large oak.

"Ranger school was good for something," she said. She had been walking back and forth atop the rocky ledge. Mahegan could see she was worried.

"Good for lots of things," Mahegan replied. He exited the hole by doing a dip press and swinging his legs to one side. He rolled onto the rocky surface and looked up. There was dense forest in each direction, the thick trunks of pine trees creating a maze. It was overcast and late afternoon. Without the cover of darkness, they had to move.

It was a lot of coincidence that every time he went near Alex Russell, bad guys showed up minutes later.

Then he heard more noise in the cave and the helicopter circling above.

CHAPTER 21

JACKKNIFE WAS BREATHING HARD, THINKING, RUSHED, PACING IN A PLACE it was hard to pace. They had made some good moves and they had made some bad moves; rather, Jake Mahegan had made some good moves that disrupted their good moves.

Satisfied that they had made no bad moves, Jackknife was content to believe that their path was still viable. The murder of General Savage's ex-wife using his own pistol that was still registered to Mahegan was a stroke of brilliance. Jackknife never considered the outcome of any action to be a result of fate or chance or luck. Jackknife's own brilliance—and that alone—was accounting for the success of the operation so far.

The decapitation of the military leadership. Stalling cars on the highways using a latent remote access Trojan planted in the service networks of most major car dealers to mask the true objective of stealing the nuke. Freezing individual and business bank accounts using an exploding remote access Trojan. Sure, Gavril and Zakir were executing, but these were all part of Jackknife's plan, precursors for sure, but still setting the conditions for the final act.

An unprecedented act of terror.

Jackknife believed that by locking down General Savage and his rogue team of commandos they had achieved a level of freedom of maneuver that allowed for mission accomplishment.

Assessing their progress so far, Jackknife was concerned, however.

The entire plan revolved around keeping Savage and his vigilantes at bay until mission completion. Mahegan was the one loose cannon. The other three were not a threat at the moment.

Jackknife had to keep close tabs on Mahegan. Mirror him. Monitor him.

It was the only way.

Mahegan needed to live long enough to provide Jackknife the precise information Mahegan had found during his raid during Operation Groomsman. That information, after all, was what this entire mission was all about.

Once Jackknife knew what Mahegan had found, then, of course, the man could die.

CHAPTER 22

MAHEGAN LED CASSIE THROUGH THE THICK FOREST, UP THE STEEP incline and back toward Alex's condo.

They stopped about a half mile away on the west side and used Cassie's binoculars to study the house. Two motorcycles were parked in the driveway and crime scene tape encircled Alex's house like a fat, yellow pinstripe.

"That sucks," Cassie said.

"It's only because of me. Nothing you or Alex did," Mahegan replied.

Cassie laid her hand on his arm and smiled at him. "Don't be so sure of that, wild man."

Mahegan nodded uphill and said, "We've got to get to the other side of the parkway and find the best spot."

"Then we better get moving," Cassie said.

They walked to the north, making sure to stay below the military crest of the ridge and out of sight of the police who were securing Alex's town house. They trudged up the mountain, Mahegan carrying the bigger rucksack, with Cassie hefting the one he had taken from the two attackers. They used orienteering techniques, mostly one called "handrail," where they would walk just below the crest of a ridge and follow it in the general direction they wanted to move. This tactic avoided the massive ups and downs of the ravines and valleys that were marginally navigable but would have been a straight line to their destination.

While the navigation took a longer route, it ultimately saved time. By Mahegan's count, they had traversed nearly ten miles doing about three miles an hour. The sun was perched atop the mountain ridges far to the west, sinking fast. He got the acrid whiff of burnt leaves. The weight of Cassie's rucksack didn't bother him, but his shoulder gnawed at him, the war injury that would forever remind him of his best friend, Sergeant Wesley Colgate.

Mahegan took a knee next to a towering white pine. Cassie followed suit. She slipped off the small backpack.

"What is Alex going to think?" she asked.

"Why do we care?" Mahegan replied.

"She's a part of this somehow."

"We don't have a lot of time. Is it germane to what we're getting ready to do?"

"It could be the key to everything going on," Cassie said. "But I'm not sure."

"Well, indecision has never been my thing. Let's get going."

Mahegan led Cassie past the Blue Ridge Parkway. They walked through a drainage pipe that was big enough to allow both of them to remain upright. At the base of the cylinder, bear paw prints and the distinctive smaller print of a bobcat dotted the silt. The split hoof print of deer was also evident. The bear print, though, seemed to be the most recent, nearly obliterating the others.

Mahegan recognized the far ridge where they had parked the car about a half a mile away. It was possible that the commandos had sentries patrolling the forests, but by his count he didn't believe they had enough men to cover the vast area above their base camp. They just needed to get to the high ridge he had seen from the tower.

With dusk creeping in, he led Cassie through the dim light, picking their way through the pine trees. As they approached the spot he had noticed from the watchtower, he lay down on his belly and had Cassie do the same. They low-crawled across the rocky ledge to its edge.

He could see the circular ring of huts and a few men carrying rifles, moving quickly from one building to the next. They were atop a sheer drop-off of over two thousand feet. About a mile across the valley was a similar rock face and cliff. At the base of the cliff he could barely make out the black outline of a mine entrance. He had seen this as well from the tower.

Though he had been compromised while up there, the intelligence could bear fruit. If Savage, O'Malley, and Owens were being held captive, that was as good as any place in the proximity to the base camp.

"See there," Mahegan said. He pointed at the dark outline of the mine shaft.

"I can barely make it out, but yes."

"Let's scoot back into the wood line and suit up," Mahegan said.

"We can't do this at night. It's suicide," Cassie protested.

"It's the only way. Our timing is perfect. Just enough light to see and just enough darkness to hide. They'll only hear the fluttering of silk. And of course, I'd much prefer you cover me from up here, Ranger."

"Don't Ranger me. You go, I'm going. You may be crazy, but you haven't seen crazy yet, Mahegan," Cassie said.

Something in Mahegan made him believe her. She was earnest and tough. She would go with him. They crawled into the first cut of trees and opened the nylon bags. They helped each other get situated. Mahegan's suit fit a little tight but not too bad. The AR-15 he tucked inside made it even tighter and a tad more awkward. Steering could be a problem.

Cassie checked him out and slapped him on the ass, saying, "Good to go."

He conducted a mini-version of a parachute inspection on Cassie's suit, even though these weren't parachutes.

"Good to go," he said, then patted her on the shoulder.

Cassie was carrying her rucksack inside her suit, while Mahegan was carrying the backpack from the terrorists inside his. They walked to the edge of the cliff.

Mahegan looked at her, and she returned his gaze and nodded.

* * *

Cassie Bagwell followed Jake Mahegan to the edge of the cliff, so many options running through her mind. She was one of the first female graduates of the U.S. Army's elite Ranger school and the first to complete Ranger training without being recycled. Her fellow male Ranger students had nicknamed her "Nails," for being as "tough as nails."

Given the political correctness reigning around women in special operations, the instructors forbade the nickname, but it still stuck. During the Darby phase in Georgia the biggest physical suck took place with the five-mile runs that seemed faster than the advertised eight-minute pace. Also, the next-to-impossible obstacle course called the Darby Queen was a major challenge. Male Ranger students several decades ago had given the obstacle course that name because she was a bitch, pure and simple. The course had been designed by men for men, and there were some things her five-foot-seven, wiry body was not meant to do, such as the over and under crawl that required weaving between wooden planks separated by five feet. Her wingspan was just that, and it took all of her strength to slide her arms and hands and body and legs from splintered plank to splintered plank.

But she had made it. She was a natural at leading patrols, and she was strong enough to carry the radio and the machine gun, which she had to do simultaneously several times as ordered by one officious prick of a patrol leader . . . who never graduated. At the end of the three-week Darby phase, her spot reports from her fellow Ranger students were solid, if not a tad sexist. *Keeps up well. Surprised she's doing so good. . . . Helps out when she can. . . . Doesn't smell too bad. . . . Pretty strong for a girl. . . . Her daddy helped her get in but she's doing ok. . . .*

Then came the mountain phase up in Dahlonega, Georgia, where her childhood love of rock climbing and rappelling had her teaching her fellow Ranger students knot tying and rock-climbing techniques late at night. The peer evaluation reports got stronger. *Helped me learn knots. . . . Pulling her weight (even though she don't weigh much). . . . Just read that her daddy was a dick, didn't want her in here. . . . Starting to smell pretty good. . . . Hell of a rock climber.*

The final phase in Florida was where she truly excelled. Land navigation, compass reading, and just plain sucking it up with no sleep and little chow. She could taste graduation with every gulp of the Yellow River as she patrolled with her Ranger students through the muck toward some obscure objective. After she passed her Florida patrol, making her three for three on her patrols, she was given an honor graduate patrol. The instructors made her the patrol leader for a parachute assault onto a drop zone, which she planned and executed perfectly. At assembly, she wasted no time in forming her troops up for move out, certain that the instructors would give another student an opportunity to lead, as was customary at every natural break in the action. But, no, she planned and executed the jump, the assembly, the movement to the objective, and the ambush.

Two men fell asleep in the ambush location and didn't fire their weapons at four a.m. when the vehicles entered the kill zone. Those two men had caused her to fail the honor graduate patrol, but she was okay with that. Honor grad would have been great, but she was happy with her black-and-gold tab. After graduation, she went downtown on Victory Drive in Columbus, Georgia; partied with her male graduates; and got the standard black-and-gold Ranger tab tattoo on her left shoulder.

While she was in Ranger school, she had missed much of the publicity about her father. He had openly spoken out against his daughter and other women serving in Special Forces. He had not attempted to parse his words.

"My daughter has no business in Ranger school and should she graduate, which is unlikely, she has no business serving in Special Forces," Bagwell had said at the time two years ago.

Back at Fort Benning preparing for graduation the next day, Cassie had been asleep in her bunk, the only person in the desolate female barracks. *The only female graduate.* She could feel her body reestablishing itself after losing twenty pounds she didn't have to lose. The fat and calories she was putting away in the mess hall were restoring her muscles, but she was still weak.

Which was why when they came for her, she was slow to react.

She was sleeping and sluggish in waking. The blanket was quickly over her head, and she could hear two male voices as someone tied her feet to the metal bunk. Another man was choking her, saying, "Say a word, bitch, and I'll slit your throat. Just look at it this way. Your daddy sent me."

She continued to struggle, but these were strong men who had ambushed her. Soon her hands were tied to the metal posts beyond her head. One man cut away her gym shorts with a knife and said, "Oh my. Lookie here."

Cassie had been sleeping with her knife taped to the metal rails, and she slid her hand slowly up the slick metal, could feel the handle as the man used his knees to pry her legs open. The binding was tight but just loose enough for her to manipulate the knife in her hand. The man above her stuffed a cloth in her mouth, and she was having a hard time breathing. She was able to grab the knife handle as she turned her legs inward, trying to prevent the man from gaining further access.

Fumbling with the knife, she cut the poorly tied rope as the man had defeated her last line of defenses and began to say, "Oh yes."

But the knife came arcing down on his left shoulder and he howled in agony. "What was that?!"

The man between her legs was no longer there. She felt him roll off and thud onto the floor. She instinctively turned her knees inward as she flipped the knife in her hand and stabbed behind her, where the man was beginning to choke her.

With this thrust she found his thigh, and he too began howling. She used the precious seconds when neither man was restraining her to cut the ropes on her wrists and ankles. With that task done, she began chasing the two men who had assaulted her.

But the lights came on as they exited through the back door of the barracks. Cassie was standing there in a bloody gray Army T-shirt with no shorts.

Staring at her father.

"Did they . . ."

"Did they what?" she asked, breathing heavily. Her adrenaline was pumping. Blood dripped from her knife. Her eyes darted wildly searching for her attackers.

"Penetrate?"

"What? No, they didn't *penetrate.*" She said the last word as if she were spitting it out.

"Good. Then there's nothing to report." Her father turned on one heel and began to walk out.

"Wait a minute, you bastard," Cassie shouted.

General Bagwell stopped but kept his back to her.

"You don't walk out on me after this!" Her chest was heaving. Her legs ached from doing her best to prevent her assailant from gaining access. She was barely conscious of the knife in her hand and the three short steps she was taking as she lifted the blade.

"Stop, Cassie," her father said, sensing her approaching.

Cassie stopped, if only because she remembered being a little girl and responding so quickly to her father's voice. Like a puppy. Sit. Play. Roll over. At one time she had adored the man. Now she despised him, and not only for ridiculing her Ranger training, which she had done as much for herself as she did to say a giant *Fuck You* to her father.

"Why, so there can be more secrets, *Daddy*? So you can pass me more shitty intel? So you can . . ."

"Stop it!" He turned and stepped toward her but stopped. She held a knife in her hand low down by her thigh. An uppercut would slice open his abdomen, and Cassie was feeling it. "There will be no talk of classified information in this barracks!"

"Then what is there to talk about? Just a little rape attempt? No, we can't discuss that either, can we, *Daddy*?"

"When I'm in uniform, you'll address me properly, Captain. Do you understand?"

But Cassie was feeling weak. Her energy was leaving her rapidly. Mind spinning wildly. Two men had just tried to rape her and here she was arguing with her father. The entire scene was beyond comprehension. Secrets. Why did there have to be so many secrets, she wondered.

And then she passed out.

That night was a blur to Cassie, but still something with which she struggled.

Her father had said it was best to keep it quiet, that this was why men and women should not be in units together, that he had been right and she had been wrong.

The next day, he didn't show up at her Ranger graduation. One of her West Point classmates had pinned her tab on her. She cried openly that day, not with tears of joy but with hate and anger toward her father. How could he? True, he was old school, but Cassie knew that she was a leader and that Ranger school was first and foremost a leadership school. It opened the doors to promotions, advances that would provide her leadership roles where she could make a true difference in the Army and in foreign policy one day. That was all that she had ever wanted to do. And to deny her that and let her attackers go? She wondered if he even looked at her as his daughter anymore.

Then the second blow came when she had figured it all out. Four years ago while serving in Mosul in charge of special intelligence, her father had called her using a burner cell phone and directed her to meet with a French special agent, who claimed to have useful information. Despite the personal issue with her father, she was a professional. She *had* respected him, respected his combat service. She knew that until you were out there in a thin-skinned Humvee riding around with the potential for a bomb to rip your legs from your body, you didn't know combat. And Cassie knew combat, too. She wasn't your ordinary intelligence officer. She actually rode or flew along on missions to see firsthand what was happening on the ground. Her Humvee had been rocked by an improvised explosive device near Mosul as she checked on the Iraqi Army's progress against ISIS. No one was seriously injured in that attack, but still, it counted. She was there, braving the risks of the front lines.

Only to redeploy to Fort Bragg with just her mother to welcome her. Operation Groomsman had been a debacle, and her father was ashamed of her, presumably for supplying the pearl of intelligence that led to the bombing.

"He won't come down," her mother had told Cassie.

"I'm good with that, actually," Cassie had said.

Her mother had just hugged her and shook her head. She didn't know. Then, two years later, after Ranger school, she'd had enough.

"I'm going to see him at Fort Myer," Cassie said. She had driven the five hours in her car and stormed up the steps of her father's government mansion, walking past the guards and the aides and the chefs and the staff.

She found him seated at a large oak table in his study. There was a man seated with his back to her. Without looking at her, her father said, "Not now, Cassie."

"Not now? When?"

"Not. Now."

He used his commander's voice. His chairman's voice. As if the world should shudder and bow to his directive.

"Well, fuck you, Daddy."

The unknown man's shoulders stiffened. Her father looked up at her through leaden eyes.

"You just insulted a superior officer," he said. "Not only a superior officer, but the chairman of the Joint Chiefs. I could have you arrested and disciplined for insubordination."

"No, I didn't do any of that," she said. "This is just a daughter telling her father he can go fuck himself."

"That what they teach you in Ranger school?"

"You wouldn't know, would you, slick sleeve?"

Slick sleeve was the derogatory name for someone without a Ranger tab on the left shoulder sleeve.

She watched his eyes go dark before he spoke.

"This man is my Judge Advocate General. My lawyer. I'm signing my will. You are not in it. Thanks to all of the negative media attention you brought me with this stupid Operation Groomsman, I've had to hire private attorneys who cost a fortune."

"Some stupid operation? That stupid operation killed innocent civilians who just wanted to get married," Cassie said. "And you set me up!"

"Oh, please don't tell me I raised a daughter who for one second believes anyone in the Middle East is innocent of anything," snapped General Bagwell. "And set you up? Whatever are you talking about, Cassie? We haven't talked since before you deployed."

Cassie seethed. He had his built-in deniability with the burner phone, and she had spoken over the tactical phone in her headquarters. There was no log of phone calls. There was nothing she could prove. But she knew in her heart that her father had established the liaison for some reason.

"Fine. You can deny it," Cassie said. Her voice was soft and steady. "How about this? You let two men try to rape me and then tell me not to report it? How's that sound, Mister JAG." She poked the colonel on the shoulder and then turned and hustled past the same staff and chefs and aides and guards barely outracing her father's shout of "Out of my house, now!"

Two years ago. Not a word since.

Now, standing on the rock ledge with Jake Mahegan, she knew exactly what she was doing.

Because she knew why her father had directed her to meet with clandestine French agent Yves Dupree when she was in Mosul four years ago the day of Operation Groomsman.

Mahegan looked at Cassie, who appeared deep in thought.

"Snap out of whatever it is you're thinking about. You're leading the way here since you're the expert at this."

"Never said I was an expert." Cassie smiled. "Just said I like it."

She spread her arms and her wingsuit ruffled with the slight breeze that was pouring down over the lip of the cliff. She stepped forward and did a slow motion fall face-first over the cliff.

Mahegan followed her, spreading his considerable wingspan. Her boyfriend's wingsuit was slightly smaller than what he hoped for, but he had to work with what she had. Having never used a wingsuit before, he found his first few seconds of flight cumbersome and frankly, nearly out of control. Mahegan was a big man and he wasn't certain that these flying squirrel suits were ample enough to lift someone six and a half feet tall and 240 pounds.

Mahegan calculated that he needed to keep his forward velocity greater than his downward velocity. For every yard he dropped, he wanted to do at least two yards forward. He spread his legs and his arms as wide as they could go. He opened his fingertips and turned his palms into the slipstream, attempting to have them act like the flaps on an airplane that provide lift.

He stabilized after a few seconds and found himself hurtling in a straight line across the valley toward the mine shaft opening. Cassie was a spec in front of him, diving and twisting along the terrain that Mahegan was so close to colliding with. He flipped forty-five degrees to turn away from the lip of a ridge that had tall pines poking into the sky like spears on a redoubt. Pine needles brushed his face with the smell of sap. His wingsuit scraped against the spindly branches.

Tilting back toward Cassie's path, he had some clearance. The velocity with which he was falling or flying, he wasn't sure which, created a windstream that caused his eyes to tear. He felt the drops streaming across his cheeks, reminding him of hanging out the door of a transport aircraft as a jumpmaster was about to send sixty paratroopers from the rear cargo doors of a C-130 aircraft in combat.

He and Cassie had discussed landing only briefly. It was intuitive to him that he needed to angle almost straight up to get maximum wind resistance to slow his movement to an acceptable level such that he wouldn't break every bone in his body. As he calculated his landing, they passed over a creek that shined with the rising moon in that instant between twilight ending and the onset of full dark. Several canoes were overturned and bunched together. The circular outline of the gravel drive that serviced the cabins and their inhabitants slipped beneath him. Briefly he thought of the irony that an old Bible camp might now house jihadist terrorists fighting in the name of Islam.

The far mountain wall drew close quickly. It loomed large and ominous ahead. Cassie flared upward at a seventy-degree angle. There was nowhere to glide for a soft landing. The face of the mountain ended abruptly at the valley floor, almost in a perfect ninety-degree angle. Cassie floated toward the mine shaft opening, now not visible at all, looking like a large bird, gliding effortlessly, hunting prey, looking for the evening kill.

He, on the other hand, looked like a B-1 bomber that had taken shrapnel and was attempting an emergency landing. He was now barely above the trees. These were oaks, birches, and maples. Mountain trees in the valley. Cassie spread her entire suit as wide as she could get it and then inexplicably fell into a delta dive, like a hawk speeding toward a rabbit.

Then she disappeared.

She was either a messy wet spot on the side of the mountain, or she had found the mine shaft.

He followed suit. Slowed as much as possible, lost a lot of altitude, his boots raking the tops of trees, which helped him slow even more. Without warning, Cassie's landing zone appeared.

There was a wide gravel road that angled into the mine shaft from both directions, forming an inverted Y of sorts. The entry to the shaft was at least fifty yards long, hidden by the tall trees. Megan dove toward the ground, as Cassie had done, and felt the ground rushing toward him. Instinctively, he spread his legs and arms, gathering as much air as possible, as if he were parachuting. He slowed some more, felt the gravel, knew he was low enough not to slam into the side of the mountain, then collapsed his arms and legs until he felt his feet hit the ground. He tried to run in order to keep up with his velocity, but his mass was too much. He tumbled over his head twice and then stood up, stumbled some, found a rock pile, and rolled toward that as he unzipped his wingsuit.

All combat was the same. Only the methods of entry changed. And the first rule of combat was to put your weapon into operation immediately. As he stepped out of the wingsuit, he had the AR-15 up and scanning at the ready. Noiselessly, he wadded up the wingsuit and collapsed it into its self-contained nylon pouch.

He stuffed that in the bottom of the small backpack, moving the grenades to the top as he kept the AR-15 up and scanning.

Their plan had been to link up at the mouth of the mine shaft. He didn't immediately see Cassie, which didn't necessarily concern him right away. She was an Army Ranger, so that counted for something in his book. He felt a pebble strike his boot and heard another land against the rock he was using as cover.

Cassie was huddled on the outside of the mine shaft opening on the far side from his location. She was maybe twenty yards away from him. Two guards had come running out of the mine shaft, perhaps having heard his less than perfect landing. The guards stayed together and began searching in his direction, walking directly at him. He didn't notice any unnatural protrusions from their heads or helmets and guessed that they were not using night vision goggles. Retrieving his knife, he prepared for their advance. The goal was to kill or disable them without their shooting a weapon, alerting the others. It would be a tough challenge, given there were two of them and one of him.

One guard walked past him within three feet, less than a yard even. He could smell the man's sweat. The other guard was still on the opposite side of the rock.

"What did you hear?" one man said in an Arabic accent.

"Rocks," the other man replied.

As the lead man turned his head to the right, away from Mahegan, Mahegan leapt up and grabbed the chin of the guard as he jammed the knife through the man's neck. He immediately wheeled in preparation to first defend against the second guard and then attack to disable. He wanted one man to answer his questions, and since they both spoke some English, it gave him hope that he could get some answers.

Mahegan turned to find the man on his knees, his head hung low as if he were praying, and Cassie Bagwell sticking a knife in his throat.

He would not be questioning either of these men.

"Let's grab the weapons and ammo and get in the mine shaft," Mahegan said. They inspected their respective kills and came away with two pistols, two assault rifles, and several magazines of both kinds of ammunition. Their commander had decided to up-arm the guards tonight based upon the skirmish earlier today, Mahegan presumed.

"Follow me," Mahegan said.

He stepped into the mine shaft and turned on the flashlight on the rail of his AR-15, which he held at arm's distance in case someone decided to shoot at the light. He swept it in an arc, studying the shaft. An old rail line ran down the middle with about five yards of uneven terrain on either side. The shaft was at least fifteen feet high in most places. As they walked on either side of the centerline rail, Mahegan shined the flashlight on several large alcoves off the main shaft. In one was an assortment of assault rifles and green metal ammunition containers. An ammo bunker. While important and interesting, he wasn't looking for weapons and ammo. He needed to find his teammates. Another alcove contained a lacquered wooden canoe, probably used on the river that cut through the base camp, a remnant of the Bible camp. It sat perched atop a boat trailer. Again, interesting, but not germane unless it could offer them a way out of the base camp.

After walking about one hundred yards by Mahegan's pace count, he found what he was looking for: a door that was no more than a set of steel bars.

"Watch my back," Mahegan said.

He used the keys he had removed from the guard he had just killed. After unlocking the steel bars, he walked ten yards into the alcove and saw O'Malley and Owens hanging from shackles, looking like slaves awaiting purchase or punishment, or both.

He went out to Cassie, reached in her rucksack, and retrieved a small hatchet.

"Come inside the door and guard in both directions," he said.

"What did you find?"

"Two of my friends. We'll keep searching, but I want to free them up," Mahegan said.

O'Malley and Owens were unconscious. They were probably dehydrated and weak from no food. He felt the men's necks for a pulse and got weak ones. He chopped the chains around O'Malley's wrists as he held the bearded man with one arm so he didn't fall forward. Then he chopped the chains securing the man's ankles. O'Malley was completely free. Mahegan removed a water bottle from his cargo pocket and held it to O'Malley's mouth. He coughed and spit, but he awoke.

"Here, drink this," Mahegan said to O'Malley.

He repeated the process with Owens. Chopped the chains holding the wrists. Chopped the chains holding the ankles. Poured water on his head. Made him drink. When both men were mildly coherent, Mahegan tapped them both lightly in the face.

"It's me, Jake. I'm here to get you out. I've got a rifle for each of you, and we're probably going to have to fight our way out."

Both men nodded. They were pale and gaunt. Their shoulders were probably separated from hanging from shackles for days. But he needed them to fight as he knew they could. Cassie found the key to unlock the shackles and removed them quickly before returning to her post.

"Noise," Cassie said.

"Let's go, guys," Mahegan said, helping his two friends to their feet.

"Jake, man." It was all Owens could say. Owens's eyes were wide and wild, like he thought he might die any second at the hands of the men who had been torturing him.

It took a few minutes for the men to orient themselves, but Mahegan would rather risk the time to have them halfway healthy. He knew that Owens and O'Malley at 50 percent was twice as good as any half-baked Syrian terrorist.

"More noises from the mouth of the mine shaft," Cassie said.

"You guys good?" Mahegan said to his two friends.

"We're half naked. Pants don't fit. Barefooted. And an AR-15 piece of shit with two mags of ammo? Why don't we just fix bayonets?" Owens said.

"Yeah, you're ready. Let's go," Mahegan said. He smiled inwardly, glad his friends were alive.

"Cassie, you take rear security. I'll get us to the next prison cell. Patch and Sean, you guys stay in the middle and don't shoot anything unless I say," Mahegan said.

He had little time to get the remaining captives: General Savage and Cassie's parents, at a minimum. He used the rail-mounted Maglite to find his path in the pitch-black tunnel. Walking along the centerline railroad track with the AR-15 in one hand and the small hatchet in the other, he felt Patch Owens's hand grabbing his shirt, and he was sure that Sean O'Malley was clasping Owens's shoulder or belt. It was their standard protocol when operating in extremis in blackout conditions. He could also hear voices speaking in Arabic near the mouth of the mine shaft.

The light caught a wooden box in the distance. He slowed his movement and felt his teammates slow with him. No one said anything. They knew better. Mahegan was in charge. The enemy was 150 yards away, at a maximum, and every second counted. They walked along the rail line that most likely fed railcars into the bowels of the shaft during the mining heydays. Mahegan could visualize the pit ponies back in the mid-nineteenth century pulling the car loaded with gold, mica, smoky quartz, or even rubies. As he walked there was a faint gurgling in the distance, but before he could process that information, another set of iron bars appeared to his right.

Mahegan shined his flashlight inside the dank prison cell. A naked man was staked to the wall in much the same fashion that O'Malley and Owens had been. Mahegan quickly used the hatchet to chop through the chain—bound by a heavy gauge lock—securing the door.

"Secure the door. Watch my back," Mahegan said to his newly formed team. He entered the small cave. It was a cutout from the main tunnel, as if miners had dug twenty yards into the wall of the mountain and, finding no gold, decided to stop.

At the end, hanging by shackles, was a gaunt and badly beaten Major General Bob Savage. His gray hair, typically bristles, was longer than normal. He showed at least a three-day growth of beard. Looking almost Biblical hanging from the wall, Savage had been brutally beaten, tortured, by someone looking for information. Savage knew many of the nation's secrets, but Mahegan was certain that if there was one person the country could count on to protect classified information, it was Savage, no matter the pain.

And there had been pain.

Mahegan washed the light over Savage's mangled body. Bruises along the rib cage indicated beatings. A bamboo shoot three inches long sticking from Savage's middle finger on his right hand indicated brutal torture. The shoot was stained black with dried blood. The light showed deep bruises on his face along with one-inch knife cuts, some appearing deep.

Before Mahegan moved farther into the cave, he shone the light along the floor, seeing a few dried water bottles, days old. He figured the guards had drunk those, not Savage. He shone the light high and caught the glint of a wire reflecting back at him. The wire led to a small camera aimed at Savage. He must have missed the camera in the cell that held O'Malley and Owens, if there had been one.

Knowing now he had no time to spare, he reached up and disabled the camera by removing it from the nail that held it in place. He recognized it as a Mini Tiny Spy closed-circuit camera. Most likely there were others in the mine shaft, so he considered their position burned.

"Patch, Sean, need some help," he said in a hoarse whisper. He turned back around, looked at his former boss, and said to his blank face with closed eyes, "This is going to hurt." Knowing his former boss was in immense pain, he needed to remove the torture devices and try to cleanse Savage's wounds. Mahegan grabbed Savage's hand and pulled out the bamboo shoot from beneath the fingernail. Mahegan felt it scrape as it gave way and was free of Savage's hand. Some blood came with the shoot, but Savage's body remained limp and unresponsive other than a slight shrug as he autonomously reacted to the pain.

"I'm abler than them," Cassie said. She walked in and lifted Savage's arm with the bleeding hand while Mahegan used the hatchet to sever the chain. With both arms free, he worked on the leg shackles, loudly banging through the chains.

Savage fell forward onto Cassie, who held strong with his considerable but diminished weight.

"I've got a pulse, but it's not much," Mahegan said, securing the hatchet in his cargo belt.

"We're going to have to carry him," Cassie said. "But we've got to get him some water first. He's dehydrated."

"Enemy, twelve o'clock," Patch Owens said.

Mahegan lifted Savage from Cassie, who had been bracing him upright. Savage was six feet tall and to Mahegan felt as if he weighed about 180 pounds. There were no clothes in the cave, but Mahegan quickly retrieved his flying suit and stuffed Savage in it as best he could. It provided him some amount of dignity and gave Mahegan a manner in which to drag him if necessary. The suit would be unusable, but he didn't plan on needing to jump off any other mountains, either.

Owens and O'Malley were holding their fire. They had downed three water bottles apiece and had gone to work on the pouch of Clif Bars that Cassie had packed. That left six for Savage, Cassie, and him. He and Cassie could get away with one apiece if they could get four down Savage's throat without him choking. Mahegan was reasonably certain that O'Malley and Owens could respond to a threat.

"One hundred meters, boss," Owens whispered.

None of them had any night vision capability, but Mahegan had the flashlight under the rail of the AR-15.

"Get inside the cell," Mahegan said. They filed past him as he laid inside the door opening and aimed the muzzle toward the mine shaft opening.

Backlit by the somewhat lighter shade of black from the opening of the mine shaft, two men walked toward Mahegan. He had no doubt there were others waiting at the mouth, but that was a long-range problem as far as he was concerned. He felt a foot on his left buttocks and heard Cassie whisper, "Don't worry. Not getting fresh. Just taking aim."

She was standing above him, rifle aimed along the tunnel toward the attackers.

"I've got left; you've got right. Shoot immediately after I do," Mahegan whispered.

"Roger," she replied.

They were in a somewhat protected position, the solid mine shaft wall of granite and dirt protecting everything but their heads. Presumably the guards knew the approximate location of the cell, if not its precise position. The two men stopped at the cell from which he had freed O'Malley and Owens.

Once they realized the cell was open and empty, the two men began running toward them, though Mahegan still believed that the attackers had not seen their position. As they ran ahead clumsily, their black outlines became more prominent. He felt Cassie's foot shift slightly, perhaps tensing to take the shot . . . or receive one.

Mahegan sighted along the enhanced tritium-illuminated iron sights, aiming for center mass of the man on the left. With less than twenty yards between Mahegan and the running men, Mahegan slowly squeezed the AR-15 trigger until it released and sent a 5.56 mm bullet into the abdomen of the attacker. Cassie's shot was less than a second later, and she felled the man on the right. Both attackers stumbled forward and slowed, dropping to their knees. Mahegan placed another shot in the left man's face while Cassie fired the newly acquired AR-15 at the man on the right. Both dropped dead in their tracks.

The shots rang loudly in the mine shaft, echoing along the tunnel toward the opening. Mahegan watched for others, but none immediately came rushing forward. No doubt there was a camera showing some of what had just transpired and someone was coordinating an effort to close off the entrance. He had no sense that there was a ventilation shaft, had felt no breeze move air in any direction. He picked up the same stench of urine and feces that he had smelled since entering the first cell. It was as stagnant as a farm pond.

Unlike the cave that he and Cassie had escaped from near the

French Broad River, here there was only one way out—the entrance where up to twenty fighters might be lying in wait for them.

Mahegan said, "Keep watching the entrance. I'm going to check these guys out."

"Roger," Cassie replied.

O'Malley and Owens crawled out of the cell, both wanting to help. Mahegan told them, "You guys watch Savage. Make sure he's okay."

Owens said, "Old man's barely alive. You need firepower. We've got that."

Mahegan looked at Owens in the dark and saw a glint in his weak eyes. He wanted to contribute. O'Malley was the same. Owens had an AR-15, but O'Malley was empty-handed.

"Got a weapon for me, man?"

"Here, use this," Cassie said, handing him her Berretta pistol.

"Peashooter? Damn," O'Malley said.

"Focus, people," Mahegan said. He moved out to the two shot men, checked for pulses, and determined that both were dead. They were dressed in black cargo pants and tight-fitting shirts. They had carried AR-15s and wore tactical vests that contained extra ammunition magazines and, to Mahegan's satisfaction, hand grenades and smoke grenades. He scavenged it all, distributing it to Cassie and his two teammates.

"Okay, you guys defend here while I go deeper and look for Cassie's parents," Mahegan said. "Use these grenades. You've got enough ammo to hold them off for about ten minutes. I won't be longer than that. And here's a rifle, Sean." O'Malley pocketed the pistol and took the AR-15 from Mahegan.

"You're not going without me," Cassie said. Mahegan understood that she wanted to be present when and if they found her parents, but he needed someone coherent to stay with his three teammates. He shined his flashlight into the dark mine shaft that seemed to give way to a natural cavern. Blackness swallowed the beam of light.

"Okay, let's take them with us," Mahegan said. "Because I doubt we're getting out that way except by brute force."

Mahegan looked over his shoulder where five men stood vaguely silhouetted by the tunnel opening over one hundred yards away. Oddly, they weren't pouring out a fusillade of bullets or rockets, but Mahegan was certain that was to come. The single rail line ran straight down the middle with about five yards of clearance on either side of the sloping, curved ceiling cut into the rock. One man tentatively lifted something onto his shoulder and immediately Mahegan said, "RPG!"

The rocket-propelled grenade left the tube and began smoking toward them as Mahegan pushed Cassie back into Savage's cell for protection. The rocket steamed past them in a blazing trail of fire and smoke. Mahegan watched as it continued deep into the cavern and saw it explode another hundred yards into the abyss. The explosion was muted, as if muffled by another layer of something. Mahegan remembered visiting the caverns in Linville, not too far away.

Several years ago, he and his team had conducted a training mission in Linville in preparation for combat in Afghanistan. Linville was unique because it had an underground river that provided ingress and egress in a variety of places. While he didn't notice any ventilation shafts on his walk into this shaft, if it gave way to a natural cavern, as it appeared to, given the ragged edges of the tunnel, there was a chance that a water system flowed through the labyrinth.

"This way, quick," Mahegan said. He recalled studying the map and saw Fletcher Creek, Mills River, Long Branch, and several other streams cutting through the mountains. It was possible, he thought, that this cavern led to water somewhere.

Mahegan fired his AR-15 at the figures approaching from the mouth of the mine shaft. It was suppressive fire, nothing more. Bullets came barreling back on them, pinging off the sides of the cavern and rifling along the walls of the corridors.

"Stay in the middle," Mahegan said. Owens and O'Malley, both naked from the waist up, scarred and bruised, carried Savage, using the wing flaps of the wingsuit as a makeshift poncho litter.

"Get on the tracks," he said, telling them to walk along the middle of what was left of the rail line. "And Cassie, pull rear security."

They walked in single file with Mahegan leading them down the dilapidated rail line along the narrowing mine shaft. The shaft gave way to a natural cavern. There were no more support beams, and the walls were jagged limestone that opened considerably after another one hundred yards. Cassie was firing three-round bursts every few seconds, forcing the attackers to duck, take cover, and delay firing anything bigger than a rifle at them.

They approached the box that Mahegan's flashlight had spotted. A fifteen-by-five-foot wooden container sat atop a flatbed railcar. He led them off the rail, and they squeezed past the wooden crate. Instantly, Mahegan thought, *Missile.* This group of insurgents was hiding a weapon of mass destruction inside the cave. With no time to stop and further inspect, he pressed ahead, thinking. The presence of this crate and whatever it held explained the low rate of fire they were receiving and the unwillingness of the enemy to advance. In the short term, the crate provided Mahegan and his team some temporary protection. Long term was an entirely different story, but he would deal with that once he had his team safe.

"Hell's that?" Owens asked from behind him as they walked.

"Dirty bomb, probably," Mahegan replied. "We'll come back to it once we're safe." Something, though, tugged at the back of Mahegan's mind. Could he use the bomb, if that was what it was, to their advantage now to aid in their escape? The railcar had a hitch tongue where a locomotive or crew of men could pull it out of the tunnel. It did not appear to be self-powered.

Mahegan found a right turn off the main cavern and led his team in that direction, thinking that Cassie's parents were not being kept in this part of the complex. As if they were in sync, Cassie said, "My parents, Jake. Let's not forget them."

"Not forgetting," Mahegan said. He searched with his flashlight and saw that the thirty-foot-high ceiling of the cave was populated with thousands of bats. The gurgling he had heard earlier became louder, and he grew more hopeful for an exit other than brute force back through the mine shaft.

"Where are they?" Cassie asked as she backed around the right-turn corner of the cave.

"I'm searching everything I see. There have been no more cells," Mahegan said. "They could be in another part of the camp."

Cassie was silent for a moment as they continued to walk, then said, "Okay. Let's find a way out, then."

Mahegan listened and followed the bubbling sound, louder now, using his flashlight to find their way. The terrain was rough and uneven, not often trod, if ever. Owens and O'Malley were having a hard time but were sucking it up. Separately they would mutter the occasional curse word as they stumbled, but Mahegan understood they would have a hard time walking on a flat road, much less the jagged calcium and gypsum crevices they were traversing. His flashlight caught the first glimpse of water, a shallow pool ebbing against the ledge upon which they were walking.

"You always were a damn genius, Captain Mahegan," Owens said in his Texas drawl.

"We're about one minute from having our asses kicked, Patch. Call me a genius when we're out of this shit hole and secure."

"Roger that, boss," Owens muttered.

Mahegan waded into the water and felt the gentle, grainy slope scrape against the bottom of his boots. The gurgling was now a full-on rushing noise, and Mahegan searched for the sound with the light. He felt the wall made of flowstone and gathered hope that he had found an egress that didn't involve pushing the railcar into the waiting hordes of terrorists. He shined the light into the middle of a pool of water that at first glance seemed stagnant, but after a moment the subtle movement of water away from him was evident. He was standing in a recess pool probably carved out over a million years. The main stream was about twenty yards in front of him.

Ahead, was a river or swift stream tumbling through the cavern. It appeared out of the wall to his far right, maybe fifty yards away, and disappeared again into the wall to his far left, maybe seventy-five yards away.

"No way Savage can handle that," O'Malley said from behind. "Not sure any of us can."

Mahegan turned and saw his friend's bearded face. O'Malley's wide, green eyes reflected both a concern about their predicament and malnourishment.

"We've dealt with worse, Sean," Mahegan said. "We're going to have to try." Mahegan nodded at the right turn they had taken about fifty yards away. The tips of crisscrossing beams of light searched for them like prison guards looking for escaped convicts.

"Gather around, team," Mahegan said.

O'Malley and Owens laid Savage on the thin film of water that was barely covering their boots. Owens knelt down and cupped some water into Savage's dried lips. Cassie stepped forward, and they formed a circle around Savage's prostate body.

"I'll lead us down. Sean and Patch, can you hold Savage by the feet and head, kind of like a water slide? Cassie, you bring up the rear?"

"Been doing it okay so far," Cassie said, looking at the approaching flashlight beams. "And we don't have much time."

"We can do it, boss. But we have no idea what's on the other end and how much of that is under water. We could all drown."

"Drown or get shot, take your pick. I'd rather see what's at the end of this rainbow," Mahegan said.

Cassie's AR-15 sang with two three-round bursts.

"Whatever we're doing, we better do it," she said, pulling the trigger again.

Mahegan helped position Savage in the middle of the rushing stream, which was bitter cold. Now, they could add hypothermia to the list of life-threatening possibilities.

"Water's freezing, man. We've got to go," Owens said.

"Follow me," Mahegan replied. He sat in the water in front of Owens, who was holding Savage's feet. Behind Owens was Savage, whose head was being held by O'Malley as O'Malley hooked his legs beneath Savage's arms and over his torso. Behind them, Cassie was kneeling in the water keeping the attackers at bay.

Above the din of the rushing water that was climbing up his torso as he inched forward on the sloping flowstone, the high-pitched tone of a grenade spoon releasing pinged loudly. He felt the water begin to move him forward and downward, knowing he had caught the flow. He had Owens's feet hooked around his chest and felt them moving with him. As his head went underwater with the rush of the river, he heard Cassie's muted voice: "Grenade!"

Mahegan was plunging feet-first in a near-vertical dive when he heard the muffled explosion. He hoped Cassie survived and was still with them, but there was absolutely nothing he could do about it as he was free-falling through the darkness, submerged in water and unable to breath.

CHAPTER 23

Yves Dupree signed the document that transferred all of Charles Sledge's power as the chief executive officer to him, the General Counsel, who would now be the interim CEO.

It was approaching midnight on Friday, the day after Sledge had been murdered, and he had already notified all next of kin, made the funeral arrangements, and executed myriad legal documents that pertained to his will and considerable estate.

Dupree cared about none of that. In fact, he had a lackey associate do most of the work while he attended to other, more important matters. Dupree was especially interested in the Sledge's new, clandestine project he had recently introduced as Blackstone. It was a multilayered information assurance program that protected the accounts of their millions of retail bank customers.

In his corner office at the United Bank of America building in downtown Charlotte, he stared at the screen and could not believe what he was seeing. He had helped implement Blackstone because the classified briefings they were receiving from the government indicated that a significant cyberthreat was targeting banks and infrastructure. After today's debacle with millions of cars being stopped, he had immediately opened Blackstone to reassure himself.

Blackstone was spinning across his monitor a series of numbers associated with bank accounts. Each number was between .01 and .99, and it reflected the amount of money skimmed from each of the accounts. Every time Blackstone attempted to block the skim, an image of an actual cartoon rat appeared and knocked out a feckless-looking mouse. *Hacker humor,* Dupree thought. And every time Blackstone attempted to follow the source of the Trojan, the same cartoon rat appeared and lifted cartoon railroad tracks, spreading them apart, ties flying in the imaginary air, indicating that the path was blocked. With nearly 50 million customers, both individual and business, the skim would net about $25 million for the hackers.

Not a bad day's hack.

But he also noticed something equally interesting on another monitor. Part of the overhaul of operations had included a real-time operations display of customer service metrics that any member of the executive team could review. There were multiple charts and graphs on the display to include items such as phone call wait times, customer satisfaction ratings, and number of customer complaints. The customer complaint chart looked like a hockey stick from yesterday to today. Yesterday it was somewhat steady and level, and today the complaint trend line had gone exponentially up.

Beneath the complaint trend line graph was a box with the top five complaints. Usually complaints included mortgage processing, fees and charges for savings and checking accounts, and foreclosures.

Today, the number one complaint by a large margin was inability to access consumer checking and savings accounts. The number two complaint concerned automated teller machines. People were unable to retrieve cash at the ATMs because their accounts were registering as closed.

Dupree looked at the spinning skim display of the Blackstone software system and saw that in the bottom, the black-and-green image showed millions of customers attempting to access their accounts with wrong passwords. Either everyone had forgotten their password today or someone had hacked their system and was changing every individual's password as it was entered so that customers would make repeated attempts, ultimately locking their account after the third try.

The number three customer complaint on the operations dashboard was customer wait time on hold. Normally in the one- to three-minute range, wait times were showing over thirty minutes and climbing.

Dupree called his chief operating officer into the office.

Chris Salisbury was a lean, serious man with a thick crop of brown hair and wire-rim glasses. He always wore his sleeves rolled up, as if he was constantly pressing his nose to the grindstone, which was usually the case.

"Yes, sir, Mister Dupree," Salisbury said. He stood in front of Dupree's desk with the three monitors.

"You see this shit?" Dupree motioned Salisbury around the desk to get a better look at the displays.

When Salisbury saw the operations dashboard, his mouth opened, he stuttered, and then he looked at Dupree.

"This is real?"

"I'm assuming so," Dupree said. "Everything is imploding. This could be the second phase of the Internet thing they've been talking about on the television all day."

"Internet of Things," Salisbury corrected, and immediately wished he hadn't.

"Seriously? You're going to check my shit when you're in charge of operations and right now nobody can access their account and nobody can get cash?"

"My apologies, sir. I'm still shocked."

"Let's meet in an hour. Go find out what you can and round up all the right people. Oh, and we're being skimmed by a Trojan to the tune of about twenty-five million dollars."

"You're kidding," Salisbury said.

"Actually, I'm not. We have an attack on our system unlike anything we've seen before. This will be public in about five minutes, so I need the team assembled and working this ASAP," Dupree said.

"Yes, sir." Salisbury turned on his heel and ran out of the large office, dodging the glass coffee table, sofas, leather chairs, and free-standing modern art.

Dupree pressed a button on his phone, and a female voice answered quickly. "Yes, sir?"

"Here. Now," Dupree said.

Within a minute, Gail Weaver walked in. She was average height and slender. Dupree considered her beautiful, which was one of the main reasons he hired her for the public relations position. She was a University of North Carolina at Charlotte graduate with a major in communications. United Bank of America had paid for her master's degree from the same institution. Two years ago she was an anchor for a local television station, where she had interviewed Dupree. He had just arrived from France, where he led HSBC operations. Somewhat of an international rock star in the banking world, Dupree took full advantage of his celebrity as the turnaround man and general counsel for UBA. After the interview outside of the building, Dupree had flashed his trademark smirk and asked her to drinks. Gail didn't hesitate to agree, and they spent the night across the street in Dupree's newly purchased swank condo.

Since then he had offered her a job, upped her salary twofold, and placed her in the top five of his companion rotation—his A Squad, as he called it. Rarely was an A squad woman not available, but on the off chance that occurred, he kept a few in the B squad, as well. Though over time and without a phone call or text message the B squad became somewhat stale. It was not uncommon for Dupree to meet a new woman, add her to the A Squad, and then bump an existing top list woman to the B Squad.

Gail was still on the A Squad, but barely, Dupree thought. She sat down across from him and crossed her toned legs.

"Yes, sir," Gail said.

"You tracking this?"

"Tracking what?"

Dupree shook his head and thought that she was most likely

going to be B Squad before the week was over. Looks had to be coupled with precision and intelligence. That was why he liked Alex Russell. She was a beautiful and smart woman, definite A Squad material.

"Our customers can't seem to access their accounts today," Dupree said with patience.

"You mean some customers or all customers?"

"All, Gail. Every single one of them," Dupree said. "Come here."

"It's midnight. Are the IT guys doing an update?"

"Don't think so," Dupree said.

She walked around the large oak desk and stood next to him as she stared at the monitor that showed even longer wait times and more complaints than just a few minutes ago.

Dupree ran his hand up the back of her thigh, feeling the smoothness of her skin and her firm butt. He slid a finger inside her thong and gently rubbed her in the most sensitive places. She didn't flinch. This was not unusual behavior for him, and often, he surmised, she enjoyed it. He *always* enjoyed it, and if it took his mind off the events at hand, then so much the better.

Her eyes fluttered at his touch, but she held it together and said, "What would you like for me to do . . . about the customer complaints?"

"I think we need a statement, because the press is about thirty seconds from calling us. The statement needs to be proactive, indicating that we are working on the issue and that the government warned of a possible large hack, that we were prepared, and that we are fighting it."

He continued rubbing his finger inside her as she responded.

"I can do that," she mumbled.

He quickly removed his hand and stood up.

"So, let's get to it." He smiled. "In fact, let's call the press and make a proactive announcement that we have been hacked, that we are fighting it, and that we are requesting that the president declare a state of emergency."

All of that was true. And he knew who was behind the hack. Gavril and Zakir, the two Bulgarian hackers he had yet to kill but most assuredly planned to. Like boxers in a ring, they were slugging it out over the Dark Web. What Gavril didn't realize was that Dupree didn't care if United Bank of America was hacked and lost all of its money.

But first he picked up the phone and called Alex Russell.

CHAPTER 24

ALEX RUSSELL STOOD AT THE SAME PERCH SHE HAD THAT MORNING, unsure of her ability to maintain her persona as Alex Russell. She had injected the last of her meager supply of PKCzeta drug into her arm when she went upstairs briefly while Mahegan and Cassie waited downstairs. She needed more. Wanted more. Had to have more.

But the more she used the drug, the more she needed it. Already, the trauma was creeping back in. Nightmares. Daymares, as she called them, hallucinations, visions.

With the cops at her townhome, she had asked the sheriff, "Am I under arrest?"

"No, ma'am," he said.

"Am I being charged with anything?"

"No, ma'am," he said.

"Have you found me helpful in this investigation?"

"Yes, ma'am."

"Do you have any further questions for me?"

"Not at the moment, ma'am."

"Good. Then I'm going out for a while. You've got five police officers here. You've got a SWAT team in the valley, and you've got a helicopter up above burning gas."

Actually she had heard the helicopter pull off station to refuel, she presumed, but she had made her point.

She had left the sheriff standing there slack-jawed as she backed her Land Rover out of the garage and punched the button to lower the door. She wove past the police motorcycles that were parked in her driveway, waved at the cops who stared at her with confusion, and then sped back to her concealed perch just as the sun was setting.

She shivered again, her mind unraveling.

"Valid target," she whispered to no one.

She needed her boost, was jonesing for a PKCzeta protein inhibition and blocking shot. She craved the needle again, even hours after giving herself that shot.

Licking her lips, she watched as the men in black cargo pants and shirts massed at the entrance to the mine shaft. She knew Mahegan must be inside the tunnel. Why else would they be shooting a rocket-propelled grenade in there?

After the police had raided her townhome in search of Mahegan, she had watched with interest as the SWAT team first surrounded her vacation home and then entered after she came out with her hands up. She allowed them to search the entire house before telling the police that Mahegan had kidnapped Cassie Bagwell at knifepoint. She wasn't sure why she had purposefully misdirected the police. She knew she was struggling with the bad memories from Operation Groomsman and no matter how hard she tried, couldn't shake the demons that kept her awake at night.

Looking through the binoculars she watched men scurry into the tunnel, as if in pursuit. Had Mahegan found Savage and the others? She thought about General Savage and her love/hate relationship with him and his ex-wife, Vicki Savage—the now remarried and murdered Vicki Sledge. Alex would not claim credit for destroying the Savage's marriage, though she certainly could if she wanted to. Savage was a righteous, no-bullshit killing machine 99 percent of the time. Alex, though, had met him too many times at his Wood Lake farmhouse for late-night discussions about the job, combat, continuous rotations into theater, and battle losses. She had become his "work wife," which unexpectedly led to her fulfilling most of the role of any wife, including sex. Neither of them were proud of their transgressions, but neither were they embarrassed or ashamed. It had happened and that was that, as far as they were both concerned.

But Alex's divergence from herself had been the catalyst for Savage to sever the romantic relationship. After Operation Groomsman four years ago, their liaisons had lessened until they finally ceased altogether last year. She still saw him at work, and oddly their interactions were not awkward. Two professionals doing their jobs, dedicated to their country and missions. Or so he must have thought.

The wind licked Alex's face and she thought of the scrape of Savage's rough beard as he would kiss her. She missed that. Did she want it back? She wasn't sure. As she smelled the gunpowder wafting up the mountain, she was reminded of the shooting range behind the farmhouse and the storm doors that led to the COOP where all of this action had started a day ago.

Who was she, she wondered. Savage's JAG? His lover? A murderer? A traitor? Alex couldn't keep it all straight. She knew one thing for certain: She was going insane. Only the drugs helped her maintain any semblance of professional acumen in the office.

She felt her phone buzz in the pocket of her black dungarees and retrieved it. Yves Dupree. What could he want?

Sure, she had slept with him, also. He was a playboy and had a stable of women, but she also needed information from him. She knew things about Yves Dupree that no one else knew. She knew that he had lived in Paris prior to the November 2015 attacks. She also had been able to trace his rather complicated list of limited liability companies, one of which had cash withdrawals over $20,000 in the weeks leading up to the Paris attacks that had killed at least 130 people. And her dossier on him showed he was pivotal in Operation Groomsman.

She shook her head and said to herself, "So, Yves, what do you want now?" Lifting the phone to her ear, she swiped the answer bar on the screen and said to him, "Yes?"

"Alex, how are you?"

"Peachy," she replied. Keeping cool and aloof, although difficult to do, seemed to be her best option at the moment.

"I thought I would tell you that we are being hacked in a big way," Yves said.

"Define 'we,' " Alex replied.

"The United Bank of America. UBA. Our customers. Our businesses. First there are kidnappings and murders of military leaders and their families. Then there is a remote access Trojan delivered by automobile service centers to millions of cars across the country, causing them to stop at precisely nine this morning. And now there is a full-scale cyberattack on one of the biggest banks in the nation."

"Tell me something I don't know," Alex said.

"Right. I'm wondering where General Savage and his homeland security team might be."

"I have negative knowledge at the moment, Yves."

Alex continued watching the mayhem in the valley. She needed Savage back alive. She wanted Mahegan alive as well. She wasn't sure what she wanted out of Dupree, except maybe money and another good bout of sex. It all depended on who she felt like being on any particular day. Her throat clenched a bit as she remembered a day and time where she was the focused combat JAG fighting the good fight for America. Now all that had changed, and she was talking to a thieving Frenchman, of all people, on the phone as she watched a giant clusterfuck happen in the valley.

How could things go so wrong? Had she forgotten something? Was her memory really that bad?

"Yves, baby. Stay calm. I'll find Savage. Everything will be okay," she said.

And she was crazy enough to believe that it would be.

CHAPTER 25

MAHEGAN ROCKETED ALONG THE SMOOTH FLOWSTONE AS IF HE were a space capsule plunging into the ocean after a moonshot. He had been underwater for twenty-four seconds by his count, unable to take a breath. He was vaguely aware that he was still clenching Owens's feet beneath his armpits.

While he was an advanced swimmer and waterman, most people couldn't hold their breath for more than thirty seconds without freaking out. His mind shifted to his teammates behind him. Could Savage survive? Owens? O'Malley? Had Cassie even made it into the river?

He was in a sudden free-fall. Mahegan welcomed the feel of air and water rushing past him. He gobbled a breath somehow, even though water continued to rain down upon him, forcing him downward. Opening his eyes was difficult. He was inside the heavy flow of a waterfall. The further he fell, the more he could see. Eventually, the faint relief of ridges and valleys, some lighter shades of black, some darker, came into view. The moon cast its nighttime glow through the falling shards of water, making Mahegan sense he was inside a twirling kaleidoscope. The farther he traveled from the lip of the cavern, the more the water spread and dissipated. He broke the first rule of the paratrooper and looked at the ground beneath him as it rushed toward him.

The moon was reflecting off a large body of water, which gave him hope that their fall would be absorbed by the forgiving buoyancy of the reservoir below. He crossed his feet and held his arms to his chest, clutching Owens's ankles against his ribs. He hoped the daisy chain of people above him remained intact.

Mahegan's feet hit the water, and he continued plowing deep, as if propelled by his team above. He felt Owens's feet jar loose, and Mahegan opened his arms so that his friend would be free to kick to the surface. Though he was still torqueing into the water, Mahegan began flapping his arms to slow his descent. He needed to surface, find his team, and get them to land where he could oxygenate them if necessary.

Mahegan hit bottom, flexed his knees, and then pushed off, boring his way to the surface, splashing upward and sucking in a giant gulp of air. He felt the shockwaves of more bodies plunging near him. He paddled back two strokes as he watched Cassie fall into the water. He assumed Savage and O'Malley had already made entry. Quickly Owens and O'Malley surfaced with a limp Savage between them. Mahegan recognized their faces in the pale moonlight, the only glimmer of light in the utter darkness this deep into the mountains. Owens and O'Malley floated Savage onto his back. Mahegan could see they had him moving in the right direction toward a small slice of shoreline.

"I'll get Cassie," Mahegan said.

"Think she got hurt," O'Malley said.

O'Malley would know. He was the last to leave the cavern before Cassie.

Mahegan dove into the clear water and saw Cassie's pale face amidst the black water. Her short blond hair was lifting slightly from her scalp. Her arms were above her head, but she was sinking, not rising. She had the rucksack on her back, and her left arm seemed to have a chunk of skin scalloped out, a dark trail of blood caught in the moonlight beneath the water like a smoky vapor. Her wound could have been from enemy fire or from a rock cut as they were barreling down the tube. He swam to her and lifted her immediately. Grabbing her by her torso, he kicked upward. A bubble of air escaped her mouth. She had not done well in the twenty-five-second underwater portion of the escape.

If she had been shot, most likely she would have lacked the wherewithal to suck in a deep breath prior to submersion into the funnel of water. He kept kicking with his boots as he reached for his knife and cut the straps on her rucksack. Holding the rucksack in one hand and Cassie in the other, he continued thrusting his way to the surface.

Finally cresting, he pulled hard toward the shore, where he could see Owens administering mouth-to-mouth to Savage as O'Malley held an AR-15 up at eye level, searching for threats. Even though his friends had been out of the service for a couple of years, their combat skills returned easily.

Reaching the shore on all fours, he said, "She's not okay. There's a first aid kit in this. Grab it." He handed the rucksack to O'Malley, who rested the rifle against his shoulder and pawed through the contents. Mahegan stood and dragged Cassie to the sandy outcropping, then immediately began pumping her chest, followed by forcing oxygen into her lungs.

"She was shot in the arm," O'Malley said. "Five-five-six round. Lucky thing. I saw it happen. Bastards came around the corner right when we were going under. Instead of jumping into the river, she turned to fire, grabbed the grenade, and threw it back at them. Ballsy move."

"Stop her bleeding and I'll get her breathing," Mahegan said between heavy chest compressions and mouth-to-mouth.

In his periphery a few feet away Owens was working on Savage, saying, "Come on, old man, you ain't dead yet."

Mahegan tilted Cassie's head as she began to vomit. She spit up some water, but mostly bile and digested Clif Bars. He kept compressing her until more vomit came up, this time mostly water. She coughed, gasping for air, and opened her eyes.

"You're okay. Stay still. Sean's working on your arm. You've been shot. No biggie," Mahegan said. She was confused, disoriented. Spittle drained on either side of her lips and chin. She had done well, not that she needed to acquit herself of anything. He spent maybe a second more than he wanted contemplating her actions of the last twenty-four hours, then nodded and stood.

He hustled to where Owens was working on Savage, who began coughing and puking, though Savage sat upright and put his hands on either side of himself.

"Where the hell am I?" he said, spitting out water and coughing, his voice sounding like the gravel upon which they sat.

"You're in good hands, boss," Owens said to the general.

"Patch? Whiskey Tango Foxtrot." Savage shook his head, revealing a spark of the flint that was Savage's signature stare.

"We'll explain in a bit. We've got to get Jake and Sean moving with Cassie," Owens said.

Savage shook his face again and wiped his mouth, looking older than Mahegan had ever seen him. He turned his head toward Mahegan.

"Jake? They told me you were behind all of this."

"Not me, General, though I did just save your ass."

"Technically, we all did," Owens said.

"What do I tell you guys about taking credit for shit?" Savage barked.

"Well, the good news, General, is that we don't work for you anymore," Mahegan said.

"The hell you don't. The nation is under attack. Those bastards have hacked everything. Even Zebra. They sent us all fake messages that you were in trouble. Fucking *en fuego.* So we all came to rescue your ass and got ambushed by a bunch of terrorists who immigrated under the refugee protection status. I was conscious for most of the torture and faked passing out, hoping they'd slip up. They did."

"They tell you what was in that crate near your prison cell?"

"They didn't tell me jack, son, but I listened when they thought I was dead. These are Syrians who infiltrated with the refugee flow that our genius leadership advocated," Savage said.

Mahegan nodded. That confirmed his suspicions. A combination of sophisticated cyberattack coupled with a ground force to exploit the chaos.

Savage coughed again. "What the hell is Cassie Bagwell doing here?"

"She's the daughter of the chairman—"

"I know who the hell she is," Savage barked. "She's that Ranger woman. Why is she here?"

"Her parents have been kidnapped," Mahegan said. "Just like you, Patch, and Sean."

"Bart Bagwell? Kidnapped?"

"Yes. And his wife," Mahegan said. "A sniper killed General Sizemore in Iraq. A terrorist team raided General Jackson's family on Fort Bragg and killed them. General Leland's computer at CENTCOM was found with child pornography on it. He has been arrested by the FBI. And then there was you, Patch, and Sean. And the president and his cabinet are locked in the basement of the White House. Today there was a cyberattack on about a million vehicles. They just stopped running at nine this morning, wherever they were. Wrecks everywhere. Fatalities. Casualties."

"Classic," Savage said.

"Decap op," Owens said.

"Roger," Mahegan added. "Hamper our ability to respond as the Syrians hit us."

"Only means one thing," Savage said.

"What's that?" Mahegan asked.

"That somebody knows who you guys are. You've been burned as my off-the-books team," Savage said.

"We get that, but who?" Mahegan said. "What do you know about Alex Russell?"

"Alex? What does she have to do with this?"

"She was in the COOP. I avoided an ambush that I'm assuming was similar to the ones you guys faced. I immediately went to the COOP, as per protocol. She showed up about twenty minutes after I did. Did you give her the combination?"

Savage paused, thinking. Mahegan could see him shake his head. The sound of rushing water drowned out their conversation, as well as the sound of anyone who might be attempting to approach them.

"Alex Russell," Savage whispered. "I'll be damned." Savage

sucked in a deep breath. "Just get us moving, Jake. I'll tell you everything you need to know once we get somewhere safe."

Mahegan nodded, formed the team, and led them through the valley, following the stream downhill as it fed out of a dam. The going was rough, but they needed to get as far away from the terrorist base camp as possible so that they could regroup, share intelligence, and develop a plan.

The feeling of teamwork, however minor, was something that Mahegan missed, but not until the past couple of hours had he realized how essential men such as O'Malley and Owens were to him. Mahegan was a loner, true, and he could operate well by himself, but the concept of reliable teammates was something that had always been important to him.

Mahegan led the team as they trudged through the dense forest. The moonlight was sufficient for navigation, and Mahegan caught the reflection of a white, dirt trail off to their right. He led the team up the hill, through some dense underbrush, and up a ditch. Normally he would avoid a road, considering it a danger area with terrorists in the vicinity, but he needed to trade off speed for security, so he moved his team there. Unless the terrorists had drones or some type of tracking mechanism, Mahegan felt the risk of compromise was minimal given their need to find shelter. The cool night risked hypothermia for the three men who had been prisoners, and he needed to get them to warmth.

The road switched back and forth in a series of hairpin turns as it followed the ridgeline, avoiding diving into the severely undulating terrain. After an hour of walking, they came upon a wide gravel road to the east, their right. They had been moving mostly east and then had started angling north. Now it looked like he had found an old campground. As they walked into the open area, they came upon a rundown A-frame that looked as if it might have once served as camp headquarters.

"In there," Mahegan said. The building was cut into the woods so that it was barely visible. The circular drive upon which they walked was riddled with overgrown alfalfa and rye grass, some patches reaching chest high. Mahegan walked up the stone porch to the building, tested the rusted doorknob, and leaned his shoulder against the warped door. It gave and he stepped inside, using the flashlight under the rail of the AR-15. Clearing the building room by room, he found nothing but rotting wood and spiderwebs. In the back rooms, there were a few bunks without mattresses. In the front there was a kitchen without running water and a family room with a fireplace.

They were all cold from a combination of being wet, sweating on the walk, and the crisp evening, but a fire was out of the question.

"This is as good as it gets for tonight," Mahegan said.

"At least it blocks the wind," Owens said.

Mahegan looked at his charges highlighted by the sliver of moonlight cutting through the milky windowpane. Savage leaned against the closed door at his back. Mahegan could see pain in the man's eyes as he tried to control his shivering body. Cassie slid her back against the wall until she was sitting upright, legs splayed out, arm in a sling. Owens and O'Malley were standing in the kitchen, looking out the windows.

"We can stay here four or five hours, tops," Owens said.

"I'm thinking until sunrise. We get some rack. Divide among the five of us whatever is left in Cassie's rucksack. Drink water. Make a plan. Just like old times," Mahegan said. "But we've got to get you guys warm, too."

"Roger that. Build a fire," O'Malley said, pointing at the empty fireplace.

"Maybe for a short while. They'll come after us," Mahegan said. Then he had an idea.

"What was in that damn crate?" O'Malley asked no one in particular.

"I'll tell you what they said when they thought I was dead," Savage said. He leaned forward from the door and walked toward his former charges.

"We've got headlights coming down the road," Owens said. "I'm counting three vehicles. Look like pickup trucks but not sure. Maybe two miles out."

Mahegan looked at the AR-15 he was carrying. He had maybe half a magazine. He quickly walked to Cassie and started pawing through her rucksack.

"Three mags of 5.56, two mags of 9 mil, five grenades, five Clif Bars, two pair of socks, a space blanket, a pack of matches in a waterproof bag, some kite string, and maybe four water bottles left. That's what I've got," Cassie said. "Oh, and the hatchet in your belt." She grimaced as she pointed at his waist.

"You good to move?"

"I'm good. Hurts, but I'm good."

Mahegan took the hand grenades and ammunition magazines and passed them out to O'Malley and Owens, who each had an AR-15 that they had secured from the first two Syrians they had ambushed in the tunnel.

"You got anything to get me out of this stupid-looking Batman outfit?" Savage asked.

"Best we can do right now, boss. Helps you fly if you need it," Mahegan said with half a smirk.

"I'm freezing my ass off, Mahegan."

"You always tell us not to snivel. None of us have any extra gear. We'll keep you safe. Just stay alive."

"You can use this," Cassie said, holding up a folded space blanket, a reflective coating on one side. It was a Mylar wrap used by emergency personnel.

"No thanks, Ranger. You need that more than me," Savage said. Mahegan couldn't determine whether Savage was being sarcastic or not with the "Ranger" comment.

"We need to get moving," Owens said, clicking a fresh magazine into the well. "They're maybe a mile out, winding down the road and coming right at us."

"Okay, everybody out the back. Cassie, I need to borrow your ruck. I'll link up in a few minutes. Patch, you take charge and get everyone in defensive posture. Give the general a pistol if we have to arm him."

"Why?" Savage asked. "So I can shoot myself?"

"Go," Mahegan said. Patch Owens took charge, moving O'Malley and Savage toward the back door and helping Cassie stand. He ushered her toward the rear of the building.

Mahegan got to work with the hatchet and the contents of Cassie's rucksack and finished in less than three minutes, then met his team in the dense forest behind the house.

"Smoke?" Owens asked.

"Yeah, smoke," Mahegan said. "Everyone okay?"

"We're okay, but Savage told me what was in the crate. It ain't good," Owens said.

He looked at them, their eyes peering back at him as if they were feral animals.

"It's a damn tactical nuke," Savage muttered as the first shot echoed toward them through the night.

CHAPTER 26

ZAKIR WAS FURIOUS.

He had stood at the edge of the flowing river inside the cave and still wondered how the Americans had escaped.

It was Mahegan, he was sure, but he still was confused as to why Mahegan was not under control. He had been assured that the commando would not be a factor.

Now he led a column of three pickup trucks toward Mahegan and the former captives. Zakir had placed tracking devices in the pants of two of the prisoners. With bare feet and bare chests, and now soaking wet, he doubted they would think to remove their only article of clothing. It had taken a few minutes for their position to appear on Gavril's computer screen.

Busy with the skimming operation of five major banking networks, Gavril was slow to notice the alert that the prisoners were outside of the compound. Zakir, though, had prompted him, and Gavril shared the screen with his computer in the mountain base camp so that Zakir could follow the two escapees. Zakir made the assumption that they would all stick together, as the blinking lights on the computer seemed to indicate so far.

Zakir waited until he could determine the direction Mahegan and his men were moving before chasing them. When they moved to the road, he used Google Earth to scan likely destinations, saw three possibilities, and determined that they would likely enter the first structure they could. The temperature was dropping into the low fifties, and while that was a very comfortable temperature for hiking at night through the mountains, it would not be comfortable for the wet and hungry prisoners who had escaped.

It was after midnight, and he had other pieces of the plan to put into action. He couldn't afford the time required to snuff out this menace, but then again could he afford not to? Their entire plan had been predicated on disabling Savage and his crew of independent operators. Thus far, they had been executing well.

The cars had been disabled. They had skimmed millions of dollars from personal and business bank accounts. But these were preliminary missions setting the stage for the slash-and-burn tactics to come. Meaningful destruction coupled with psychological fear—and there was much to fear.

Into the handheld personal mobile radio, Zakir said, "Stop here."

The three pickup trucks held up short of the wooden building, their headlights off now. The moon and ambient starlight were highlighting the weatherworn structure. Two years ago, in his scouting of this region for their base camp, Zakir had studied this building in depth. He knew the floor plan and the surrounding area. He also knew human nature. The prisoners had been beaten. Mahegan had been on the go for two days. They had exchanged fire with his men. They were traveling with a woman who had possibly been injured in the gunfire. Their adrenaline would be dumping right now.

"Smoke," he said, pointing at the chimney. He chuckled. "They've built a fire. Just as I suspected." From the comfort of his pickup truck bench seat, he radioed his men. "We will approach from the west along that ridge with the shallow ditch. Follow my lead."

Zakir had his men park the trucks a quarter mile away, and then walk through the woods to the west of the building. He kept his eye on the smoke, spotlighted by the brilliant moon and drifting lazily to the east.

"Remember," he said to the team leader in Arabic, "we must

keep Savage and Mahegan alive if possible. Kill the others . . . and kill them all if you can't avoid it."

He knelt next to a large tree and looked across the open area, maybe twenty yards, to the building. To his right were six men, three teams, who would surprise Mahegan and his sleeping crew. He had handpicked six of his best to perform this mission. Already he had lost two men in the assault on the fire tower, two men near the general's prison cell inside the mine shaft, and several others. His team of highly trained professional killers had now been whittled to fourteen. This was his primary assault force, and his battle calculus told him he needed at least fifteen men to execute the final mission. If he included himself, he could still accomplish his task.

Killing or capturing Mahegan and Savage would pave the way to successful mission accomplishment.

He tapped his first man on the shoulder and pointed at the house. Standing, he watched the first two men dash across the open area. He was not surprised that they had received no fire from Mahegan and his team. Now, more than ever, he was convinced they were asleep. Zakir tapped the second two-man team, and they dashed across the dirt lot and skillfully lined up behind the first two men on the near side of the front door. Finally, he said, "Stay with me," to the last two men. "We will provide covering fire."

Zakir's heart was racing. He had fought in combat with ISIS in Syria and northern Iraq after Operation Groomsman. With every kill he felt a sense of despair instead of the fulfillment he sought. Whether burning someone alive in a cage or beheading them on camera, Zakir knew that he needed to come to America to kill the man who had killed Malavdi, his best friend.

But Jackknife—who was truly in charge—had forbade him to kill Savage or Mahegan before Jackknife said it was time. They needed to be off the battlefield, neutralized, but Jackknife, too, had an axe to grind with Mahegan and Savage, apparently.

Zakir didn't care as long as the men died at his hand. Tonight or tomorrow, it didn't matter. They would all be dead soon, regardless.

He watched as the lead man ran up the steps and used his boot to kick in the door. Instantly a yellow flame licked out and an explosion blew apart the front part of the house. Zakir had been watching with both eyes open and was now momentarily blinded in the night. He felt the two men to his side stiffen, as if they wanted to run to the aid of their comrades, but Zakir said, "No, wait. Watch."

When he regained his vision, Zakir spotted two of his men on their backs several yards from the building. He assumed they were dead. The two men who had been the third and fourth in the stack against the building were crouched, turned away from the heat, but still preparing to enter the inferno to find Mahegan and Savage, their last orders. He had trained his men well. Suddenly, both commandos dropped to the ground as if they were puppets and someone had cut their strings.

Without warning, Zakir felt the supersonic rush of a bullet snap past him. He heard the impact on one of his men kneeling against the opposite side of the tree. Another shot rang out. How had their position been compromised? He stood and ran quickly back to the trucks, where he attempted to crank the engine.

As the engine churned, he shouted into his handheld radio, "Launch the Skunk, now!"

Mahegan had led his team from the south of the building to the far east side, expecting the terrorists to follow the natural drift of the terrain, park, and walk to assault and support positions, as any reasonably trained unit might do.

He tapped Owens on the shoulder and pointed north, toward the trucks, indicating for him to keep an eye on any terrorists attempting to escape back toward their rides. Those trucks would soon become Mahegan's ride if his plan worked. To his left was O'Malley, whom he had sighted on the men running across the hardpan. Mahegan had Cassie and Savage directly behind him.

They carried pistols for self-defense but were wounded and not part of the plan.

As the terrorists stacked against the wall, Mahegan tapped O'Malley, the sign to shoot once the first man opened the door. The two hand grenades that Mahegan had rigged using the kite string exploded and created the havoc he desired. O'Malley's AR-15 was on single-shot mode, and he fired it exactly four times, two of which might have been overkill on the bleeding men who had been first in the building. The flames that churned at the front of the wooden building were enough for O'Malley to use the iron sights. He shot the third and fourth men in their heads, dropping them instantly. He watched as O'Malley put two more bullets in the dying men, who had been first to enter the building.

Mahegan felt the momentum shifting his way, their way. Ever since he had been ambushed in Pinehurst he felt as though he were at least one step behind. Now, in this tactical setting, he had some control, could use his skills.

He tapped Owens, who had found the three men in the small ditch to the northwest of the property, where Mahegan had expected them to coalesce. It was an obvious rally point: well concealed, large trees for protection, and positional advantage above the building. Mahegan had built the fire to seduce the terrorists into believing that they were resting and drying out, which they desperately needed to do.

Owens used his AR-15 to snap off two quick shots, then he angled the rifle to take a third shot at a running man, perhaps the last of the group to be alive. As Owens was sighting, Cassie tumbled into him, knocking his aim off course.

"Damnit," Owens said.

"What the hell?" Mahegan said, turning around. Cassie was attempting to get up, holding her pistol in her good hand. Her other arm was in the sling.

"Sorry," she said, sheepishly. "Was trying to help."

"Focus, Patch," Mahegan said, turning back around and ignoring Cassie.

"He's in the truck. I've got a shot—Damnit, what the hell?"

Cassie bumped Owens again as she was standing up in the thick underbrush.

"I swear to God that was an accident," Cassie said. "I'm not used to this sling."

They watched the pickup truck disappear up the mountain road as if it were a vanishing ghost.

Mahegan stared at her from his kneeling position. They had killed six of seven terrorists. Probably would have had seven of seven if Cassie hadn't stumbled.

"Why are you even moving?" Mahegan asked her.

"Pain," Cassie said. "I'm eating some pain right now and just needed to move."

Mahegan eyed her suspiciously, wondering if she had intentionally caused Owens to botch the shot. Refocusing on his plan, he said, "Sean, help Cassie and Savage. Apparently she's not as able as we thought. Get them to the remaining two trucks. Get inside and turn the heaters on. Look out for IEDs or booby traps. Doubtful but possible. They hadn't planned on us living."

"Roger that, boss," O'Malley said.

"Patch, let's you and me go inspect these dudes."

"With you," Owens said.

And like that, they were all moving as if they were back in Afghanistan or Iraq or Syria. The teamwork, the comradery, all of the things that Mahegan had lived for and fought for. True, he loved his country, but he loved his men even more. He had fought for them, and he would die for them. Those emotions came back with force as he and Patch Owens slowly moved across the hardpan in front of the smoldering building in the middle of the night in the Pisgah National Forest.

They inspected each dead man. They had papers and documents in their pockets. Without taking the time to analyze anything, Mahegan and Owens stuffed everything in their cargo pockets. The two men who had entered the booby-trapped building had died instantly, shrapnel chewing off half their faces. They were burned badly and hot to the touch. Mahegan scraped whatever charred remnants of information he could from their outer tactical vests and cargo pants pockets. They collected four AR-15s and twelve magazines of ammunition. Two of the men also had Sig Sauer pistols, not unlike Mahegan's Sig Sauer Tribal but not nearly as well kept. One of the two men in the ditch was still alive.

"One head shot and one in the upper chest?"

"Lucky to get the head shot," Owens said.

"This guy's moaning. Let's see if we can't patch him up and get him to talk," Mahegan said. "Also, grab the uniforms off the others. I think you and Sean are burned with your pants."

"Trackers?"

"Yes."

"Roger. I'll go get one of the trucks and we can slide him in the back," Owens said. "Help me get the uniforms."

They quickly removed the uniforms from two of the dead men and bundled them up.

"Okay, this is a pretty good haul. Do that and then we'll figure out our next move," Mahegan said.

Owens returned quickly with a Mitsubishi extended cab black pickup truck. It looked relatively new. Owens helped him with the wounded terrorist, and they slid him into the bed.

"He's got a sucking chest wound. I put an MRE wrapper on it and wrapped some flex tape around his chest. This guy was carrying a damn U.S. combat ration."

"That's good news. Means they're running out of shit to eat," Owens joked.

Mahegan said, "Let's get rolling."

They were in the Mitsubishi and pulled up next to O'Malley, who had Savage lying down in the back portion of the cab and Cassie sitting in the passenger bucket seat.

"Where to?" O'Malley asked through his open window.

"These things probably have trackers on them. And I wouldn't be surprised if they had drones or if they were setting up ambushes along the roads, so keep some distance," Mahegan said.

"Where we going?" O'Malley asked.

"To Target," Mahegan said.

As he looked through the windshield, the first round fired from the drone was headed directly at the windshield.

CHAPTER 27

ALEX RUSSELL HUGGED HER KNEES IN THE FREEZING COLD AS THE wind whipped past her. The temperature had dropped significantly, and she was not properly dressed for an evening on top of a windswept mountain in late September.

She used a night vision goggle to observe the activity down below, wondering what was happening. She had seen three trucks leave but only one return. What did that mean?

Had Mahegan rescued Savage and the others?

She began having another one of her nightmares, though she was wide awake, shivering and needing the needle. She needed her pills, too, so she dug a cold hand into her pocket and shook the bottle with a disappointing rattle. She could tell there were only a few pills left in the prescription bottle. She chewed hard through two clonazepam, swallowing them dry. Almost instantly she felt her mind begin to smooth out, but she stayed with the dream, her fugue state.

She became Ameri Assad, her alter ego. Ameri was a bad, nasty bitch.

Ameri had meant to kill Mahegan on that road, but he had vanished into the woods before she could react. Not usually Ameri's problem, but silly Alex had taken her meds, confusing the issue as to who was truly in charge. If it were Ameri, well, she shot first and asked questions later.

While Alex Russell still had questions for Jake Mahegan and

what he had seen on the ground during Operation Groomsman, Ameri Assad couldn't give a rat's ass. To kill him now would leave Alex's questions unanswered, but Ameri was fine with unanswered questions even if they were important questions to Alex. Awake and disoriented, Alex gave way easily to Ameri, who would appear instantly, like a doppelganger.

The moon sweeping the sky and stars swirling around her, she stood in the middle of the night appearing as disoriented as she felt. She lifted her arms upward as if she were doing a sun salutation, but to the moon. Chuckling to herself, "Yes, a moon salutation. Perfect."

She ran her hand along the smooth contours of her Berretta pistol, removed it from her hip holster, and placed the barrel in her mouth. She bit onto the hard metal, tasting gun oil, smelling the round that was chambered. She placed her finger on the trigger mechanism and felt that it was taught, maybe a pound or two of pressure to fire the hammer.

She laughed a deep-throated laugh, the barrel bouncing on the roof of her mouth. This was how Ameri felt about Alex, that Alex deserved to die for what she had done. Combat stress, post-traumatic stress disorder, other stressors such as what was happening right now in the valley below her, all combined to make Ameri well upward and outward.

Ameri made Alex begin to pace on the ridgeline between the towering birch and pine trees, muttering. For four years Ameri had been torturing Alex. Sleepless nights, endless days, relentless thoughts. Twenty pounds lost from a lithe frame that couldn't bear to lose ten.

But somehow she stuck with it. Stayed with the unit and stayed with Savage, who never let a loyal soldier leave his grasp. And while she knew where Savage had been, in the mine shaft, he was of limited use, other than to serve as bait for Mahegan, which had worked. Now she had no idea where they were but was certain they would be back, either as captives or hunters. Her perch was just fine to watch the action and strike when she wanted.

Ameri forced Alex's mind back to that awful day four years ago during Operation Groomsman. The memory was fuel for Ameri's ability to materialize. Without the haunting confrontation, Ameri would not exist. Ameri knew that those PKCzeta shots had begun to erase the memory of the brutal bombing that she had watched in real time and then hundreds of times over and over in slow motion, seeing the Hellfire missile strike her sister's SUV and then the JDAM bombs raining down like lethal lawn darts, exploding and maiming.

Yes, Alex Russell had given the valid target order to kill her sister, though she had not known her sister, Fatima, was in the convoy.

The trauma, the despair, the wanting to take it all back but knowing that she couldn't. Two words. Valid target. Two words said so many times they became meaningless.

And why had she given the clearance? The intelligence seemed to signal that al-Baghdadi was in the convoy. Intelligence provided by Cassie Bagwell and her special intelligence team in Mosul. Unrelated to JSOC, Cassie's intel unit provided high-value target information to General Savage's killers. Even if al-Baghdadi had been in the convoy, would it have been worth the loss of her sister?

No, of course not, which was why Ameri Assad appeared before her like an apparition, scolding her, dominating her, and now guiding her to a righteous solution to her problems.

Ameri removed the pistol from Alex's mouth slowly, reminding her who was in charge. She aimed the pistol at Alex's forehead and made a "bang" sound.

Bang.

Yes, it was Alex's voice and Alex's hand, but it was Ameri who was alive in her mind. It was Ameri who could return Alex to full mental health or take her down a spiraling path of insanity. Ameri's solution, of course, meant that she would in effect work herself out of a job. If she resolved Alex Russell's mental issues by killing Savage and Mahegan, or at least having someone else kill them, then Ameri would be able to let go and be with her sister, with Allah.

So Ameri grabbed Alex Russell's face by the chin—of course it was Alex's hand—and made her stare at the memory that Ameri played like a high-definition video in Alex's mind.

Savage had been there, next to her in the forward command post. His dominant aura permeated the small van as they had leaned close together, shoulder to shoulder. She could smell his sweat.

Savage had turned to her as they watched the Predator streaming video of the SUVs flying down the road in column toward a high-walled compound a mile away.

"Need to make the shot in the next fifteen seconds," Savage said.

Alex hesitated, taking deep breaths. She knew her sister was getting married to a man from Bulgaria. She had been invited but had kept her Syrian lineage hidden all these years. She couldn't afford to give away her identity just yet. She had been raised in Newark, New Jersey, as Alex Russell, not Ameri Assad, her birth name. Thirty years ago, when Ameri was just a toddler, her father had turned on his brother, the president of Syria, Hafez al-Assad, attempting a coup that was never reported. An *Et tu, Brute* type of internal attack that failed. Hafez had no problem personally executing her father and mother while sparing Ameri and her sister, Fatima.

Ameri turned on another Netflix original in Alex's mind. This was a movie of when she was four years old and playing in the dirt lot next to their home in Damascus. She and Fatima were pushing a baby carriage with their prized porcelain doll, a gift from a visiting dignitary, someone who had met with their uncle, the president. It was a Queen V Fashion Royalty Doll, and they had no business bouncing it around in the rocky, windswept field. But Fatima and Ameri were sisters and best friends, just a year apart in age. Ameri was the eldest and therefore was responsible for Fatima. They took turns holding and rocking the valuable doll as they stood next to their home in the Malki neighborhood. Beautiful jasmine trees lined the road, and even at that young age Ameri appreciated that she lived in a good neighborhood flush with other children her age. But Fatima was her best buddy. They were taking turns holding the Queen V doll that they had named Queenie, or *Kuayni* in Arabic.

Fatami began trying to sing the Syrian lullaby, "Fly, fly, dove . . ." as Ameri was handing Kuayni to Fatima. Ameri looked over her shoulder. Two black SUVs stopped in front of their house. Three men carrying small machine guns exited the first. Two men from each SUV went into the house, and she heard gunfire. One man from each SUV walked directly toward them. Ameri pulled Fatima close, each clutching Kuayni. Suddenly, one man snatched her by the waist, her cotton dress fluttering in the breeze, her white socks falling around her ankles over her shiny black shoes. She screamed as another man snatched Fatima.

"No!" Ameri was reaching her hands out, clutching nothing but air. Fatima was doing the same as Kuayni shattered, its face oddly watching Ameri as she cried for her sister.

"Ameri!" Fatima shouted.

"Fatima!" Ameri shouted.

They were locked in separate SUVs. The men who had gone in the house quickly returned to the vehicles. Ameri heard one man say, "It is done."

That was the last she had seen Fatima. A boat ride and a plane flight later, she was with a new family in Newark, New Jersey, crying herself to sleep every night, singing, "Fly, fly, dove . . ." and wondering where Fatima might be, longing for her.

Time marched on and assimilation became paramount. New friends, new sisters and brothers, albeit not blood, became her life. She even began to like her new identity as Alex Russell.

Alex had moved on, Ameri tucked securely in a file cabinet in her mind. But it turned out that the file cabinet was a weak prison cell door that Ameri easily breached on the day of Operation Groomsman.

The marvels of social media had allowed a curious but infinitely more objective Alex Russell to find Fatima. Fatima had met a young boy named Malavdi in the orphanage near her Syrian village. They became friends and then later became lovers. Malavdi had moved. He was a computer expert who lived in Bulgaria. He was an orphan, not unlike Fatima and Ameri. Fatima had returned to Syria, working in the refugee camps with the United Nations. She spoke many languages and had become invaluable as an interpreter for all sides of the conflict. She had met men such as her uncle Bashar, who was now president, without his knowing who she was, nor did she tell him. Fatima had also met men such as al-Baghdadi as she translated for Syrian rebel forces attempting to negotiate a land dispute. All of this was captured on Facebook, Twitter, and Instagram.

Then Fatima and Malavdi vacationed a few days near Gavril's apartment on the Black Sea in the small town of Burgas. She became pregnant. There was an announcement on Instagram when they became engaged. The picture of Fatima and Malavdi holding each other with the Black Sea in the background warmed Alex's heart. Her sister had found love. And as if to signal Ameri, Fatima had written, "Fly, fly, dove . . ." on the Instagram post and put the hashtag #sisters.

But Fatima, ever the optimist it appeared, insisted that they get married in the village in which she had grown up along the Iraqi border near the town of al Hasakah, a confluence of five rivers that created the Khabur River, which fed the Euphrates. They were holding the wedding in a large compound in the tiny village of Marqadah, which placed them perilously close to the Iraqi border. The refugee camp was long gone, but her childhood village remained.

Of course as Operation Groomsman began to unfold, Alex Russell was in combat mode, focused. She wasn't tracking the names of towns, just the legitimacy of the target on an open road. How could she know it was Fatima and Malavdi's wedding party?

Stop it. Stop it. Ameri scolded Alex at her rationalizations.

"You gave the permission," she said. Of course it was Alex Russell's voice, but it was Ameri Assad talking.

She *had* given General Savage the "valid target" go-ahead for a mission that killed not only civilians but her sister.

And that son of a bitch Mahegan had seen the carnage first-hand. Inspected the bodies. Filed the report. Had information. Information that she still needed.

After Mahegan and his men had raided the wreckage, most likely executing the survivors, and then departed, she and Savage had flown into the scene with a small security team. She remembered the smell of burning rubber and flesh. The simmering heat that encapsulated the area like walking through invisible doors into an inferno. Then she put it all together. Hasakah. Marqadah. The towns. The road. The wedding date. Then the sound of her voice screaming seemed disembodied then as it did now with every nightmare. Did she know at the time that it was her sister charred black in the SUV? None of the bodies were recognizable. But she *knew*, and it was enough then to send her over the edge. When positive identification came back on the victims, Alex Russell took leave for two weeks, found her doctor through that liaison in the Caribbean, and finally wound up with her doctor and his Boradine experimental PKCzeta treatment. She ate benzodiazepines as if they were candy, anything to suppress the memory and the wild thoughts cycling through her mind.

She paid the doctor for the ability to self-administer the PKCzeta treatments that helped begin the erasure of her memory. Two solid weeks she had been strapped to the table and given the shots and eaten the pills and came out the other side feeling not normal, but like she could fake normal.

And that was good enough.

But there was Ameri, who appeared out of nowhere. And Ameri was pissed off. She was no longer the scared child reaching out her hands to her younger sister as men carted her away. She was a grown woman capable of righting every wrong.

Ameri wanted to fight America in America, not Syria. Ameri wanted to kill. She was bloodthirsty but knew that her survival within Alex consisted of being able to make Alex survive and fake being Alex when she needed to be Alex, like when walking through the halls of the JSOC compound or reading over inane legal documents, all of which were necessary fodder to keep up the illusion of Alex Russell.

So Ameri was patient, nudging Alex to perform properly during the day but giving her free reign off duty. The drugs actually hurt Ameri, because the drugs were making Alex forget the horrible murder of her sister, a murder in which she was complicit.

Ameri knew that Fatima and Malavdi had paid a price that warranted retribution. Ameri would seek that revenge through Alex Russell. She would find a way to make General Savage and Captain Mahegan pay a price worse than being burned to death by a Hellfire missile.

They would feel hellfire.

Alex walked along the rim of a ledge that dropped at least one thousand feet straight down. She held her arms out as if she was walking a tightrope, balancing. In her right hand was her pistol, making her lean more toward the open air than the land to her left. She sang the children's song *"Hamama, nodi, nodi . . ."*

Dove. Fly. Fly.

She slipped but caught herself, or more properly, Ameri caught Alex. Alex was too valuable for Ameri to let her die, just yet. Once the mission in America was complete, then Alex could die and Ameri could be with Fatima.

Until then, there would be no resolution.

Then Alex realized why she slipped. Finding sure footing on the ground, she retrieved her night optic and looked through the night vision goggle. The blinking infrared lights helped her spot the eight-propeller drone hovering and firing rockets over the ridge about two miles away.

CHAPTER 28

THE MISSILES WERE SMOKING DIRECTLY AT HIM AND HE ATTEMPTED to avoid their impact, swerving the truck, nearly careening over the lip of a vertical drop.

There was a succession of loud thuds that chewed up the dirt road.

"What the hell?" Owens shouted.

"We need some night vision goggles. They've got a damn Skunk Copter up there," Mahegan said.

"Paintball?"

"No, those are rockets. They've upfitted it."

The unmanned aerial system swooped low, spitting .50 caliber chain gun rounds at them and stitching the side of the truck like a rivet gun. A Skunk Copter was a riot control drone the size of an average skateboard with eight mini-helicopter blades and weapons systems attached beneath. The eight blades were necessary to carry the heavy payloads of paint and rubber bullets. Obviously the Syrians had transformed this riot control platform into a kinetic death machine.

Mahegan needed to find cover.

"We'll ditch the trucks when we get over the ridge and down by the river. Then we can figure this out," Mahegan said.

Mahegan swerved off the road as the drone came in for another run, the machine gun spitting heavy metal at them until it suddenly veered away.

"This is going to have to do," Mahegan said.

They were in a rare flat spot with a wall of a mountain to the left and about fifty yards of level terrain to their right. O'Malley's truck stopped behind them.

They gathered in front of the vehicles, and Mahegan said, "Sean, Patch, take off your pants and put on these bloody uniforms."

"I love it when you talk dirty, Jake," O'Malley quipped.

"Well, you've got tracking devices in your pants."

"See what I mean?"

"Keep it in your pants," Cassie said.

"I keep it in my sock, young Ranger," O'Malley said. "But good comeback. Total respect."

"Okay, Cassie, carry your ruck. I know you're sucking, but I'm carrying the prisoner, and Patch and Sean are helping General Savage."

"I'm good with that," Cassie said. "I grabbed the first aid kits from beneath the truck seats. These are pretty new and well stocked."

"Okay, good thinking. Let's move. I hear that damn drone buzzing again."

Owens and O'Malley changed while Jake positioned the wounded terrorist on his shoulders in a fireman's carry.

Mahegan led his team onto the flat wooded surface next to the road and then began a series of steep switchbacks until he found an obvious trail that ran north.

Above him he heard the incessant whine of the drone circling the trucks about a mile away now. Rockets rained down, and the trucks exploded into bright fireballs that partially lit his path.

Then he heard the helicopter blades.

Setz flared the helicopter when the eight-propeller drone appeared. She caused the Blackhawk to list to the north and then dive to get away from shrapnel.

"What the hell was that, Bev?" Oxendine barked.

"A drone just fired about five missiles into two pickup trucks on a dirt road to our seven o'clock. We're about five miles from where we took the SAM shot. There's something in the mountains here beyond Mahegan," Setz said.

"We don't know that. This could all be Mahegan. The cars, the banks, the kidnapping. Everything."

"The banks?"

"Have been getting word that most everyone's bank accounts are shut down," Oxendine said.

"That's not good," Setz said.

McQueary chimed in. "We found two dead Middle Eastern men in that cave. Mahegan had probably been there and killed them, but the two dead men were kitted up to do harm, Agent."

Oxendine thought it over. They had picked up McQueary and his men, who had called in the sheriff's team from Alex Russell's house to confiscate the bodies and treat the cave as a crime scene.

"Did you find any weapons on the murdered men in the cave, Q?"

McQueary paused. "No, Agent Oxendine, we didn't. Their holsters, magazine pouches, and knife sheaths were empty. Maybe they were just dressing up to play war . . . or maybe Mahegan knows something we don't and killed two terrorists."

"Unlikely. Mahegan killed three defenseless civilians in Charlotte last night, a military police officer, and now two hikers. That's how I'm seeing it."

"Well, I'm thinking your hatred of Mahegan has you blind, then, Agent."

The two men traded hard stares.

"Your mission is to kill or capture Mahegan. End of discussion," Oxendine said.

"I'll let you kill him, hero," McQueary said. "I'll capture the dude, then you can put your pistol to his head real brave-like."

"I'm the commander of this mission, McQueary. You're being insubordinate. Do I need to relieve you of command and put someone in charge who will properly execute the mission?"

"None of my men will obey an unlawful order. That's the first thing you need to know. The second thing is that . . . accidents happen."

"Hey guys, I hate to interrupt the lovefest back there, but on my thermal I'm seeing five people walking on a trail about a mile to our south," Setz said.

"Five people?" Oxendine said.

"Yes. They're carrying rifles, and one has a large rucksack. They're in black uniforms, except one guy is wearing something that looks like a clown suit."

"A clown suit?"

"No other way to describe it. Arms and legs are connected. It's like it is all one thing."

"That sounds like a jumpsuit," McQueary said into his mouthpiece.

Oxendine looked out the window but saw nothing but blackness.

"So to summarize, we've got two burning trucks, an eight-prop drone, and five people with weapons. Plus one highly trained SWAT team," Setz said.

"There's that," McQueary quipped. "Anywhere to put us down up here in these mountains? Not feeling the night rappel."

"There's a scenic overlook about two miles up I could probably squeeze into. Or I could put you next to the burning trucks. There's space there, but I'd be worried about getting too close to the fire."

Just then the aircraft rocked and two of McQueary's men barked out simultaneously, "Enemy fire, nine o'clock."

"Davis is hit. We need a medic!" McQueary said.

"Roger that," Setz said, banking hard away from the drone and the five personnel on the ground.

The pilot broke contact to fly to the helipad at Asheville's Mission Health Center.

"McQueary, we're going to do a false insertion and drop you and your other three men a mile up the road. You'll ambush and arrest the five people walking on that trail."

"So not a false insertion then," McQueary said. "An actual drop of personnel."

Oxendine didn't have time to quibble tactical terms with the insubordinate SWAT team commander.

Setz said, "Gotta make it quick, guys. I'm not having anyone dying on my helicopter. The golden hour and all of that."

Setz was referencing the fact that if they were able to get the wounded to a qualified doctor within an hour, the chances of survival were ninety percent higher than if not.

The helicopter took fire from the drone and Mahegan realized that the enemy in the mountains had not only been following them using tracking devices but also been able to cue in on them by finding the helicopter.

No longer concerned that they had any tracking devices on them, Mahegan had to find a way to disarm the drone. The best way was to find a cover and concealed position from which to shoot it down.

With the wounded Syrian on his back, Mahegan led the team along the narrow trail to an area that had a slight overhang, providing them some protection from above. The forest was thick, and it was doubtful that the drone could get a clean shot at them.

He laid the wounded man on the damp ground beneath the rock overhang and turned around. Cassie's outline was visible against the studded wood line, her rucksack prominent and full. Owens and O'Malley held up Savage, who seemed to not be doing well. He needed medical attention and water.

"Sean, Patch, you guys interrogate this guy. See if you can get him to talk. I'm going to head up with Cassie and try to find a spot to knock down that drone."

"Bossman, that thing fired up the helicopter. It has some serious firepower on it," Owens said.

"That's why we need to get rid of it. Between the cops chasing me for whatever reason and the Syrians planning whatever they're planning, we're the only ones who know what is happening."

"I'm in," Cassie said.

"Sean, you're the medic and the comms guy, so help Savage. Patch, you're the operator, so figure out what these guys are up to. I'm most concerned about that wooden crate in the mine shaft."

"You got it," Owens said. "Drones, surface-to-air missiles, cyber-attack, and assault rifles. This isn't some hick from Gooberville with a truck full of explosives. This is a well-synced attack."

Savage sat down and put his back against the wall of the over-hang. He had finally accepted the space blanket from Cassie and huddled into it. They were looking at the trail fifteen feet ahead. The moonlight filtered through the high canopy of pines, birch, and maples. Owls hooted their nightly call to kill as bears growled and deer rutted.

The whump of the Blackhawk blades drowned the nocturnal symphony as the helicopter descended over the ridge. The blades changed pitch, so Mahegan knew that they had briefly stopped somewhere, perhaps to offload the SWAT team along the natural egress off the mountain and east toward civilization.

"I'm thinking the SWAT team is on the ground. It looked like six guys when they came to Alex Russell's house," Mahegan said.

"Alex Russell?" Owens asked.

"Yeah, why?"

Owens looked at Savage and said, "Man, she's been acting strange over the last month. Savage was tapping that when he and his wife separated and then she went off the deep end."

Savage looked up at them. "Alex has issues," he said. "Yes, we had an affair. But her issues go well beyond that. Everything for her goes back to Groomsman."

"She asked me about Groomsman. What's the big deal? What does she want to know?" Mahegan asked.

"That operation was a clusterfuck from Jump Street. Captain Bagwell there and her HVT hunter team sent over a nugget of information that al-Baghdadi's phone was in that convoy. Sure enough we tracked it, and it was his phone," Savage said.

"I'm aware, General. I went in and retrieved the pieces of it. Remember? We found the SIM card with the one picture of al-Baghdadi flipping the bird."

"Of course I remember," Savage said. "You were about a quarter mile away and securing the outer perimeter when I came in with my security team and Alex. She saw the carnage and couldn't handle it. Just completely lost it. Once we got back to the states I gave her some leave. You guys may think I'm a hard-ass dick, but I'm loyal. I kept her on but kept her stateside. No more deployments."

"That intel was good," Cassie said. "It was a solid lead."

"No doubt," Savage continued. "As Jake said, the phone was there. Baghdadi just planted it. My question is, now that you're here, where did the tip come from?"

The moonlight reflected Cassie's alabaster face.

"It was a HUMINT feed," Cassie said. "One of our operators on the ground gave us the intel, and because it was a high-value target, I immediately passed it to JSOC. You guys."

"Right. Who was the source?" Savage said.

"Even if I remembered we can't talk about that here in front of this prisoner or outside of a secure facility," Cassie said.

"He'll be dead when we're done with him, so no worries there. Plus your dad tried to pin all of that on me, which I was fine with. I made the call, so I should have taken the heat."

"My dad is a weasel," Cassie said. "He's ashamed that I went to Ranger school and . . ." Cassie paused.

"And what?" Savage pressed.

"I get that, but a good leader supports his daughter and his generals. He didn't support you after Operation Groomsman," Cassie said.

"Not going to argue with you there. Still, what was your human intelligence?" Savage asked.

Cassie paused. "The French had a team on the ground in Syria. Their DGSE, that's the CIA equivalent, reported al-Baghdadi in the convoy and gave us the location and the phone number. The number matched what we had been tracking, and when we listened, the voice matched what we had on file."

"I know how to spell DGSE, Captain," Savage said. "Who was your source?"

Mahegan listened intently. Savage was driving at something that he needed to know. Perhaps it was what Alex Russell wanted to know as well.

"He had a call sign of Jackknife. That was all we knew. I had a liaison in my ops cell and he passed on the intel from Jackknife. I'm told Jackknife was one of their best field operatives," Cassie said.

"You were played, damnit." Savage barked louder than Mahegan preferred.

"I was not played. That intel was legit," Cassie defended.

"Jackknife is my call sign. Only my operators know it. There's no way that some random French guy in the field uses that call sign."

"It's not impossible, General. People have the same call signs frequently," Cassie replied.

"No. It was a message to me. We were in too much of a rush to chase the back end of the intelligence. Someone wanted the people in that convoy dead and used us to do it," Savage continued.

"But who? And why?" Cassie asked

"Was there a guy named Dupree involved? Slick Willie type? He was the lead DGSE guy on the ground. Tight with your dad," Savage said to Cassie. Mahegan watched Savage bore his glare through Cassie's eyes, locking on, staring her down.

Cassie paused.

"Yves Dupree was my contact," Cassie admitted

"Whatever led you to him? Of all the human intelligence sources out there, you have to pick a bankrupt banker turned DGSE?"

"Bankrupt banker?"

Mahegan chimed in now. "That's right," he said. "Our financial intelligence team traced transactions from wealthy Syrian refugees to Yves Dupree, who was DGSE and working for the UN High Commissioner for Refugees. We sent the information to HQ in Baghdad, but it ended up in the black hole. We moved on to the next mission. But Dupree was definitely on the take."

Savage didn't let go of Cassie. "So who hooked you up with Dupree?"

Cassie leaned against the rock formation that created the overhang above the trail.

"Jesus," she whispered.

"Who?" Savage demanded.

"Easy, boss," Mahegan said.

"Don't 'Easy, boss' my ass. I called that strike in, Jake," Savage said.

"My dad. General Bagwell. Made a call on a secure burner phone and told me Dupree would be in a Mosul souk and had information for me. I went and met him and thought we had al-Baghdadi."

"Bart fucking Bagwell. The bottom of his boots never met a back he wouldn't step on. I'll be damned," Savage said of his West Point classmate.

"So who did he want dead?" Mahegan asked.

"What?" Cassie gasped.

"You were set up," Mahegan said. "If this is all about Operation Groomsman, then your father wanted someone in that convoy dead."

"Alex's sister was killed in that raid," Savage said.

The team was quiet for a few long moments. The rhythms of the wild overtook their space with the roars and ruts of animals nearby.

"Oh my God," Cassie said. And Mahegan could see she wasn't totally shocked. He decided to get back to Alex Russell.

"This is no coincidence that your parents have been kidnapped by the same people that captured these three," Mahegan said to Cassie.

"When were you going to get around to that little tidbit of insignificant intelligence, Mahegan?" Savage barked.

Mahegan looked at his former boss, huddled in the space blanket, shivering but tough as nails.

"Was too busy thinking in the present saving your precious asses," Mahegan snapped back.

O'Malley and Owens both sarcastically said, "Thanks, bro, you're the best. I mean, we love you, man." Then they did knuckle punches with eyes cast downward in mock deference to Mahegan, who smiled.

"Yeah, I can go tack your asses back up on that wall," he said.

"What have you done for me lately?" Owens said.

"You guys never change," Savage said.

"Yeah we do, boss. It's just been a while," Mahegan said. "We're onto something here. Bagwell tells Cassie to meet Dupree. Dupree gives Cassie bogus intel, but it is corroborated by an actual phone and an actual voice recording where we got a match. You make the call," Mahegan said, pointing at Savage.

"Actually, I turned to Alex and she said, 'Valid target,' " Savage said.

"Right, but who did they want to kill? Fatima? Who was Fatima marrying?" Mahegan asked. "That seems like a more likely target, or someone else in the wedding party."

"We got it all in the investigation. She was marrying some Bulgarian guy named Malavdi something or other. And an SUV broke down before we hit the convoy. Two survivors."

"That seems convenient," Mahegan said. "Names?"

"Actually," Savage said, "they were pretty big fish in the cybercrime world. We fed all that up the chain to Bagwell—"

"This thing starts and stops with General Bagwell," Mahegan said. "He was kidnapped first."

"A lot of things happened at once," Cassie said, defensive.

Mahegan shook his head. "Among many, one. It's an old Native American saying. If you want to disguise what you're really doing, do a lot of things. If your real target is Bart Bagwell, why not kill a bunch of generals to hide that and slow down the people trying to figure out who you are and why you're doing it."

"About right," Owens said.

"And this may explain what Alex wanted from me," Mahegan said. "I knew Dupree was bad news. Had run into him a few times but didn't know he was connected to Groomsman . . . or your father. She wanted me to confirm Dupree was in the mix." He looked at Cassie and continued. "Somebody knows Bagwell was involved. I don't believe your parents' kidnapping was random. And now Alex has gone off the deep end and may be using something. One minute she's about to freak out, then she goes upstairs and she comes down rubbing the inside of her forearm and is smooth and level. If she knows your dad was involved, we may not be able to save them."

"I saw that," Cassie affirmed, still shaken, but coming back to the point of the conversation. "I know." She lowered her head.

"Would Alex want revenge on us enough to orchestrate an attack of Syrian terrorists against the homeland?"

"Alex is Syrian," Savage said. "One night she was at the farmhouse and I heard her singing in her sleep. She was singing a Syrian lullaby. Fly, fly, dove. I asked her about it the next morning, and she defended and denied until I took her into the basement and strapped her to the lie detector I keep down there. She confessed not knowing that the damn thing doesn't work. Said she was an orphan, dumped in Newark, New Jersey. Went to undergrad at James Madison in Virginia and then got the legal scholarship from the Army and went to UVA law school. Commissioned as a JAG, and the rest is history."

"If she's Syrian and we're dealing with Syrian terrorists, there's a chance she's been the one coordinating all of this," Mahegan said. "It takes a smart, diabolical mind to plan and execute everything."

"She's smart and diabolical," Savage said. "But I don't know that she's a traitor. She is a U.S. citizen. Would she kill someone? Sure, for her reasons. But would she plan an attack on her homeland just because we killed her sister? I don't know about that. Doubtful, but possible."

Mahegan just realized that Savage also had no reason to know that his ex-wife, Vicki Sledge, had been murdered and that he, Jake Mahegan, was the prime murder suspect.

"You always told us to give you the straight information, General, so I'm going to give it to you straight," Mahegan said.

"Get to it, son," Savage said.

"Two nights ago someone shot and murdered Charles Sledge, Danny Sledge, and your ex-wife," Mahegan said.

Savage paused.

"Okay. They have a suspect?"

"Yeah, me. The murderer used your pistol that I bought you

and you were supposed to register in your name. That helicopter is coming after me because I am the number one suspect in the murder of your ex-wife."

"You do it?" Savage asked flatly.

"No, I was dealing with some of these Syrians just like you guys were, except of course I didn't get taken off the battlefield."

"Damn, bro. Ouch," Owens said.

"Well, I can only put up with so much bullshit from the general," Mahegan said.

"You'll put up with whatever bullshit I sling your way, son," Savage said. "Now that's something Alex Russell could do. She hated Vicki, and Vicki hated her. Alex wanted to taste the power, and I, unfortunately, let her. Vicki found out about it and they went after each other like two cats with one litter box."

The timing would have been tight, but it was possible that Alex shot the Sledge family in her fugue state, then drove to Savage's farm where he met her. She could potentially have been suffering from posttraumatic stress that sometimes created delusions and hallucinations in its most severe forms. He perhaps had seen that in Alex Russell. That Savage believed she could have murdered Vicki Sledge and her family was something. The general didn't parse words and if he saw that in her then Mahegan believed it could be true.

He needed to find Alex as much as he needed to knock the Skunk drone out of the sky and ultimately prevent whatever the Syrians next phase threatened.

"Okay, Cassie, let's go," Mahegan said. "Patch, you're in charge."

"Thanks, bro," Owens said with sarcasm. "Got comms?"

Mahegan paused and reached into his pocket. Cassie's SIM card was still there in the bottom.

"This got wet, but let's see if it works," Mahegan said. Cassie burrowed deep into the rucksack and retrieved her phone.

"The screen is cracked," she said. She took the SIM card and slid it into the side of the iPhone, then hit the power button. The screen flickered and died.

"I don't know," she said.

"Keep it on," O'Malley said. "It might come back to life."

"Sean would know," Mahegan said. "Tech genius."

"Roger," O'Malley said.

"Okay, if it doesn't work and if we don't come back, rally whenever we can at the COOP," Mahegan said. "What are you guys going to communicate with?"

"Roger," Owens replied. "Sean will figure something out. Smoke signals. Something. He's a tech genius."

"Smoke signals," O'Malley reiterated.

"Well, whatever. Here's her number," Mahegan said. He had scribbled it on a piece of paper he found in a baggie in Cassie's rucksack as he stuffed the phone in her cargo pocket.

Mahegan led Cassie from beneath the overhang and began climbing the terrain above, which was the lip of a forty-five-degree rock face that rose as far as he could see into the darkness. The gray granite appeared formidable, but Mahegan did not want to wander aimlessly into the SWAT team that he believed had been placed below them at the mouth of the valley that led to Asheville.

"Let me go first, Jake. I'm the climber. You can follow me. I'll pick the safest route," Cassie said.

"With one arm?"

"I'm better with one than you are with two," she quipped. Mahegan figured he could catch her if he was behind her, so he let her lead the way. They crawled single file up the face of the mountain until they reached a plateau that afforded them a view into the opposite side of the valley where their evening had begun with the flying suit jump.

"We're in the open here," Cassie said.

"We need to be," Mahegan replied. "Now you can watch my back."

Mahegan sighted through the iron sights of the AR-15 using the ample moon and starlight. He heard the buzz of the drone as it flitted through the valley, out of sight.

Cassie lay behind her rucksack to the rear of Mahegan. He could feel her leg touching his, thigh to thigh. She had his back.

The drone briefly lifted above the ridgeline to his south before it dipped again.

"The skunk is bobbing and weaving, looking for us," Mahegan said.

"Roger," Cassie said.

A gunshot rang out from beneath them, near the overhang they had just departed. Then a succession of others, indicating an exchange of fire. He heard shouting and then abrupt silence.

"SWAT guys. Looking for us, finding them. Hope no one was hurt."

"Good thing we're up here," Cassie said with a hint of sarcasm.

"Not entirely unplanned," Mahegan replied.

The drone appeared less than a hundred yards to the south, hovering and spinning with its eight rotors making it zip through the air like a wasp. Mahegan could see a few small, twelve-pound tactical munitions. They were lethal bombs maturing through the research and development phase, which meant that the missile had probably been capable for several years. The bean counters in the Pentagon were loath to let any technology be used in the field unless everyone in the approval chain had their asses covered completely, even though those bureaucrats would never need the weapon in combat.

The drone spun in his direction, the night optic glinting with moonlight.

"Skunk, twelve o'clock," Mahegan whispered.

"Take the shot," Cassie said.

Mahegan aimed low, using a three-round burst capability. He squeezed the trigger three times in rapid succession, aiming at the body of the drone. Sparks flew from one of the rotors. His shots struck metal casing. Nine bullets had to do some damage.

Still, the drone fired two rockets toward their position atop the ridge. One rocket skipped like a pebble skimmed along a lake surface and careened into the black void beyond them. The second rocket impacted just beyond Cassie, creating a buckling effect of the ledge upon which they lay. Mahegan fired three more shots at the drone, which was now teetering and spinning wildly without the synchronization of its eight blades. He thought he scored another hit. He turned when he heard Cassie's voice. She wasn't behind him anymore.

"Jake," Cassie said. There was fear in her voice.

Jake spun around and saw that Cassie's rucksack had tumbled over the edge and was hanging by a small pine stump. Cassie was below the pine stump that was poking three feet up through the shale.

"I can't hold on long," Cassie gasped.

Mahegan popped out his magazine, cleared his weapon, and reached it out to Cassie, whose hands were slipping from the flimsy pine. Her shoulder wound left her no choice but to let go and precariously hold on with one hand.

CHAPTER 29

ALEX RUSSELL WATCHED MAHEGAN AND CASSIE DUEL WITH THE drone. She hoped what she was watching was not a hallucination. Her PKCzeta shot had all but worn off, so she couldn't be 100 percent certain.

The night vision goggle was up again. Mahegan was scrambling to reach an assault rifle to Cassie, who was dangling from a flimsy tree root with one hand. She scanned laterally and saw the drone was damaged but still flying with one rocket hanging from its rail. Whoever was controlling the drone was most likely watching this literal cliffhanger play out. One well-placed rocket could kill both Mahegan and Cassie, who would fall about a quarter mile into the valley below. No way she would survive that.

Alex had a few decisions to make, and all involved her pistol. Mahegan and Cassie were no more than one hundred yards from her perch. Interesting that they ended up close to her. Interesting how everything seemed to revolve around her. Tonight, the last twenty-four hours, the effort she had put into becoming a model citizen and army officer.

She wondered where Savage was. Why didn't Cassie and Mahegan have him with them? That's what she had wanted. Savage. He was her focus. She wanted him in every sense of the word. No one was going to stop her from making him see what she had to show him.

Alex retrieved her pistol and aimed it.

As she contemplated her shot, Ameri Assad said to her, "Just kill him." Ameri was referencing Mahegan, of course.

Just kill him.

Three words, one less than the four that Alex Russell had uttered that had killed Fatima.

Yes, sir. Valid target.

That Ameri was able to appear tonight—right now, at this moment—was testament to the power of the memory that haunted Alex Russell. The shift from calculating lawyer to vengeful Syrian was sudden and severe. Ameri was there in full force, moving the pistol in Alex's hand from her aim on the drone to aim at Mahegan, his back exposed as he was leaning over helping Cassie.

Just kill him.

Alex didn't fight with Ameri, couldn't fight her. Ameri controlled her whenever she chose. This was the moment, she presumed, that Ameri had been waiting for. While cognizant of what she was doing only because of the fading effects of the needle she had poked in her arm several hours ago, Alex felt helpless.

Just as helpless as she had been last night when she had driven to Charlotte to visit the Sledge family.

Yves Dupree paced in his office.

Gail was doing the public relations thing. With the twenty-four-hour news cycles, he had to keep feeding the beast with updates and information.

Dupree walked to one end of his tongue-and-groove oak floor, stared at the bookcase with law and finance books he'd never read, turned around, spotted the Carolina Panthers' stadium through the floor-to-ceiling window, thought about the college game at noon today, then walked to the far wall with its credenza and assorted knickknacks.

Had he made any mistakes?

He didn't think so. The calls to Alex Russell could be explained by his duties as the executor of Charles Sledge's last will and testament. Those were the only weak points that the police could exploit, but so far the police hadn't asked him a single question beyond last night's brief session with Special Agent Oxendine, who had issues of his own. Oxendine was busy chasing Mahegan, fueled by his own jealousy of the special operations warrior.

Dupree had studied Mahegan and General Savage ever since his duties as the senior French DGSE agent on the ground in Iraq and Syria from late 2011 to 2013. Early on, though, he focused his attentions on the commander and had established a strong individual relationship with General Bart Bagwell. He regularly invited the general into the French version of a Sensitive Compartmented Information Facility on the forward base in Mosul.

They became friends, as much as any two strangers thrust into combat could. The routine visits led to the random firefights while traveling to different parts of the city, which led to a camaraderie and bond that by Dupree's calculation was simply the lonely man at the top syndrome. Who else did he have to talk to when he could enjoy the occasional cigar and cognac at Dupree's compound? With security at the perimeters, it was just Dupree and Bagwell talking and sharing information. The French lived differently, he admitted that much. Dupree's budget was higher than the average intelligence chief in country. The compound was an estate, heavily guarded with lots of secret entrances and exits.

"What I'd do for a good, random blow job," Bagwell had said one night.

"Well, General, if that's a request, I'm afraid I don't lean in that direction, but it can certainly be arranged."

"Nah, just thinking out loud," Bagwell had said.

But Dupree knew that in the intelligence business, leverage was everything. At their next rendezvous Dupree updated the general on his assessment of the burgeoning Arab Spring, which was spot-on, he liked to think. After the usual round of booze and cigars, Bagwell went to the usual restroom in the guest bedroom off the parlor. Dupree had prepositioned two well-paid ladies in the room, and he remembered looking at his watch after forty minutes of waiting for the general. Either they had killed him, or the old man had some stamina.

He had come out of the bedroom muttering, "Sorry. Took a little longer than usual."

Dupree had seen the glimmer in Bagwell's eyes.

And later he had watched the video, which he saved.

Bagwell enjoyed what Dupree figured must have been his first threesome. It was an unbridled display of raw sexual release. He took very little convincing, and soon they were all three on the bed.

Turned out to be the best thousand dollars Dupree had ever invested.

When he had his idea for cashing in on the UN High Commissioner for Refugees' inability to process the flood of refugees in Damascus, an area that General Bagwell was responsible for, he had invited the general back over for a routine update.

"I have an idea," he had told Bagwell.

"Not sure I can support that," Bagwell had said.

"Oh, but I think you can, my friend," Dupree had said. He showed the general the video. After an initial angry reaction, Bagwell succumbed to protecting his career once Dupree had assured him that all he needed the general to do was to make sure that his financial intelligence task force reported only to him. It was a slight organizational change but had to happen for Dupree to be successful. Bagwell made the change. Dupree set up the joint bank account to reassure Bagwell, and then cigar nights became even better as they laughed over how much their bank account was growing and enjoyed even more women—what were twenty videos when there was one video?

The laughter came to a screeching halt, though, when Dupree wanted to rotate out of Mosul and explore a private sector job with HSBC Bank, using his law and business degree credentials. Before he could leave, the Carbanak bank heist not only emptied their account but also led to the revelation of their identities by some rogue Bulgarian hackers. Bagwell had been promoted to chairman of the Joint Chiefs of Staff and now a sex video was the least of his worries.

Dupree was left nearly penniless once that fund was raked. Bagwell, he was certain, would be fine unless exposed. Sitting alone in his Mosul compound, Dupree could feel the Arab Spring tightening its noose around him.

But then the Bulgarians had contacted him. He had been given instructions to fly to Burgas, Bulgaria, to meet with three men named Gavril, Zakir, and Malavdi. They had "located" his money and determined who had "stolen it," they reported. But they could not provide him an online report. He had to visit them in person.

He flew into Burgas after connecting from Sofia. From the airport, he took a short taxi ride to the Lazuren Briag Hotel on the Black Sea. He had waited patiently in the sand dunes across the street as he watched two men enter the café in the hotel. After ensuring they had not been followed, he walked into the café and sat at their table.

"Gentlemen, the Black Sea is as beautiful as they say," he had said.

"I think you will enjoy it more after our conversation," the man named Gavril had said.

"Shall we go for a walk?" Dupree said.

"A ride," Gavril said.

They walked to Gavril's car, a ten-year-old Opel Astra. Sitting in the backseat, Dupree checked to make sure the locks were operational from inside the car before closing the door. They drove about five kilometers before arriving at a small apartment building. They walked into the ground floor and then took the stairs to a dark basement filled with servers and small wall-mounted air conditioners.

In the middle of the basement was a semicircular, elevated command post that had wires running beneath the raised access floor panels. Six forty-inch monitors sat side by side, with a keyboard for each.

"Before we show you who has your money, we need a guarantee

from you that you will help us with something," Gavril said. "In exchange for your cooperation, we will not expose that you and General Bagwell had a Swiss bank account worth nearly seventeen million dollars."

Dupree studied the short, bald man. He seemed to be no threat. The one named Zakir, though, was over six feet tall and silent. His shirt was tight along the arms and chest. The man was strong, and Dupree had no desire to fight him, though he had no doubt he could kill him if he had to. Ever since Dupree's assignment in Syria with the French DGSE, he had been an efficient killer. Malavdi was smaller and wiry and could have been a threat, but less so than Zakir.

"Of course I need to know what the favor is," Dupree said.

"It is painless for you," Gavril said. "Zakir here will do all of the hard work."

"I'm no stranger to hard work, Gavril. What is it you want me to do? And when do I get my money back?"

Zakir spoke up, finally.

"We need the UN High Commissioner for Refugees to hire me," Zakir said.

Dupree coughed. "What makes you think I can do that? I'm French," he said.

"Please, Mr. Dupree. We 'found' your money. Do you not believe we can also find out who you really are? Before Mosul, you served in Syria posing as a midlevel manager with the UN High Commissioner for Refugees. You had a call sign named Jackknife. Shall I continue?"

Dupree shook his head. "I'm convinced. Why do you need a position with UNHCR?"

"That's not a relevant question, Mr. Dupree," Zakir said. "Just get me a job in Syria. I'll take it from there."

Dupree nodded. "That can be arranged. Now let's get on with it."

"Just be assured that you will not see any of your money until Zakir is assigned to UNHCR in Syria."

"I understand. Now please show me who has my money," Dupree said.

And they did.

All of his money was resident in an account under the name of General Bagwell.

"Bagwell has my money?"

"Perhaps. This is our leverage. We let you off the hook, because now it is just his bank account, implicating him fully. We hold this until we have what we want."

"I can get you visas to the United States," Dupree said.

"So can we. Zakir just needs a job," Gavril had said. "Malavdi is to marry soon, and we may want to relocate his fiancée, who is Syrian. Is that too much to ask?"

"No. Consider it done," he had said.

"And, perhaps we like your business model," Gavril had said, coughing and laughing. The two younger men had smiled. Dupree figured that was the play, to take over where he and General Bagwell had left off in their funneling of Syrian refugees. The crisis was growing worse by the day, and more and more wealthy Syrian citizens were fleeing, which of course overwhelmed the system and would drive prices on the "travel agent" black market through the roof.

Dupree had ultimately pulled the appropriate strings, and soon Zakir was working with the UNHCR in Damascus.

Dupree left Burgas that day with $500,000 more in his bank account than he had when he arrived. So it had been a worthwhile trip.

After returning to his Mosul compound in 2013, he met one last time with General Bagwell before the man became the chairman of the Joint Chiefs of Staff in America.

CHAPTER 30

Special agent Tommy Oxendine couldn't believe the report he just received.

When he stepped off the helicopter to use the men's room and make some phone calls at Mission Health Center in Asheville, he learned that somehow he had missed the report that the two military police who had been shot in Moore County and dumped in the Uwharrie were Syrian terrorists.

He stood outside the emergency room watching the injured being trucked in by old pickup trucks and some new ambulances.

The document he was holding said that the fuel situation was becoming dire because fuel trucks had to navigate their way to dozens of airports and thousands of gas stations, just in North Carolina. While the patch to the automobile Trojan was effective and working, the mechanics still had to input it on every vehicle, one at a time, except where over-the-air rekey worked, which was in about ten percent of the cars. People had drained most of the fuel stations in the area, expecting Armageddon, and raided the supermarkets, which were now barren.

He looked up at Setz, who was staring at him through the cockpit window of the helicopter sitting on the hospital helipad. Oxendine held up a finger as he finished reading the report. He called his boss, the director of the SBI, Winston Black III, whom he awakened at this early morning hour.

"Calling me at home, Oxendine?"

"Sir, there's a national crisis going on, we've got two wounded, and there's a murderer on the loose."

"Don't lecture me, Oxendine. I assume you haven't caught your man, so get to your excuse," Black said.

Oxendine could visualize his boss in his inside-the-Beltline mansion in Raleigh sleeping in a room with a high ceiling and perfectly matching chintz. Nothing about Black's life in any way paralleled Oxendine and his hardscrabble upbringing, his modest living, or his aggression in the field.

"We have indications of a terrorist cell operating in North Carolina. When I piece together the facts that we found two Syrian terrorists dressed as military policemen in the Uwharrie and my helicopter has been fired on by a surface-to-air missile and a drone, something larger than hunting down Mahegan is going on. Don't get me wrong—Mahegan is still good for the murder. I just felt like you should know so you can tell the governor."

"Why would I call the governor to tell him you haven't caught Mahegan?" Black asked. "You have an entire SWAT team at your disposal."

"And we're close. They're on the ground about to capture him," Oxendine said.

"Well then, you'll want to talk to Yves Dupree," Black said.

Oxendine racked his brain. "The bank guy?"

"Yes, the bank guy, as in the heir apparent to the throne at United Bank of America. The acting CEO. He has provided some useful information to the governor. Apparently, he's a donor."

Oxendine rolled his eyes in frustration. Setz was pumping her arm up and down, the signal that they needed to move quickly. There was probably another medevac coming in, and Setz needed to open the helipad for inbound traffic. Oxendine also found it instructive that Black had not asked about the two wounded SWAT team members. One was gut shot and the other had metal shards in his face and eye from the bullets striking the side of the aircraft.

"Can't you just tell me what he said? I need to get back on the chase of Mahegan and get into that valley to see what is there. It may require more than one SWAT team," Oxendine said.

"Under no circumstances will you gather any more forces than you already have, Agent Oxendine. Is that clear?" Black said.

"I'll let you handle it, then," Oxendine said. "We may even need the governor to call out the national guard on this."

Black roared with laughter, causing Oxendine to hold the phone away from his ear.

"The National Guard? The governor's already got them out in the streets helping to move cars, pick up stranded motorists, and secure sensitive locations. Where have you been?"

"I'm making an official report, Director, that I believe there are terrorists in a valley twelve miles west of Asheville, North Carolina," Oxendine said. "Oh, and we've got two wounded, one critical, seeing how you're so concerned."

"You recording this for your records, Oxendine? Well, record this . . ."

"I'm sorry, we're losing the signal," Oxendine said, and shut off the phone. He jogged out to the helicopter and boarded through the open cargo door.

"We've got two inbounds trying to bring in critical patients, Agent. We've got to move," Setz said.

"Roger. Let's head back up to provide support to the team."

As Setz lifted off and began the short flight into the mountains, Oxendine pressed the UHF channel to speak to McQueary, who by now should have cornered, captured, or killed Mahegan. But first his phone rang.

Yves Dupree called the number he was told never to call, not even in case of an emergency.

"Yes?"

"We need to meet," Dupree said.

"You don't call me. Ever," the voice on the other end replied. Dupree could hear wind coursing through the microphone of the receiver

"There's a problem," Dupree said.

"It's not my problem and I'm rather busy."

"It could be your problem," Dupree said. "This is bigger than me now. Something I never expected or intended."

"There's no way it could be my problem."

"You've forgotten something," Dupree said.

"Yes? What is that?"

"I know where you are," Dupree said.

"Do you?"

"I'm looking at you right now, as a matter of fact."

He heard the pause. Dupree knew his listener would most likely interpret his comment as intended, that he was following the listener on the Internet somehow using a tracking device.

"If that's the case, then good for you. You've got your money. I've got what I want."

"You're forgetting something," Dupree said.

"Not on the phone. Meet me," the listener said.

"I'm glad you agree with me. I'm coming to you. We have very little time before we are done. See you in a bit."

Dupree hung up and called out to Gail, who came rushing through the side door. United Bank of America was at full operations, lights on, information technology team at full throttle, public relations people brainstorming potential solutions on the whiteboard, and operations personnel staring at computer screens watching millions of dollars disappear.

"I'm heading out for a bit. I'll be back before sunrise," Dupree said.

"That's four hours, sir. We're in crisis mode. I've got CNN, Fox News, and every major network wanting interviews."

"Then give them an interview. Tell them I've got my sleeves rolled up and am fixing the problem," Dupree said. "Which is exactly what I'll be doing."

"But you were hosting the governor at the Tar Heels ESPN game of the week tomorrow at the stadium," she said. "Or today, I guess." She looked at her watch.

"College football game? You think they'll be playing football with all of this happening?"

"A lot of the cars are getting fixed already, and the NCAA put out an announcement that to show the terrorists that America will not be stopped we will have NCAA football. This is a special game, as you know, between the Heels and Clemson on neutral turf to draw a big crowd from both schools. Stadium is sold out. Seventy-five thousand tickets sold."

"In other words, they don't want to take the financial hit. They make nine billion a year. So that's a billion a month, which equates to two hundred fifty million a weekend. Everything's about money, Gail. *Everything.*"

"Yes, sir." Gail nodded, her brunette hair slipping across her face. The hair and the pout on her lips gave Dupree a temporary rise, but he resisted the urge to waste another fifteen minutes on her. He needed to leave now.

He had done something at the Sledge crime scene that he remembered could come back to haunt him and he needed to resolve that issue immediately.

He took the elevator to the parking garage, hit the key fob on his Mercedes-Benz Maybach S600, and slid into the driver's seat.

As he turned out of the garage, he knew that he would never return to this building, the tallest in Charlotte. He wondered if it would even be standing if he were to return.

As he passed the gate to the stadium, he recalled four years ago leaving a meeting with Captain Cassie Bagwell in a Mosul souk and establishing a one-man checkpoint on the outskirts of the small village the wedding convoy had to pass through to get to the compound. Dupree was dressed in the olive drab uniform of a Syrian police officer. Wearing a keffiyeh, he hid his light brown hair. His deep tan was enough to fool those in the convoy. And those that weren't fooled certainly respected the AK-47 strapped across his chest and the pistol tucked into his holster.

He used a mirror to inspect beneath the vehicles of the wedding convoy. Already they were self-absorbed with happiness, inwardly focused, little patience to worry about the tedium of an all-too-predictable checkpoint. One of the drivers laughed and waved a wad of Syrian pounds in his hand saying, *"Eajilu! Eajilu!"*

Hurry up!

Under the third of five vehicles, where Fatima and Malavdi were in the backseat kissing like lovebirds, he discreetly placed a magnetized box. In the metal box was a cell phone that was transmitting to another burner cell phone he had hidden a few miles away. The two phones were playing a recent recording of an al-Baghdadi conversation he had intercepted.

He snatched the money from the driver immediately after and said, "*Adhhab, adhhab.*"

Go.

As if he was doing them a favor by releasing them.

Release them he did.

CHAPTER 31

MAHEGAN HELD HIS RIFLE AS FAR OUT AS HE COULD SO THAT Cassie Bagwell could hang on and not fall to almost certain death into the rocky crevices below.

A shot belched from a pistol about fifty yards away. Mahegan heard the report at the same time sparks flew in his eyes when the bullet pinged off the weapon.

He instinctively looked up and saw Alex Russell standing on a ridge in the moonlight. She was framed by pine trees jutting upward and by the moon casting its glow upon her as if she were the lead in a Broadway show.

Alex was in her balanced shooter's stance, the same one he had seen when he had returned to the Land Rover after dumping the terrorist bodies. Her feet were evenly spread, knees flexed, arms outstretched, hands securely gripping the pistol.

Fifty yards across a windswept mountain ridge was a tough shot, but he didn't want to give her a second chance. The wind tossed her hair from his right to left, from the north to south, typical for this time of year. At this distance the wind and altitude would impact the flight of the bullet.

He was holding the weapon with his left hand and grasping the edge of a rock crevice with his right. He was bearing Cassie's full weight on the ripped and shredded left deltoid. His face contorted in agony with every pull of Cassie's weight. He didn't expect Alex to miss again. He expected her to learn from her mistake and aim a little higher and a little farther to the left, allowing for the curve and fall of the bullet with the altitude and the wind. It was still a tough shot, but not an impossible one.

"Don't do it, Alex!" Mahegan shouted.

In his periphery he noticed the drone spiraling, trying to stabilize. It had one rocket hanging from the rail.

"Cassie, you've got to pull up," Mahegan whispered.

A second shot jumped from Alex's pistol and grazed Mahegan's calf. He felt the bite, knowing she'd aimed too far left and too high. She overcorrected. She had him bracketed.

Cassie was almost to the lip of the cliff, one hand on the rifle and the other now pulling at her rucksack, which was hanging from the tree stump. It was a rookie mistake to grasp something that was not rooted into the ground. Then three things happened at once.

The drone launched a missile wide, Alex fired again, and Cassie's rucksack broke free of the tree stump and caused Cassie to lose her grip on Mahegan's rifle. Simultaneously, Mahegan flipped backward from the impact caused by the impact of the rocket.

And then everything went black.

Alex Russell fought Ameri Assad, but lost.

Alex's pistol fired at Mahegan, who was extending his rifle so that Cassie could hang on.

The bullet pinged off the weapon, creating a spark. She realized she was too far away and had to correct for the wind, so she adjusted up and to her left. Her second shot kicked up dust behind Mahegan, or maybe it was a fine spray of blood.

She *hoped* it was blood.

Ameri saw the drone stabilize and lock on Mahegan and Cassie with a missile. She felt Alex coming back to scream, "No!" but body checked that thought and fired again. Ameri was in charge now. She would get revenge for Fatima.

Then the missile launched, Cassie fell, and Mahegan flipped off the back side of the ridge.

* * *

Zakir stood in his base camp and watched the trucks line up. They were on schedule and making their final move.

He had less than fifty percent of his fighting force still viable, but that was enough to get the Mack truck to its target by noon today. He had about nine hours to get there and execute the mission. They had rehearsed every detail, and he expected success.

He walked into the small building on the opposite side of the mountain from the mine shaft and stared at the chairman of the Joint Chiefs of Staff and his wife. They were completely broken. At some point in the night one of his men had chained the chairman to the iron bars in his cell and whipped him with a set of tire chains until the chairman's back was oozing blood.

Mrs. Bagwell was weeping.

"Is he alive?" he asked her. The general was motionless on the dirty floor of the cabin he had converted into a cell. Mrs. Bagwell stared at him, eyes fixed, mouth open, unable to speak.

"I'm alive, you bastard."

"Everything comes full circle, doesn't it, General? You defraud Syrians departing the chaos there. You get caught with millions of dollars in a Swiss bank account. You use your daughter to pass along bad information to General Savage and his men. And instead of paying us to protect this information, you kill my two best friends? And you thought you were killing us, too. That's why you had Jake Mahegan inspect the wreckage. We would be dead, except for a faulty transmission on our Suburban. American technology. Not the best, right?"

"Bart, what is he saying?"

"Be quiet!" Zakir said to Bagwell's wife.

Turning back to General Bagwell, he said, "And now you have your wife and daughter in jeopardy."

"What does Cassie have to do with this?" General Bagwell asked. His eyes darted nervously. His mouth contorted. Gray stubble peppered his face. Spittle had dried on the corners of his mouth, like a clown's permanent frown. The general was up on his knees now and holding the bars with his hands reaching out from manacled wrists.

"Everything," Zakir replied. He took a few strides and grasped two of the bars of the general's cell just above the general's head. Staring at the man's tortured back was difficult even for a hard man such as Zakir.

"You used your daughter, General, in a way that no man, much less a father, should have used anyone. You gave her the contact with Mr. Dupree. Eager to please her father and to make her mark, she met with Dupree, who told her to bomb the wedding party, only he didn't mention that it was a wedding party. He said the wedding was a ruse for safely moving al-Baghdadi. She even provided JSOC the name for the operation. And you wanted them killed simply because we were blackmailing you? And you wanted it to appear as a mistaken act of war, collateral damage? Without your Cassie to manipulate, there would have been no Operation Groomsman."

"How do you know that?" the general growled.

"What do you care? You publicly humiliate her for attending a man's school. Where I come from, both men and women can be tough. What is your problem with strong women? I, for one, love strong women. Your Cassie is a strong woman, General. She has shown great fortitude in the face of her mistake. She is reconciling."

"How do you know about . . . about all of this?"

"I make it a point to know everything about what I am doing. I know, for example, that you and Yves Dupree met routinely when you were the commander in Iraq and Syria. He was French DGSE, you know? I also know that you had a joint business venture with Mr. Dupree."

"Where are you getting your information?" Bagwell shouted.

"France is known for its wines, no? Germany for its cars? America for its . . . football? What is Bulgaria known for?"

"Dogshit," Bagwell said.

"Good one, General. We are known for our hacking capabilities. I am inside your Pentagon. I am inside your automobile manufacturers. I am inside your life. Your bank accounts. I know what you watch on Netflix. *Orange Is the New Black*? Really?"

He stepped away from the cell and continued.

"I know that you and Yves Dupree lost millions of dollars when we stole it from you. Good for us that Mr. Dupree has mixed loyalties, mostly to himself."

"Yves Dupree is a lying sack of shit," Bagwell said.

"That may be, General. You can trick a Frenchman, perhaps, but not me. I did Carbanak, General. The greatest bank heist of all time, online or actual. So I have the money you stole from the Syrians trying to leave their country. And we're giving some of it to Dupree for helping us out a bit, but I doubt he'll live long enough to enjoy it. And thanks for getting him that job at United Bank of America. We told him to ask you for it."

"Bart, what is he saying?"

Zakir turned to Mrs. Bagwell and said, "If the general doesn't appreciate the fact that Cassie is an Army Ranger, then how on earth can you *even* speak to him that way?"

Zakir then lifted his pistol and shot Mrs. Bagwell in the forehead. Her head kicked back, and blood painted a dotted line up the light green wall.

"No!" Bagwell shouted. He was rattling the cage and forcefully shouting from his diaphragm. "You son of a bitch!"

Zakir bent down and whispered, "Come here, General."

Bagwell leaned forward. Zakir placed the pistol against the general's temple. "This is for Cassie," he said. "And, yes, Fatima and Malavdi, also. Yes, it's mostly for them, you son of a bitch."

He pulled the trigger. The bullet bore through the general's brain and tumbled out the other side onto the wall. Bagwell hung by his shackled wrists, slumped over, his face a tortured mask, frozen in death.

Zakir had pieced it all together. Hacking their way through the Operation Groomsman report and then tracing the deposits to the Swiss bank account, Gavril and Zakir had learned of the "cash for green card" scheme that Dupree had established.

The rest was easy. With Zakir's job as a UNHCR refugee placement assistant, he and Gavril developed their plan after they watched the Americans bomb and destroy the wedding party.

While Zakir planned on making Bagwell's transgressions public eventually, he enjoyed solving the puzzle and watching the reaction of the general.

Busted.

Why kidnap and kill one general when you could kidnap and kill many in order to mask your true purpose, Zakir had figured. The same was true for the Trojan in the cars. Why stop just one Mack truck and four Suburban SUVs when you could stop millions?

He removed the handcuffs from the general and his wife. Placing the pistol in the general's hand, Zakir aimed it at Bagwell's wife in the adjacent cell and used the general's index finger to pull the trigger, ensuring gunpowder residue would appear on his sleeve. Murder–suicide.

He dropped a copy of the general's secret bank account statement next to the dead officer. It had a balance of nearly $17 million at one point in time. Then he slid the West Point ring from the general's ring finger and slipped it onto his middle finger, where it fit snugly. He admired the black onyx stone and twenty-four karat gold rubbed soft from years of constant wear.

Zakir thumbed the ring as he walked outside and saw that his convoy of Mitsubishi trucks and the lone Mack truck were idling with their parking lights on. The drivers all wore night vision goggles. He strode confidently to the Mack truck and stepped up to the driver's compartment, asking Ratta, "Have we secured our new passenger?"

"Yes. The team recovered Captain Bagwell. The drone kept eyes on her until the team could recover her. She is still alive. Injured, but still with us. I have her in the truck," Ratta said. He motioned to the cab with his chin.

"Good. And the weapon?"

"Yes. I have set a timer for noon today, nearly eight hours from now."

"And, finally, I see we all have the proper uniforms," Zakir said.

"Of course, Zakir. I issued U.S. Army combat fatigues to everyone."

"We must move now if we are to make our deadline."

Zakir walked around the front of the Mack truck, climbed into the passenger seat, and radioed his man in the lead Mitsubishi.

"Forward," he said.

There was no reply, but the convoy began moving with three trucks in the front and three behind. Their convoy looked similar to the one they had attacked, with an extra truck in the front and the back.

They snaked along the Bible camp road up the valley to the gravel road where the fire tower was located. They hooked a right onto that road and passed where he had found two of his men dead earlier yesterday. They turned onto the Blue Ridge Parkway and headed east, toward Asheville.

CHAPTER 32

"DAMNIT, THAT'S HIM!" SPECIAL AGENT OXENDINE SHOUTED INTO the headset.

Setz was hovering the Blackhawk over a high mountain ridge near where they had taken fire from a surface-to-air missile earlier in the day. They had returned to pick up McQueary and his SWAT team that had a brief firefight with three men, none fitting the description of Mahegan. After the initial exchange of gunfire, they made no further contact with the three-man patrol and subsequently moved to a pickup zone, where they boarded the helicopter.

Once in the helicopter, McQueary reported gunfire on the ridge, and Oxendine convinced Setz to brave a return at night. Through his night vision goggles, Oxendine could see the outstretched form of Jake Mahegan lying motionless on the eastern slope of a rocky mountaintop ridge.

"I can't land up there. Too windy and too narrow. We'll have to send down a penetrator."

"Get it ready," Oxendine said to Setz. The crew chiefs were listening and opened the port door, shoved the cable wench perpendicular to the aircraft, and spooled out some cable with a small T-seat at the end. The crew chief sat on the seat, hugging the cable, while his crewmate began to lower the cable into the rotor wash and the wind.

Oxendine unfastened his seat belt and shouted above the din of the turbine engines, "Stop!"

The crewman in the seat stared at Oxendine, who dangerously pulled at him and brought him back into the aircraft, pivoting the arm of the wench.

"I'm the one going down. This is my guy!" Oxendine shouted.

"You're crazy," McQueary shouted back at him. Oxendine was creating chaos in the back of the Blackhawk.

"I don't care who goes down there, but I'll remind you that we had a surface-to-air missile earlier in the day and two reported firefights. So somebody get down there," Setz said.

Oxendine used his large frame to muscle the crewman off the T-seat and straddled it himself, used his foot to push off the floor and rotate the winch perpendicular to the helicopter. He pumped his right fist while holding on with his left hand and shouted, "Send me down!"

The cable lowered Oxendine to within twenty feet of Mahegan's motionless body. Immediately Oxendine had his pistol up and aimed at the former soldier. He stumbled as he walked across the windswept ridge, the breeze stiffening as the morning wore on. Perhaps a front was coming through. He could smell diesel and cordite wafting upward from the valley below.

He reached Mahegan and placed his knee in the man's back. Mahegan's body was warm as he removed the Sig Sauer Tribal from the belt clip on his holster and pocketed the weapon. An AR-15 was on the rock outcropping about twenty feet away—probably Mahegan's weapon and not a threat to him. He placed his hand against Mahegan's neck, feeling for a pulse, and whispered in Mahegan's ear, "If you're not dead now, you will be before you get up in the helicopter, traitor. I am Lumbee and will not have you embarrass our people. Better to die a hero than grow old? No, better that you die right now before we are all embarrassed by you."

Oxendine felt no pulse, but he was not an expert at such things. As such, he loosened his knee against Mahegan's back, removed his knife from its sheath on his own belt, and cuffed the handle and blade along his forearm.

He slid the blade toward Mahegan's upper abdomen and felt with his free hand for the gap between the ribs, but all he felt was ropey muscles.

Finding what he thought was an opening, he slowly slid the knife into Mahegan.

Mahegan felt the knee press into his back, but he was actually wondering about the sound of a diesel engine in the valley below directly prior to the helicopter hovering above him.

But now he knew this was the SBI agent who had been chasing him for the past day and a half. He was aware of the man's knee on his back. He heard the man whisper to him a Native American saying that had always been his creed: *Better to die a hero than grow old.*

Mahegan guessed that Oxendine believed that he had killed the Sledge family. He didn't know what the man knew or believed beyond that. Perhaps that he was involved in the terrorist base camp in the valley below?

Waiting for the right moment when the agent would be focused on his own task and not Mahegan's status, he delayed until he felt the sharp edge of the man's knife press against his abdomen. With a quick movement, Mahegan used his left leg and hip to rotate the agent in the direction he was already leaning. Then Mahegan used his left arm—hurting from holding on to Cassie—to jab his elbow into the agent's left rib cage. Those two motions reversed their positions quickly. Mahegan used an old wrestling move to slide on top of the agent and clasp his knife hand. He beat the hand against the rocks until the man's knife came loose and skittered away.

The helicopter was yawing above him, but he didn't care. Mahegan removed his Tribal pistol from the man's belt and then used the agent's handcuffs to lock his arms behind him.

He stood and aimed the pistol at the agent and then the helicopter, then back at the agent. He made a circling sign with his hand intent to indicate that he was going up in the helicopter. As the hoist was being lowered, Mahegan walked to the cliff where Cassie had fallen. It was a straight drop with a few trees poking out along the way. It was unlikely anyone could have survived that fall.

Mahegan pulled the large agent onto his shoulders like a sack of flour and sat on the wobbly T-seat. The cable began to pull them up as he listed beneath the Blackhawk. There was no wooden block or protective ceramic plate on the edge of the helicopter to shield the cable from the sharp edges of the helicopter chassis. As the cable swung, it banged against the metallic edge of the cargo floor. He watched as a cable strand frayed, and then another.

They were at about fifty feet above the rock ledge, and any fall would be fatal. As they approached the cargo door opening, the cable swung outward and then inward. He used the momentum to dump the agent's body onto the cargo floor of the aircraft. The cable swung out again as the pilot attempted to maneuver the helicopter against the buffeting winds.

Another cable strand snapped, and now there were fewer strands of the twisted cable holding him in the air than those that were severed and frayed. As the cable swung back toward the helicopter, his weight was too much for the remaining wires, and the cable snapped. Mahegan leapt from the falling T-seat and grasped the bottom of the floor of the helicopter, hanging in the air. He strained to pull up, but his left shoulder wouldn't function properly. It was separated from attempting to save Cassie.

Mahegan held on, looking up at the confused men who were tending to the cuffed agent and looking at him. One man reached over and grasped his wrist while another clasped his opposing forearm. The pilot tilted the aircraft to the left to try to make it easier, but it just made things harder. Mahegan looked up and then down and saw he was now hundreds of feet above ground level.

He also saw Alex Russell aiming her pistol at the helicopter. Perhaps the pilot was conducting evasive maneuvers.

The SWAT team members managed to get his torso into the

helicopter, and from there Mahegan kicked a leg up and rolled into the cargo space between the seats.

Immediately he had four AR-15 rifles in his face with men shouting at him. Mahegan looked up and saw a still-cuffed agent standing in the back of the helicopter, balancing himself as he raised his boot and kicked Mahegan in the head. For the second time in the last hour, Mahegan lost consciousness.

"Get these cuffs off of me now!" Oxendine yelled as the SWAT team members helped retrieve the hoist arm by turning it from perpendicular to inside the helicopter.

McQueary placed the headset on the cuffed Oxendine and said, "I'll remove these cuffs on one condition and that's that I'm in charge now, Agent."

"Sure thing, buddy," Oxendine said. McQueary removed the cuffs and sat Oxendine down.

"That kick was total bullshit. He saved you. That man could have killed you, and don't think I didn't see what you were doing down there. I'm beginning to wonder what you've got to hide. Why you want him dead so badly," McQueary said.

"He's bad seed," Oxendine muttered.

"Where to, Q?" Setz asked McQueary.

"Any sign of Captain Bagwell? Let's scan the ridge for her," McQueary said. "This guy's hurt bad, but let's give a quick look. We've been asked to look for Bagwell, so let's make a run along this ridge. If he kidnapped her, maybe she escaped."

"I've got movement to my eleven o'clock. One hundred yards. Female," Setz said.

"That's got to be her," Oxendine said. "Let's go!" He had replaced his headset, and regardless of what McQueary said or Mahegan had done, Oxendine was still in charge.

As the helicopter began to slowly pitch forward, Setz shouted, "Holy shit, she's shooting at me!"

Oxendine looked into the cockpit and saw the Plexiglas windscreen shattered so that navigating would be nearly impossible.

The helicopter pitched to the right and began careening past the ridge. Was Setz hit? The copilot had been quiet the entire time, and as Oxendine studied the bullet patterns in the windscreen, it appeared she might have been struck.

"Beverly, you still flying this thing?"

"Roger, but losing control. My collective is shot," Setz said. She struggled with the helicopter and fortunately had some room to fall on the eastern side. The Blackhawk leveled out, and Setz flew to Hendersonville Airfield, which ran parallel with I-26 about thirty miles south of Asheville.

"No gas at Buncombe and no room for a crash landing," Setz said.

"We need to get Mahegan to a hospital," McQueary said.

"I've called ahead," Setz said. "There is a hospital four miles from the airfield. There will be an ambulance waiting."

"No," Oxendine said. "The doctor works on him at the airport while I question him."

"You can't be serious," McQueary said. "This man is wounded. Head trauma."

"I'm serious as a heart attack. He's involved in something happening here. Those three guys were his men. Everywhere he is, there's bad guys coming at us. We can torture our enemies overseas? We can do the same here," Oxendine said.

"You know we can all actually hear what you're saying," McQueary remarked.

"I know you can. Write it down. Record it. Mahegan is on the gray list. Possible detain. His weapon was found near a murder scene. That weapon committed the murder. I've got a Skype meeting with my evidence team and operations center when we land," Oxendine said.

The aircraft hovered slowly and began to descend into the dark single-strip runway in Hendersonville. Blue lights flashed in the distance, serving as a beacon.

Setz did an adequate job of getting the hindered aircraft to the ground safely. As soon as they landed, the SWAT team disembarked and dragged Mahegan into one of the empty hangars, where they laid him on a sturdy worktable covered in grease and airplane parts.

"Get the ambulance over here now," McQueary said.

The medics came running, and the ambulance driver followed. The weak light in the hangar was insufficient, so the medics used the headlights from the ambulance to assess Mahegan's condition.

Oxendine watched as a car raced up next to the ambulance and a man and woman in blue scrubs leapt out of the car.

"We got the call there was a serious patient," the female doctor said. "Why isn't he in the ambulance?"

"Because I said so," Oxendine said. "This man is a terrorist on U.S. soil. We need him treated, but just enough so that we can question him."

"Once a patient goes into my care . . . whoever you are . . . they remain in my care. Is that clear?"

"I'm Special Agent Tommy Oxendine, and I'm in charge here. Do what you have to do to keep him alive, nothing more."

The doctor shook her head and said, "I'm not wasting any more time with you."

She walked up to Mahegan, and Oxendine followed. Frankly, Mahegan looked okay. He wasn't sure what McQueary and the others were talking about.

Then he saw the blood coming from Mahegan's ears.

"Q, guard this place like it's your home and child molesters want your daughter," Oxendine said. McQueary nodded and deployed his men to the four corners of the hangar.

Oxendine walked to the small building that some might have considered a terminal. It looked like an abandoned brick ranch house with a glass door instead of a wooden one. Inside was a man dressed with a UNC–Chapel Hill Tar Heels jersey over a set of blue overalls. He had gray hair and a sleepy face with jowls hanging like a bulldog's.

"Can I do you for?" the man asked.

"I'm Special Agent Oxendine with the State Bureau of Investigation. You got Wi-Fi?" His adrenaline was flowing.

"I'm Tucker Thompson. I'm in charge of this airfield. You're on my turf, so back it down just a bit."

Oxendine had his man, but something was nagging him at the back of his mind. He had four text messages from Lucy Cartwright, the officer in charge of the SBI operations center. While he could get testy with Director Black, a one-and-done patronage appointee too scared to leave his office, he preferred not to piss off Cartwright, and he'd already pushed those boundaries. She was known for incisive decision making, slightly outranked Oxendine, and was well connected with both political parties. The texts referenced his forensic technician at the Sledge crime scene who needed him to call her, or preferably, to Skype with her. She had something to show him.

"Wi-Fi?" Oxendine reiterated. He wasn't backing down.

"Yeah, we got Wi-Fi out here, Special Agent. Here's the password," Thompson said, handing him a piece of paper.

Oxendine nodded, retrieved his iPad from his pack, and powered it on. Shortly, he was connected to Skype and called Cartwright. As the Skype call was buzzing, he looked up at Thompson, who pointed out a small room. Oxendine closed the door as Cartwright came on the screen.

"We've got him, Lucy. Wrapping this thing up," Oxendine said. He sat in a chair at a small gray, metal desk with several papers loosely scattered across the top. He smelled old sweat and cardboard. This was someone's office, rarely used.

"Tommy, look. This thing isn't what we think it is," she said. "We've got a team at General Savage's house in Vass, and someone stole this pistol from a shadow box."

"So? Mahegan stole it."

"No, it was a gift from Mahegan. Right there in the shadow box it has an inscription on a brass plate that says, 'Congrats, Boss.' And there's a bunch of initials, including. P.O., C.M., S.O'M. That's Patch Owens, Chayton Mahegan, and Sean O'Malley. Owens and O'Malley went missing when General Savage did, apparently. No one can find them."

"You're saying this is a group effort? Savage murdered his ex-wife? Mahegan and them are in on it or running that operation in the mountains?"

"I don't know anything about the mountains and, no, that's not what I'm saying. Remember the sliding boot prints? When kids try on their parents' shoes and try to walk, they always slip and slide. My daughter did that just the other day with a pair of my heels. Made me think of these casts Emily took from the crime scene. Someone wore bigger boots than their feet required. Someone was trying to make it look like Mahegan."

Oxendine paused, the adrenaline keeping his mind in high gear. "I don't know, Lucy. What about the fingerprints on the military police car?"

"Well that, too. Those military policemen were Syrian terrorists. The one still alive is talking. Not saying much, but the FBI is there in Moore County setting up shop now."

"The FBI! Why didn't you tell me?" Oxendine roared. He wanted to have this thing wrapped in a tight little package with a bow before the feds got involved.

"I just did. Now calm down. You can still win this thing," Cartwright said, knowing Oxendine perhaps better than he knew himself.

"Not looking to win anything," he said, knowing his voice sounded hollow.

"Okayyy," Cartwright said. "Here's what I'm seeing based upon the evidence. We have two dead terrorists in a golf lodge in Pinehurst. One was shot by a Sig Sauer Tribal and the other by an AR-15. Very distinctive hammer imprint on the shell casings. See what kind of pistol your guys got off Mahegan. Second, when we were checking Savage's house in nearby Vass, we found Mahegan's Jeep Cherokee. Government issued, but it's his. Fingerprints all over it. Was in Savage's garage. We also matched slugs found in the wall of the Pinehurst golf lodge to the two weapons—an AR-15 and a Glock 19—found in Mahegan's Jeep. The military police vehicle the terrorists used left tire tracks in the back of Savage's property, and there's a set of storm doors there. No one has been able to get past the combination lock yet, but they're trying. Somebody framed Mahegan or maybe even thought they were framing Savage, because they stole the pistol from Savage's house. There's just no way Mahegan did what you think he did. The pistol, the MPs, the boots, and last, the shooter's stance."

"The shooter's stance?"

"Yes, the bedroom has thick pile carpet. Top-of-the-line padding underneath. Mahegan weighs maybe two hundred thirty pounds, right? Big guy. The casts Emily took and demonstrations she did using some of the techs on scene show that the shooter used a square stance, feet level with one another, and weighed between one hundred twenty and one hundred seventy, max."

Oxendine thought for a moment. Clearly Cartwright was trying to convince him that Mahegan was not his man. He had to work his way through the maze of untangling his beliefs and the evidence Cartwright had just presented. His eagerness to capture Mahegan had driven him like jet fuel, but first and foremost, Oxendine considered himself a patriot and a North Carolinian. Sure, he'd never served in the military, but he'd been law enforcement all of his life. Same thing, mostly, Oxendine believed. It's about service, not personal goals and vendettas.

He sighed audibly. Cartwright noticed.

"Okay. Flushed all that you believed before?"

"You're getting me there, Lucy. Damnit. Who made you so smart?"

"My daughter. Now listen," she continued, "Vicki Sledge kept a journal. There was another woman involved with General Savage. Her father is some big shot."

Cartwright continued.

And then it all made sense to Oxendine.

CHAPTER 33

ALEX RUSSELL/AMERI ASSAD RAISED HER ARMS TO THE DEPARTING helicopter and shouted, "Kill me, you bastard!"

Calm down, calm down now, Alex, Ameri said to Alex.

"What the fuck! I'm talking to myself," Alex said.

No. You're talking to me, Ameri. I'm who you are. I'm here to help you through this. We're here to kill the Americans who killed Fatima and Malavdi. You've planned all of this. They work for you and you're calling the shots. Now we need to get back to the one place we are safe and we can finish the job.

She stumbled forward and put one foot in front of the other. With one hand holding the pistol and the other grasping pine limbs filled with sap, she wound her way to her Land Rover. After opening the door, she fell inside and closed the door. Would the helicopter shoot a missile and incinerate her? Or would she be able to get to her supply of PKCzeta shots and help her fight Ameri Assad, her split personality? The only way to survive was to erase the memory, to overdose, and perhaps even kill herself.

But had she done too much already? Had she killed? If so, how many people? Would she kill again?

The real problem was that the moment Alex Russell had a thought, an idea, an impulse, or an emotion, Ameri Assad was right there to analyze it, interpret it, and pass judgment on whether it was useful to Ameri's purposes. Like an inspector. The thought police. And of course Ameri wanted Vicki Sledge dead because it would implicate both Jake Mahegan and General Savage, the two men most responsible for Fatima and Malavdi's deaths.

But Ameri wanted total destruction. The convoy had been totally destroyed, which had totally destroyed Ameri's world, so why not destroy their world?

"Drive, bitch," Alex whispered to herself.

Drive, bitch.

Alex drove all the way down the snaking two-track trail into the valley where the Bible camp had been. She parked and walked into the cottage she knew was the prison cell. Inside, she found the chairman of the Joints Chiefs shot through the head and his wife shot twice. Murder–suicide? Doubtful. It smelled more of Zakir, who had burned Yazidis in cages. What was the difference? *To kill someone in a cage by any method is cowardly,* Ameri whispered in her ear.

Don't be cowardly.

Ameri wanted her to see this. It was fuel for Alex to keep moving.

This is who started it. Now do what you have to do, Alex.

Alex had one more task inside the base camp. She drove the Land Rover and parked it, then backed it up, got out, did what she needed to do, got back in, pulled out of the dark area, and then pulled her way up the valley the same way the Mack truck had left earlier. Alex looked over her shoulder through the rear window and saw everything that was to come.

Atta girl, Alex. Now you're talking.

Alex Russell turned her Land Rover onto the Blue Ridge Parkway and then onto I-40. She had a long drive ahead of her and desperately needed her shots.

But Ameri was in charge and Ameri said, *No. Way.*

Just be calm, Alex. You're almost there. What? Four hours? You've waited four years. What is four hours?

She struggled a bit with her Land Rover. The farther away from her condo—and the empty vials of her medication—she drove, the heavier her burden became.

Eat something, Alex.

Her hand reached out and grabbed a box of Luna Bars. They weren't anything but candy, but Alex was hungry. She'd been awake for two days now. She needed nourishment if she was to finish her drive.

Atta girl, Alex. Keep driving.

CHAPTER 34

THE DOCTOR STITCHED UP MAHEGAN'S CALF AND ABDOMEN AND tried to put his left arm in a sling, but Mahegan said, "No way."

He sat up on the makeshift operating table and looked out of the hangar. There was a SWAT team member at each corner. The sun was rising and the air smelled of a fresh mountain morning. Dew shone on the grass like a million tiny diamonds, and the impossibility of what had transpired in the last two days seemed just that, impossible.

When he stood to walk, his calf bit at him slightly, as did his left shoulder, forever the bearer of pain and anguish.

"You need a sling, Captain," the doctor said. She was probably in her forties and tall. She was a sturdy woman, in command of her presence and those around her. The nametape on her smock read, "Peters."

"Dr. Peters, thank you for patching me up, but I need to stretch my legs. They're cramping up."

"Yeah, okay," Doctor Peters said. "Go stretch your damn legs. All of you can go take a flying leap for all I care."

"Thank you. Truly," Mahegan said. He shook her hand and felt her deflate. He imagined she'd had a rough night, especially if she had been dealing with the aggressive agent. He couldn't fault the agent for his aggression, but he could fault him for his closed-mindedness. The man had to have been blind to so many clues that even Mahegan had discerned.

He walked to the edge of the corrugated metal hangar and watched the sun nose over the ridge to the east. He heard the hiss of tires on what he suspected was I-26 running north and south. Maybe it was I-40, but the way the sun was coming up and the fact that he heard someone mention Hendersonville, he was pretty sure the road was I-26.

To his right was a brick building. Next to that was a shorter man wearing SWAT team gear and a larger man that had to be the special agent in charge. They both looked in his direction, then turned away and finished their conversation. Then the bigger man broke in his direction with a long, powerful stride.

"Who said you could step outside of this hangar?" the man shouted.

Mahegan looked over his shoulder, miming that surely the man was not talking to him.

"Yeah, I'm talking to you!"

"I really don't think you are," Mahegan said.

The man stopped directly in front of Mahegan. His nostrils were flaring like a bull's, sucking and pulling at the oxygen, filling his lungs, exhaling in Mahegan's face. The man was an inch shorter than him, maybe twenty pounds lighter. He had felt his weight on the ridge and now could see that, although it would be no easy task, the man was beatable. The camouflage nametape on his tactical uniform read: Oxendine. He had flat, black eyes and a hook nose. His face bore the pockmarks of an acned youth. Sparse black hairs poked through oily pores. The man had not shaved in a couple of days.

"The doctor put four stitches where you cut me, Agent Oxendine. She asked me how it happened. I told her some asshole didn't know how to use a knife."

Oxendine closed the gap even further between them. His nose was maybe two inches from Mahegan's. Oxendine's stale, foul breath washed over his face.

"Then I told her that I easily subdued the asshole, but instead of killing him, which might have been the best option now that I've got some time to think about it, I let the asshole live. She then asked me, 'Why did you do that?' And I said, 'You know, good point, Doc.' So, if you really want to have it, let's go, Tonto, right now. I have some fresh stitches you could bravely rip out. I've got a dislocated shoulder you could come after. Calf is all shot up. But you know what? I'd still kick your ass and put your head through that sheet metal right there. And I'd leave you there as some kind of exhibit for the good people of Hendersonville. They could come here and pay five dollars to see what a genuine asshole looks like. There'd be a line a mile long just to see that. And if you tried to move your head, it would rip your neck off and you'd just be some kind of display. You so much as twitch, asshole, that's the result. I'm telling you this now to be fair. I'm not putting my knee in your spine and literally trying to stab you in the back. I'm face-to-face telling you that your head will be through that wall. Now, do you understand *me*, Tonto?"

Oxendine stood his ground, continued breathing on Mahegan.

"You can move in one direction, and that is backward, out of my face. And if you don't do that in the next five seconds—"

Oxendine moved, but it wasn't backward.

The agent's right shoulder twitched, which indicated the man was making a close quarters hand-to-hand combat move on him. Mahegan's left hand snatched Oxendine's right wrist as he locked his left elbow to immobilize Oxendine's dominant hand. Mahegan swiftly pivoted under Oxendine's right hand by releasing his pressure a bit, allowing the natural force of Oxendine's arm to elevate, creating the gap for him to slide beneath. He then used his right arm to encircle Oxendine's waist as he released the man's right wrist.

Mahegan then planted his left leg in front of Oxendine's left leg as he slid his forearm in between Oxendine's right arm and his back. He immobilized Oxendine momentarily and said, "I'm giving you one last chance."

But Oxendine continued to struggle and said, "You're going down."

Mahegan then quickly slid his left arm around Oxendine's waist as he removed his left leg and the arm bar, latching his hands together as he deadlifted Oxendine's body onto his stomach. He was vaguely aware that a small crowd had formed, including the doctor, who must have been wondering what the hell she had been brought into. Oxendine flailed his arms, reached for his knife, realized Mahegan had already tossed that on the ground, and tried back-kicking Mahegan with his legs.

But Mahegan walked step-by-step about ten yards up to the wall of the metal hangar and then flipped out of the way, released Oxendine, watched the man thud into the ground, and then put his knee firmly in Oxendine's back as the man struggled to get up.

They were parallel to the hangar, and Mahegan slowly repositioned Oxendine so that his face was pressed up against the corrugated metal. He grabbed Oxendine's hair, lifted the man's head against the forceful pull of his neck in the opposite direction, and thought, *Why is he making it easy on me?*

"That's enough, Mahegan!"

Mahegan didn't know who was talking, and he really didn't care. This mustang needed to be broken.

He let go of Oxendine's head, which slammed into the metal wall with a loud thud. While the agent was stunned from that moderate blow to his hard head, Mahegan squatted to one side, placed one hand in the man's tactical belt and the other at the top of his tactical vest, lifted him in a straight deadlift, gauging him to be about two hundred twenty pounds, swung him back from the metal hangar, took a step back, and then lunged forward leading with Oxendine's head, which banged loudly against the metal.

It didn't go through, but he did feel Oxendine go limp in his hands. He dropped the agent on the ground and turned to find five SWAT team members with their rifles aimed at him.

"What? You've spent two days with that prick. You can't tell me none of you guys wanted to do that," Mahegan said.

A few of the men smirked. He sized up the team and chose the man with the name tag. "McQueary."

"Officer McQueary. I suggest we go sit in a room where we can pull up a map and have a conversation. I heard a Mack truck or other kind of rig firing up in the valley when the helicopter came down on me. I saw a large weapon crate in the mine shaft. The crate was wooden. Like all ammunition crates, but maybe fifteen feet long and five feet wide. Like a missile or a bomb. This was when we were pulling out General Savage and two of my former Delta teammates."

"Shit. We had a firefight with those guys," McQueary said.

"No, you didn't. They warned you away. None of you would be alive if they wanted to kill you," Mahegan said.

McQueary nodded in apparent agreement.

"Let's sit down in there while the doctor stitches my leg again," Mahegan said.

The four SWAT team members, initially confused, followed their boss's lead into the brick terminal. A man dressed in a light blue UNC–Chapel Hill Tar Heels jersey and overalls smiled and gave Mahegan a thumbs-up.

"I'll be selling those tickets," the man said. "Be nice to have a genuine asshole on display."

Mahegan nodded. "I'm glad to help."

"Just get me out of here in time for the Heels game, y'hear?"

Mahegan kept walking and nodded. He guessed it was a Saturday college game.

They huddled in the office that Oxendine had used earlier. His iPad was still there on the desk, connected to something. The FaceTime display presented itself, and Mahegan pressed the green ANSWER button.

"Who's that?" Mahegan asked, lifting the device.

A young woman's face came on the screen and said, "Better question. Who are you and where's Agent Oxendine?"

"I'm Jake Mahegan here with Officer McQueary of the Charlotte–Mecklenburg SWAT team. Agent Oxendine is resting," Mahegan said.

"But . . . you're the guy we've been trying to catch," she said. The woman was midforties, hair pulled back in a tight ponytail, thin lips, no makeup, tired eyes but alert. Her face was the size of the screen.

"They caught me. What's your name?"

"Can you let me see Officer McQueary?"

Mahegan handed the device to McQueary, who said, "Hi, Lucy, it's me. Everything is cool."

Mahegan listened for code words. "Cool" could have been an alarm, he wasn't sure. McQueary handed the iPad back to Mahegan and said, "Go ahead. You've seen more than we have."

"Hi, Lucy. What's your job?"

"I'm the officer on duty in Raleigh at the Joint Operations Center in the National Guard building. We've got the governor and secretary of public safety coming in at ten a.m. for an update. Basically, I'm in charge until they get here."

"This thing might be over by then," Mahegan said. The clock on the wall read ten minutes after nine. Realistically, whatever was supposed to happen would occur in the next twenty-four hours. The Syrians knew that they couldn't sustain this thing much beyond that.

"Well, then we better get to it," Cartwright said.

"Okay, first of all, I didn't kill the Sledge family, but right now think about the concept of 'Among many, one.' It's an old Native American proverb about creating multiple events to disguise the one event you wanted to have happen. Someone killed the Sledge family. Meanwhile, the chairman of the Joint Chiefs is kidnapped. A family on Fort Bragg is slaughtered. A general is assassinated in Iraq. A general is arrested in Tampa.

"Which of those things did they really want to happen? Of course whoever planned and executed all of those missions is thrilled they all achieved success. There were probably others that failed. But my guess is, because they used a pistol I gave Savage, they wanted to frame Savage and disable him. And if whoever did this knew that Savage hadn't properly registered the gift, they wanted the police after me, too. Why, though? Someone perhaps knows that Savage has a means to disrupt attacks on the homeland and by kidnapping him and putting Oxendine on my ass for two days, that capability would be disrupted. To what end, you ask?"

"As they say on *Law and Order*, 'Asked and answered.' Please continue," Cartwright said.

"I saw a large crate about fifteen feet long inside the mine shaft where we fought about thirty or so Syrian terrorists. Your local murder in Charlotte is connected to an international terrorist plot. Savage thinks it's a nuke. My question for you is, have you gotten any reports of missing weapons?"

"No missing weapons," Cartwright said, looking away for a moment.

Officer McQueary spoke up offscreen. "Lucy, we already know that a surface-to-air missile fired at the helicopter. I was on that. It had to be a Stinger missile. So checking our National Guard armories might be a good place to start."

"Roger that, Q. The general will be coming in with the rest of the brass," Cartwright said.

Mahegan stared at the screen, forgetting that Cartwright could see him. What was he missing? A lot, he was sure, but something was hanging right in front of his face. The cars that stopped suddenly. There was something there.

"You still with us Mahegan?"

"Among many, one," he whispered.

"Right, you asked me to think about that. All I got right now is . . . nothing," Cartwright said.

The crate Mahegan had seen was big enough for a JDAM missile or even a small, tactical nuclear device, but that seemed beyond comprehension. Why stop all the cars at once? Because it was a cool thing to do? To psyche the American people? A prank that cost lives in accidents? He didn't see any of that.

Among many, one.

"Lucy, can you pull up on your computer the transit routes for ammunition? There's the Military Ocean Terminal at Sunny Point in Brunswick County on the coast. I-40 starts there. Do you track shipments there?"

"We do. Those shipments come in almost entirely on rail," Cartwright said. Her voice was confident. This was something she knew.

Mahegan continued to think about the options. He could hear the hissing of the tires on the interstate as the morning picked up. It was Saturday. People whose cars were operational were going to the mall or the big city of Charlotte.

"What about Interstate 26?" Mahegan asked.

"That's classified. You're not cleared," Cartwright said quickly again.

"Okay, that's something," Mahegan said. "I have clearance at the highest levels, but I can't prove any of that to you right now. I'll step out and you can tell Officer McQueary whatever travels on that road. But I would ask you to check your logs or whatever you've got that monitors weapons moving along our interstates and rail lines, specifically I-26. And specifically what was moving at nine yesterday morning and where it was supposed to be—"

"Oh my God," Cartwright said.

"What?" Mahegan asked. He was about to hand the iPad to McQueary but stopped and looked at her. She was staring at something to the side, as if she had put her phone down and was now working at a computer station. Mahegan could see the side of her head and the white reflection of a computer monitor, but he couldn't read any of the words. She looked back at her phone.

"Put Officer McQueary on, please," Cartwright said.

Mahegan handed the iPad to McQueary but stayed where he was. Evidently Cartwright didn't care, because she began speaking.

"The Office of Secure Transportation put out an alert late last night that it lost signal on one of its armored tractors during Friday morning's rush hour network attack."

"What's the—" McQueary began.

"It's the guys who move nukes around," Mahegan said. During his time as a special mission unit operator it was his business to track some sensitive weapon movements. He took the iPad back.

"Where was the rig when they lost signal?"

"On Interstate 40, just west of Asheville. Oh my God."

"Roger that. So we're looking for a nondescript black cab and gray trailer. Somehow these guys overpowered it and among all the noise, the reports got lost and some bureaucrats didn't want to admit that they couldn't find their truck."

"This explains the firefight we heard about in that location. We were getting calls of road rage all day long. We were overwhelmed. Says here that a search team is leaving this morning from Washington, DC, to look for them."

"It's a little late for that. The Syrians have been inside every computer network they want for the last three days. I'm sure they knew to disable the GPS on the truck. Can we call this Office of Secure Transporation and ask them if they can light it up somehow? I'll get McQueary here and the Blackhawk, and we'll chase it down," Mahegan said.

"Are you saying that they're using it as a weapon?" Cartwright asked.

"It *is* a weapon. And why steal it if you're not going to use it?" To McQueary, Mahegan said, "Grab your guys and tell them we're going to chase a Mack truck."

"What about Oxendine?" McQueary asked.

"Is he awake? If so, I'll knock his ass out again. He's useless. Let's go," Mahegan said.

"I'm awake," Oxendine said. "And you're under arrest."

Oxendine was holding his pistol up with an unsteady hand.

"Agent Oxendine," Cartwright said. "I'm the watch officer on duty. I have placed Officer McQueary in charge of this operation. You are to stand down. Anything you do from this point forward that countermands my orders will be considered insubordination."

Mahegan liked Cartwright.

"Stand down, Agent," Mahegan said. "You heard the officer."

Oxendine lowered his pistol slowly and looked at McQueary. "I'll listen to you, but not to him."

McQueary nodded, looked at Mahegan and then at the iPad.

"Any word?" McQueary asked Cartwright.

"I've secure chatted with the watch officer for the OST, who says that they've been trying for a day and a half to turn on the truck's GPS and other RFID tags. Someone must have pulled that thing apart," Cartwright said.

Mahegan reflected for a moment. Where was Alex? Where was Cassie? They were both part of this somehow. He had last seen Alex on the mountaintop, and he had heard the diesel engine of the Mack truck, so unless Alex had moved quickly, there was no way she was with the truck.

Cassie had fallen some distance. The terrain below had looked brutal and unforgiving. Mahegan's bet was that Cassie was dead, broken on the rocks below the ridge above the terrorist valley. But still, there was one way to check: her cell phone. The FBI had tracked her using her car GPS and then her cell phone. If she was still alive and if she still had her phone, then there was a possibility.

"Lucy, the FBI has Cassie Bagwell's cell phone number. See if they can ping it. It was questionable whether it was working, but it's in her cargo pocket. There was a Velcro pouch inside the pocket. That's where I put it. She might be dead on the side of a mountain not far from here, or she might be in that Mack truck."

"Roger. There's a joint operations center in the Pentagon that has an interagency task force set up. That's who I'm secure chatting with. Apparently we are now the main show. Ever since we asked about OST. They probably got their ass handed to them, but who cares? Okay, secure chat sent. FBI has rogered. Says, 'wait one.' It's bubbling."

Mahegan assumed the "bubbling" was the indicator that a text was being prepared by the individual on the other end. Cartwright was talking in excited but precise tones. She was professional and in her element. The way she had shut down Oxendine was classic, without hesitation.

"Okay, here it is. Holy shit. They've got it," Cartwright said.

"Where is she?" Mahegan asked.

"She, or rather her phone, is moving sixty-five miles per hour on U.S. Seventy-Four just outside of the town of Shelby heading east toward Charlotte."

"That's it," Mahegan said. "She's either dead or alive, but we've got to get eyes on that truck." He turned to McQueary. "My money says that they have about ten to fifteen commandos left. They'll be in trucks or SUVs on either side, making it look official. The Mack truck and trailer are nondescript. There's no way anyone would know there is a nuke in there."

"The FBI is just getting all chatty here. The missing nuke is a B61-12 that was getting transported to Tennessee to get its upgrade to make it precision guided," Cartwright said.

"That nuke is one of our lower yield nukes," Mahegan said. "Just about fifty kilotons. Hiroshima was fifteen kilotons by comparison. Just FYI. So, about three and a half times as bad as Hiroshima. We've all seen that video."

McQueary turned to his four men and said, "Saddle up. We've got to stop it."

Mahegan said, "Roger."

Among many, one.

And Mahegan kept thinking. He stared at a map of North Carolina on the wall. It had all of the airfields but also showed the major road arteries. He saw U.S. 74 and the town of Shelby. It was maybe an hour to Charlotte. What could they be doing on a Saturday in Charlotte?

Mahegan looked through the window and saw a group of men talking on the apron. The man who had joked that he would be happy to sell the tickets to view a genuine asshole like Oxendine was standing there.

Wearing his UNC–Chapel Hill Tar Heels football jersey.

Just get me to the game in time . . .

A nuke at a football game in uptown Charlotte?

CHAPTER 35

Jackknife rumbled along the highway, thinking this is still winnable. The cargo was precious and deadly and would destroy precisely what needed to be destroyed.

Mostly it would destroy the spirit of the American people, because if that venue could be attacked in today's environment, then any venue was vulnerable. And that was an important message to send.

If a simple wedding party in the Syrian countryside was vulnerable, then why shouldn't one of the most sacred places in America be vulnerable as well.

Jackknife tried not to think postdestruction. It was inconceivable, actually. Everything Jackknife had done for the past four years had been focused on this plan: recruiting Gavril and Zakir, developing the plan, orchestrating the logistics, gathering the intelligence, holding everything together, and synchronizing the entire plan.

Jackknife had tasted the blood by shooting Vicki Sledge with her husband and child. What was it Mahegan had said?

"Among many, one."

That had been Jackknife's entire strategy all along. The kill on Vicki Sledge was masked by multiple other kills that day, forcing law enforcement to try to figure out all of those simultaneous murders in a very short period. The Trojan that disabled the cars had been designed to create enough chaos for Zakir and his men to hijack the Mack truck carrying the weapon. Predictably it was lost in twenty-four hours of chaos, which was what Jackknife had anticipated based upon Jackknife's own experience with bureaucracies.

With the lack of sleep for the past several days, Jackknife welcomed the bumpy road.

Staying awake through the finale was important. Revenge would never taste so good.

CHAPTER 36

Zakir watched Ratta navigate the village of Shelby. It was frustrating to have to slow down, stop at red lights, and then speed back up. He had considered going all the way to Interstate 85 into South Carolina and then back up to Charlotte, but that route seemed longer. Now he wondered if he had made the right decision. This bumpy road was not good for their mission.

Ratta had disabled all of the RFID tags, making Zakir less concerned about being tracked by the police or military. He knew that they would soon locate his position and where he might be headed. But given even the specter of what he might be carrying in the back of the Mack truck, law enforcement would tread carefully. They would not want to shoot into the body of the trailer for fear of detonation. Likewise, the police would know what the truck was carrying and wouldn't want to cause an accident that could have the unintended consequence of explosion.

Through the windshield of the truck cab, the stores and subdivisions sprawled through the countryside. Everything seemed normal, but that was all about to change. Zakir felt as if they were going downhill most of the way, which made sense, as they were leaving the Blue Ridge Mountains and traveling through the Piedmont of North Carolina. God's country, as he had heard some people call it. They were racing down some hills and powering up others, the clutch and gears grinding beneath the strain of the steep inclines. But still, in all, they were falling away from the mountains and toward less severe terrain.

He looked over his shoulder at Cassie Bagwell, who was sitting in the sleeping cab with her back to the wall. They locked eyes. Zakir nodded at her as if to say, *I did what you surely wanted me to do.*

Cassie stared back at him. *Approval,* he wondered? She was hurt, and Zakir had done his best to stabilize what looked like a broken arm. His men had found her in a small grouping of sapling pine trees that had been strong enough to absorb her fall without breaking but flexible enough to bend and not cause her severe harm. Somehow she had managed to hang on to her rucksack, which they had collected with her. Zakir watched her head bounce with the bumpy road and wondered if she understood the enormity of what was happening. The wheels that she had set in motion with her intelligence report, which led to Operation Groomsman.

As they exited the town limits, Ratta was able to pick up some speed. They grinded up a long grade called Kings Mountain, then flew down the back side into the valley and turned northeast onto Interstate 85. From there, they were less than an hour from the United Bank of America Stadium.

The football game was to start at twelve-thirty, with the pregame activities peaking around noon, which was when Zakir wanted to be there. He knew that the closer he got to the stadium, the tougher it might be to gain full access. Just being in the proximity would be good enough. The entire world was going to come down on him. He might die fighting, but he was finally feeling the sense of justice he had been seeking.

For Malavdi. For Fatima.

The Mack truck barreled along I-85 at eighty miles per hour like a cruise missile with programmed attack coordinates. The traffic was steady and growing.

As they were passing the town of Gastonia, he looked in the passenger side-view mirror.

The helicopter was bearing down on them.

Zakir smiled.

* * *

Jake Mahegan stepped into a crewman's vest, or monkey harness, and clicked his snap link into the rappelling D ring in the floor of the Blackhawk helicopter. The wind buffeted his face through the open door, and Setz, the pilot, tilted the helicopter's nose forward to gain on the Mack truck in the distance.

There had been a brief debate about crew rest and flight safety, but Setz was having none of that, Mahegan had noticed. The pilot had started this mission and she wanted to finish it.

Mahegan leaned into the wind until the monkey harness strap was taught. He felt like a jumpmaster performing a door check, but now he was scouting for the best possible way to stop a Mack truck with a nuclear device on it. They sped away from the Hendersonville Airfield and toward Charlotte, using U.S. 74 as a centerline guidepost. By being able to track Cassie's iPhone, they would be able to interdict the truck prior to its reaching the Clemson versus UNC–Chapel Hill football game in the Carolina Panthers football stadium.

The problem was that a nuclear device would destroy everything within five miles and most things within fifteen miles. Their window to stop the Mack truck was very small if they wanted to minimize damage.

Mahegan had studied the map and recommended that the best place for a standoff would be the bridges over the Catawba River. Those were equidistant between the town of Gastonia and the big city of Charlotte. If the device was on a timer, there was very little they could do about it except try to get inside what he expected to be a well-defended truck with jihadists surrounding both the truck on the outside and the bomb on the inside. The Syrians had become a phalanx of suicide bombers.

Mahegan had asked McQueary to direct that the local fire departments near those two crossings mass their trucks and create an impenetrable barrier. He didn't give specifics of the threat but did tell McQueary to use the term "national security emergency" when talking to the police and fire chiefs of Gaston and Mecklenburg Counties. At a minimum, Mahegan wanted that truck in the river to deaden the blast and occlude its lateral burst radius. While the blast would still be devastating, its impact might be mitigated.

It was at times like these that he needed the backup of General Savage, Patch Owens, and Sean O'Malley. For example, if Savage was on hand, Mahegan might be able to get a Chinook helicopter to do what he was going to try to do with a Blackhawk.

Wondering where his teammates might be, Mahegan continued to focus on his resources at hand. He had four SWAT team members, including their seemingly reliable leader, Lieutenant McQueary. He had asked for and received one truck driver from the small crowd that had gathered near the airfield as the sun had risen on the crazy morning. They had a Blackhawk helicopter with two General Electric T700 engines pushing the aircraft over Shelby, North Carolina, en route to the Catawba River crossing of I-85 and U.S. 74. In the Blackhawk helicopter were two pilots and two crewmen that served as door gunners. They had mounted on the pintles the two M240B machine guns in the crewman's doors.

Those machine guns might be useful when the Blackhawk slowed to a hover above the Mack truck. Mahegan had developed the plan in the Hendersonville brick building, working with the SWAT team, assigning each man a mission. It would take the entire crew to accomplish the task, and even then he wasn't certain. He had gathered four thick fast ropes, lifting shackles, and other materials flown in from the Air National Guard base in Charlotte.

Mahegan had the pilot lower the cargo hook at Hendersonville Airfield, where he secured the four ropes with lifting shackles. At the opposite end of each rope were similar shackles that each of the four SWAT team members would have to secure to the trailer.

Mahegan had the task of escorting the truck driver to the connection between the cab and the trailer. Ideally they would do this before the bridges, because Mahegan did not believe the enemy would stop and could possibly blow through whatever defenses the locals were able to construct.

As he hung outside of the helicopter, the four thick ropes

swayed and bounced with the rapid hum of the rotor blades. He looked over his shoulder at the SWAT team, each man lost in his own thoughts. Then Mahegan looked over his other shoulder and saw the trucker, Jimmy Ray Cranston, who had turned his Catfish Junction hat around and was praying. The man had said he'd never been in a helicopter before, but if his country needed his help, then who was he to say no. He wore an Aerosmith T-shirt over blue dungarees and scuffed work boots. He had a denim jacket that he had removed because he was sweating despite the 150 mile an hour wind blowing through the open doors of the helicopter.

They crested Kings Mountain, the isolated terrain feature of Crowders Mountain loomed ahead. The highway was a small ribbon of asphalt angling through the valley. The helicopter banked northeast, and then there it was.

The Mack truck was surrounded by its own escort of pickup trucks with gunners in the beds of each truck.

Beyond the Mack truck the blue and red lights of police and emergency vehicles flashed maybe six miles away. They immediately began taking fire, and the door gunners pivoted the machine guns toward the nose of the aircraft when Mahegan said, "Enemy, twelve o'clock. Pickup trucks. Avoid the Mack truck."

Both gunners raked the pickups and did an impressive job on the first pass. Setz flew past the convoy and spun around for one more gun run before lining up and matching their speed with the truck. Two of the six trucks had caught fire and one more had wrecked. That left three trucks and their associated gunners. The second pass of the helicopter included a broadside sweep first of the south side with the starboard gunner firing at max rate into the one pickup on that side. Setz swung around the tail end of the Mack truck and sped past the two pickups on that side, with both gunners now unloading massive amounts of lead. The port gunner had removed his machine gun from the pintle and laid it on the floor of the helicopter next to Mahegan's feet for better aim. One of the pickup trucks exploded, and the other careened into the guardrail.

Immediately Setz had the helicopter matching the speed of the Mack truck. They dropped the four ropes, with Mahegan going first without gloves. They didn't have enough, so he gave the trucker his gloves, which seemed to be working fine as the man slid down the rope and landed clumsily on the roof of the trailer.

"I'm a fireman, too," the man said, smiling as his baseball hat blew off his head.

"Get on all fours," Mahegan said.

Next the four SWAT team members slid down the ropes and began moving to the lifting points for the trailer. All trailers were constructed to have multiple lifting points so that port container handlers could most easily move the cargo. Mahegan was praying that the top rail of this nuclear-carrying container was an extension of a solid-state body of the container. Otherwise, when they began to lift the container, they would peel the roof off it and lose any opportunity to mitigate the nuke. But it was all they had, because the ropes weren't long enough to reach the bottom of the container.

Mahegan led the truck driver to the front of the trailer and climbed down the security ladder onto the metal arms of the trailer hitch. He noticed that the cab had a sliding metal plate with a wire mesh window behind it. Spreading his feet on the yawing truck base, he had Jimmy Ray lay down on the base and used his metal fifth wheel puller to reach beneath the trailer and partially unlock the jaws of the fifth wheel.

When Jimmy Ray had the fifth wheel ready to completely set the kingpin free from the fifth wheel, he nodded at Mahegan. Mahegan's hands were on the air brake lines. Jimmy Ray had told him if he pulled the air brake lines off, the vehicle would not be without brakes; rather, all of the brakes on the cab and the trailer would engage at once.

Mahegan wanted that to happen, but only once the four lifting shackles were secured and the fifth wheel jaws were ready to open.

McQueary gave him a thumbs-up. About the time he looked at

Jimmy Ray, the truck swerved and hit a large pothole. Jimmy Ray bounced up, tumbled, dropped the fifth wheel puller, and was hanging over the edge of the speeding trailer, about to fall.

Mahegan turned, grabbed Jimmy Ray by the rear of his blue jeans, and lifted. "Push, man. You've got to push up, Jimmy Ray," Mahegan said. The man's head was nearly scraping the concrete road. Mahegan risked another step forward on the unstable platform, grabbed Jimmy Ray's shirt, and pulled hard. The trucker was able to reach back and get his hands on the platform, pushing back into the center.

"Holy shit, I almost died," Jimmy Ray said.

"We're all going to die if we don't focus. You dropped your tool. Can you reach what you have to?"

"No, not without the fifth wheel puller," Jimmy Ray said. "I got it partially open, but you didn't give me the word yet."

"Show me," Mahegan said.

They lay on the platform and Jimmy Ray pointed at the fifth wheel jaw arm handle. Essentially, pulling on that handle would release the trailer kingpin, which was the only thing holding the trailer onto the truck chassis.

"I think I can reach it. They're ready up top. You're telling me as soon as I pull this, the trailer sets free?"

"Yes. Its speed will keep it moving forward, but it will begin to decelerate pretty quickly."

Mahegan nodded at McQueary that he was going under. McQueary pumped his arm that they needed to hurry. Mahegan guessed they were less than a minute from the roadblock.

He climbed beneath the trailer and saw the fifth wheel handle about three feet away. He reached out, clasped the handle, and yanked hard.

Immediately the trailer separated from the truck. The concern now was that the helicopter had to lift the trailer up and maintain the same speed, decelerating over time. Mahegan watched as the trailer began to lift off the ground. He crawled back to the truck platform and could plainly see the greasy, black fifth wheel and couldn't believe that was all that was holding a trailer to a truck, but it was.

The Blackhawk was lifting the trailer now, and the operation was going smoothly. The airbrake cables were stretched to their maximum as Setz continued to slowly ascend with the trailer. The problem with disengaging the air brakes too soon was that the truck would begin to brake, and if the trailer wasn't above the top of the truck, the trailer would strike that, causing the helicopter to nose over and face-plant into the road.

Not to mention causing the truck to flip over, which was still a possibility.

"Hang on," Mahegan shouted.

Jimmy Ray grasped an iron handle on the back of the cab, squeezing until his knuckles were white. Mahegan looked up at the trailer and thought it was high enough. Then he looked back at the truck cab and saw that the black slider was open.

Cassie Bagwell was staring at him through the wire mesh bulletproof back window of the cab, shaking her head, as if to say, *No.* With no time to contemplate her actions or what she intended, Mahegan noticed that the trailer was fully in the sky above them. The air brake lines snapped off and spun into the air with a sizzling sound, like that of frying bacon. The truck brakes locked, pinning Mahegan and Jimmy Ray against the back of the cab as smoked boiled all around them. The front heavy truck began to nose up, and the driver must have turned the wheel, because it spun a full turn and threw both Mahegan and Jimmy Ray outward, both hanging on to their respective grips.

Jimmy Ray went flying first and Mahegan followed, both landing thirty yards away in the grassy median. Mahegan rolled maybe ten times before he stood up as if he had just done a parachute landing fall in twenty-knot winds. Gaining his bearings, he checked on Jimmy Ray and found that he was injured but not badly. Maybe a broken leg.

Mahegan pulled his Tribal from his hip holster and said to Jimmy Ray, "Stay there, I'll get you a medic."

"Can't move. Not going anywhere."

Mahegan took a step, turned around, and said, "Good job." Then he was running to the cab that had stopped spinning. The driver's side was faceup with the passenger's door flush with the concrete of the highway. The back windshield was buckled and crushed, which did not portend well for Cassie.

He climbed up the backside of the cab near where he had been holding before the air brakes released. He could hear movement inside the cab, and he clawed to the top of the driver's door. The smell of leaking diesel permeated the air. Black smoke was boiling from the hood. While diesel had a higher flashpoint than automobile fuel, a fire was a real possibility with the kinetic force the truck had just endured.

Leading with his pistol, Mahegan stood over the driver's door and saw a man's head moving toward him slowly. His face was a mess, rivulets of red blood running into his open mouth where he was missing teeth, fresh wounds from the truck accident. He could see the man in the passenger seat was also injured badly, but his hand was reaching for a gun. A quick glance confirmed Cassie was unconscious, maybe dead, in the sleeping compartment.

Mahegan shot the driver in the face. Then he shot the hand of the man in the passenger seat. How he had survived, Mahegan didn't know. Mahegan opened the door, laid on the dead man, and stuck the pistol inches from the passenger's face.

"What's in the trailer?" Mahegan asked.

The man remained silent, even with the Tribal bore speaking to him its silent threat that it could erupt with a life-ending explosion any moment.

"Malavdi. Fatima," the man whispered. His words were raspy.

Mahegan figured there were internal injuries causing blood to drain into the man's throat. He registered the names.

"Groomsman," the man said. "Finally."

All of this action had revolved around Operation Groomsman ever since Alex Russell had squared off with him in the Uwharrie National Forest.

"What is in the trailer?" Mahegan shouted this time. He heard sirens in the background, knowing that he had maybe fifteen seconds to kill the driver if he wanted to.

He didn't need to. The man began to speak, pressing his tongue to the roof of his mouth, but his head lolled over against the highway concrete through the shattered passenger window. Mahegan quickly scrambled into the sleeping compartment and grabbed Cassie, who was dead weight.

She had glass cuts on her face and was bent awkwardly against the cab because her captors had tied her hands behind her back and bound her feet. That was why Cassie was only able to signal *No* with her head. But what was she trying to tell Mahegan? He knew that without the extra reinforcement of this special truck designed to haul nuclear weapons, all of them would have been dead. He felt a weak pulse on Cassie's neck.

"Help me, Jake," she whispered. Her lips parted slightly, and Mahegan's heart leapt, glad she was alive.

"I'm here, Cassie," Mahegan said.

He heard the ambulance arrive and then the paramedics as they began climbing onto the cab.

"Clear in here with one injured friendly!" Mahegan shouted. He holstered his Tribal and saw the first man was a SWAT team member, but not one of the men he had met.

"Weapons down, hands up," the man yelled. He led with an AR-15 inside the cab. The cop's face was a pinched expression of fear and focus.

"Two friendlies, one injured," Mahegan reiterated.

"Hands up," the man said.

Mahegan held his hands away from his body. "She needs an ambulance now. Get her into the ambulance now. I'll feed her up to you. Those two dead guys? They're the bad guys," Mahegan said, using his commander's voice.

After a moment, Mahegan's heart sank. He heard the baritone of Tommy Oxendine approaching the vehicle.

"Out of my way. This is my scene!" Oxendine shouted. Soon he was on top of the vehicle next to the SWAT team member. Oxendine locked eyes with Mahegan as Mahegan began to slide his hand toward his pistol.

Oxendine's hand came through the window as he said, "Feed her up to me. I've got her."

Mahegan hefted Cassie onto his shoulder as he practically stood in the back of the cab with Cassie hugging him, as if they were slow dancing. Her head was on his neck, next to his cheek. Her lips brushed his cheek. She held on to him as tightly as she could. "Thank you," she whispered, then passed out.

"Send me down a backboard, Oxendine," Mahegan said.

Oxendine didn't hesitate. "Backboard! Now!"

Soon two paramedics were sliding the backboard through the open door. Oxendine guided from the top while Mahegan slipped behind Cassie.

"You're going to be fine," Mahegan said to Cassie, but he wasn't so sure. He noticed a slight spot of blood at the corner of her mouth. He was concerned she had internal injuries as the others appeared to have.

He secured two straps around her and fed her up to Oxendine and the paramedics. They moved her slowly so as to not worsen any injuries. Mahegan sensed the smell of diesel growing stronger and knew the risk of fire increased every second.

He watched Cassie's feet disappear and heard a bucket line of paramedics passing the backboard into the ambulance.

"Fire!" someone outside the truck screamed.

Oxendine reached down and Mahegan grabbed both of his forearms as the lawman pulled him through the driver's door. The engine exploded, and for the second time in ten minutes Mahegan flew into the median, but this time Oxendine had hugged him tight and leapt from the truck frame, deliberately aiming them at the grassy area.

Mahegan looked up and saw Oxendine on his back. The man stood and shook his head as if to loosen cobwebs.

"Damn, that was righteous," Oxendine said.

Mahegan lifted onto his elbows enough to see the ambulance crossing the bridge toward Charlotte and hopefully the best doctor on duty.

"Where's the trailer?"

"They offloaded Q and his team, then dropped it in a rock quarry about ten miles from here. The team's trying to get down there. We might all be kissing our asses good-bye anytime now."

Mahegan looked at Oxendine, something hanging in the back of his mind.

It felt strange lying in an interstate median with no cars passing him on either side. The morning sun was giving way to noon. To his left he could see the roadblock less than a half mile away, the gap for the ambulance still there.

They were ten miles from Gastonia and ten miles from Charlotte. He remembered looking up and seeing the Blackhawk carrying the container with ease. The helicopter's max sling load was roughly 10,000 pounds. An empty shipping container weighed half of that. A fortified trailer might weigh twice that, but the Blackhawk had lifted that trailer with no problem. A fortified trailer with a nuclear missile on board would be even heavier. Still, the Blackhawk did not seem to have been laboring.

He looked at the police on the bridge. His mind flashed back to that first altercation with Alex Russell in the Uwharrie National Forest.

So tell me, Jake Mahegan, what is it that you care most about? she had asked him. He had answered her and she had said, *That's right. Teammates. JSOC. Friends. All that happy horseshit.*

As recognition flashed in his mind, he turned to Oxendine and said, "Have you got anything on Alex Russell?"

"Yeah. You know her?"

"Yes. She was Savage's JAG officer. Been acting strange," Mahegan said.

"Real name's Ameri Assad. She was an orphan from the Assad line of presidents or whatever they have in Syria. One of them murdered her parents and split the kids. Put one in east Syria near Iraq and another in Newark, New Jersey. Tell me, Ameri got the raw end of that deal."

Mahegan's mind was in high gear now. "There's nothing in that container," Mahegan said, pointing at the gorge where the Blackhawk had dumped it. He thought of Cassie shaking her head. She was sending him a signal. He stood and said, "Get Setz back here now. And get me a bomb specialist."

"She's refueling and probably dead asleep on the tarmac at Charlotte Airport," Oxendine said.

"I'm telling you, call her. Now."

"I need to do something first," Oxendine said.

"Call her," Mahegan insisted.

Oxendine squared up with him and embraced him. "I'm sorry," Oxendine said. "I'm sorry, brother. I was wrong."

Mahegan pushed Oxendine away and said, "Okay, great. Get Setz, the SWAT team, the bomb guy, and let's get going."

Oxendine stepped away and spoke into his radio. "Mahegan thinks he needs you. How soon can you be here?"

Mahegan watched Oxendine, looked to the east, and willed the helicopter to be in the air.

"Ten minutes?" Oxendine shrugged.

"Tell her she's got five. Maybe," Mahegan said.

"She heard you," Oxendine said, showing him the radio. Mahegan heard the helicopter engines whining over the speakers.

"Where we going?" Oxendine asked.

"To hell, probably," Mahegan said. But he was really thinking that he needed Owens and O'Malley, two of the best bomb guys he knew.

CHAPTER 37

ALEX RUSSELL APPROACHED THE GATE OF FORT BRAGG, NORTH Carolina. As usual on a Saturday, there was a steady stream of families and soldiers coming and going from the largest military base in the country.

Known as the home of the airborne, Fort Bragg was also home to a four-star general's headquarters and multiple three-, two-, and one-star generals' headquarters. The sprawling military compound had several access points from all directions. One passed by all of the drop zones such as Sicily, Salerno, Normandy, and Holland, odes to the 82nd Airborne Division's combat jumps in World War II. Others provided access through more residential and commercial areas.

Alex chose the busiest gate nearest the high-ranking officers' quarters to enter Fort Bragg because those military policemen were the most pressured to keep things moving along. God forbid some general's wife has to wait in line, Alex thought.

She thought of Vicki Sledge and the look on her face before she had shot her. Priceless. While Ameri Assad was fully in charge of Alex Russell, Alex felt some satisfaction with that pull of the trigger. But it was Ameri who had decided to shoot the husband and son. Alex didn't have that in her. Alex had fallen in love, for whatever that was worth, with General Savage about the time that Ameri began to take shape in her mind.

Now Alex/Ameri drove the Land Rover SUV with its trailer

hitch pulling the fifteen-foot-long boat trailer with a canoe on top. Covering the open well of the canoe was an old gray tarp secured with quarter-inch lines woven through eyelets every two feet.

Ameri kept saying, *Keep calm, keep calm, keep calm.*

Alex, though, was a nervous wreck. If she had ever needed the PKCzeta shot, it was now. She wanted to get rid of that controlling bitch Ameri, and now.

But she couldn't. Like a possessed woman, she stayed in line, pulling the trailer with a canoe from the camp.

One damn heavy-ass canoe, Ameri laughed in her head.

Alex was behind a family in a Buick Encore that she only imagined had been shut down yesterday by the virus that Gavril had uploaded to millions of cars around the country.

As the military policeman waved the family forward, he turned to Alex and waved her up next for inspection. Alex had her military ID card in her left hand. Just beneath her right hand in between the seat and the console was the same Berretta she had aimed at Mahegan three days ago and with which she had shot him this morning.

Do your best bitch resting face, Ameri said.

Alex looked at the private at the gate, who crisply saluted her.

She returned the salute and returned her hand to hover just above the pistol.

"Been canoeing, ma'am?" the private said as he flipped the identification card over and scanned it. The scanner beeped and the private frowned.

Alex's hand lowered toward the pistol as the private scanned again.

"Yes, been canoeing, Private."

This time the scanner made a different beeping sound and the private smiled.

"Daggone thing has been acting up all day. Gotta be careful in them canoes, ma'am. You have a good day," the private said, and waved her through.

One down, one to go, Ameri said.

One of the general officer headquarters that Fort Bragg housed was the Joint Special Operations Command, the home of General Savage and the former workplace of Jake Mahegan, Patch Owens, and Sean O'Malley. Alex Russell worked there as well and still had all of her credentials to get through the second gate, which led into the compound.

Alex drove another few miles, being careful to drive at the posted speed limits, which was usually thirty-five miles per hour. She approached the gate and saw the golf-ball-looking structure that was a series of antennae and radar dishes, like a giant cell phone tower that could communicate anywhere in the world. Alex knew that inside the headquarters on any given day was a full staff of soldiers, sailors, airmen, and marines along with dedicated civilians.

As she nosed the Land Rover into the chute to pass through the gate, she reached for her credentials and looked up at the guard, who was a private military contractor, former unit member, and would not be easily fooled if he had been warned.

He turned toward Alex. His face showed immediate recognition of who she was, which was why she shot him through the skull. She noticed the man was wearing body armor and a helmet, so they were on some kind of alert, possibly driven by her actions. His head kicked back as the pistol bucked in her hand. Because the gate was closed, the cantilevered arm was down and the tire shredders were up. She opened the SUV door and entered the guard shack where she raised the arm and lowered the tire shredders. Then she turned and fired a bullet into the combined electronic countermeasures jammer and communications device.

Alex drove through the gate and tugged the canoe into the parking lot. She parked on the far side where she could see Pope Army Airfield. Her SUV was a good quarter mile from the headquarters and the lone vehicle parked this far away from the building. Some of the JSOC members used the parking lot to store their boats on the weekend if they were going fishing early in the morning before work or heading out for a late-afternoon ski trip. She backed the trailer in between two boats, a Skeeter bass boat and a Boston Whaler center console. Her canoe looked perfectly at home.

She stepped out of the SUV and rolled back the canvas of the canoe enough for her to see the nose of the warhead and the timer affixed to it. She punched in the code—Fatima's wedding date, of course—and then set the timer for one hour. While Ratta had set the timer, she adjusted it to give her more time to get somewhere safe. She activated the countermeasures, as well. That would give her time to get at least thirty miles away. It was really Ameri Assad who wanted to live. Alex preferred to die, but Ameri was deriving too much joy from exacting revenge for her little sister.

She unhitched the trailer and let the tongue rest on the asphalt. Then she drove to the gate, passed through the entry she had left open, stopped, closed the gate, lifted the tire shredder, and lowered the arm. In her periphery was a Humvee, but it was unmanned. No threat. She continued through the gate with something nagging at the back of her mind.

No time to waste now.

Leaving in her wake one dead gate guard and a B61-12 nuclear warhead set to detonate in less than an hour, Alex drove to the For Sale by Owner lot on Fort Bragg. There was one young man with the high and tight haircut of a paratrooper. He was placing a sign in the windshield of a white Jeep Wrangler. Not her first choice, but it was more about availability.

"Looking for a trade?" she asked him.

He turned around and she held a pistol at his heart, then pulled the trigger. The young man slumped to the ground, dead.

Good work, Ameri told her.

She scavenged his body quickly for the car keys and his cell phone, which she would dump after making a few calls.

Alex got into the Jeep Wrangler and began driving east. *Almost done, Alex. Good girl,* Ameri said. *You know where to go.*

CHAPTER 38

MAHEGAN FELT THE AIRCRAFT SLOW AND PITCH UPWARD AS IT CAME in for a rolling landing in General Savage's Vass, North Carolina, backyard. On the helicopter were Tommy Oxendine, Setz, and her copilot.

As they were landing, Oxendine said into his headset, "Bingo. FBI finally did something. I told them to follow that asshole Yves Dupree from UBA and they captured him and some short bald, Bulgarian guy near the train station in Uptown Charlotte. Name's Gavril, supposedly the uncle of that guy named Malavdi."

"We killed Malavdi and Fatima in an errant bombing in Syria. That's what this is all about. Alex Russell's sister was going to marry Malavdi. We killed them," Mahegan said.

"Guy's supposedly singing like a bird," Oxendine said, looking at his phone, secure chat text scrolling through. Oxendine's face darkened.

"What?" Mahegan asked.

"Oh shit."

"No nuke in the trailer?"

"No nuke in the trailer."

"Alex Russell has it and she's taking it to JSOC headquarters. That's her target."

What do you love the most, Jake Mahegan?

"What makes you sure of that?" Oxendine asked.

"Something she said. She doesn't care about killing a football stadium full of people. She cares about revenge on the people who killed her sister. This is all intensely personal. She's lost her shit. Gone psychotic," Mahegan said. "I saw it. Just didn't realize to what magnitude."

"What's here at Savage's place?" Oxendine asked.

"Maybe the rest of my team. It's worth two minutes to find out," he said. "While I'm in there, see if you can get a fix on Alex Russell's SUV. She's probably had all her stuff protected or disabled, but there's got to be a way. Phone. Something."

The helicopter touched down near the storm shelter doors where Mahegan had first met Alex Russell.

Instantly he knew that no one was in the shelter, but there was activity in the house. He ran up the back steps to find Savage, Owens, and O'Malley in the kitchen. Mahegan came barreling into the house with his pistol drawn, expecting to also find Alex Russell holding a pistol.

Instead, they were loading their weapons and running out the door toward him.

"Heard the chopper. Knew it had to be you," Savage said. "Where are we going?"

"HQ. Got to be there. Patch, Sean, you guys have got to diffuse a nuke. That's what I know."

"No prob, bro," Owens said. O'Malley shrugged as they jogged to the helicopter.

They boarded the aircraft and sped toward Fort Bragg, the nose pointing low and the rotors kicking out dirt and grass like a lawnmower. As they approached JSOC headquarters, a dark Land Rover was heading out of the back gate toward the high-speed road along the drop zones.

"Could be her," Mahegan said. "Call Moore County police. Black Land Rover. Dark-haired female. Also call the base commander. Lock down the gates."

Setz switched some dials, spoke into her mouthpiece, then came back on and said, "Communicated. Where am I going?"

"Parking lot. I'm getting comms that a gate guard was shot," Oxendine said.

"Okay, keep talking to everyone, Oxendine. You stay on the aircraft with General Savage. I'm going on the ground with the others."

Mahegan looked out of the open door and saw the parking lot and the fifty or so cars near the headquarters building. Then he looked to his right, across the asphalt, and saw about five boats.

"The boats," he said, remembering the canoes from his wingsuit flight into the mine shaft.

Setz dropped them about fifty yards from the five boats. Mahegan immediately saw the low trailer with its tongue on the asphalt. On it was a canoe with a canvas covering the top.

"A million bucks says there's a nuke in that canoe."

"No bet here, boss," Owens said. They jumped off the aircraft, which then pulled away into a high hover, nosed over, and began heading west toward the last known location of the black Land Rover.

Pulling back the canvas, Mahegan looked down and said, "Better hurry."

They had nine minutes.

CHAPTER 39

ALEX RUSSELL/AMERI ASSAD SANG, "FLY, FLY, DOVE . . ." THOUGH IT was more of a hoarse whisper sneaking past her dusty, chapped lips. Her eyes were fixed on nothing in particular as she drove through the gate of Fort Bragg back into the civilian world.

She was smart enough to know that at least by now every law enforcement agency in the state, maybe the nation, would be looking for her vehicle, so she hoped that somebody put a missile on it and destroyed it, avoiding any kind of DNA incrimination.

But she doubted that would happen, which was why she never relied upon luck. What she did rely upon was her own ingenuity. Whether it was Alex Russell longing for General Bob Savage or Ameri Assad seeking revenge for Fatima, both personalities had proven themselves to be resourceful.

Alex drove the Jeep Wrangler into Fayetteville, North Carolina, the town directly outside of the gate at Fort Bragg. She looped around on a series of roads that took her to the town of Spring Lake and then took back roads the entire way to her preplanned objective. She wasn't surprised that she had made it this far in her plan, though she'd had moments of doubt.

There were few places where she felt safe, where she believed she could ride out a nuclear blast that would decimate JSOC headquarters, and all of Fort Bragg for that matter.

Ratta, the Syrian engineer and overall handyman, had connected the timer to the warhead and created the best antihandling device possible in the short time they had available. The canoe had a series of battery-powered infrared beams crisscrossing above the smaller catalyst bomb. Those infrared beams, if broken, would send a wireless electrical impulse to the bomb and detonate the nuclear warhead. While she couldn't deny that Mahegan and his teammates were pros at handling crisis situations, she couldn't see them finding a solution for this one even if they found the canoe to begin with. She was confident that an hour lead time was sufficient to reach her destination for the evening.

After tonight, Alex would will herself to visit her doctor and continue to try to erase the horrible memories of Operation Groomsman. Part of her knew that she would have fresh trauma that might tip her over the edge into complete psychosis, if she wasn't already there. When she had learned the Mahegan snatch mission in Pinehurst had failed, she had to improvise in order to lure Jake Mahegan into her clutches. Key to the plan was removing the formidable team of Mahegan, Owens, and O'Malley. Zakir and his men had brutally tortured General Savage for good reason, harming him physically and psychologically. Alex's love and respect for the man, though, only grew as she received the reports of the beatings he endured for forty-eight hours. Cassie arriving on the scene had been a surprise, but Alex had adapted.

She thought about all the players involved in Operation Groomsman: General Bagwell had Yves Dupree plant the phone in Fatima's SUV at a checkpoint. Dupree provided the intelligence to Cassie Bagwell when he was operating as a field agent for the DGSE in Syria. Cassie had passed the intelligence to Savage's team. Savage had the target vetted and turned to her . . . and she had confirmed.

"Yes, sir. Valid target."

And her life had changed dramatically ever since.

She had made her "destroy list," just as snipers had their kill lists. Ameri had appeared for the first time in many years and began the gradual takeover of Alex's psyche by having her make a destroy list. Ameri believed that she and Alex had endured unimaginable suffering, which was exactly what she wanted them to inflict on everyone in that kill chain.

Ever since that day four years ago, Ameri had begun her slow, methodical takeover of Alex. Alex was the car and Ameri was the driver. Everyone saw the vehicle, but the tinted windows made it hard to determine who was driving. Alex emerged just enough to be believable until it was time for Ameri to take control, which she did with greater ease by the day. Like a virus that adapted to a vaccine, Ameri had found lodging in Alex's psyche, immune to the treatments applied to mitigate her posttraumatic stress.

With Alex Russell's firm grip on the steering wheel and Ameri Assad's nefarious plan unfolding, Alex/Ameri drove to a wooded area where she could securely park the Jeep Wrangler and find cover for the imminent blast.

Mahegan ripped the tarp off the canoe and watched O'Malley prepare to go to work on the auxiliary detonation device that would act as the catalyst for the nuclear explosion. It was a small bomb on a bigger bomb.

"Uh-oh," O'Malley said.

Mahegan looked at his friend and teammate and knew that if O'Malley had concerns, they all had concerns.

"Oh man," Owens said.

Mahegan's personal mobile radio chirped. It was Savage.

"No glory on the black SUV. Just a family heading out the back way. Nothing to do with our issue," the general reported.

"Roger," Mahegan said. The Blackhawk had caught up with the vehicle in a couple of minutes. The timer showed less than four minutes until detonation.

"Alex Russell got away," Mahegan said. "Let's not let her get away with this."

O'Malley looked over his shoulder. "Bossman, this is bad."

"Antihandling device?" Mahegan asked. Even though it was broad daylight, O'Malley was wearing a pair of night vision goggles that allowed him to see possible infrared beams associated with antihandling devices.

"Sort of. There are about twenty IR triggers tacked underneath the rim of the canoe. They're all shooting infrared beams over the detonator, which is basically a mortar shell with a timer. If I reach into the canoe to try to defuse the mortar, I'll break a beam that will send a wireless impulse of electricity to the trigger right there and we all get vaporized." O'Malley pointed at the trigger device affixed to the timer. Mahegan could see the time ticking down like sand through an hourglass.

"So this is an IED. Just one with a bigger bomb."

"Roger," O'Malley said. "Two bombs, actually."

Savage radioed in again and Mahegan answered, "Send it." He stared at the mortar shell. It was an 81 mm explosive shell meant to deter enemy infantry in the close fight.

"Got the bomb fixed?" Savage asked. His voice buzzed with static.

"Working on it," Mahegan said, thinking.

"Fix it. I'm heading your way. Don't want to ride the thermal."

"Getting close to two minutes," Mahegan said. His left arm ached from all the abuse it had taken on the ridge. The pain made him think of Wesley Colgate, his best friend who had been blown to bits by an IED. The bomb trigger had eluded the jammers on Colgate's vehicle because the enemy had secured American technology that was able to find gaps in the bandwidth that electrical bomb triggers could sneak through.

But Mahegan wasn't trying to get an electrical trigger through the bandwidth. He needed to block all of those infrared triggers from sending a miniscule electrical impulse to the receiver atop the bomb that would detonate the nuclear weapon. He needed a jammer, just like Colgate had on his vehicle that horrible night.

"Patch, the gate has to have a jammer," Mahegan said.

"It does. Can control it from inside the guard shack or from inside the HQ—oh shit. Right," Patch said.

Mahegan and Patch ran toward the gate, a hundred yards away. They weren't sprinters, so it took them about fifteen seconds.

They saw the dead gate guard, didn't pause, and found that Alex had destroyed the ground-based jammer with a pistol shot to its face.

"Shit," Patch said.

"No time," Mahegan said, thinking. He looked through the open door of the guard house and saw an up-armored Humvee parked with a machine gun mounted on top.

"Colgate," Mahegan muttered.

"What's Wes got to do with this, man?"

"Everything," Mahegan said. He burst from the guard house and ran to the Humvee. Owens followed and jumped into the passenger seat. A Duke Version 3 vehicle-mounted electronic warfare jammer, one of the best in the world, was mounted above the center console. The question was, could it overpower and neutralize the fifteen or so passive infrared switches on the canoe?

They would have to find out.

"One minute!" O'Malley shouted as Mahegan fired up the Humvee and raced it toward O'Malley with Owens hanging on to the side as if he were kite surfing.

"Crank that up all the way, every bandwidth possible where we know passive infrared switches convert to voltage," Mahegan said to Owens. "I don't care if we shut down every phone call in Fayetteville."

"Same game, different location," Owens said as he played with the dials on the big green metal box mounted in the console.

"You good?" Mahegan asked. "Because I'm telling Sean we've got this."

"Forty-five seconds," O'Malley said, his voice resigned to their looming fate.

"We're jamming everything right now. I don't think any impulse can get from the passive infrared motion detectors to the bomb circuitry. Go, it's a simple bomb and a complex antihandling device."

O'Malley handed Mahegan the night vision goggles, performed the cross, and closed his eyes as Mahegan laid his hand on his back as if to say, *You die, I die, too.*

O'Malley's hands slowly reached into the canoe. Mahegan used his free hand to hold the goggles up to his face. The beams were crossing in every direction from every aspect of the canoe. He heard the Humvee idling and thought he could almost hear the crackle of electronic waves coming from the Humvee's jammer. The idea was to overpower the receiving antenna of the smaller bomb's trigger device to prevent any other signals from reaching it, coded signals that would be saying, *Detonate.*

Mahegan watched O'Malley's hands dive beneath the infrared lights and then he heard the Humvee cough, felt O'Malley flinch, heard the Humvee engine humming again, didn't hear an explosion, and saw that there were twenty seconds left for O'Malley to do a two-minute bomb defusing job.

But O'Malley was a pro, and he snipped the sending wire from the detonating bomb to the nuclear warhead, lifted the mortar shell, and flung it like a football as far as he could toward the open space of the mostly empty parking lot. O'Malley, Owens, and Mahegan dove beneath the Boston Whaler sitting next to the canoe. Mahegan pulled his two friends in close. They had been tortured, starved, and beaten but had "rangered up" and joined him in the hunt to protect the nation. The least he could do was put his body in between them and the coming explosion.

The mortar round exploded upon impact with the asphalt and sprayed deadly shrapnel in every direction. Metal fragments raked the Humvee in front of the canoe. Mahegan checked his buddies. Other than some shot nerves, everyone was still in one piece.

"Hope that was the end of it," Savage chirped over the radio.

Mahegan lifted his radio and said, "Hope ain't a method, General. But whatever you do, don't park that aircraft near this nuke."

Worried about the kinetic energy from the spinning blades, Mahegan directed the helicopter to the entrance road near the guard shack. The Blackhawk landed and Mahegan, O'Malley and Owens boarded. Placing the headset on, Mahegan said, "You need to get bomb disposal, the FBI, all the nuke geniuses, everybody down there. That's a live nuke just cooking in the sun."

"Roger that," Savage said.

"Alex Russell?" Mahegan asked.

"No clue," Savage said.

Mahegan paused and then said. "That's one whacked-out woman. I have a plan, but I need to see Cassie first."

Savage eyed him and said, "You got it."

Mahegan stared through the open door of the Blackhawk as it lifted away from the JSOC headquarters and ferried them to the hospital at Fort Bragg. Landing on the helipad, McQueary said, "We done?"

"I think we're solid. Good job," Mahegan said.

"Roger that. Looking forward to some shut-eye. You guys are impressive, man."

"Not nearly as you," Mahegan said. "Take these guys to Pope to be debriefed. I'm going into the hospital. Then you're done. Great job and thanks."

"Roger that, Mahegan," Setz said.

He looked at Oxendine and nodded. "You should go with Savage and the team here. Be part of the back brief."

Oxendine nodded, knowing not to question Mahegan after the last forty-eight hours of misjudgment.

Mahegan stepped off the Blackhawk, ducked beneath the whirring blades, and walked into Womack Army Medical Center at Fort Bragg. He found Cassie's private room after bumping into a special operations physician's assistant he knew. The man led him through the labyrinth of hallways to Cassie.

He knocked, thanked the PA, heard Cassie's voice, and stepped into the room. She was sitting on the edge of the bed pulling on her hiking Tevas. Cassie was dressed in sport gear, including running shorts, sports bra, and tank top.

"Doing some PT?" Mahegan asked.

Cassie looked up and smiled.

"Can't. I'm winged. But I *am* getting the hell out of here."

Cassie lifted her left arm, which was covered with a desert tan sling. "They claim I broke it when you dropped me."

"Dropped you?" Mahegan asked.

Cassie stood and walked toward him. She placed her hand on the back of his neck and pulled him toward her. Leaning forward, Mahegan felt her lips brush past his face as she whispered into his ear, "Next time we're on a mountaintop and I'm hanging from a tree branch with an armed drone shooting missiles at me and you've got a psycho bitch shooting a pistol at you, try to stick with me, okay?"

Mahegan put his hands on her waist, her slung arm an awkward divider between them.

"Deal," he said.

Cassie leaned back just enough to put her lips against his, kiss him fully, and then pull back.

"Then let's go find Alex Russell. I suspect she's still out there."

Mahegan ran his hand down her spine, not wanting to break the moment, but knew that she was right. Plus, he had the bad news of her parents' murder to pass to her. The FBI and state law enforcement had crawled over every inch of the Bible camp and found the cabin where an apparent murder–suicide had taken place.

"What?" Cassie said. Mahegan's eyes softened, a slight narrowing as he pondered how to deliver the news.

"Your parents," Mahegan said.

Cassie slowly shook her head, muttered "No," and fell into Mahegan's arms. He held her like that for several minutes, felt her sob against him until she got control of herself. Warm tears slid across his bicep as she turned her head, looking away, embarrassed that an Army Ranger had a temporary display of emotion.

"Alex did this," Cassie said. "But he started this entire mess."

"Understand. They found a bank statement and connected him to a financial scam with Syrian refugees. Cartwright from the operations center updated me on the search in the mountains.

It's not pretty. While there is no way to fix what's happened with your parents, I do have a thought about Alex," Mahegan said. He had lost his parents in horrific fashion as well, so he understood a little bit of her agony.

In part to change her dark thoughts to something constructive, he told her his plan regarding Alex, and she agreed.

CHAPTER 40

IT HAD BEEN THREE DAYS AND THE BOMB HAD NOT DETONATED. ALEX Russell was sitting on her haunches, wild eyed like a baying animal, cornered and desperate. She was in a small alcove off the tunnel leading to General Savage's Wood Lake Mansion, which she knew better than the general knew it himself.

After they had unhitched the canoe with the nuclear weapon, Ameri had Alex park deep in the woods behind Savage's estate and then race to the COOP. She had spun the lock dial in broad daylight, banking that Savage and the others were consumed with chasing down the bomb.

When she didn't hear an explosion, she had been dumbfounded. Something had to have malfunctioned. Ameri scolded Alex. *You stupid bitch. How could you fuck this up? The easiest part. Just park the nuke and drive away.*

Alex was ashamed, downtrodden. She had sulked in the COOP, pulled her hair straight out, saw her wild eyes in the mirror, pounded her fists against the wall, and began to lose all control.

"You're Jackknife! You can do anything!" she shouted in her empty chamber. True, she had given herself Savage's call sign because she wanted to be like him while wanting to kill him. Oddly, like a distant, dimly lit buoy in the ocean, a realization that she had gone completely insane clanged in the far reaches of her mind. Properly chastised, though, Alex began to feel Ameri calm her down. *One final mission. Can't mess this one up, Alex. Have to complete it. Have to kill him.*

Ameri had guided Alex back toward internal composure, lowered her heart rate, and led her to the light switch. Alex had flipped the light switch in the COOP and watched the server diodes blink in the darkness. The green and red lights reminded her that she'd given Gavril and Zakir all the information necessary to navigate their way into the Zebra code, leading to the kidnapping of Savage, O'Malley, and Owens. The beginning. The opening gambit that was supposed to remove the key chess pieces from the board, providing her the freedom to maneuver and enhancing her opportunity of success.

But Mahegan had avoided capture. He was every bit as good as advertised.

Still, Alex and Ameri had destroyed most of the kill chain: Dupree, Savage, and General Bagwell. Dupree was in detention, caught with Gavril based on a tip she had fed to the police. General and Mrs. Bagwell were dead in the cabin, shot by Zakir, Bagwell's own vices having undone him. Savage had been freed because of her inability to take Mahegan off that chess board. And like chess, Mahegan was the pawn that had found the eighth rank and returned not just one valuable piece to the board, but three: Savage, O'Malley, and Owens. That team was formidable, but she had still tricked them, delivered the nuke to JSOC HQs.

While Cassie was technically in the kill chain, she was just a functionary, passing along information. General Bagwell and Dupree had manufactured the intelligence to kill Malavdi because Malavdi, Zakir, and Gavril had emptied their bank account by accident. And while it would have been a good thing to kill Cassie, at least she was in the hospital, having survived what Alex had at the time believed would be complete destruction of the Mack truck by a missile.

So she waited in the tunnel beneath Savage's home, an alcove off the main tunnel that only she knew about, and one that gave her access without tipping the security cameras or passive infrared switches. They would not expect her here, not after three days. She had carried a small backpack with a knife, pistol, and enough food for several days of lying in wait.

She was ready for whenever Savage returned home to his lair, surprised he had not come sooner. Until now, the floorboards above her head had been deathly quiet. She had become claustrophobic but persevered on her rations and water bottles. She peed in a hole she had scraped in the dirt using her knife, then covered it up to hide the ammonia smell.

She used the K-bar knife to scrape in the dirt, the doodling of a maniacal killer. Then her knife stopped, her eyes flicked up, her mind listened, her body remained perfectly still.

She heard the front door open and a single pair of footfalls enter the foyer and ascend the wooden steps.

He's home, Alex. Kill him.

He entered the foyer. She heard him throw his keys on the antique hall stand and pause, probably checking himself out in the mirror, thinking he'd looked better.

She heard him trudge up the steps, imagined his aging frame struggling after the abuse he'd been through. She listened for the shower but didn't hear anything and guessed he was going straight to sleep.

Where she wanted him.

She heard the bed creak under his weight and then gave it a full thirty minutes. She heard no other footfalls in the house. The wind had picked up, causing the pine trees to whistle a bit. Alex looked at her watch. It was almost eleven p.m. Another five minutes. Could she wait that long? She'd waited three days, she could wait another five minutes. Just to be sure.

Then Ameri was in her mind, saying, *Go now.*

Alex stood slowly, her knees popping like firecrackers. Other than the aching bones, she was stealthy. Two days ago, Alex had unlatched the door that led to the master closet so that she could silently push it inward and brush past his Army uniforms.

Leaving behind her detritus of food wrappers and water bottles, she moved slowly, one foot in front of the other along the dirt floor of the tunnel. Reaching the end of the narrow passageway, she felt for the metal ladder rung and found it. Grasping the third rung, she placed a foot on the first one and began to climb. She was stealthy, moving like a cat tiptoeing through the night, stalking.

The ladder was bolted to the frame of the house and was straight up. It had been built as an escape route for Savage to get into the tunnel and the COOP. Reaching the master bedroom closet panel, she shoved on it slightly and felt it give noiselessly. She had put Vaseline on the hinges the same day that she had prepared the hatch for her entry.

She stepped through the entry, totally focused now. She was within yards of her destination. Her big decisions now were, *Shoot him or stab him?*

Both, Ameri told her. *Enjoy the close kill. Look into his eyes. Slide the knife into his heart. Then put the pistol to his head and a bullet through his brain.*

There he was, a lump on the bed. She recognized the soft snore she had slept next to after sex. Savage was a good lover but was quick to sleep once they were done. He wasn't one for cuddling or holding. He was a hard man who lived a Spartan life of killing the enemies of the nation. She admired him for that. But he also made a bad mistake in killing her sister, Fatima.

For that he would pay.

Alex stood over the bed holding a knife, not unlike she had the time the doctor had awoken and talked her down out of her fugue state. This time, though, she would not be talked down. Ameri was in control. She held the knife in her dominant right hand and the pistol in her left. She studied the rhythmic breathing of Savage's back. He was sound asleep with his head buried in the pillow. She found the spot on Savage where she wanted to slide the knife.

She leaned forward and placed the knife against his back, its razor-sharp tip easily cutting through the fabric.

* * *

Jake Mahegan sensed Alex's presence as she climbed the ladder and opened the emergency door that Alex had built into the compound once the COOP was completed. Savage had been unaware, because he was often deployed for months at a time, but Owens had sent a microdrone inside the COOP not too long ago that used infrared and thermal imaging to map the interior. Increasingly, special mission units were using these drones to measure dimensions of walls and view the interior of buildings before assaulting.

Owens had found that the imaging showed a thin false wall where previously there had been nothing but dirt all around the COOP. Owens had inspected, found the tunnel, and reported it to O'Malley and Mahegan. Always suspicious of their enigmatic former boss, Mahegan, O'Malley, and Owens kept the information to themselves, assuming Savage had built the passageway. When Mahegan had mentioned the passageway to Savage, the general had expressed ignorance. That was when Mahegan knew where Alex Russell was hiding. They had found the dead soldier's Jeep Wrangler hidden in a creek bed beneath some freshly broken pine saplings less than a mile from Savage's estate.

Mahegan lay perfectly still, breathing steadily, even adding a faux snore into his exhale. Cuffed along his left wrist was his Blackhawk knife, blade locked open, and his trusty Sig Sauer Tribal was in his right hand.

He felt the tip of the knife against his back. It wouldn't take Alex Russell long to realize the knife was pressing against a ceramic body armor plate.

He felt the knife searching for an opening as if she thought she was simply pushing against a bone. Mahegan used his left arm to impose a powerful thrust over the sheets and into Alex Russell's left arm. He was thrusting blind but was happy that the first cut had found solid purchase on her body. He quickly slid his right leg underneath his body and spun so that he was able to slide out of the bed on the side where she was.

She was prepared, though, and slashed the knife across his

chest, its blade flashing in the sparks created by the metal on ceramic high-velocity contact. They squared off like two wrestlers in a ring. There was maybe fifteen feet of room in either direction between the west wall of the house and the bed and in between the south wall and the master closet. Mahegan had worn the body armor at the insistence of Owens and O'Malley.

"What if she comes out of the closet spraying and praying, dude?" Owens had asked.

"Just make sure you guys stay out of sight and out of audible range until she makes her move," Mahegan had said.

"Why not just drop some smoke grenades down there and flush her out?" O'Malley advised.

"This is personal now. Plus, there may be more ways out of there that we don't know about," Mahegan said.

"I don't know, man, I checked that thing out pretty good, but it's a possibility."

"Still, we could block both ends of the tunnel," Owens said.

"Do we know she's in the tunnel? For sure? We do that and she's watching somehow, maybe with her own drone, then we lose her. This is what she wants. She blames Savage for killing Fatima. This is the bait to flush her out. We go in there and she's there, it's a booby trap or death trap for us. We go in there and she's not there, she's in the wind. She's either in the tunnel or in a spider hole somewhere waiting for Savage."

So Mahegan had driven Savage's Ford F150 pickup truck into the garage and parked it next to his Jeep Cherokee. He had entered through the door, dropped the keys in the tray, and made his way upstairs, trying to take forty pounds off his footfalls to match Savage's weight. He had removed his boots, which he didn't want to do, but also thought that Alex might be able to see the shape of his Doc Martens through the outline of the bedspread and sheet. Not wanting to fight in socks, he had removed them and was now barefoot, which was second best to having a good pair of boots to kick in Alex's head.

He watched Alex circle and saw in her eyes that she had gone completely crazy. She was mumbling something to herself that sounded like *run, no kill him, run, no kill him, where's Savage, no kill him.* Her hair was stringy and lifting into the air as if static electricity was pulling it upward. She wore the same clothes she had been wearing—the dark cargo pants, black top, and tan outer tactical vest. Her arm was bleeding from the knife wound he had inflicted, but she seemed unbothered by the pain. She smelled like urine and body odor, perhaps from days of living in the tunnel.

"What did you see, Mahegan?" she asked him. Her voice was eerily an octave higher, as if it were a different person speaking. She was a woman possessed. People who were operating disconnected from reality, perhaps high on something, or in this case dominated by intense hatred, were people that had no fear and felt no pain.

She lunged with the knife and grazed his left shoulder. He used her momentum to throw her up against the wall. She still clutched the pistol in her left hand. When Alex's back hit the wall, she bounced off it like a pro wrestler bounces off the ropes. She came at him hard, head first, wild eyes looking upward, showing the whites beneath her irises. She was fast and quick, slashing left and right as if she was flipping nunchucks. Mahegan sidestepped but still caught the butt of her pistol against his injured left shoulder, which screamed at him with pain.

Mahegan's back was to the wall, and Alex was coming at him again from the direction of the bed.

She stopped short, lifted the pistol, and fired.

Alex was a smart fighter. She had demonstrated her skills on the ridge as well as when she was hiding in plain sight daily. Savage had given him her background in martial arts, but even he was surprised at her quickness. She had charged him twice to get him to believe she would charge a third time, and he did, but that was when she leveled the pistol at his face from ten feet away and pulled the trigger.

The bullet slapped into the wall behind him. Her aim was marginally off as it had been on the cliff. Mahegan raised his Tribal and snapped off two quick rounds, both impacting the center mass of her body.

Blood began to blossom on her tactical vest.

He watched her fall to her knees. She attempted to lift her weapon, but couldn't. Reaching into her tactical vest, she removed a hand grenade and placed it to her teeth to pull the pin.

Mahegan shot her in the head, but not before the pin stayed between her clenched teeth and the grenade bounced to the floor. Mahegan dove toward the grenade, palmed it, and hurled it toward the window. If it went through, he might live. If he missed, he would die.

The tinkle of broken glass was followed immediately by a loud explosion.

Alex Russell was moving toward him with the knife, like an ice climber. He had only grazed her scalp, but the body shot had done its damage. She reached out, stabbed the knife into the hardwood floors, and pulled herself forward. Repeated the process.

Mahegan stood, kicked the knife away, and said, "Alex, I'm sorry about Fatima. She died next to the man she loved. What more can you ask for? You? You get to die alone on the floor of the man you loved."

Alex/Ameri stared at Mahegan. Her eyes focused on him, flashing with hatred before they went blank with death.

He walked out of Savage's bedroom, his clothes bloody and his conscience clean.

EPILOGUE

MAHEGAN LOOKED AT CASSIE FROM ACROSS THE ROOM, THEN stared back into the ocean. He stood at a floor-to-ceiling open window that led to a balcony. Curtains fluttered inward with the trades whisking off the Atlantic Ocean. It was early October and the nightmare of Alex Russell was a good two weeks behind them. Mahegan had attended the funerals for General and Mrs. Bagwell and had been by Cassie's side the entire time.

After leaving Arlington Cemetery, it had been Cassie's idea to get away to Bald Head Island at the mouth of the Cape Fear River. No cars were allowed on the island, and they had to take a ferry over from Southport.

"Less chance of General Savage finding you and giving you another mission," Cassie had said as she presented the idea to Mahegan. "And I'd like to spend some down time with you."

Mahegan pulled the salty air into his lungs. He had grown up in the Outer Banks, breathing sea mist since he was a baby. He thought about Patch, Sean, and General Savage. He had saved his teammates. Cassie had helped and at the same time lost her parents. That counted for something, maybe a lot.

He had wrestled with the undeniable pull of attraction toward Cassie during the mission and after but had kept that feeling at bay, like a winter frost extending into spring. Mahegan had not been lucky in love, as they say. He'd lost everyone he'd chosen to be close to or he had received missions on the heels of making a decent connection.

But here he was with Cassie, who was lying naked in their bed in a rented cottage on Bald Head Island. She rolled over and stared at him in his boxer shorts.

"You're looking pretty good standing there all semi-naked and stuff," Cassie said.

Mahegan smiled. "Feeling pretty good."

He looked at her left shoulder and saw the Ranger black-and-gold half-moon shaped tattoo.

"Whacha thinking about?" Cassie asked. She rolled partially, still nursing her left arm.

"Not much. Mostly my mom. She's gone, but I think about her every day. I think about what she taught me and how she always told me it was better to die an honorable death than to grow old."

Cassie paused, looked beyond him at the ocean, and then caught his eyes. "I'd kind of like to do both."

Mahegan smiled again and thought for the first time since he was fourteen years old that he might like that, too. He walked over to the bed, lowered himself carefully next to Cassie, and pulled her onto his chest.

"Me too," he said.

ACKNOWLEDGMENTS

First, thanks to the great team at Kensington Books: my editor, Gary Goldstein, communications director, Vida Engstrand, publicist, Karen Auerbach, publisher, Lynn Cully, and president Steven Zacharius. They all worked hard to make *Besieged* a better book and I'm grateful for this team every day.

Likewise, Scott Miller and the team at Trident Media Group continue to prove they are the best in the business. Thanks to Allisyn Shindle, Emily Ross, and Brianna Weber for the way you all crush it every day on behalf of all of Trident's authors.

A special thank you to Richard Wilkins and Beverly Setz, who won the Wilmington, NC character name auction for charity. The substantial proceeds went to Songs From the Sky, a nonprofit documentary film about the 82nd Airborne Division Chorus produced by legendary filmmaker Paula Haller. Beverly Setz did a great job as the Blackhawk pilot ferrying Tommy Oxendine around North Carolina.

Another special thank you goes to Cheryl and Chuck "Q" McQueary, who donated generously to the NC Heroes Fund in the Raleigh, NC charity auction. The funds support our active duty service men and women through the NC Heroes Fund. Chuck McQueary made for a tough SWAT team leader, his moral compass keeping Oxendine in check.

Thanks to Rick French of French/West/Vaughn, the national

powerhouse in public relations. A huge shout out to Charles Upchurch, who provided man-to-man coverage 24/7 through some crazy news cycles as we launched *Three Minutes to Midnight* paperback, *Besieged* hardcover, and prepped for *Direct Fire.*

As always, research continues to be a favorite aspect of my writing and I hope you enjoyed the story. I look forward to delivering the next Jake Mahegan novel to you.

—AJT

Kensington Publishing Corp.
Joyce Kaplan
900 Third Avenue, 26th Floor
US-NY, 10022
US
jkaplan@kensingtonbooks.com
212-407-1515

The authorized representative in the EU for product safety and compliance is

eucomply OÜ
Marko Novkovic
Pärnu mnt 139b-14
ECZ, 11317
EE
https://www.eucompliancepartner.com
hello@eucompliancepartner.com
+372 536 865 02

ISBN: 9781496760692
Release ID: 156593254

www.ingramcontent.com/pod-product-compliance
Lightning Source LLC
Chambersburg PA
CBHW020938180826
50016CB00030B/156
9781496760692